An English Ghost Story

KIM NEWMAN

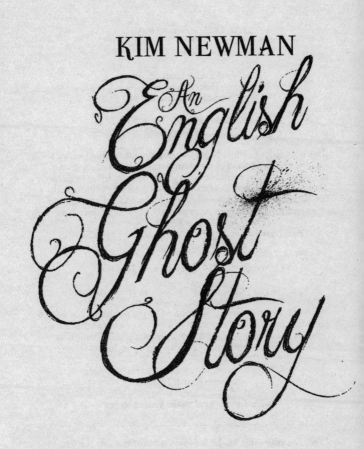

An English Ghost Story

TITAN BOOKS

An English Ghost Story
Print edition ISBN: 9781781165607
E-book edition ISBN: 9781781165591

Published by Titan Books
A division of Titan Publishing Group Ltd
144 Southwark Street, London SE1 0UP

First mass market edition: September 2016
1 3 5 7 9 10 8 6 4 2

Kim Newman asserts the moral right to be identified
as the author of this work.

Copyright © 2014, 2016 by Kim Newman

A CIP catalogue record for this title is available
from the British Library.

Printed and bound in the United States.

Did you enjoy this book? We love to hear from our readers.
Please email us at: readerfeedback@titanemail.com

To receive advance information, news, competitions,
and exclusive offers online, please sign up for the
Titan newsletter on our website:
titanbooks.com

For Helen

Spring

They would fall in a clump, like ripe apples. Mother, father, daughter, son. Touched by the charm, their persistent – though thinned – love would flare. As only once before, at the birth of baby Tim, the family would be a whole, united by fiercely shared feeling. Things that had seemed important would be trivial, and things that had seemed negligible would be potent.

The Hollow awaited the family with a welcome. It needed them. Unpopulated, it tended to drift. Without people in residence, it might disperse on the winds. That afternoon, the place was on its best behaviour, spring green promising summer gold.

When Dad bought a Mercedes-Benz A-Class hatchback, Jordan's brother Tim had called it a 'hunchback' and the car had been 'the hunchback' ever since. Dad, proud of his purchasing power, resisted the name for a while, but eventually gave in.

For the long drive to the West Country, Jordan had made a mix tape of season-specific tracks: 'April in Portugal', 'Spring Fever', 'Apple Blossom Time', 'Springtime for Hitler'. If she had to spend a whole day with her parents and brother, hitting the road at an unreasonable six in the morning, she needed a mental cushion.

On the motorway, beyond range of GLR traffic reports, Dad made a show of being willing to give her tape a listen. Jordan relaxed in the back seat, as her music opened what felt like a cage. After a couple of tracks, the mood in the hunchback turned sour.

'No one your age can *really* like this antique crap,' said Mum, over Judy Garland's 'April Showers'. 'It's not natural. *I* wasn't born when this was recorded.'

Like a weasel, Tim backed Mum up, though he was really too fixated on his Game Boy to register anything outside his bubble of kill-fantasies.

'Da-ad,' Jordan appealed.

'I have to concentrate, Jord,' he said.

Aptly, Sarah Vaughan sang 'Spring Will Be a Little Late This Year'.

'Our daughter has the musical taste of a sixty-year-old drag queen,' Mum told Dad. 'One day, she'll make someone a wonderful fag hag.'

'What's a "fag hag"?' asked Tim.

'Never mind, Timmy. I'm calling a family vote. Hands up who wants music from this decade.'

Mum put up her hand and so did Tim. Jordan folded her arms, angrily. Dad shrugged, while still holding the steering wheel. Mum declared two for, one against and one abstention. Jordan's cassette got ejected.

As navigator, Mum controlled the in-car entertainment. She set the tuner to the kind of non-antique crap someone Jordan's age was supposed to like.

'This is definitely more *now*,' said Mum, pretending to enjoy rap. Jordan thought the track was called 'Poppin' a Cap in Mah Bitch's Skull'. Mum shook her head just out of time to ranted misogyny.

'Aren't you supposed to be a feminist?' she mumbled.

Mum turned round and glared at her. Tim made a gun-finger and popped it at Jordan. When her little brother grew up thinking violent killer pimps were heroes, it wouldn't be her fault.

She had known this would happen... but she'd still spent several hours compiling her spring mix.

Jordan had resisted this jaunt, but Mum and Dad made a show of including her – and even Tim – in discussions about the move out of the city. The ultimate threat was that if she didn't take part in viewings, she couldn't complain about the house they wound up stuck in.

Her parents were striving heroically to keep their own rows about the proposed move to a strained minimum so as to present a united front to the kids. 'You'll be living there too,' one or other of them would say when Jordan's attention wandered from the sheaves of listings provided by rural estate agents. She always had to bite her lip to keep quiet about her secret plan. She wasn't going to stay in the backwoods. Once she had her A levels, she would head back to London, get a flat with Rick and find a university place in the city. She'd secretly spent her sixteenth-birthday money on a streamlined art deco kettle. Still boxed under her bed, the Alessi would come out when she was setting up her own home. The best thing about this family exodus was that a year from September, she'd be living over a hundred miles away from the rest of them.

After turning off the motorway, they found themselves driving along winding lanes, craning to make out contradictory signposts for oddly named hamlets. The level of tension ratcheted. Dad held back sharp comments about Mum's map-reading skills. Today, they were scheduled to view four places around Sutton Mallet, a village in Somerset that was clearly marked but elusive. If you wanted to get there, it seemed you shouldn't start from here.

'This map must be out of date,' said Mum at last, giving up.

'More likely, it's too new,' said Jordan, pointedly. 'These roads haven't changed in hundreds of years. Perhaps the map-makers are embarrassed by how *antique* they are.'

Mum gave Jordan one of her cold looks. Jordan sank back, chafing her shoulder against her seat belt.

'Sector fifteen cleared,' Tim said. 'All hostiles liquidated.'

The beep-beep-beep of Tim's handheld device, a mild irritant three hours ago, was now as painful as regular tapping against an exposed dental nerve. He reported his kill-count every few minutes. His thumbs apparently made him the premier mass-murderer of the age, though he claimed his genocides were justified in a time of war.

Fifty minutes late, in a collective bad mood, they arrived at the first viewing. They piled out of the hunchback. Jordan had chosen a sleeveless blouse for the journey. April chill ice-stroked her bare arms.

The place was a tip. Described as 'in need of renovation', the house was a derelict shell on a bankrupt farm. Vast sheds still stank of cattle carcasses. The business had been wiped out by mad cow disease. They stood about, depressed by the cheery chatter of Rowena Marion, the estate agent handling their first two viewings.

'It's ghastly,' said Jordan, loud enough for Mrs Marion to hear. 'Like an extermination camp for cows.'

Mum looked as if the criticism were aimed directly at her, which it was. All the places would be like this. Jordan had dragged herself out of bed before dawn for an agonising waste of time.

'I think it's a "no",' said Dad, understating.

'Early days yet,' shrugged Mrs Marion, who must have known the farm was unspeakable but still thought it worth showing in the hope the townies were cracked enough to go for it. 'This is the first place you've seen, yes?'

Dad admitted that it was.

'I think you're going to love Clematis Cottage,' Mrs Marion confided, blithely. 'Follow me and have a look-see.'

The next viewing was a dear little cottage in the village itself. What the listing concealed was that there was no driveway from the road to the 'extensive adjoining property' and no suitable place to park within a hundred yards. They cruised past the place, momentarily struck by its picturesque qualities. By the time Dad found a half-hearted lay-by on the other side of the village green, they knew it was a loser.

Trudging back along a grassy verge, Jordan had to lean into a prickly hedge when a tractor passed. Mrs Marion, not ready to give up yet, was there before them, on foot.

The owner – an eighty-year-old keen to move into a nursing home with the fortune he had been told he would realise on his property – loitered like an eager puppy, promising tea and chocolate digestives. Jordan sympathised, but it was cruel to inflate his hopes. They were in and out before the kettle whistled.

They left Mrs Marion – the pensioner should feed her poisoned biscuits – and had a grim pub lunch, saying little about the show so far. Dad had a pint of the local bitter, which was stronger than he expected. Mum had to take over the driving for the afternoon. Not hungry, Jordan couldn't even finish a packet of salt-and-vinegar crisps.

Next up was a new estate agent, Poulton and Wright. And a place even further outside the village than the hell-farm.

In the back of the car, Jordan looked at the photocopied listing. The property they were to see was called the Hollow. The photograph didn't give anything away; in it, she could hardly see the house for the trees.

'Don't get your hopes up, folks,' said Dad as they turned off the main road. 'This was always the long shot.'

Mum and Dad were tense after the dud viewings. Each was storing up blame for the other to shoulder.

When a thing failed to work out, no matter the degree of shared initial enthusiasm, it automatically became sole intellectual property of someone else.

They drove down a single-lane road across flat moorland. From a long way off, they saw trees and what looked like the tips of towers.

A car stood on the verge by the open gate of the property. A youngish man, cagoule over pin-striped trousers, waited, leaning against the gate-post. As Mum fussily parked, Jordan looked over the new estate agent. He had spots and the too-ready smile she'd distrusted in Rowena Marion.

But the Hollow was different from Kow Kamp Funf and Clematis Cottage.

Jordan saw it all at once, from the road, and was *certain*. This was the place. It was like her first kiss, Doris Day's 'Que Sera Sera', the taste of strawberries, her car accident. Instant and all-encompassing, wondrous and terrifying, a revelation and a seduction.

Zam-Bam, Alla-Ka-Zamm!

The strangest thing was she knew her parents felt the same. Mum actually turned and smiled at Dad, who let his hand stray to her wrist for the tiniest of intimate squeezes. Tim looked up from his game, the Elvis lip-curl he'd shown the loser places replaced by open rapture.

'Kew-ell,' said Tim.

Jordan was caught up in the spell.

Just this once, nothing else mattered. Her mind was settled in. The shock passed and she got comfortable with the feeling. It was like coming home.

They got out of the hunchback in a tangle and

overwhelmed the agent. If he expected city folk to keep their cards to their chest and strike a hard bargain, he was surprised.

'I love it,' said Mum. The shift was miraculous: suddenly, she was relaxed and open, uncontrollably smiling. 'I just love it.'

Jordan saw she had been wrong. The spotty agent's smile wasn't fake. Of course, he had *known*. He had been waiting by the Hollow for a few minutes, and he was familiar with the property. He could feel it too.

The *charm*.

This was what they needed. A new place, to start all over again, to put the past behind them, to build something. Yet an old place, broken in by people, with mysteries and challenges, temptations and rewards.

They might as well cancel the remaining viewing.

'I'm Jordan,' she imagined herself saying to her new friends, 'I live in the Hollow.' No, 'I'm *from* the Hollow.'

Was the Hollow the house or the land? The name was misleading. Weren't hollows dents in hills or woods? The property rose a little above the surrounding moorfields. An island that had come down in the world, it still refused to sink into the Somerset Levels.

Her arms didn't feel cold. A million tiny dandelion autogyros swarmed on warm winds.

'Brian Bowker,' said the agent, 'from Poulton and Wright's.'

His spots were mostly freckles, though some had whiteheads. He looked as if he was blushing all the time, perhaps a handicap in his business. Unlike Rowena Marion, he didn't try to hide his West

Country accent. He didn't sound like a yokel, though; it was just a way of talking, a burr.

Dad shook hands with him.

'This is the Hollow,' said Brian Bowker, standing aside and making a flourish as if signalling stagehands to haul open the curtains.

Tim had to be restrained from running. Jordan did the honours, hugging her little brother with a wrestling hold. Mum and Dad put arms around each other's waists and a hand each on a child's shoulder, as if for a family portrait.

'We're the Naremores,' said Dad. 'I'm Steven, this is my wife Kirsty, and our children, Jordan and Tim.'

'Pleased to meet you all,' said Brian Bowker.

'I think this is it,' said Mum, out loud.

The agent's smile became a grin. 'You ought to look closer; not that I should say that.'

'We will, old man,' said Dad, 'but I think Kirst is right. I can feel it. Have you sprinkled fairy dust about the place?'

For once, Jordan wasn't embarrassed by Dad. She knew what he meant. It wasn't just the spring-blossom; the air seemed to *dance*. This was the season of the songs, the happy songs about love blooming with the greenery, not the melancholy songs of faded flowers remembered in fall.

The house stood in the middle of a roughly square patch of land, boundaries marked not by hedges or walls but still ditches from which grew bright green rushes. A moat ran alongside the road and the Hollow had its own bridge, wider than it was long, for access. Mum, cautious after the dispiriting fuss at Clematis

Cottage, had parked on the road. That felt wrong: they should have driven through the gate and across the bridge, up to the barn, which was large enough to garage a fleet of cars.

Apple trees grew in what Jordan supposed was a deliberate pattern. The largest lay on the ground, roots exposed like a display of sturdy, petrified snakes, hollowed-out body sprouting a thick new trunk, fruiting branches stretching upwards. Tim was enchanted by this marvel, which had been smitten but survived. He had to be called away from exploring before he disappeared entirely inside the wooden tunnel of the original trunk. A couple of trees beyond the house, at the far edge of the grounds, were too close together, upper branches entangled and entwined, like giants kissing.

'The property used to be called Hollow Farm,' said Brian Bowker, consulting his clipboard, leading them along a paved path that wound through the trees. 'It goes back as far as there are parish records, to the Middle Ages. In the nineteenth century, the surrounding fields were sold off to one of the big local farmers and it became just the Hollow. The householders kept only this small apple orchard. You'll still get all the cookers and eaters you need.'

Jordan could hear the trees. They moved, very slowly. Each leaf, twig, branch and trunk was rustling or creaking, whispering to her. There were trees all over London, but any sounds they made were too faint to be heard above traffic and shouting. City trees were furniture, but these were living things; worlds in themselves, populated by insects, birds, squirrels.

'In the barn, there's a cider-press,' said Brian Bowker, 'disused since the thirties. It'd cost a fortune to fix, I'm told. A shame. Miss Teazle, the last owner, didn't work it, but liked having it there.'

The walk was further and the house bigger than Jordan had thought they would be. The house stood on raised stone foundations – Dad said something about a high water table and flood country – and was an obvious patchwork of styles and periods. Matched follies, the towers seen from the road, rose to either side, above a greenish thatched roof, topped by hat-like red tile cones with gabled Rapunzel windows. Aside from the towers, it was a farmhouse built at twice life-size. The ordinary-scale front door looked tiny. Ivy had been encouraged to grow, perhaps to cover the jigsaw-sections of red brick, white plaster and grey stone. Over the centuries, parts of the house had been replaced when they collapsed or people got tired of them. It had grown independent of any architect's designs or council's planning permission, evolving to suit its inhabitants.

Brian Bowker unlatched the front door.

'You might want to put locks on the exterior doors,' he said, 'though Miss Teazle never felt the need.'

Dad was horrified.

'This isn't exactly a high-crime area,' the agent said, 'but times have changed since the old girl was a young thing. It won't be a big job to make the house secure.'

Brian Bowker stood aside so they could step into a foyer. A combination of veranda and conservatory, it had a pleasant, damp straw smell. The ceiling was so low Dad banged his head on a dangling light-fixture – which would be the first thing to go. It took moments for Jordan's eyes to adjust to the green gloom. Plants were all around, some overgrowing their pots, extending tendrils across the stiff, brushy doormat. Something like ivy grew *inside* the foyer, twining around a wrought-iron boot-scraper, creeping up a trellis. A row of brass hooks was ready for a burden of coats. Several pairs of boots were tumbled together by the door. A bright yellow pair of wellies looked scarcely worn.

'Miss Teazle's things are still here,' said Brian Bowker. 'Her relatives in Australia want to throw in furniture and bric-a-brac. A lot of charity-shop stuff, but there might be treasures. She was rich, after all. Now, come on through and see this…'

He touched a section of the wall. A pair of doors slid open like secret panels, with a woody scraping sound. Beyond was cool darkness and a windowless hallway. The agent shepherded them inside and along a cramped corridor to another set of doors, which he pushed open.

As one, the family gasped. Brian Bowker chuckled.

Jordan would not have guessed a room in a private home could be so large. It was fully twenty feet high and twice that long. After the murk of the hall, it was filled with warm, wavering sunlight. Opposite the doors, French windows were inset into a panoramic expanse of picture windows. The view was impressive – not just the orchard, but the expanse of moorland. Facing away from the village, the house might have been at the edge of civilisation.

'Thanks to Dutch elm disease, you can see a

long way from here,' said the estate agent. 'From the towers, you can see Glastonbury Tor. That's all safety-glass, by the way. The original panes didn't come through the hurricane in 1987.'

That night – a few years before her brother was born – was among Jordan's first memories. Waking up with the windows of the flat rattling, angry elements threatening to blow them in, roaring winds and car alarms. Snuggling with Mum and Dad on their sofa, away from breakable glass. Then the mess on the streets next morning.

The room had a fireplace taller than Dad, several sets of upholstered furniture, a twelve-foot polished oak dining table, many nook-like retreats and hiding places. A Victorian chaise longue, with dark floral pattern cushions. Just the thing for her to be discovered draped across by Rick, transformed into her gentleman caller.

A brass chandelier hung from stout, bare beams; out of use, sconces dusty and clogged with old candle wax. Streetlight-like freestanding lamps were arranged around the space. Faded carpets, Turkish or Arabian, lay like quilt squares on the flagstone floor.

'This is the oldest room,' said Brian Bowker. 'The hearth and floor are fifteenth century. So is one of the walls. The house has been knocked down and rebuilt over and over. The towers are a nineteenth-century addition. An unusual feature. The big windows were first put in by Miss Teazle, after the war. She was born in this house, never lived anywhere else.'

The last owner of the Hollow had been a writer.

'I remember her from when I was a girl,' said

Mum. 'The Weezie books when I was little, then the Drearcliff Grange School series. Old-fashioned even then, but we all read them. I see things in this room that were in the stories: that's the fireplace Weezie hides in when she plays sardines. Louise Teazle must have done that when she was a girl, hidden in there. And written about it later. I expect all writers do that, fill their books with bits of their lives.'

Jordan had heard of Louise Magellan Teazle but never read her. When younger, she had read Alan Garner and C. S. Lewis. Now, she had lost the habit. There was too much else to do.

She imagined hiding from Rick in the fireplace and letting him find her. She was sure he would love this place too, when he saw it.

Brian Bowker showed them every part of the house. The two towers were the most obviously inhabited, connected to the house by the hall and four rather dark, cube-shaped rooms full of fascinating junk. These would need a lot of work to be reclaimed as guest rooms or storerooms. There were two completely fitted bathrooms, and two separate toilets – one outside, in a shed-like structure – which made Tim ecstatic at the thought of 'a bog for each of us!' In the West Tower were the kitchen (she saw precisely where her Alessi would look its best), a walk-in larder that was a room in itself, a master bedroom that hadn't been used since Miss Teazle's parents' day, and a maid's garret which Tim instantly claimed for his own.

The East Tower was smaller. Louise Teazle had used the ground-floor room as a study.

'Good grief,' said Dad, 'that's an Amstrad.'

An old word processor stood on a desk between an upright manual typewriter and a daisy-wheel printer. Jordan let her fingers linger on the word processor's keyboard and got a tiny static tingle.

'You can tell a writer lived here,' she said.

The walls were covered with bookshelves, and there were three old wooden filing cabinets.

Above the study was the bedroom the writer had slept in all her life. This, Jordan realised with a thrill, would be her room. It contained a canopied single bed, a frail-looking rocking chair by the window, an antique writing desk, a wash-stand with a matching basin and jug, a dressing table with an attached mirror and an odd little chest of drawers. Ancient toys and old-lady things were arranged like a museum exhibit. It should have been sad but somehow wasn't. Jordan believed Miss Teazle had stayed keen throughout her long life, not letting her childhood dim but never finding memory a trap. The bed had new sheets and a duvet, the colourful cover clashing with the pastel designs of the wallpaper. Something to be fixed.

Brian Bowker took them out through the French windows. Neglected, wild patches had been vegetable and herb gardens. Tiny blue and white flowers grew everywhere, even from the thatch of the roof and between the stones of the paths. Was there a book in the study about which plants were which? If not, she would get one from a library. She wanted to learn about birds and butterflies too. Rick had said to look out for mushrooms, poison ones and druggy ones.

Tim ran wild like a six-year-old, flashing back a few years to the golden age before his current personality had set in. He even swung from the low branches of a tree, as if raised in a jungle by apes. Mum and Dad laughed, relaxed, not worried about traffic or lurking paedophiles. This was what being a kid must have been like in the old days, when the Beatles were pop stars and television was black and white.

They called Tim and were shown the barn. The cider-press turned out to be a vast, complicated contraption with interesting wildlife sprouting from its innards and a wooden tub which still smelled of long-pulped apples.

A workbench was fixed to one wall. Outmoded tools were neatly arranged on hooks above it.

'Are there power points?' Dad asked.

The agent pointed them out. 'Put in when they took out the old generator and hooked the Hollow up to the mains. The place didn't even have a phone for years.'

'Sounds heavenly,' said Mum.

Dad laughed.

'That's all changed now,' Brian Bowker assured them. 'The utilities are all in order.'

Tim was especially taken with what looked like a child-sized tractor but turned out to be a sit-astride grass-mower.

'We've tried to keep the place trim since Miss Teazle passed away. A lass from the village comes in every couple of weeks to mow the orchard and hack the weeds. This is a very fertile patch. Miss Teazle had a pair of goats to nibble the grass, but they're gone now.'

'Frisky and Whiskey?' said Mum. The agent looked baffled. 'Those were the goats in the Weezie books.'

Dad raised his eyebrows. Mum wasn't embarrassed.

'It all comes back,' she said, tapping her head. 'All sorts of things are stored away up here.'

'Anything useful?'

Jordan tensed slightly but Mum laughed. Dad gave her waist a squeeze and kissed her.

The barn had a second storey, reachable via a wooden ladder and a hatch. They all looked up.

'There isn't anything up there,' said the agent. 'Miss Teazle was quite infirm. She wouldn't have been able to manage the climb.'

'I'll do a recce,' Tim announced. He swarmed up the ladder, disappeared through the hatch, clattered around in the dark, and poked his head back over the edge.

'There's a door,' he reported, 'in the wall, leading nowhere.'

She stepped out of the barn and saw what her brother meant. Twenty feet above ground was a wooden door, with a gibbet-like structure above it. The door rattled as Tim shoved it from the inside. It swung open and Tim leaned out over the drop, grinning broadly.

'That was for lowering bales of hay down into the yard,' Brian Bowker explained. 'You might think about keeping it bolted shut to prevent accidents.'

They took the point.

'Come down, Timbo,' said Dad. 'Before you do yourself an injury.'

Dad and the agent were both relieved when Tim vanished inside the barn and reappeared, dusty but unhurt, at ground level.

Brian Bowker knew he had a sale. He was talking as if there was a done deal and the Naremores were moving in a week from Tuesday.

Mum and Dad didn't contradict him.

They all left the barn, for a last look around.

Jordan felt funny. She was – she realised with a shudder – happy. After all she'd been through these last few years, she was home. A fresh start in a new place. It felt right, in a way she had either forgotten or never known.

Her secret plan was revised. The Hollow changed everything. Rick would understand; he always let her do the forward thinking.

Afternoon sunlight made a green-gold haze about the place, an aura of contentment. Shapes formed and wisped in the light patterns. Jordan imagined they were reluctant to see her go, eager for her return.

She couldn't wait to tell Rick about the Hollow but stifled an excited impulse to beg Dad for the car phone. The thought of calling her boyfriend now – with Tim and her parents eavesdropping – made her squirm inside. The family had been here less than half an hour and already she knew it was where they would settle.

In the hunchback, on the way to the last viewing, to a perfectly nice house that would have no chance of winning their hearts, Tim kept on about 'his room', listing places where his things could be put, and new things he would need. Usually, when he spun methodical fantasies upon impossible premises, he would continue until one or other of the family was forced to shoot him down. This time, they let Tim run on and on. This time, they understood exactly what he meant.

Mum pressed the play button on the in-car cassette player. Music filled the car, 'Spring Spring Spring' from *Seven Brides for Seven Brothers*. Jordan shivered again, not with cold but love.

She looked back, out of the rear window, and kept her eyes on the Hollow, even when only the tip of the taller tower was visible. When they were on the main road, she turned around and felt the need to count heads. All four of them were in the car but it was as if they had left someone vital behind.

As soon as the family was away from the Hollow, they missed their new home, each in their different way, each feeling at bottom the same thing. But they took the sights, sounds and smells with them, to well up unbidden in their minds as the next few weeks stretched into the next two months and they impatiently went through the business of buying and selling, as if homes could be made with money and contracts.

Besides memories, the family – as a single entity and four discrete individuals – took from the Hollow something else, something subtler and more lasting, something they shared but never got round to talking about. The magic was private and should not be spoken of out loud, for fear that it would evaporate like dew in the sun. It was as if they had exchanged vows with the place, leaving something of themselves behind and taking something of it away.

At long last, after what seemed an age, summer came and the family returned to the Hollow.

Weezie and the Gloomy Ghost

by

LOUISE MAGELLAN TEAZLE

Illustrations by Mr Kees Van Loon

This book was first published 11 October 1932
by Alder Bough Press

Reprinted fifty-two times

Paperback edition first published 1965
by Kilpartinger & Co. Ltd
Reprinted fourteen times

Magic edition published 1979
by Pyramid Children's Books Ltd

Reprinted ten times
This edition reset and illustrations
reoriginated 1988, reprinted 1988

Published 1990 by Mythwrhn
an imprint of Real Subscriber Books Ltd
The Pyramid, 112–56 Cardinal Wolsey St, London E14 4DL
and New York, Delhi, Auckland, Cape Town and Toronto
Reprinted 1991 (twice),1992, 1994
Reissued 1997

A CIP catalogue record for this title is available
from the British Library

Once, not so long ago and not so far away, there lived a good little girl named Weezie. Really, she was not so little as all that any more and perhaps not so good either. Her Mama and Papa said that since she had shot up so much the summer before she should be called by her proper name, which was not Weezie but something horrid.

When people used her proper name, she would pretend not to hear. She had been pretending for so long now that she really did not hear. She would go on humming to herself and ignoring her parents until they would finally give in and call out, 'Weezie, my Weeze, please not to tease!' Then she would look up and come indoors at a run.

Weezie liked to wear her blue pinafore, though its hem was well above her knees and Papa said she looked like a heron in it. She was still having lessons from Miss Emily Ginn, her governess. She would have to go away to a school when the leaves started to fall from the trees.

She lived with her Mama and Papa – and Miss Emily Ginn, Peter the Man, Katie the Cook and the goats Frisky and Whiskey – at Hilltop Heights, a big old house in the countryside far away from the city. Only Weezie knew, for she was clever in a way grown-ups had forgotten, that others lived with them. She knew Hilltop Heights was a Haunted House.

Everyone who ever lived at Hilltop, even when there was just a hill there without a house, had stayed on.

Oldest among the ghosts was Club, a Piltdown Man. He was not very bright and had little forehead to speak of, but was Weezie's best friend in all the world. His special place was in the hayloft, which had once been his cave. Weezie and Club made drawings together, of the strange animals that had lived in his time and the strange people who lived now. Club was a highly talented artist and would certainly be as wealthy and respected as Mr Van Loon if he were alive today.

The other ghosts were her friends too.

Sidney the Saxon and Guillaume the Norman, who had fought with thick, brittle swords. Goodie the milkmaid and Crispin the Fey, who had eloped together to spite proud Queen Titania and shared a love that was still sung of. Rupert the Cavalier and Noll the Roundhead, who had fought with thin, tempered swords. Adventurous Captain Harry Persimmon, who had sailed the seven seas and had a leg eaten by cannibals and an arm eaten by a shark; and his stay-at-home brother Jarge Percy, who had lived to a hundred and twelve without ever walking beyond sight of Hilltop Heights.

Sometimes, the ghosts played jokes. When a psychical investigator came from London to look over Hilltop Heights, they perpetrated such fearful pranks that Weezie had to become very grown-up and tell them all off. It was not nice to turn a man's hat inside out in mid air in front of him, even if he did lisp. When the investigator mentioned 'ectoplasmic manifestations' it came out as 'ectoplaththmic manifeththtationthth' and half a gallon of spit.

Hilltop Heights was an enchanted place. Every cupboard and carpet had its special qualities. In Weezie's room was a magic chest of drawers. The top drawer always had the same thing in and the bottom drawer never had the same thing twice and the middle drawer was always a jumble of surprises. Weezie loved surprises.

The ghosts were Weezie's friends.

One ghost, however, was not: the Gloomy Ghost.

She didn't know his real name and none of the others did either. He didn't show himself as he had looked when he was alive but instead lingered about a dreary part of the hill as a thick black cloud or a pool of murky slime. He clung low to the ground and seeped into the house like damp. Whenever the Gloomy Ghost was about, even on the sunniest and happiest of days, it felt like a long, rainy Wednesday afternoon. Weezie thought of him when she had toothache, and imagined his shadow gathering under the eaves when Miss Emily Ginn made her recite the seven times table.

Whenever china was dropped or a toe stubbed, the Gloomy Ghost was there. Whenever jam spoiled or a window broke, the Gloomy Ghost was sensed leaving the scene of the crime. But the worst habit of the Gloomy Ghost was that when he was most up to mischief, he would arrange matters so that Weezie, and not he, would take the blame.

She had lost count of the suppers she had missed and the times she had been sent to her room to learn her lesson. When that happened, the other ghosts would keep her company and endeavour to cheer her up.

They meant well and kept trying to help with her history lessons, but whenever Sidney and Guillaume or Rupert and Noll tried to tell her about the days in which they had lived they got into arguments and forgot about her.

Then, when even the nice ghosts were ignoring her, Weezie felt in her bones an icy shudder. The Gloomy Ghost's chuckle. He could only be happy if she was not. When she was unhappy she leaked tears and screwed up her face until she became what Papa called 'a Sneezy Weezie'. She hated to be called 'a Sneezy Weezie' more than she hated spinach and wasps, which were the worst things in the world. The only thing she hated more was her horrid, horrid real name.

The only times the Gloomy Ghost laughed out loud was when someone called Weezie 'a Sneezy Weezie'. At those times, it was all Weezie could do not to blub like a baby.

All the ghosts had special places in Hilltop Heights, like Club's cave or Goodie and Crispin's herb garden. The Gloomy Ghost's special place was a sad copse down by a stagnant stream. When not making mischief for Weezie, the Gloomy Ghost lay on the rocks like a pool of black slime or hovered low about stunted roots like a thick mist. More than anything, he liked it when Weezie got some of him on her blue pinafore and she had to wear something else until it was laundered.

Once, as a glorious summer morning was dawning and the ghosts were calling to Weezie to play outside in the sunshine, black ink was spilled over Papa's ledgers and trailed across Mama's best carpet by Weezie's shoes. It was useless to protest that she had not been wearing the shoes, had in fact outgrown them months ago. There was blame to be had and she would have to take it.

In her room, jailed for a whole day, she was a Sneezy Weezie. There was nothing else for it.

Why was the Gloomy Ghost so gloomy?

None of the others could tell her. He just was what he was.

She wished now that the ghosts had been nicer to the psychical investigator. He might have been able to tell her what to do about the Gloomy Ghost.

When finally let out of her room for supper, which she was to take today without dessert as a punishment, she was determined to sort the Gloomy Ghost out.

Things could not go on like this.

After supper, when it was almost dark and the summer day was gone for ever, she went out to the Gloomy Ghost's copse and stood over his black pool of slime.

'Why are you so horrid to me?' she asked, out loud. 'I've never hurt you, and nor has anyone else.'

The black pool rippled.

She thought the Gloomy Ghost was laughing and stamped her foot. A loose stone splashed into the pool.

Suddenly, she felt awful inside.

The Gloomy Ghost was not laughing. He was crying, harder than she had in her room.

She forgot that she was very angry.

For the first time, between sobs, the ghost spoke.

'You gave me your toothache,' he said. 'And that hideous multiplication table. Ghosts feel only what people near them feel. Whenever I came near you, you felt only nasty things. Seven times seven.'

She was surprised. She had not understood.

'And why do you call me Gloomy? I don't like it at all. No more than you like to be called Sneezy or...'

He used her real name, her horrid name. Hearing it was like a slap.

Weezie's heart ached. She thought back and couldn't remember when the Gloomy Ghost started to be gloomy. It seemed to be ever since she had known of him. But, she realised, she had been the one who gave him his name. The others had picked it up from her.

To him, it was as bad as her real name was to her. He hadn't chosen it and he hated it. If he was called Gloomy, he became gloomy. Worse than gloomy, cruel and mean. But, underneath, he wasn't like that. He wasn't like anything. He was a ghost.

She wanted to comfort him.

'There, there,' she said, letting her hand lie close to the pool but not touching the slime. 'What would you like to be called?'

'I... I don't know. I've forgotten my name.'

'Poor thing.'

A tear leaked from her eye and dropped into the pool. Where it fell, the black became clear as water but thinner than liquid, like pure light.

'I think I'd like to be called Merry,' said the Gloomy Ghost.

'The Merry Ghost?'

The pool rippled. Some slime accidentally got on Weezie's hand and before she could think not to she had wiped it on her pinafore, leaving a black streak. She frowned, but made herself not get angry.

The streak faded to nothing.

The black pool rose up and became white, taking shape.

The Merry Ghost was a little boy, younger than Weezie but about her height. She could see through him, but he had a definite form. He was smiling but his eyes had no practice at not looking sad so they gave him away.

Her tear coursed through him, through the ghost-stuff of his body, until it touched his phantom heart.

He smiled and reached out to hug Weezie.

His arms were clean but cold, and she shivered in his hug. It was a comforting shiver, a happy chill descending after a hot, stuffy day indoors.

From then on, the ghost was no longer gloomy.

Until she went away to school, Weezie was best friends with the Merry Ghost and Hilltop Heights was the happiest of haunted houses.

They had many other adventures, and perhaps you'll hear about some of them one day.

* finis *

Moving Day

Sun rose over the Hollow. Birds sang, and flew from the trees to the eaves of the house. Water boatmen skipped on the duckweed in the ditches. Early summer dew burned off in a trice. Apples, ripe early, hung in the orchard, ready to be eaten.

The Hollow was coming to life, in anticipation.

Brian Bowker drove Steven out to the Hollow and handed over the keys, along with an oilskin packet of papers and deeds. Steven shook hands with the estate agent, who lingered an awkward moment – not setting foot on property no longer under his custodianship, his right of access given away with the keys – and left, wishing the Naremores joy in their new home.

Steven opened the gate and let it swing inwards on its new hinges, then crossed the bridge. He found himself striding proudly up the drive, until he stood between the shadows of the towers. He got on his

37

mobile and told Kirsty they owned the Hollow. She said the movers had called and were on their way from London.

After ringing off, he wandered beyond the house and stood alone in his orchard, looking at his trees and his house, feeling the spring of his grass under his soles. At last, he could relax. For the first time in what must have been years, he was completely calm, secure, safe.

His wife and kids were back in Sutton Mallet, at the B&B where they'd spent the night. The family's belongings were in a removal van on a motorway. Steven's business was out in the aether: telephone numbers, e-mail addresses, websites, domain names and bank accounts in the process of transfer from one physical address to another. This moment of possession was his alone.

On behalf of the family, but his.

There had been a bad moment when the survey came back with a list of needed repairs, but the Teazle estate had dropped the asking price. In his profession, Bowker could almost pass for human. He'd gone out of his way to fix the deal, arranging for the urgent work to be done before exchange of contracts. Steven's ambition, however, was still never to be in a kitchen with an estate agent again.

Since that first visit to the Hollow, he'd been back several times, frustratingly chaperoned, suffering agonies of doubt. What had been obvious that first time was hard to recapture. He should not have worried. He knew that now.

Experience led him to expect disappointment, to

suspect a fast one being pulled. The hardest part was overcoming his instinct to distrust. He had to concede the possibility something good was being gifted.

It was still here. What they had all felt.

He looked up at the West Tower, at the window of the room he would share with Kirsty. In the flat – in the *old* flat – their double bed had to be jammed into a corner, leaving only a thin L of path around it. To get dressed or undressed without banging elbows or knees, they'd had to go into the bathroom. The master bedroom at the Hollow had space for a king-size bed, a dressing table, a full-length mirror and matching his-and-hers chests of drawers with room left over. Should they ever want to, they could fit in a hip-bath, a spinning wheel, a Nautilus machine and a pinball table. The walk-in wardrobe was the size of Tim's old room.

The window caught the sun and flashed like a mirror held by a partisan signalling an all-clear to comrades.

Because he could, because no one could stop him, Steven let his body go limp and fell to his knees, feeling the cool of the grass through his jeans, then pitched forward onto his face and rolled over to look up at the sky.

He lay on the land he owned. Tree branches crowded his vision. Green and gold fruit hung, waiting to be plucked and eaten. They must all have apples. It would be a ceremony. Eating the fruit would seal the pact.

His mobile trilled. He let it ring for long seconds.

Overarching branches shielded him from the sun. He did not have to squint or blink. He could focus on the gentle movements of the trees. They had been beckoning; now they were welcoming.

Steven felt as if he were being hugged.

Jordan kept an eye on the road ahead. It wasn't a winding country lane but an arrow-straight Roman causeway across a moor. It would be all too easy to drive into a ditch if the road took a sharp, unexpected kink. Mum, car phone wedged between shoulder and jaw, ran over her things-to-do-list, talking equally to Dad over the phone and Jordan and Tim in the car.

Mum was sensitive about her driving – she'd been in two accidents, and once lost her licence for a year – so Jordan didn't mention any minor veering or the incident of the startled cyclists. She would only speak up if a Naremore life was threatened. Tim had a dent in his forehead, near the hairline, from the worse of the two crashes. He was always careful to fasten his seat belt now, even when sitting in a parked car. Jordan had been in the accident too, but only sustained minor bruises. She remembered the instant of grinding terror, though.

Jordan saw Mum had spotted the turn-off. They had their own signpost: THE HOLLOW ½M. On large-scale maps, the place was listed as if it were a tiny village separate from the already-tiny-enough Sutton Mallet.

The signpost was a pick-up point for the school buses she and Tim would be catching come September. Because of a discrepancy in the educational systems of town and country, it was easier to let them miss a month or so at the end of this academic year and start fresh in the autumn, after an extended holiday which stretched ahead like an eternity. Tim would be joining Class Six of primary school in Huish Episcopi. She would be in the second year at Sedgwater College.

Her old college let her sit her mocks a month early, to help with the move. She had done as well as expected. Exams had never been among her problems. That was one of the reasons few noticed the problems she did have: as long as she got marks in school, all must be right at home and in her heart.

There was no point thinking like that. Things were different now.

She could hardly believe it herself, but last night in the cramped B&B room, even before they were in the Hollow, she had breathed easier and slept well. Weights which had pressed down on her for as long as she could remember were lifted. She wanted to call Rick as soon as possible, and tell him how she felt, how things were changing. Without Rick, she might not have made it through the dark forest to this clearing.

Mum's list ran on as she drove along the turn-off that became the drive of the Hollow. At this rate, her parents would still be on the phone to each other when they were face to face.

'Nearly there, Steven,' said Mum. 'I'll click off.'

She put the car phone in its dashboard cradle, and checked on Jordan and Tim with glances up at the rear-view mirror and to the side.

'You two have everything sorted? We've a lot to get through today.'

Getting the major moving-in done in one day was

important to Mum and Dad. They wanted to sleep soundly in their new house and wake up the next morning to find themselves at home.

For Jordan, it would be different. It would take months of exploring and teasing and rearranging and experimenting before she was settled. It would be like when she started going out with Rick, and wasn't quite sure what to make of him but knew it would be all right in the end. She looked forward to the long business of moving-in. It would be an adventure, just as Rick had been – was still – an adventure.

'Your LL has been noted and processed, ma'am,' said Tim.

'LL?' queried Mum.

'Lengthy List,' Jordan explained.

Tim's acronyms often annoyed Mum, but now she laughed, half-turned and accepted her son's salute.

Tim wore baggy camouflage trousers, a green-black T-shirt and an SAS-style black beret. For this mission, he had tiger-striped his face grey and green and gold.

Jordan sometimes thought her little brother inhabited one of those weird zones. Then again, she was hardly one to speak up. None of the Ne'er-do-well Naremores could stand for the Average Normal Party.

'Where's he got to?' Mum asked.

They were driving through the gate, over the bridge – less rickety-rackety after the concrete fix-up required by what Tim called the SS, Sinister Survey – and onto (into?) the Hollow. Mum looked around for Dad.

They had agreed, in a way Jordan thought was

sweet, that he should not go into the house – *their* house – without them. The family should take the first step inside together.

Dad should be outside.

'You could always give him a bell,' Jordan suggested.

Mum instinctively reached for the car phone before realising it was a joke.

'HH,' she said, exaggeratedly. Standing for 'ha-ha', it was a Timism the whole family had picked up on.

'Is Dad a casualty?' Tim asked.

Jordan and Mum looked where Tim was pointing, between the garage and the house. Dad was lying flat on the ground in the orchard, limbs stretched out in an X. Hearing the car, he sat up sharply, flyaway hair sticking out, displaying a goofy grin.

'Definitely a casualty,' Mum confirmed.

It was a day of firsts and rituals. That was important. They linked arms and octopus-stepped over the threshold, cramming themselves into the foyer. Then they laughed as Steven searched his pockets for the keys which he had only just put away, refusing to let his arms free until they were properly inside. He had forgotten the inner foyer doors, which led into what Tim called 'the secret passage'. All the doors and windows were newly fitted with locks. The keys were still shiny and hard to tell apart, but he instinctively slid the right one into the lock and it turned easily.

Kirsty and Jordan set out to make a ceremonial pot of tea. There were cups a-plenty in the kitchen, though they had to be rinsed of months' dust. Kirsty had brought tea-bags and milk from the village shop. While the womenfolk saw to their chores, Steven and Tim went out to fetch apples.

'The golden ones are sweet and for eating, while the green ones are tart and for cooking,' said Kirsty.

'You should get the gold ones,' added Jordan.

'HH,' said Steven and Tim, together.

In the orchard, Steven put on an ironic caveman voice and told his son, 'Men hunt, women cook.'

'Women can hunt,' said Tim.

'Absolutely, Timmy.'

Steven hefted Tim, who was getting to be quite a weight at ten up onto his shoulders and hoisted him towards an apple-bearing branch.

'I can't reach, PP.'

PP. Paternal Parent.

'I can't heft you any higher.'

'It's all right.'

Apples fell past Steven and thumped on the grass. Four exactly.

'The branch bent. I couldn't reach it, but it could reach me.'

'If that isn't a welcome, I don't know what is.'

He crouched and let Tim vault off his shoulders. Straightening up, he saw the branch still swaying, having given up its gifts. Tim snapped off a salute to the tree, which Steven solemnly echoed.

Tim pulled the front of his T-shirt out into an apron-pocket and piled in the apples. His white tummy and arms undermined his junior commando look, made him less Tim o' the Green.

This could work, Steven thought. No, he must be

more positive. This *would* work.

The past two months had been eerily quiet. At first, he felt he was walking through a landscape dotted with unexploded bombs, some sticking obviously out of the dirt, others buried just below the surface. An explosion would almost have been a relief. At least, a big bang would mean things getting back to what passed for normal. Then it dawned on him. A tiny green shoot of an idea, poking up through the blasted landscape. Could this be hope? Had everything really changed?

The family had made an unspoken pact. Their mission, as Tim would have put it, was to get back to the Hollow, to occupy the position and to hold off all-comers. With that end in view, sacrifices Steven had expected to be forced after screaming matches were made with quiet dignity. It was not just about Dad being a crackpot.

Before they saw the Hollow, the mooted move had been an act of desperation, a last chance. It had been this or call in the lawyers, the therapists and – God help him but it might have come to it – the hit men. Since their first sight of this place, he had begun to feel they were not escaping from anything but escaping to something.

Now they were here, safe.

While the removal men carried family belongings into the house, Tim executed a complete reconnoitre of the territory. With two cups of tea in him, he piddled in all four of the toilets, achieving a satisfactory FF (First Flush) in each. He had enough pee left to spray a few drops into the ditch at the far border of the property. Holes plopped in a green mass of duckweed, took slow moments to fill in. In the city, only the homeless piddled in the open air, but the country welcomed the watering.

That first time, Tim had carried out only the most perfunctory reconnaissance. Mum and Dad had been back to the Hollow while prepping the relocation. The BS had gone along on one of those expeditions, but he was held in reserve, confined to quarters. This was the key deployment. It was on him now. He had to get the lie of the land, assess its potential. Once mapped and known, landscape was an ally.

First, he inspected the perimeter. He began at the bridge, looked over the clean concrete support pillars which had been put in recently. Plants were already swarming up around them, green rust spreading in tendrils. He slid down the thickly grassed slope to the slow-flowing stream and looked under the bridge. He dipped his hand in the cool water. In a pinch, it was potable.

He found an unrusted steel strut which made a perfect hand-hold and slipped under the bridge, curling up and jamming his knees against the concrete underside to keep his feet out of the water. There was just enough space to crawl along, hanging upside down, reaching from strut to strut, without getting wet. Emerging into sunlight, he awarded himself ten merit points for the small manoeuvre but deducted five for forgetting to time himself against his stopwatch. If he didn't know his time, how could he better it?

Beyond the bridge, he stayed down in the stream-bed and made his way to the corner of the property, where a T-junction fed the ditch around the Hollow. The moat was shallow, a reflecting runnel of green water in the centre of a strip of muddy, reed-thronged marsh. Insects crawled and buzzed, some fabulously strange.

Tim made his way around the ditch, until he was back where he started. The Hollow's moat consisted of two flowing streams connected by still cross-channels. The moor, neutral territory, was divided into fields by these ditches. Far off, he could see sheep.

His hands and arms were brown now, with grey patches where mud had dried in the sun.

The perimeter secure, he mentally divided the property into quadrants: orchard, garage/barn, house, drive. The garage/barn and the house would warrant extensive individual patrols, but orchard and drive were open territory. At present, the drive was occupied by the movers' vehicle. Tim found a spot by an outlying tree, in a clump of bushes dotted with tiny yellow flowers. He blended in to watch the removal men at work. Since the secret passage was narrow, they had to lug the bigger items round by a side path and through the glass doors. He was pleased none of them spotted him. They were not potential hostiles, but this was fresh country and he needed the practice. He had to become part of the land.

He thought about the orchard. He felt good about the place. The tree had dropped apples into his hand. An operative could live off the land in that quadrant, find shelter and provisions. Vegetation would conceal him from enemy eyes.

The largest of the trees had fallen once, but grew still. The trunk had split open and its inside was rotted out, but it had survived and flourished. A thick, healthy limb extended from the main trunk, spreading living branches from the hollow bole, sound wood growing from the dead. This was a good place. When prying eyes were gone, he would work with an entrenching tool and make himself a lair. PP had said something about helping Tim build a treehouse, but that wasn't quite in the plan. He envisioned a hide, which would be secret. From the outside, it must just look like a fallen tree. Hostiles would stroll past without knowing they were mere feet from his lair. He had a code-name ready, Green Base.

The old campaign, the city mission, was over. No victory could be claimed, since it was abandoned before objectives were secured. A black demerit against him, which he would have to work hard to wipe out. Though it had not been his decision, forces had withdrawn and he had pulled out along with the rest of them.

Here, there would be a new campaign.

At the Hollow, there was a chance for G and G. Gold and glory.

A fresh apple fell, nearby. Tim reached out and it slapped right into his hand, a perfect catch.

Earlier, he had shared fruit with the family.

This was just for him.

The Hollow swallowed everything they had brought from London. When heaved into place by the removal men, their desks and chairs stood out, clashing with what was there. But if Kirsty looked again a few minutes later, she couldn't tell what was old and what was new – except the obvious Naremore gadgets Miss Teazle had lived and died without: widescreen TV, computers, CD and DVD players, fax, microwave.

Kirsty's old things, bits of furniture from the flat, were newer than things which had been here for ever, or at least since Louise Teazle was a girl. Decisions must be made soon. Stuff would have to go. Their leaved dining table looked like a sideboard next to the Hollow's main table, which was long, wide and solid enough for a catwalk.

She was ready to be ruthless. Someone in this family had to be. First for the chop: a dusty five-bar electric heater which stood in the huge fireplace. Its inadequate grille and visibly frayed fabric cord were accidents in the making.

The Hollow was a project worthy of her full attention. She had ideas about how it could be made to work for them. At the moment, Steven thought of it as only a home, but Kirsty saw more, a potential business asset. She wasn't ready to set out her ideas yet, but when she did they would be stunners.

They already had post, dumped on an escritoire in the passage. She carried it into the main room. Letters had come from electricity, water, satellite TV and telephone suppliers. A technician would be out tomorrow to hook up more phone lines and the satellite dish was due at the end of the week. She glanced at an electoral register form and a set of leaflets from the council and read several cards from people who had received their change-of-address note.

'You haven't dropped out of the rat race,' wrote Bobbie, 'you're just running faster than the other rats.' What had her sister meant by that? Probably nothing; it was widely accepted that Bobbie was barking.

When she picked up a slim packet, borders edged with the self-invented hieroglyphs Vron used on everything, an uneasy plunge of anticipation troubled her stomach. She had no idea how her best friend was really taking the family move, whether she saw it as a betrayal or an abandonment. She turned over the jiffy bag several times, trying to puzzle out runes she knew were impenetrable. To the horror of the Post Office, Vron once sent Steven a birthday parcel blatantly marked 'contains Anthrax and Poison', CDs of the metal bands he didn't like. After a deep breath, she slit open the packet. Out slid a shiny, modern paperback. *Weezie and the Gloomy Ghost*, first of the Weezie books. Inside the book was an Escher postcard with 'Luck' lettered on the back.

Kirsty thought Vron didn't believe in luck, then remembered her friend's actual statement was that she believed people made their own luck. Thinking for a moment, she decided it was a fair post-break card, a helpful note – though 'Good Luck' would have been less ambiguous. The picture, of impossible lizards climbing impossible stairs, meant something she would puzzle out later. Everything Vron did meant something. The book would be useful. She would re-read it, perhaps aloud to Steven and the kids... though she'd better keep back who it came from. Vron was still a touchy subject at family meetings.

A cream envelope was addressed to 'The New Owners'. Mr Bernard Wing-Godfrey, President of the Louise Magellan Teazle Society, asked permission to pay a visit to discuss matters relating to the late authoress. He congratulated the Naremores on being lucky enough to live in his heroine's house.

Did Wing-Godfrey mean Weezie or Miss Teazle?

She hadn't read a Louise Magellan Teazle in thirty-five years. Suddenly, looking at the little girl on the cover of the book, a penny dropped. Weezie was short for Louise, doubly short for Louise Teazle. They must have called Louise 'Weezie' when she was little. Kirsty paged through *Weezie and the Gloomy Ghost*, looking at the Van Loon illustrations. Hilltop Heights was the Hollow taken off a moor and put on a hill. One picture showed Weezie's home in full, in the distance beyond the copse where Weezie stood with the transformed Merry Ghost. The two towers were unmistakable. Kirsty wanted to share this with Steven, soon.

She looked around, remembering what she had said on the viewing day, that she could see things from the stories in the big room – what would they call it, the hall? – and all around the house.

Kirsty had never known such a happy place.

And now she lived here.

She had been told about happy places, but never been able to believe in them. Until the break, Vron had told her that what she needed to do was find a happy place inside herself and move into it when things got too much. Vron said you could furnish your happy place from memory and whimsy. When she had tried, Kirsty imagined a big room filled with items that meant something to her. She hadn't got very far before it all fell apart.

Like a lot of Vron's ideas, the happy place theory was barely workable. But before giving up, Kirsty had remembered to include Weezie's magic chest of drawers, with the top drawer that always had the same thing in and the bottom drawer that never had the same thing twice and the middle drawer which was always a jumble of surprises.

There was a three-drawer chest in Jordan's room. She was sure she had seen it. An idea clicked in her mind and a wish warmed her heart.

Kirsty went up, above Miss Teazle's study, and looked in on her daughter.

'Hello, Mum. What's up?'

Jordan had her three matching pink suitcases open on the bed.

The chest of drawers was in a corner. Kirsty was drawn to it. She touched its stained surface. The brass handles were tarnished. It had taken some punishment over the years. Louise must have had a kitten; old scratches marred the bottom drawer.

(that never had the same things twice)

'Would you mind if I had this in our room?'

'That thing?'

'It's too small for your collection.'

A taller chest of thinner drawers was in the middle of the room, final resting place undecided. Its drawers were sealed with masking tape.

Jordan thought a while and Kirsty found herself on tenterhooks. What if her daughter refused? After so long without a blow-up, was this worth one?

'Feel free, Mum.'

Kirsty was relieved and hugged Jordan, suddenly, harder than she intended.

'Oof. What's that for?'

'Because I have the best family in the world.'

Jordan looked at her, not sure if she were serious or setting a trap. Kirsty couldn't blame her, not after everything.

'So do I, Mum.'

Tears started in Kirsty's eyes. Happy tears.

With clothes unpacked and things provisionally arranged, Jordan could relax, easing into her room as if it were a warm, scented bath. She picked a suitable disc from a Perspex rack and fitted it into her portable CD-tape-tuner: the Chordettes, *Sentimental Journey*. She lowered herself into the rocking chair, gingerly in case it snapped to twigs under her weight. The chair was just her size. She settled and put out a foot, resting it against the low window-sill. She eased herself gently back and forwards, in time to 'Carolina Moon'. The movement was strangely sexual.

Her favourite photograph of Rick was tucked into a corner of the dressing-table mirror, where he could gurn at her when she played with her face. As she rocked, his tiny eyes seemed to follow her.

When Dad and Mum told her the family was moving to the West Country, Jordan threw one of her wobbliest wobblies. She refused to eat for a week and retreated to her cupboard-like old room. Putting on her eyelashed sleep mask and earphones, she played heartbroken Patsy Cline directly to her brain.

She thought only one thing: leaving London meant losing Rick. The whole move was cunningly designed to make her utterly miserable.

It wasn't as if coming by a boyfriend had been easy. She was one of those girls boys were afraid of. It was odd, because she had always had more boy friends than girl friends. Talking to fellas was easier because she had more to talk about with them. All the boys she had been friends with until the last few years went mad with puberty. They either started looking at her with that expression that really did have to be called 'undisguised lust' no matter how silly it sounded, or wanted to pour out their hearts about how they were tragically smitten with some twitty girl Jordan wouldn't have given the time of day.

She wasn't tribal, either: while classmates were deciding which Spice Girl to emulate, her role models were Doris Day in the tart romantic comedies of the early 1960s and Audrey Hepburn in *Funny Face* and *Breakfast at Tiffany's*. She listened to all kinds of music, but mostly liked singers from the 1950s and early 1960s. For a while, she had worn a headband like Jackie Kennedy and dressed for college in a powder-blue suit with matching shoes and gloves. When asked why she favoured odd styles, she could only say they felt right to her, embarrassed even by terms like 'vintage' and 'retro'.

The thing about Rick was that he hadn't been at the same schools as her from the age of six. They had met in college as more-or-less adults and didn't have any history. He noticed her in the common room, when she was smoking her third ever cigarette. She had bought a long pink holder in the Oxfam shop and had to take up the habit to make use of it. He was a sci-fi freak and said she looked like Lady Penelope from *Thunderbirds*. He had unmanageable red hair and crooked teeth, but she had known at once about him, as she had known at once about the Hollow.

If it had been a few years ago, the move would have meant starting all over. Tim had already forgotten his city friends and was ready for country duty. But she was different.

As soon as she saw the Hollow, she knew that moving wasn't leaving, wasn't a straight swap. Dad was bringing his business with him, prepared to work out of a virtual office. Mum wouldn't cut herself off from the support network she'd built up in London. Map distance meant very little these days.

Her parents knew she had slept with Rick. She had put up with their lecture about being 'sensible', though she gathered that as teenagers they'd been gob-happy, pill-popping, joylessly promiscuous punks. There were photos of Mum with her hair in a Mohawk ruff. The major concession Jordan had extorted in return for her cooperation with house-hunting expeditions was that Rick would be able to sleep over at the flat. As it happens, they had only been able to take advantage of the ruling twice and on one of those times her period had been on and they couldn't do anything. She had been assured with a solemnity on a par with a clause in a peace treaty ending a thirty-year border war that Rick would always be welcome at the Hollow, to stay for as long as he wanted. He was leaving college in a month's time and would come down for a long visit. Then he was taking a year off to work as a cycle messenger before going to the University of the West of England in Bristol, only fifty minutes away from Sutton Mallet. It took longer to get across London in the rush hour. She was already determined to get into UWE. It made perfect sense. The Communications degree Rick was taking was ideal for her. The puzzle pieces all fitted.

She would be happy in this place. Rick too.

Back in the city, she was still a kid because everyone she knew thought of her that way. They looked at her style choices and thought she was playing dress-up, but this was the way she was, was who she was. It wasn't going to change.

Here, at the Hollow, she would be treated as a young lady.

From her window, she saw Tim dart from tree to tree, finding spots of cover. This was his paradise too.

As she rocked, she remembered caresses. Afternoon sunlight fell upon her, warming her face and hands and throat like soft, warm fingers.

Clear voices told Jordan what she could expect from love.

Steven gave the removal men bottles of beer from the cool-box. It was a hot day and they'd unloaded in double-quick time.

The three blokes from the city, sweaty from work, sat on the grass by his drive, blinking in the sunlight.

Already, he was apart from them. They were alien but he was at home. He was from the Hollow. He was a Hollow man.

'Lovely spot you've found here, Steve,' said Ben, the driver. 'Idyllic.'

Ben's shifters – a friendly Rasta called Trey and a silent lad, Jimmie – drank their beer and looked up at the towers. This must be totally beyond their experience.

'Wonderful for kids,' said Ben. 'Specially your younger pair. Loads of places for hide and seek. They're already at it, I see.'

'Tim's gone to ground,' Steven admitted.

They looked past the house, into the orchard.

'It's like "how many animals can you see in this picture?"' suggested Trey.

Steven laughed. Tim was crawling by the fallen tree, keeping close to its shrinking noontime shadow.

'What's your little girl's name?' Ben asked.

'Jordan?'

'No. The littler one. With the straw hat.'

'Don't understand your banter, old chap,' said Steven, stiffer than he meant.

'She was watching us inside, from the fireplace,' said Ben. 'Wasn't she, lads?'

Reluctantly, Trey nodded. Steven noticed he had crossed his fingers, all eight of them.

'Pretty little thing,' said Ben. 'With ribbons.'

'Not one of mine, I'm afraid. Must be a stray.'

'There was no girl,' said Jimmie. He didn't have the thin voice Steven had imagined. 'Just shadows. Playing tricks.'

Ben let it drop. Steven was puzzled. Something was

odd here, but he'd have time to hunt it down. He was going to have a lot of time.

He had arranged with his major clients to take things easy for the next month while he got the Hollow sorted out. Then, he would be open again for business and better than ever.

Steven wasn't a stockbroker, an accountant or an investment counsellor. In the pits of the crash, ejected from the brokerage where he'd worked for most of the eighties, he had found a gap in the money market and made up his own job. He found individuals or institutions with funds to invest and brought them together with individuals or institutions with projects which needed finance. He was an intermediary, a deal-maker. It was a game, really: putting together financial jigsaws. Tatum, his personal assistant, was keeping his city office open, but the business was in Steven's head and computer files. When he worked it out, he was surprised at how little he needed to be in London. Well over half his clients weren't city-based. He just hoped there would be enough for Tatum to do to justify her salary. Especially when he took on someone local to handle secretary-assistant chores here.

'Talk about peace and quiet,' said Ben. 'Listen to that.'

A few birds. Tiny tree-shifting sounds. Kirsty pottering about in the house. No traffic, no voices, no car alarms.

'And breathe the air.'

Steven took in a lungful and didn't choke.

'Wait till someone spills a load of cow's muck on the

road,' said Trey. 'Then talk to me about your effluents.'

'I hope you know what you're doing, Mr Naremore,' said Jimmie. 'This isn't the city.'

'True,' said Trey. 'No clubs, no cinemas, no tube trains, no Saturday nights. Prob'ly can't get espresso for a hundred mile hereabouts.'

'Oh yes I can. I've brought my own machine.'

Trey laughed, dreads shaking.

'We're here to escape from Saturday nights,' Steven said.

'That's not what I mean,' said Jimmie.

'I'd go mad inside a week,' said Trey.

'Just be careful,' said Jimmie. 'Shadows can be deceiving. You need to shine your light all around.'

Kirsty put a bowl of apples, which Tim had gathered, on top of her new chest of drawers, the Weezie chest. She remembered how it went, and recited to herself.

'"The top drawer always had the same thing in and the bottom drawer never had the same thing twice and the middle drawer was always a jumble of surprises."'

She pulled open the top drawer. It was empty. And the bottom drawer. Empty too. The middle drawer was stuck. She had to scrape a seal of paint with a nail-file before she could jiggle it open. It was crammed with bent, rusty wire coat hangers. A jumble, certainly, but not really surprising. She took out the hangers and twisted them into a modern artwork which she shoved into one of the Sainsbury's bags they were using for the rubbish. Hanger-hooks speared through the plastic like claws.

So much for Weezie's magic chest of drawers.

When she was a little girl, Louise Teazle must have had more imagination than Kirsty's children. Of course, she had grown up to be a writer. She had to have imagination. Sometimes Kirsty wondered what was wrong with her kids. Shouldn't they be crazier? They were both far too responsible. At Jordan's age, she'd been a wild woman, with biro-tattooed knuckles and safety-pin piercings. Her daughter's watchwords were 'neat' and 'nice'. There was hope for Tim, though, when he grew out of this military thing.

A magic chest of drawers shouldn't be empty. She pulled out the bottom drawer and popped in an apple. She hadn't noticed but there was an old newspaper lining the drawer, faded to match the brown of the wood. The headlines were about Chairman Mao and Christian Barnard. She shut the drawer.

Pleased with herself, she put apples in the two other drawers.

Weezie, she remembered, had to feed her chest of drawers with cake, to keep it magic. Louise's mother ('Mama') must have gone spare if she really did that, left pieces of cake in with the linen to mould.

She looked out of the window.

Jordan sat in her rocking chair in her own bedroom window, in the opposite tower. She looked like Norman's mother in *Psycho*, which made Kirsty giggle. Steven was in the drive, bonding with the removal men over beer. Tim was in the orchard, creeping up on an invisible enemy.

From here, she could see her whole family.

Knowing where everything was calmed her. Vron said Kirsty was deathly afraid of letting things get away from her, that she needed perspective. That was one of Vron's metaphors, but here it was literally true. All along, what she had needed was not Temazepam or primal scream therapy but a tower tall enough to look down from, to be sure everything was all right.

She wanted an apple. An apple from the orchard.

There were some still in the bowl, but she decided to take one out of the chest.

She opened the top drawer. There was no apple.

She felt inside, reaching and finding that the drawer had no back. The apple must have fallen.

The middle drawer was stuck again, so she pulled out the bottom drawer. Two apples lay on the newspaper. She laughed, realising the magic had worked. The top drawer, which had been empty when she first pulled it out, always had the same thing in it. Nothing. The bottom drawer, which had also been empty, never had the same thing twice. First it was empty, then it had one apple, now two apples. Of course, there was an explanation. The apple had fallen from the top drawer to the bottom. All magic was like that, she supposed: it came with an explanation.

She gave the middle drawer a wrench, not really expecting a jumble of surprises. The drawer came open, and she looked down at a pool of apple sauce.

Time to make a full report to the PP. Tim snapped off a salute, and ran down the intel he had gathered from his recce.

Dad nodded. Usually, he barely took in Tim's reports. Today, first day of the new mission, he paid attention.

'There are no hostiles within the perimeter,' Tim reported. 'This is a safety zone.'

'That's good to know, Timmy.'

'The IP is friendly.'

'International pachyderms?'

'Indigenous population.'

Dad flashed a proper smile. 'Of course.'

'I'll run information-gathering sorties over the next week, so we know what animal life we've got around the place.'

'Did you run across a little girl in a straw hat?'

'No, PP. Should I have?'

Tim was genuinely puzzled.

'Not really. You can stand down now, Timmy.'

Tim let his breath out and slumped a little.

'You look tuckered out, soldier. Better hop off to the bathroom and get that camouflage off before the MP catches you. There'll be an inspection later. Best not have dirt under the fingernails.'

Tim recognised Dad was playing along. The PP only half-understood the mission. Brass were like that everywhere, Tim supposed. But they were over him for a reason. His job wasn't to question authority.

He made his way to one of the bathrooms.

He would be careful to look out for this little girl in a straw hat. She was probably not hostile, but he couldn't be sure until he'd cleared her himself.

In the bathroom, he methodically cleaned his face, hands and arms. Then he changed into civvies.

* * *

How could that happen?

It wasn't exactly apple sauce. There were pips and a stem in there, and shredded peel. She touched it, but didn't dare taste. It was as if a whole apple had been put in a blender and given a couple of minutes.

A jumble of surprises?

She shut the drawer and pulled it out again.

Still apple sauce, but she found out why the drawer kept sticking. One last hanger-hook, broken off, was caught in the runner. It had come loose now and lay in the apple mess.

She looked in the top drawer. Still empty.

The bottom. No apples, no newspaper. A shiny copper coin. A 1948 half-penny. She shut the drawer and pulled it out again. No apples, no newspaper, no coin. A single, limp, white glove. She took it out and slipped it on. It was elbow-length, with a pearl button at the wrist. It felt warm, as if it had just been worn. She liked the glove. It was elegant, seemly, fitting, and it fitted.

She closed and opened the drawer again, hoping for a match. This time, there was a dried, pressed flower. A rose. That gave her pause. Rose was her middle name, and Vron's. A word of power between them. When they signed messages 'Rose', it signified something of paramount importance. They had called their music venture Rose Records. She picked up the rose with gloved fingers.

It was as if she was being spoken to, with symbols. A very Vron-like way of going about things.

No. She was being silly. The chest must be a conjuring prop. There were hidden blades in the middle drawer, and a false back to the whole thing. When she opened and closed the drawers, she was tripping tiny levers, shifting objects around. It was no surprise Louise would have such a thing. She wrote about magic, so people would have given her magical presents. Had it been made for one of the television adaptations of Weezie?

She opened the top drawer, the one that always had the same thing, nothing. It did not disappoint her. She took the plastic bag of bent coat hangers and jammed it in. The bag barely fitted and she had to bend and break the hangers further, ripping the bag to uselessness, to get the tangle to lie flat enough for her to close the drawer.

She counted slowly up to five and opened the top drawer.

Nothing.

She closed and opened, closed and opened, closed and opened.

The hangers were gone for ever. This was better than a kitchen waste-disposal unit. She found other things that needed to be thrown away – bags and wrappers and ruptured cardboard boxes – and disappeared them.

She picked up the chest of drawers. It wasn't heavy. It couldn't contain an intricate mechanism. It wasn't connected to any hidden chute. She'd humped it here from Jordan's room and knew it was just a piece of furniture.

It was magic. That was all there was to it.

* * *

Steven was in charge of the family's first proper meal at the Hollow. Kirsty had produced a bean salad in Tupperware and a joint of cold ham for lunch, which had been eaten outside with the removal men. Now the family were alone together and could break bread – Delia's pasta carbonara, actually, but with warmed French bread on the side – at their own table.

Tim set the places. Jordan picked the wine and the music (she had to tell Steven who it was, Julie London). The children collaborated on the carrying-out of bowls and bottles from the kitchen to the big room, which he realised now was to be called the Summer Room. Never before had Steven cooked in a room different from the one where they ate. It meant a whole new tier of jobs to be parcelled out.

Kirsty came down from the tower, in her backless cream evening dress, with one white glove. She had put her hair up.

Steven was stunned.

Tonight, when the kids were in bed, there was another inaugural ceremony to be seen to. When they had got their first flat together, they had christened all three rooms in one night, with dozes between bouts of lovemaking, and had enough left over in the early morning for afterplay in the tub of the tiny bathroom.

Counting the inside toilet, the secret passage, the larder and the foyer but not the outside toilet or the barn-garage (which might bear investigation), there were sixteen rooms at the Hollow. Maybe more, if some of the wardrobes were reckoned and further exploration of the unused store-rooms disclosed secret nooks. At thirty-eight, Steven wasn't sure if he was up to it in a month, let alone a night. And there'd be awful complications with Jordan's and Tim's rooms.

Looking at Kirsty, though, he wondered.

These last years – God knows how many? – their lives had been changing. Properly looking at her had sometimes been difficult. There were always people – the kids, Vron, others – and things – work, craziness, medication – in the way. They had both turned into strangers.

His wife was still a stranger, but not in a frightening way.

Behind her, the moors were twilit. A moon hung up high, light scattering in through the wall of glass, falling all about the Summer Room. The view was spectacular, endlessly changing but eternally the same. From this room, the landscape they saw was exactly as it would have been to a Monmouth rebel or a Roman legionary standing on the same spot. Only the occasional winking red aeroplane light among the stars let slip that this was nearly the twenty-first century.

And his wife was the same. Eternally the same, eternally a surprise. He remembered how she had been when they met, and understood that in recent years she had just channelled her wildness into other things. Now, it was being directed back at him and his mouth was dry with excitement.

'Where's the other glove, Mum?' Jordan asked.

'Does everything have to be symmetrical, darling girl?'

Kirsty made a flourish with her fingers.

Steven was suddenly very hungry indeed.

They all took their places at the table, clustering at one end around a candelabrum Jordan had found in one of the unexplored rooms. Candles dripped on white cloth. The big bowl of pasta had to be passed from person to person. It was almost too heavy for Tim.

Steven hadn't had to say grace since school and wasn't about to start now. But something had to be said. He could not let this moment pass.

He lifted a glass of wine.

'A toast, I'm afraid. We have to have one. Jordan, pour Tim some wine.'

No protest came from Kirsty, whose eyes and earrings sparkled with candlelight. Tim put aside his orange juice and Jordan grinned at her brother as she decanted a half-measure of Chilean red. Steven was determined to do this properly.

'To us, to the Naremore family, and to our new home. We would like to thank the Hollow for having us, and we hope that it will keep us always.'

'Here here,' said Jordan, chinking her glass against Tim's.

The sparkles in Kirsty's eyes were tears. Steven's chest tightened with unbidden memories of other tears. The glass in his hand was crystal, very easy to shatter with too heavy a grip.

Kirsty dabbed her eyes with the back of her new-old glove and touched his glass with hers. She mouthed 'I love you' at him and took a deep drink.

'Magic,' she said out loud.

They ate.

* * *

Jordan lay on her old mattress in her new bed. She was a little tipsy. Halfway through the meal, she realised her parents were looking at each other the way she and Rick looked at each other. It was the feeling she associated with Peggy Lee singing 'Fever', that finger-snapping, languid beat of mutual desire.

Right now, in the other tower, her parents were having sex.

She was more aware of it than she ever had been in the flat, though her room there had adjoined her parents'. One or other of them had been sleeping out of the flat or on the front-room sofa for what seemed like three-quarters of the time.

She supposed it was a good thing, Mum and Dad making love. But, still, well... *ugh!*

The landline wouldn't be hooked up until tomorrow and she hadn't been able to exchange more than a few words with Rick's father on Dad's mobile. She gathered Rick wasn't at home. She hadn't expected him to stay in, missing her, though that would probably have made her feel nice.

When she had a phone in her room, she would be able to talk to Rick every night. She tipsily pondered this phone sex thing. How did it work exactly? Like Rock Hudson and Doris Day in their split-screen baths in *Pillow Talk*?

She didn't feel alone or lonely.

There were tiny movements in the room. The chair by the window was rocking, not vigorously, not noisily. It was a comfort. The rocking was in time to 'Fever'.

All at once, she fell asleep and dreamed.

* * *

She kept her glove on, enjoying the feel of him through satin, hooking her arm around his neck. In the dark, they were new people, without all the baggage of a marriage. Kirsty forgot everything beyond the bed.

Afterwards, she was too exhausted to sleep. The rhythm still beat in her body, and she still felt him close, pushing gently against her, pressing down tenderly. He had most of the duvet but she was warm enough, wondering if her skin was glowing with the heat she felt inside.

Steven had dropped off and was sighing in his sleep. He only snored when he had the flu.

She slipped out from under his arm and rolled off the bed, landing like a cat.

Perspiration dried on her back.

The moon shone through the curtains. She crawled across the floor, feeling the bare boards between the rugs, relishing the scent of the old wood, and sat cross-legged in front of her magic chest.

'Thank you, Weezie,' she whispered.

She peeled off her glove, finding her arm and hand slick with sweat, and popped it into the top drawer. She made the glove go away, padded back across the room, and slipped into bed. She gently wrestled a stretch of the duvet onto herself, snuggled against the comforting presence of her husband, and surrendered to night and darkness.

The family all dreamed the same dream. They were together, at the Hollow, on the crazy paving patio beyond the French windows of the Summer Room, looking at the orchard, which was crowded with more trees than they had imagined. The sun was high but its light was as gentle as the moon. Everything was alive and moving lazily: the trees, the birds, the house, the grass, the streams.

From out of the orchard came a little girl in a straw hat and a white sailor suit, with blue ribbons around her hat and waist and knees. She was solemn beyond her years but bright and friendly and all that they could wish she was. She was a friend and a sister and a daughter and a comfort.

With her, hanging back cautiously in the green shadows of the orchard, were playmates. The little girl looked at the family, fixing on each in turn, seeing right into their hearts. She understood at once that they were not what they had been in the city but were reborn in this place, at the Hollow.

Once she had decided that it was all right, her playmates came out of the trees.

The family were seized with joy.

Settling In

As weeks passed, the family settled, explored, discovered. They filled the Hollow, fitted in nicely.

They lost their city pallor and began to tan. They ate healthily and never got tired of apples. They were not bothered by insects, even at dusk. Midges swarmed in pestilential clouds across the moor but turned aside at the ditch-moat of the property.

In tune with their surroundings, the family were at last in tune with each other. They listened, they cared, they were tolerant, they loved and were loved.

They were constantly surprised, but never shocked.

For the first time in their lives, they felt perfectly safe. In learning to live in a new place, they learned to live with each other, to appreciate each other's mysteries.

The Hollow, they decided, was a happy place.

In the octagonal room, Steven experimented with seven different positions for his desk before realising Louise Teazle had been right all along. He set up his computer in exactly the spot hers had been. Kirsty and Tim were off foraging at the County Stores in Taunton, which left Jordan at home to help arrange his office.

'Sit in your chair,' said his daughter. 'Give it a whirl.'

He pulled his chair close to the desk and sat down, getting the feel of the position. A significant chunk of his life would be spent here. He stretched fingers to touch his keyboard. Jordan adjusted the back of the chair.

'Comfy?'

He was.

'You have to watch out for repetitive stress injury,' Jordan warned.

In London, he had felt the beginnings of back pain and semi-arthritic aches in his finger joints. What with everything else, he'd never even mentioned it to anyone but Tatum. A few twinges didn't count for anything set beside the rest of the problems.

In the Hollow, it all cleared up. It had probably been psychosomatic.

'In Computer Studies, we had a whole lesson on setting up a work station,' said Jordan.

She measured the distance between his chair and the desk with finger-spans, and did mental calculations. She took a ruler and sized him up, as if for a sitting-down suit. When thinking, she looked younger than she was.

'I'll tape an X on the floor,' she said, 'to show where your chair should be. It's what we had to do. After a couple of months, you can pull up the mark.

By then, you'll be settled. Where do you keep your masking tape?'

'It's in one of those.'

She looked at a stack of cardboard boxes. 'Shouldn't they have been unpacked *weeks* ago?'

She was almost funny, trying to be strict.

(not screaming)

He ummed and ahhed about having been busy. She put hands on her hips and tutted. Her navel winked at him above her jeans' waistline. Before her Audrey Hepburn craze set in, she had agitated for permission to get her belly button pierced.

Steven saw an opportunity. He tickled her. She screamed

(not the old kind of screaming)

with laughter, and hauled his chair off its X spot, then spun him around.

He laughed too.

It struck Steven that he couldn't remember the last time he had been alone with Jordan. He and Tim were together often, doing Dad–son things with tools. When the home front was at its worst, the only cause that united him with Kirsty was worrying about Jordan. As a trio, they had been through several, hideous sessions, more like an encounter group than a family argument.

That was another life.

He stopped spinning.

'Dad,' Jordan said, 'has Mum heard from Veronica?'

The name still turned him cold.

'Not since we moved,' he said. (She hadn't, had

she? The new Kirsty would have said something.)

'Good,' she replied, kissing his forehead. 'Veronica used to frighten me.'

'Me too,' he confessed. 'But she was Kirst's friend. Your Mum needed a friend.'

(Veronica called herself a healer.)

'She wasn't anyone's friend, not really.'

Jordan was sharp about people. It was one of her problems, actually. When she was in her darkest self, she always knew the worst thing to say. The truth.

'I think you're right,' he said.

This bright, sunny, funny girl was a delight and a wonder. One of the great discoveries of the Hollow. He had to think hard to remember the old Jordan.

'There's something wrong with Veronica, isn't there?'

'Yes, Jord,' he admitted. 'I don't know what it is or how she gets her hold over people, but she's not like us. Not like the way we are now.'

'Does Mum miss her?'

Steven thought hard. 'No,' he decided. 'Mum has us. It was the choice she made. The choice we all made. To come here, and be a family.'

(What did the witch think about Kirsty's choice?)

'I'm glad,' Jordan said. 'I can't imagine how it would have been if we hadn't found the Hollow.'

'What makes you think the Hollow didn't find us?'

He had to say that. It had been in his mind from the first sight of the place.

Jordan sat in a window-nook, sunlight on her hair, and got comfortable. Steven was impressed at how relaxed his daughter was. She had always been intensely self-conscious, but that was gone.

'Dad, have you noticed?'

She was looking at him, light behind her. He knew what she meant, what she wanted to talk about. He was excited but a little anxious. It was enormous, when he thought about it. He had a sense of privilege that Jordan had chosen to raise it with him, not Kirsty.

'Little things,' she said. 'When you go into a room, it's as if someone has just stepped out. I keep thinking it's Mum or you, but it can't be. There's a rocking chair in my room. Sometimes, it rocks by itself.'

'Does it frighten you?'

She shook her head. 'Not at all. I don't think it should.'

'It's a mystery,' he said. 'I've come across them too. Things change when you're not looking, rearrange themselves. Always for the better. I was thinking of opening those boxes, and letting the fairies do the unpacking but I think that's not in the programme. We have to make an effort, or it doesn't count. But let's start a mystery collection. Mum and Tim can join in. In the end, we'll get to the bottom of it.'

'I suppose,' she said, doubtful.

'The fun of mysteries isn't the explanation,' he said, tweaking her nose. 'It's the wondering.'

His computer came on, by itself. Startled, he pantomimed fear, with ridiculously exaggerated face-pulling and contorted limbs.

'Spooo-ooooky,' he said.

Jordan laughed and launched a cushion at him.

'One for the collection,' he said, glancing at his screen.

HH, it flashed at him. HH HH HH, filling the

screen. Then his file manager was there, neat as it could be.

'Did you see that?' he asked Jordan.

'What?'

'Nothing. It was for me.'

After supper, Jordan sat in her rocking chair, examining the book. It was something she had found, or which – to pick up on Dad's thinking – had found her. Running her fingers along a row of shelved spines, this was where she had stopped. *The Haunting of Drearcliff Grange* was a hardback with an unfaded jacket. The cover showed a wood-panelled corridor after dark, lit by a single candle. Four alarmed girls in straw hats and school blazers cowered away from a see-through knight in armour who was raising a solid-seeming battle-axe.

The book was yellow and dusty at the top edge, but good as new. If this was Louise Teazle's own copy it had probably never been read. Having written it, she knew how the story came out. From the flap copy, Jordan learned it was the fifth of the Drearcliff Grange School books. A first edition, from 1944. Had either of her dead grandmothers read it then, during the War? Mum said girls still read Louise Teazle when she was at school.

On the first page, a girl called Gillian Gilchrist ('Gill-Gil') was up late at night on a dare, alone in a disused part of the school. To get into a secret club, the After Lights-Out Gang, she had to creep out of her dorm (what did that mean? a shared room?

something like a hospital ward?) and spend a whole night in the West Wing. The rest of the gang – Angela the Boss, Catty Korner and Sarah-Suzanne Symmes – had told her the wing was haunted.

Knowing what to expect, Jordan read the rest of the chapter. Phantoms appeared, but Gillian was ready for them. 'Stow the rot, fillies,' she sneered. 'Can't fool I with a sheet dipped in chem-lab phosphor. That bloodstain is most unbecoming, Angela. And try to clank your chain with a little more *spirit*, Sarah-Suzanne.' After several more or less alarming apparitions, Gillian was grabbed by a sinister shadow-figure. It turned out to be the new gym mistress, Miss Ilse Haller.

In the next chapter, it transpired that the After Lights-Out Gang had indeed intended to sneak into the West Wing and terrify Gillian, but were detained by a snap air-raid drill. With Gillian missing at head-count, a search was carried out for her. Now, the gang was in hot water with Miss Beeke, the fearsome headmistress. Also, Gill-Gil was worried that the spooks might have been real.

Jordan assumed that the ghosts would be spies or smugglers in disguise. Miss Haller, who was supposed to be a Czech refugee, was most likely a Nazi spy.

Still, she read on.

The old slang was stranger even than the Rat Pack hipster talk she loved and tried to affect, but it had its own appeal. An all-girls boarding school was as bizarre to Jordan as a nunnery, but she recognised character types among the staff and pupils from the schools she had been at. She wasn't sure how many of the odd turns of phrase were deliberately comical, but got a sense that Louise Teazle sometimes slyly pulled her readers' legs. Gillian, an evacuee from 'reduced circumstances', suffered the other girls' snobbery, but showed courage ('spunk', not a word Jordan had heard with that meaning) and won acceptance. Sarah-Suzanne, surprisingly clearly a femme lesbian, nurtured a terrific crush on Gillian, which the heroine tried to deal with kindly.

Spies did appear, posing as members of a hockey team from a rival school, and plotted to kidnap Miss Haller, whose father was a scientist Hitler hadn't been able to force to work on a poison-gas rocket. But the ghosts were real, the spirits of Englishmen who had died defending their country in foreign wars, called up by Gillian herself, unconsciously wishing on a potent magic stone (part of the wall in the West Wing), to defend Miss Haller from the Nazis.

In the final chapter, the ghosts saw off the spies and word came through that Miss Haller's father had been smuggled out of Germany. Gillian said goodbye to the ghosts, who treated her with strange respect since it was subtly implied that she was destined to die for England in a future war when women would be front-line troops. She was finally initiated into the After Lights-Out Gang, with a midnight feast and a masked ritual.

The book didn't take long to read. Jordan was left with a sense of having understood only the surface. It was a fast adventure, with a lot of comedy and broad social comment, but she suspected depths. The only men in the book were absent fathers or ghosts. Even the Nazi spies were teenage girls. Whenever Gillian argued with Miss Haller or the After Lights-Out Gang, it was as if Louise Teazle were talking to herself.

The world of the book seemed real to her. An evening had slipped away as she read. It was dark outside her window. She looked at the West Tower of the Hollow. The light was on in her parents' room but Tim's window was dark – he must be asleep already.

Ghosts, she wondered. Were there ghosts?

'Someone to see you, Mum,' her daughter announced. Kirsty looked up at Jordan. She was filling out her simple summer dress a little more. Her bare arms and legs had lost the anatomy-diagram stringiness that had been cause for concern. Her skin was the pale gold of not-yet-ripe eating apples.

A set of white filigree lawn furniture had been discovered in one of the spare rooms. Steven had put the tables and chairs out on the crazy paving where Kirsty liked to sit.

Jordan stepped to one side and let the visitor come through the French windows.

'You must be Mr Wing-Godfrey?'

'Bernard, please.'

The president of the Louise Magellan Teazle Society was a middle-aged brown man. Brown hair, eyes, suit, shoes and socks. And brown skin, though he wasn't Indian or Middle Eastern. He was just a brown Englishman.

'Would you care for some tea, Mr Wing-Godfrey?' asked Jordan, a perfect miniature hostess.

'As for nectar, my dear.'

'I'll fetch some, then. Mum?'

Kirsty declined. She had been drinking iced lemon tea all morning.

'What a lovely girl you have, Mrs Naremore,' said Bernard. 'Shows the Drearcliff spirit, I'll be bound. I see you've been doing your homework.'

Books were piled on the lattice table, the Weezie stories and the first of the school series, *A New Girl at Drearcliff Grange*.

'I've been cataloguing the library.'

Bernard's eyes gleamed as if Kirsty had mentioned a treasure trove. For him, Louise Teazle's library must seem a pirate's cave: first editions of all her books, of course, along with foreign and reprint editions – Kirsty couldn't recognise all the languages Louise had been published in – and the books she had loved herself. If there were unpublished manuscripts, early drafts or personal journals, they had not shown up so far. Kirsty expected real treasures would be hidden, perhaps guarded. When the Hollow wanted her to find anything, she would be led to it.

'And I've been reading again, refreshing my memory.'

'You read Teazle as a girl?' asked Bernard.

Kirsty shrugged. 'Didn't everyone?'

'Most girls, a few boys, until, say, twenty years ago. Even since then, there has been a great deal of interest. She has always been in print. Specialist presses keep her work alive. I have been on television, several times, talking about the Society. Our members are very active.'

Jordan came back with tea and withdrew into the house.

Bernard let out a satisfied 'Ahhh' with his first swallow.

'Didn't your school friends give you a hard time for liking Louise?' asked Kirsty. 'I'd have thought boys even then thought she was soppy.'

'I came to Teazle late in life, Mrs Naremore. She meant a great deal to me at a trying time. I was confined, against my will, far from home. Her books were, quite literally, my lifeline.'

Kirsty wasn't fazed by Bernard's odd admission. She felt she understood this man.

'Have you been here before?' she asked. 'When Louise was alive?'

'It was not my place to impose on Miss Teazle.'

Even Bernard's fingernails were brown. Not dirt, not bad health, not even stained. 'Only now have I, as it were, plucked up the necessary courage.'

'I hope you're not disappointed.'

He looked at the orchard. Tim was hidden in there somewhere, as green as Bernard Wing-Godfrey was brown.

'Our members are most envious that you invited me to the Hollow. It is sacred turf to us, of course. The Avalon of Teazle.'

Kirsty didn't know how to take that. She ought be made uncomfortable by this odd fellow, but was at her ease. He was reverent of the Hollow. She should extend him a welcome.

'We were wondering whether you would be averse to opening your home to a select number of us, on a strictly limited basis of course. We would not want to invade or swamp you. We should winnow out the applicants. Only the most presentable would pass. The Society is not without funds. We would, of course, reimburse you any expenses, and indeed be prepared to pay a fee for the privilege of access. I am empowered to gift you with quite a substantial figure. To help with the restoration. We could also provide advice. Some of us have made a deep study of Teazle. We know where everything goes, you see. We know how things should be.'

'I don't follow you.'

'This table and these four chairs, for instance. You have them at the wrong end of the Puzzle Patio.'

The Puzzle Patio was in *Weezie and the Hopscotch Hobgoblin*. It was also, Kirsty realised, this crazy-paved stretch outside the French windows.

'They should be over by the tower, near the kitchen door. So Katie the Cook can hand Weezie apple juice through the sink window. More importantly so, when she stands on a chair, she can see through the tree telescope and over the moor to the standing stones.'

'I'm not sure the stones are real. I think Louise made them up. She was probably thinking of Glastonbury Tor. We can see that from the picture window.'

Bernard seemed saddened by Kirsty's lack of trust in Teazle. He put down his tea and stood, then tugged Kirsty across the lawn towards the kitchen door. She did not resist.

He turned her round and pointed, between the trees, putting a hand on the small of her back to encourage her to stand on tiptoes. She became as tall as a child standing on a chair.

'The branches of that tree make a fork, a sight-line. The tree telescope. See the mump with the stones.'

'You're right.'

Kirsty felt light, as if she might drift upwards. From just this spot, looking through a tunnel-like curl of branches, she saw, miles off across the moor, a hillock with five upright stones around an altar-piece.

She leaned to one side and tried to look around the tree. Another tree was in the way. She leaned to the other and the side of the barn cut off the view. She walked out on the lawn, past the tower, almost to the ditch. The land sloped slightly and a far-off copse blocked view of the stones.

It was remarkable.

'Here is where the table should be,' said Bernard.

She went back to the patio and found herself agreeing with him.

'The full resources of the Society are available, Mrs Naremore – Kirsty, may I call you? We feel you have been chosen by Dame Fortune to be custodians of this place that is so special to us all. We owe you our support, our help, our labour.'

He kissed her on both cheeks and left.

If she didn't hear the cough of his car leaving the drive or see his empty cup on that wrongly placed table, she wouldn't have been surprised to learn he had never been there.

By now, she knew a ghost when she saw – or sensed – one.

* * *

On the long table in the Summer Room, Mum had laid out an array of oddments she had found in the storerooms. Jordan supposed the stuff ought to be called Teazleiana. Mum had brought the collection out to show her visitor. Colouring books and diaries, cuddly Weezie dolls, a spinning top with Weezie's ghost friends painted on it, Weezie and Drearcliff Grange jigsaws, a Gloomy Ghost money-box, Drearcliff badges and boaters, a Weezie whistle. The playthings of her grandparents' generation. No game cartridges, action figures, boxer shorts, videos, pogs, graphic novels, collectible cards, temporary tattoos.

She picked up a stereoscope, a device like a set of plastic binoculars with a slot for a rectangular card. Holding it to her eyes, she saw Weezie dancing with the stones in sharp, unmoving 3D relief. There was a set of cards, showing other scenes from the books. Another item struck her; a circular picture under glass, an illustration of the After-Lights Out Gang, four girls in askew boaters. When she picked it up, the faces fell away, leaving blanks.

It was one of those hand-held games, not like Tim's beep-beep-beep Game Boy (not heard from so much these days) but an old-fashioned puzzle. The girls' features – eyes and smiles – were on loose pellets which had to be rolled *just so* to plop into their proper places, dimples in the blanks. Getting features on faces was easy, but usually with mismatched eyes or a smile in an eye socket. The four friends – Gillian, Angela, Catty and Sarah-Suzanne – had differing eye colours and smiles, naturally.

Having rearranged the faces in comic strangeness,

Jordan shook the game and tried again. This time, almost without trying, she set everything right. She put the game down, quitting while she was ahead.

She went outside. The brown man was gone. For someone obsessed with Louise Teazle, he hadn't lingered. It was a shame he hadn't seen the toy and tie-in collection. Perhaps he intended to come back for a closer look, to stay longer.

Mum was preoccupied with something else, a new project.

'Help me carry the table across the lawn, Jordan. I think it'll be happier over by the kitchen door.'

Jordan knew she was right.

The garden table wasn't heavy, but awkward. Jordan walked backwards and Mum edged forwards. They got a rhythm going and the job was done in no time. When set down, the table found grooves in the grass, like the features had found the dimples in the girls' faces. It might almost have taken root.

There were four chairs to shift too. Jordan and Mum walked over to the crazy paving, where the table had been, and picked up a chair apiece. When they were back at the table's proper place, the other two chairs were waiting for them.

They looked at each other, and all around, smiling.

After several LRPs, Tim had determined the IP were friendlies. Each time he trailed back to Green Base, fresh tribute was laid out, a token of gratitude for his vigilance in protecting this little patch. Five apples piled like a pyramid of cannonballs, a circle of wild flowers threaded stem to bud like a necklace, a chipped stone arrowhead. This morning, it was a bird's nest with three pale blue pebbles he took at first for eggs.

He whistled with admiration.

The IP were good, better than he could hope to be. Part of the scenery, they never showed themselves outright. They could stand against a tree or the side of the garage, or even lie flat on the green grass, and seem to be entirely natural, a stain on the wood or a low hillock. He was winning their hearts and minds but wasn't sure they'd ever step into the open. They had long memories. Not everyone who had occupied this position had been as careful as Tim, as well-disposed towards the locals. Battles had been fought. He found old shrew-skulls and flattened cartridge cases, even burn-marks on the trees. The IP were wary of any new forces on the big board.

He squirmed around inside the main dug-out, which was shaped like an overturned canoe. Its opening was netted over with strands of ivy he was careful to shift aside but never break. Inside Green Base was more room than anyone would suspect. He looked up inside the hollow trunk and saw green-filtered daylight pouring through holes among the branches.

Making his way upwards, he climbed twice his height before he could go no further. He would have to carve hand- and foot-holds if he wanted to scale the inside of the tree all the way to the high plateau. He planned to make his command post there. Being small meant he could go where few others could, but a certain amount of hacking with an entrenching tool was needed to make the narrow chimney passable.

A peaty abscess under the roots was just big enough to curl up in. He should enlarge and shore up the space into a burrow for supplies. He had a list: bottled water, dried fruit, chocolate, biscuits, salt tablets, comics, his Swiss army knife, a flannel, toothpaste, sticking plasters, a torch. Already, he had scouted several fall-back positions (in the hayloft, under the bridge). Soon, he would be ready for all eventualities.

From inside the tree, he looked out, green-streaked face fitting a face-sized knothole. His eyes should seem like highlights on leaves.

The MP and the BS had moved the lawn furniture to a spot by the kitchen door, where they were laughing at nothing in particular. He watched them a while, keeping an eye out for hostiles. The women were in no danger presently. It was an all-clear situation.

He took his head out of the hole and slipped silently down to ground level. He could manage that manoeuvre in under five seconds, though it took a full half-minute to ascend to the look-out point.

A new tribute waited for him.

He picked up a Y-shaped forked stick, stripped of bark and sanded smooth. Between the tines was a strip of rubber with a leather patch threaded on it. Tim took the patch and pulled back. The rubber wasn't perished. A catapult.

Now he knew what the pebbles in the nest were.

That the IP had issued him with such a thing was a sign of trust. The weapon put him on a level with them, as if he had joined the Doomsday Club.

He slipped a pebble into the leather grip and pulled

back, feeling the strength of the rubber in his forearm. He sighted upwards, on one of the sky-holes up in the tree-top, and let go. The pebble flew upwards, just clipped the edge of the hole, and shot out into the world beyond.

'Kewl,' Tim said to himself.

He was fit to survive.

'How was the Louise looney?' Steven asked.

'Surprisingly sweet,' said Kirsty.

He slipped an arm around his wife's waist and snogged her, not minding his embarrassed daughter. They were outside, in the early evening. They would share the long summer evening hours before nightfall.

'The man was brown, Mum,' said Jordan.

'Touch of the sun-lamp?'

'No, not burned. Brown.'

'He implied that he had spent a lot of his life overseas,' said Kirsty.

'Implied?'

'He didn't say anything outright, but mentioned he'd spent a time far from home. "Confined", was his expression.'

'So he's an escapee from Devil's Island? Inherited his collection of Teazle books from a guillotined poisoner, read them over and over in the Hole, between whippings and leprosy outbreaks? Only Sneezy Weezie and her blessed spooks kept him sane.'

'HH,' said Jordan, but Kirsty was thoughtful.

'You might not be that far from the truth. There's something about the name. Bernard Wing-Godfrey.

I've come across it before.'

'I can check him out on the net.'

Steven had spent the day online, doing background checks on an oil-surveying company that seemed dodgy on the surface but might have hidden strengths. The dial-up connection was more reliable here than in London, where his modem often cut out in the middle of a research session. He enjoyed the detail-work, reading between the columns of dense figures scrolling across the screen.

He liked finding out trivial things sometimes, to keep his fingers flexible.

'Why've you moved the lawn furniture?'

Jordan looked archly at Kirsty.

'If you laugh,' Kirsty said, 'I'll leave you for a bass player.'

That was an old joke between them. It hadn't come up for ten years or so, and he was surprised – delighted, even – that it didn't hurt. At times, too recently for comfort, it would not only not have been funny but would have been the height of intramarital cruelty.

'I'd advise you not to press this point, Dad.'

'Fair enough, Jordy. I withdraw the question.'

A pebble fell out of nowhere and bounced off the table, flaking a patch of white paint from the filigree. They all looked up at the tower.

'It's a mystery,' Steven said. 'One for the collection.'

Things happened when he turned his back, or was in the next room, or while he was nodding off. Nothing sinister, but often interesting. It was as if everyone were preparing a huge surprise party for him, though his birthday had been four months ago.

Three of their birthdays fell in a two-week cluster. Only Tim had managed a party this year, and that had been a foaming disaster. Steven was torn between wanting to forget things as they were before the Hollow and needing to remember so they never happened ever again.

Before the Hollow, things had been dire. Coming here meant pulling back from the edge.

Somehow, he wasn't worried any more. He was working on never being worried again.

The mystery collection was growing, though.

First was that girl in the straw hat, as mentioned by the removal men. She hadn't shown up since, though Steven noted that Louise Teazle heroines always wore straw hats. He would have joked that the sensitive shifters had seen Weezie's ghost, but fictional characters didn't leave ghosts. Miss Teazle had lived to be eighty-three, so she should have left an old lady ghost. Unless you could pick which age you were as a phantom.

Kirsty insisted Miss Teazle was gone.

Then there were other things. Feelings, half-heard sounds, fortuitous circumstances, items that came to hand when they were wanted, apples that fell when you were hungry (and were ripe well before the greengrocer's), phone calls that came just when you needed them.

It was as if the Hollow adjusted to suit them.

At first, he always bumped his head on a lampshade in the secret passage. Now he could walk under it and just barely brush the fringe. The cord didn't seem to be shorter and the flagstone floor certainly wasn't lower. As if the passage, and the whole house, changed minutely, to make him comfortable.

There were rules for the mystery collection. Phenomena that two or more of them could bear witness to were admitted. Like the falling pebble. It was a Dad–Jordan thing, though. Tim kept mum about whatever he saw, like a good soldier. Kirsty added her few contributions reluctantly. She shared the way Steven felt, but was wary of speaking out loud about it, as if that would break the magic.

'Show him your mystery, Mum,' Jordan said.

Steven raised eyebrows and opened his hands.

'It's not a mystery, dear. It's a circumstance. If you stand just so, you can see a stone circle.'

'Brown Godfrey showed her, Dad. He got it from Weezie.'

Kirsty manipulated him into a certain position. He saw she had marked it with a heel-mark in the turf.

'I have to tip-toe,' she said. 'You have to scrunch.'

He let his knees sag a little. Kirsty held his head and pointed at the fallen tree.

'No,' she said, 'look *through* the tree.'

There was nothing. No circle of stones.

He didn't say he didn't see it.

'I tried looking from our window,' Kirsty said. 'And Tim's attic room. The top of the tree gets in the way.'

He walked out into the orchard, Kirsty and Jordan trailing him. Kirsty was smiling broadly now.

'It won't work,' she said, 'only from this spot.'

'The tree can't be in the way if the tree is behind you.'

But leaning against the tree-trunk, he still saw nothing.

'I vote this goes in the collection,' he said, puzzled.

'It's not a mystery,' insisted Kirsty. 'It's just that there's only one place you can see the circle from. It's geography.'

'And your Louise looney knew this from reading a book? A book that's sixty years old?'

Kirsty shrugged. She looked almost as young as Jordan.

'So, you're telling me the tree had fallen down already, back then, when Louise was writing?'

'I suppose so. It could be hundreds of years old.'

'It hasn't grown since, nor any of the other trees? The view hasn't changed? What about drainage schemes and Dutch elm disease? The moor is a living landscape. It shouldn't stay exactly the same from one year to the next. This, my darling, is a mystery.'

'It goes in the collection, Mum. Along with the chairs.'

Kirsty looked at them and agreed. Steven wondered what the mystery of the chairs might be.

'I'll bet if we cut down the tree, the circle would vanish,' Jordan said. 'You wouldn't be able to see it from here.'

A small green pixie emerged from the tree-trunk and made them all jump and laugh.

'Don't cut down the tree,' said Tim.

'That's not in the big plan, son,' said Steven.

Tim, relieved, saluted. Steven noticed the boy had a new catapult. His soldier would have to listen to a thorough briefing on the uses and abuses of the device. Some weapons were too terrible ever to be used outside strictly controlled test conditions, especially with the huge panes of the picture windows in shot distance.

'Reporting for rations, ma'am,' said Tim.

'Tea is just coming,' said Kirsty.

Kirsty was sparing with her use of the chest of drawers. She had an idea that, like many magical things, it only worked if she was alone with it. She didn't want to enter it into Steven and Jordan's collection, not yet. She worried that to label something a mystery was to impose a meaning which was also a limitation. This was not an experiment, this was life. It was too important to risk.

She used the top drawer occasionally, to get rid of make-up smudged tissues or rubber bands, but stayed away from the middle drawer. She was not sure that, at this point in her life, she needed a jumble of surprises. Vron had shown her she had a problem with order and chaos, see-sawing from one extreme to the other. A jumble was too much like real chaos, the stuff that had seemed so much of a threat and a promise and a danger and a delight.

The temptation was the bottom drawer.

She thought of the things she found there as Cinderella gifts. She was scrupulous about using them only for a brief time, disposing of them before dawn by putting them into the top drawer, the drawer that was always empty, the drawer that was always the same, the drawer that made things disappear.

Thus far, apart from the glove, she had found a garter, a single earring (the drawer never gave matched pairs of anything), a hand-mirror without glass, a modern plastic toothbrush that dislodged a tiny string of beef that had been caught between her molars for a day and a half, a china doll whose torn dress she had repaired with a few neat stitches.

Today, she found the last five pages of an Agatha Christie novel she had taken out of the library when she was Jordan's age. That copy had been missing those pages. The pages had been sliced out cleanly so she hadn't discovered the vandalism until she reached the end of the penultimate chapter. Reading the solution now, after twenty years, she found the details of the unsolved murder had lingered in her memory more vividly than those of dozens of whodunits she had finished. Knowing the answer satisfied her in a way she would never have imagined. Why hadn't she just gone into a shop and read the last chapter before now? Had she been waiting for this magic gift?

She posted the pages, one by one, into the top drawer, then pulled it out. They were gone.

Steven came up, curly hair wet from his bath, and sat on the edge of the bed.

'One mystery solved,' he said.

She turned, afraid he had noticed something about the chest of drawers.

'Wing-Godfrey's all over the net,' Steven said. 'I've book-marked all the Louise Magellan Teazle sites for you. There's one with old photographs of the Hollow, from before the War. Wing-Godfrey's society has a really crap web designer. You might tell him that.'

'HH,' she said, wondering whether to bean Steven with a pillow.

'After the Louise sites I found more mentions, in newspaper archives. He was a hostage in Lebanon, ten years ago. He was with a textiles company. Some fringe fundamentalist group chained him to a wall, kept him in a cellar for years, threatened to chop his head off. It was a big story. Like Terry Waite and John What's-His-Name.'

Kirsty was struck with sympathy. 'The poor man.'

'The kidnappers gave him the only English books they had. Can you guess?'

She beaned him with the pillow, which he was too slow to dodge.

'Got it in one,' he said.

She imagined the brown man in his cell (how had he got so brown indoors? Oughtn't he to have been pale?) with only Weezie for company. No wonder he had come out of it a bit of a fanatic. The business with the lawn furniture suggested he was something of a fundamentalist himself.

'Think of it,' Steven said. 'All those years without sight of a real woman. He must have worn out those schoolgirl books. Which do you think were his favourite illustrations? Gymslip scenes, probably. Are there any canings at Drearcliff Grange? Rosy third-form buttocks taking six of the best.'

'HH,' she said, not thinking him funny.

He crawled back on the bed and waited for her. His fantasy had got him going. A half-erection was rising through his bathrobe.

'Come into my study, girl,' he said, in a low, funny voice. 'You've been naughtier than any nymphet it has ever been my unpleasant duty to chastise. Matron will not be the same again since that disgusting affair with the school hamster and the curry powder. And Prefect Jemima reports that you have been smoking crack behind the bicycle sheds with the baker's boy.'

Kirsty swivelled on her stool, amused despite herself.

Since coming to the Hollow, the sex had been a constant double-plus gold-star bonus. Vron would never have believed it. Kirsty and Steven had rediscovered and renewed themselves.

'Pull down your navy-blue knickers and come here, wicked minx. You are about to suffer the soundest seeing-to any Head Girl at Drearcliff has ever received. Come morning assembly, every part of your lithe young body will be a-throb with unspeakable pleasures.'

On impulse, she edged open the bottom drawer and reached inside. She found a limp length of cloth and pulled it out. A school tie, in the colours of Drearcliff Grange. She snapped it like a whip and Steven yelped.

'I'm going to bind you fast, sir,' she said. 'Then we shall see if you can take punishment with as much relish as you hand it out.'

She held the tie between her fists, like a garrotte, and walked slowly across the room.

Steven laughed in terror.

On the telephone, Jordan remembered to be cool. She shrugged and pouted as expected, and was noncommittal. As soon as Rick rang off, she yowled with glee.

He was coming to the Hollow!

Next weekend. Then, *everything* would be perfect. Rick was going to love the place and they would explore it together. She had been holding back, not joining Tim or Mum in their expeditions, promising herself she would discover the territory alongside her boyfriend. She was saving some of the surprises to share with him.

He had no news from the city. College was over for the year. For Rick, it was over for good. He had to wait for his results. She was sure he would get the grades he needed for UWE. She did her girlfriend bit and fed him support.

Rick said he had run into Mum's strange friend near the old flat. Mention of Veronica was like a black claw in a cream cake. Jordan called her the Wild Witch, and Dad had far worse names for her. Jordan was surprised Rick only vaguely remembered who the woman was. She must have bored him with horror stories of the Wild Witch's malign influence. When he had tentatively said Veronica didn't seem so bad, Jordan had seriously wanted to strangle him.

Here, at the Hollow, they were safe from wild witches.

When he was here, Rick would be safe too.

She realised she was the only one up. Tim's bedtime was eight and Mum and Dad had taken to going to bed earlier and earlier. Jordan still wasn't a hundred per cent keen on thinking about that, but it made a welcome change from open warfare.

She was in the Summer Room, curled on the overstuffed sofa, with the cordless phone still stuck to her sternum and a shawl wrapped around her.

Dad had spent a day hooking up their giant-screen television with satellite and other gadgets, but even Tim hadn't watched it much. There were other things to do at the Hollow. At first, the TV, like other Naremore additions, had stood out among the furnishings that had come with the place. Now, it blended in. The television cabinet even matched the smoky-brown rosewood look of the dresser and the table.

It was a familiar shade, the dominant colour of the house.

She thought of watching a favourite film. *Bye, Bye Birdie*, *Move Over, Darling* or *Charade*. Other girls her age liked Tom Cruise or Leonardo DiCaprio, but her top male film stars were Cary Grant and Rock Hudson. Rick had made fun of her for her Doris Day enthusiasm, until she introduced him to mid-sixties Ann-Margret and Stella Stevens. She liked the hard, sparkly colours, the brashness and confidence even of neurotics, the brassy orchestrations of the theme songs. For his birthday, she had bought Rick a sports jacket with a fine hound's-tooth weave. She wanted them to be like the chummy but peppery couples in the films, who constantly teased each other but were hipper and smarter than the rest. They were a team against the phonies and the squares.

Here, she didn't need to watch the films any more. They were in her mind, in her heart.

Was it too soon to call Rick again?

It was. Pity.

She stood, shrugging out of the shawl, and walked across the room to replace the phone in its cradle.

When she turned back, her shawl was still in the air, as if settled around invisible shoulders. The old thing had come with the house; it was a faded white crochet with long tassels and a pleasant woolly smell.

Jordan remembered to close her mouth.

The shawl hung in the air, looking like a cartoon ghost with eyeholes and a trailing shroud.

Jordan laughed and the shawl swirled upwards in a spiral, tassels spinning, until it was a magic carpet. It rose almost to the ceiling and stretched out like a table-cloth, then gently floated downwards and draped perfectly over the back of the sofa.

She clapped, slowly.

The break with the world she had known, had almost grown up in, didn't frighten her. Her bare feet tingled, with the beginnings of excitement. Could she conduct the ghost shawl, make it dance at the lift of a finger? She decided it would be impolite. She was too old for toys. This wasn't a gimmick or a game – no hidden fishing line or computer imagery – but a revelation, an epiphany.

She was as comfortable with the Hollow, and whatever shared it with her family, as she was with Rick, as she had only recently become with her brother and parents, as she hoped to be with herself.

She was smiling and crying at the same time.

Tatum seemed spooked by the size of the study. She was the first person from their London life to come to the Hollow. Steven had suggested she stay over – one of the spare rooms was quite liveable now

– but she wanted to drive back for a late party with her fiancé.

Steven had naturally set up shop in the study, though he was considering eventually having the hayloft converted into an office suite. He liked the idea of a workspace separate from the house. For the moment, Louise's old lair suited him fine. Her books and papers were in boxes now. Kirsty wanted to go through them before she shared with Wing-Godfrey's Society. Jordan and Kirsty had gone on reading jags, scurrying through the children's books, reporting on every Hollow reference the authoress dropped. He had put his own files into the cabinets and begun to occupy shelves with active folders.

Tatum had held the fort during the interregnum. She ran down deals that were tied up, in development or scotched. He was impressed his personal assistant didn't blame herself for the one that had blown up. It wasn't her fault, but it would have been like an overeager junior to think it was. No black mark against her.

During the worst of it, he could rely on Tatum. She had thrown in her lot with him and would stick to him, no matter what. Even before this absence, she had shouldered more than her share of the gruntwork. While he was preoccupied, it had been possible that the whole business would be taken away and torn to pieces. Tatum had seen them through. He had written her in for a percentage on top of her salary. Within a year or two, he would have to make her a partner to keep her aboard. She could handle the city, the face time in crowded coffee bars and the running from one meeting to another, while he sat here in the country, hooked into the world of information, processing like a human computer.

He laid out a couple of long shots for her. It was like Kirsty's supposed trick with the tree and the standing stones. You had to stand in just one place and look just the right way to see something invisible from everywhere else. In the last week, he had managed it three times, sighting through fiscal tangles to see opportunities being born like new stars.

Tatum slipped his print-outs into her leather document case. He saw she had the scent of blood.

'This place, Steven, it's…'

She shook her head. Tatum had one of those thin faces, with smile brackets around her mouth, which work better than they should. She wore her hair in a severe bob that set off her purple horn-rims.

'I know,' he said. 'It's taken years off me.'

'All this paper,' she said, indicating the bookshelves and boxes. 'My eyes are watering from the dust.'

'None of us have had that.'

'You've gone native.'

He laughed. 'Listen to that quiet, Tate.'

'It sets my teeth on edge, Steven. I'd feel exposed. You're miles from anywhere. Anyone could come by and walk in. You'd be cut off.'

'That doesn't happen. Only in the city.'

Tatum and her fiancé had been mugged last year. Marco had lost two front teeth. She was understandably paranoid.

'One more thing,' she said, taking a folder out of her case and laying it on the desk. 'This is the last of the Oddments accounts. You're entirely clear of the mess, but Kirsty is still in a hole. I've talked with the outstanding creditors. If pushed, they'll carry her for six months. Of course, they think you'll cover your wife if it comes to that. If they forced her into bankruptcy, they'd get pennies for pounds. You'd not be legally obliged to pay off her debt. Even as it stands, you can pay or not. It's your decision.'

'Can I settle now?'

'It's your decision, Steven. You've enough in the accounts, even after expenses like me, but it'd leave you stretched. I'd let it roll.'

Last year, Kirsty had started up a small business, Oddments, on the advice of the insidious Vron, selling bizarre antiques over the net. It had been unsuccessful and proved more of a money pit than anyone could have expected, culminating in several major crises and one big collapse. Tatum obviously resented the shackles Oddments clapped on the expansion of Naremore Consultancy Services. Steven, more than anyone, sympathised with her, but that trouble was past, part of the life left behind. Here, things were different and he just wanted to clean up the last of the mess.

'Pay them off, Tate. I feel lucky.'

Tatum took that on board.

'It'll be done. Here are the figures. If you make out and sign the cheques, I'll take them back with me.'

She watched as he wrote the cheques. This would take a bite out of reserves already depleted by the move. But the house down-payment had come along providentially. The new 'things can only get better' government had changed planning laws, which meant long-ticking investment finally paid off with an unexpected gush of green. That was the beginning of the magic, providing the family with the money to escape from London and their mire of personal problems.

'Don't worry,' he told her. 'It's about freedom.'

Tatum took the cheques and proofread them. There was an extra among them.

'Veronica Gorse?' Tatum asked.

'Kirsty made her a partner.'

'On what investment?'

'Not money. She was supposed to be the keen eye for treasure. She put the "odd" in Oddments.'

'I can't believe you're paying her off. After everything. Gorse has no legal claim. She's lucky you don't start proceedings against her.'

'It's worth it never to have to deal with the mad creature again.'

His PA shrugged. At one point, Steven had seriously suspected the muggers who attacked Tatum and Marco were Vron's flying monkeys. They hadn't taken anything, just thumped and run.

With the cheque written, Steven felt another stone was removed from his cairn. He would tell Kirsty later, tactfully. It was over and done. She had new interests now.

Tatum looked around the room again and shivered inside her shoulder pads.

'I hope this is what you really want, Steven,' she said. 'I really do.'

'Oh, it is, Tate. It really really is.'

* * *

In the Hollow, Tim never missed with the catapult. He could bring down an apple with a pebble. Merits for its use within the boundaries no longer awarded. When he took position on the ditch-bank and fired over the border, aiming at a patch of marsh-grass or a gate-post a field away, the shot usually went wild. But, if he turned round and picked out a particular tile on the roof of the taller tower, just above his own bedroom window, a tile he knew was there but couldn't see from this far away, he could clip it dead centre and check later to see the rough chip raised by the impact of the stone.

He called his catapult the U-Dub, for UW. Ultimate Weapon.

He did not fire at birds or squirrels or even insects. That, he knew, was not in the rules of engagement. The U-Dub was not a first-strike weapon. It was for defence. If a bird came at him with claws and beak out for his eyes, it would be a go to put a stone into it. But the birds of the Hollow weren't hostiles.

Still, he felt safer with a strong defence capability.

They sat, all four Naremores, at the long table, empty plates pushed away. Kirsty plunged the cafetiere and poured out cups of coffee, half and half with warm milk for Tim, midnight black for the rest of them. Jordan took a chocolate biscuit with hers. Six months ago, that would have been a miracle on a par with Weezie's chest of drawers. It was magic hour, the sun nearly down but the sky still light. Shadows took a long time to gather in the Summer Room.

For minutes, no one said anything. The family were together, just enjoying that.

Finally, Tim asked, 'Is the Hollow haunted?'

It was the first time any of them had used the word out loud.

Jordan looked eagerly at Kirsty and Steven. She had something to say, but didn't want to go first.

Kirsty knew it was time to talk.

'Yes, my darling,' she said. 'I think it is.'

'Then why aren't I frightened?'

That was the question.

'I don't think the Hollow is haunted that way,' said Steven. 'The mystery collection is enough to convince anyone this is no ordinary house, but it's not like haunted houses in books and films. Those are bad places, where terrible things happened. You know, built on a cursed Indian burial ground, an unavenged murder victim walled up in the cellar. If there are ghosts here, they aren't haunting us. It's as if they're sharing. Is there an opposite of *haunted*?'

'Un-haunted?' suggested Jordan. 'Blessed?'

'What about *charmed*?' ventured Kirsty.

Steven was taken with that.

'Yes, Tim… Mum's right. This is a *charmed* house, a happy house. Good things have happened here and they linger like warmth. It's in the air, like that silence after a concert, just before the applause starts.'

Kirsty drank her coffee. The grind brought here with other half-used jars and tins tasted different. That could be the water, of course. At the Hollow, they didn't need to filter. She had stopped taking sugar in tea and coffee.

'Do we want to talk about the magic,' she began, hesitantly, 'or are we afraid that if we do, it'll go away?'

'Magic?' queried Steven.

'Yes, *magic*,' Jordan was eager to confirm it. 'Things moving, things appearing. Presences.'

'Are they what's behind the mystery collection?' asked Steven. 'Ghosts?'

'Not exactly, or not just,' said Jordan.

'The IP are friendlies,' said Tim. 'They extend full cooperation.'

'You've *seen* them, Tim?'

'You don't see them, Dad. If you saw them, they wouldn't be them.'

Kirsty thought about it.

'I haven't seen anything either, but I've been given things. In a way I can't explain.' She was wearing a bracelet from the bottom drawer. 'And I've felt it. We've all felt it. Even you, Steven.'

Her husband took her hand and squeezed her fingers. He did not think she was mad. Another miracle.

'I've seen something like a ghost,' said Jordan.

Kirsty was surprised. She had never suspected.

Tim raised his arms and went 'woooo-wooooo'. Everyone laughed, including Jordan.

'Yes, that sort of ghost. A floating white thing. The shawl on the sofa, moving by itself. Dancing.'

'I haven't seen anything like that,' said Steven. 'I must have angered the spirits or something.'

'I don't think so, Dad,' said Jordan. 'It's different for each of us, but it's different again for all of us together.'

'So who is it?' Steven asked. 'Louise?'

'More like Weezie,' said Kirsty.

'Didn't Miss Teazle die only last year?' asked Jordan. 'It's older than that. I think the Hollow has been this way for a long, long time. It's in the ground as well as the house, in the trees and the streams.'

'Maybe we're on top of an Arthurian burial ground?'

'I'm not sure it's to do with the dead.'

Steven was puzzled by Jordan's statement. 'Ghosts are the dead, surely? Spirits left behind, business left undone. They avenge their murders or haunt their heirs.'

'Those would be unhappy ghosts, Dad.'

Kirsty had a thought. 'In the Weezie books, the little girl is friends with ghosts. There's a grisly ghost in the first one – no, a *gloomy* ghost – which is like your idea of a ghost, the "woooo woooo" misery and chain-rattling ghost. But she meets it, makes friends with it, and it changes. I think Louise turned her own experience into a story.'

'Cashing in?' laughed Steven. 'Maybe we should too? Have haunted holidays.'

'No, dear,' Kirsty said, serious. 'Louise wasn't like that. I think she was like the house. She wanted to share.'

'Well, thank you, Weezie,' said Steven, raising his coffee cup. 'And thank you too, whoever or whatever you are. Thank you, ah, for having us.'

Kirsty lifted her cup too. And Jordan, and Tim.

A delicious shiver ran through her, and she knew her family shared it. It wasn't like a wind. The windowpanes didn't rattle and magazine pages didn't riffle. It was warm and cool at once, like a caress.

'That was, um, enlightening,' said Steven.

The red glow of sunset was splashed across every

pane of the picture windows, bathing the Summer Room in petal-pink light. The windows formed a giant screen. Images swirled in the panes, turning the wall into living stained glass. Kirsty recognised the colours of the watercolours which illustrated the Weezie books.

The orchard and the moor were still there, but strings of phantom light wound between the trees. Shapes danced a midsummer gavotte. Faces formed in the interplay of the trees and the flowers and the light. It was as if music were playing, setting her inner ear a-throb, rhythms syncing with the tides of her body. But there was no sound, just a burst of clarity.

'We should go out there,' she said.

The French windows opened by themselves. A shimmering curtain hung above the crazy paving. Tim ran out first, dragging Jordan by her hand. They plunged through the curtain as if it were a waterfall, and joined the others in the orchard, the others who were indistinct but definite.

Every song Kirsty had ever loved ran through her head, from 'Right Said Fred' through 'Hey Jude' and 'Anarchy in the UK' to 'Common People' to 'Becoming More Like Alfie'. Her husband got up, and pulled back her chair as she stood.

'I think we should join the children, darling,' he said, offering his arm.

'I love,' she said, beginning the sentence she had clung to for so long it had lost all meaning, then tripping as her tongue ran up against a barrier in her mind.

'No,' she said, concentrating to make the barrier

go away. 'I do, Steven. It's back again. It was here, at the Hollow, waiting.'

He brushed her face with whisper kisses.

'I love you,' she said, and her heart was free.

He scooped her up like a bride in a cartoon, and carried her through the shimmer into the orchard.

Jordan woke up in the orchard with the dawn, face glazed with dew, her brother curled up against her tummy. She blinked in the light, expecting the hammer of a hangover headache to strike, but there was nothing. She could think and breathe and see clearly.

Tim mumbled and rolled up into a ball.

She stood. Sparkling cobwebs hung between the rushes. She had wound up making her bed by the stream, in a natural depression. Dawn-warmth smoothed away her momentary goose-flesh.

Mum and Dad were here too, somewhere. She wasn't worried about them.

It was like the first healthy day after a bad cold.

The morning after the best-ever love.

Everything was fresh. Her mouth tasted different, cleaner, sweeter. She ran her hands through her hair and found it finer, untangled, heavier.

She was comfortable in herself. She didn't feel fat or scrawny.

If only Rick were here.

The longing was a worm in the apple. Soon, he would share this with her, with the family.

Last night, she had danced.

Now, she wanted breakfast. When was the last

time she had eaten anything before midday?

The smell of fresh bread emanated from the kitchen, and the soft whistle of an old-fashioned kettle.

Tim snapped awake.

'Come on, soldier,' she said. 'Reveille.'

Mum leaned out of the kitchen window, beaming and beckoning.

'How many eggs?' she shouted.

'Infinite eggs,' Jordan shouted back.

'I'll try my best.'

Jordan and her brother entered the house by the kitchen door.

With the morning post was a package, addressed to 'The Naremore Family'. Recognising the tiny hand script, Kirsty claimed and opened it. Why was Vron's first communiqué since the Weezie book addressed to the family rather than her? Did that mean anything? Should it worry her? She didn't think anything could worry her any more.

Jordan ate like a soldier and amused Tim with her chatter. Steven watched the kids, not realising his wife was watching him. She saw his laughter lines crinkle, recognised those same lines in Jordan, even in Tim (who took after her). The magic was all around. She was safe.

Inside Vron's packet was another book. A battered paperback with a fiery spectre on the cover. *Ghost Stories of the West Country*, by Catriona Kaye. Volume 46 in The Dennis Wheatley Library of the Occult. A peek inside showed a charity-shop stamp and a column of crossed-out prices which began with an optimistic £2.50 and sank to a despairing 45p – which was exactly the original recommended retail price listed on the back cover. This 1976 edition, with an introduction by Wheatley, was a reprint of a book first published in 1962.

Though she'd never heard of Catriona Kaye, Kirsty remembered Dennis Wheatley. His black-magic books were still liable to be confiscated by tutting teachers when she was at school. She'd tried to read one, but found it stodgy and annoying – she'd skipped to the quivering black mass the other girls had gone on about, then given up on it. She skimmed Wheatley's introduction. A full third of the wordage described the menu served at the society dinner where he'd met the authoress for the only time (the consommé was excellent, apparently). Then, he dismissed Miss Kaye as 'an impertinent, though not unintelligent flapper' and copied out the original back jacket copy ('a fascinating pot-pourri of spine-chilling tales') to pad his piece to two pages. *Ghost Stories of the West Country* wasn't an anthology of made-up stories – at least, not in the sense that any writer invented them – but a collection of accounts of 'true hauntings' in Somerset, Devon, Dorset and Cornwall.

A woven bookmark – one of Vron's unique creations, her own black hair with a carefully maintained white streak – stuck out, about halfway through. Kirsty opened to that point and read a few sentences.

'What have you got?' Steven asked.

'Essential information,' she said, holding the book up to show the title. 'Apparently, we live in "the most haunted spot in England".'

'Tell us something we don't know, Mum,' said Jordan.

'Let me read this, and maybe I will.'

That morning, the family all read the chapter. First Kirsty, then Jordan, then Steven, then – with serious concentration, and many questions – Tim. When they had all taken aboard what the book had to say about their home, they reconvened their meeting of the night before, under the midday sun with the heat lying heavy all around.

'So,' said Kirsty, 'what do we think?'

From

Ghost Stories of the West Country

by
CATRIONA KAYE

Chapter Three

'THE MOST HAUNTED SPOT IN ENGLAND'

Plenty of nominations stand for the title of 'most haunted house in England'. 'Ghost-hunter' Harry Price staked a claim for Borley Rectory in Essex, while Lord Halifax advocated Haverholme Priory in Lincolnshire. In my experience, the most haunted *spot* in England is an apple orchard in Somerset.

Currently the home of Louise Magellan Teazle, most-loved of our children's authors, Hollow Farm has been the site of supernatural manifestations for at least a thousand years. A mile or so outside the hamlet of Sutton Mallet, the property has been cultivated ground since well before the Domesday Book. Once an island in the marshes, it became part of the Somerset Levels after the construction of the King's Sedgemoor Drain in 1798.

I first visited the orchard in 1923, when Miss Teazle was little older than her famous heroine Weezie. She already showed the pluck that makes her books enduringly popular with children and adults alike. A surge in poltergeist activity disturbed the young Louise's elderly parents but affected the cheerful, open girl not a whit. She confided in me that she considered night-time rearrangements of the furniture little more than conjuring shows staged for her entertainment. I have returned in recent years to find the ghosts tamed if not dispelled, a circumstance I ascribe to the geniality of their present landlady, who has – as generations of children understand – an ability to get along with anyone, and confesses to be more than happy to share her home with phantoms.

That it is the *ground* and not any particular building upon it which sustains the haunting is demonstrated by the phenomenon of *ghost trees* which, in certain circumstances, appear to grow *inside* structures (a farmhouse and a barn) built where they once stood. These trees seem more solid than any walls that fail to confine them, and their branches spread through obstacles as if they were mere impertinences. I cannot bear witness to these spectral growths and Miss Teazle admits they've been little-seen since she was a girl. However, an anonymous 1824 *Blackwood's Magazine* article (signed by 'a Gentleman') and a series of journal entries penned in 1879 by Timothy Bannerman (parson of the nearby village of Alder) describe the ghost trees at some length. These, incidentally, are the major nineteenth-century accounts of the haunting of Hollow Farm. The *Blackwood's* contributor claims to have collected a piece of ghost-tree bark for examination. He reports that it dwindled to 'a smear of black stuff' (presumably, the matter we would now call ectoplasm) while wrapped in a kerchief.

A local story connected with the ghost trees is extant in many forms. The folk song 'Apple Annie's Fancy' (familiar in the arrangement by Percy Grainger) is best known, though the most elaborate is the dialect tale R. H. Barham collected as 'Nancy of Thick Green: A Legend of Wessex' in *The Ingoldsby Legends*. This has it that in the sixteenth or seventeenth century, the daughter of the farmer who then owned the orchard, named variously Anne or Nan or Nancy, plucked an apple from a ghost tree and ate it. This inculcated in the lass a powerful addiction to ghost fruit which led to a condition of self-neglect that continued until her premature death. She has since been numbered among the spectres of the Hollow, heard singing among the trees, creating a sense of melancholy and lassitude in unwary auditors. A recent tradition is that the spirit is heard to sing 'Apple Annie's Fancy', though that ditty must of course post-date the tragic death described in its penultimate verse. If Annie can sing her own theme song, she must have learned it after her death, suggesting a capacity for scholarship seldom ascribed to shades of the departed.

The *Blackwood's* Gentleman and the Reverend Mr Bannerman note that during the moments when phantom figures were visible and voices audible, the 'ceiling of the farmhouse became itself ghostly' or 'grew transparent as thick, ill-blown glass' and that stars were clearly discernible in the sky above. Bannerman, a keen astronomer, wrote 'the constellations were not in their familiar places but awry, as if we saw not the night sky of today but the heavens of some distant, remote past or futurity when the stars were in different positions'. To the clergyman, this was the most alarming of the phenomena he was witness to at Hollow Farm. Miss Teazle sets little store by either of these accounts, pointing out that neither the amateur man of letters nor the professional man of the cloth actually lived on the site. 'The old place likes to put on a show for visitors, my dear,' she said to me, when I called upon her to discuss this chapter, 'as you well remember.'

This is, indeed, so. In 1923, in the company of the trance medium Irene Dobson and the psychic investigator Edwin Winthrop, I spent a night at Hollow Farm. We saw recognisable human shapes formed out of light and darkness and witnessed the independent movement of objects as heavy as a writing-desk and a sturdy divan. Miss Teazle's mother was distraught at her inability to keep items of crockery for more than a few weeks before cracks appeared. I saw a row of crystal glasses broken as if exploded from the inside and had to extract splinters from Mr Winthrop's hand, binding his wounds with a tea-towel. Madame Dobson, an undoubted talent whose name was later tarnished by convictions for fraud, claimed to have communed with angry spirits. They resented our intrusion but had taken a particular dislike to Mr and Mrs Teazle. The ghosts' intention, it seems, was to drive them out – as a succession of tenants and owners had been driven out in the previous two hundred years.

Our little parapsychological expedition can take no credit for the sudden cessation of hostile manifestations, but Miss Teazle assures me that after our visit there was a moderation of the persecution. Her parents travelled abroad and died while she was away at school. When she returned as young mistress of the Hollow, the place was still haunted but the quality of the haunting had changed. She was able to make accommodations with 'the older tenants'. Now, Miss Teazle reports that though she has never been alone at the Hollow, malignity or mischief – which she frowns on intently – are rare. 'I'm used to living with people who aren't there,' she claims. 'Sometimes, they spill out of my head but mistake their way halfway to the page and escape for a while. It's probably good for them, you know.'

No such fortune was experienced by the Maitland-Middletons, owners of the Hollow from 1851 to 1883. When the last of the Gouches, who farmed the property for generations (Apple Annie is presumed to have been a Gouch daughter), died without issue, the Hollow was bought by Ronald Maitland-Middleton, a visionary architect and transcendentalist philosopher. He sold the surrounding fields, retaining only the orchard and the house. Maitland-Middleton added the towers that are such an unusual feature, giving the large but hitherto humble Gouch house a castellated, somewhat pretentious air. He was killed in a fall from one of his towers, shortly before completion of the building work. His daughter, Primrose, told Timothy Bannerman her mother was convinced Maitland-Middleton was murdered by 'unknown and unknowable forces' who resented his 'casting of light into darkness'. Susannah Maitland-Middleton devoted her life to her husband's memory and turned the Hollow into a species of school, offering instruction in his beliefs to the materially wealthy but spiritually bereft. Maitland-Middleton proposed that houses be built upon a spiritual as well as a physical foundation, maintaining that every dwelling should be a church, as much a home to angels as to earthly tenants.

When the Reverend Mr Bannerman visited the Hollow, Susannah Maitland-Middleton was well advanced in years and her unmarried daughter driven half out of her mind by decades of living in a house that was 'home to wicked angels'. In his journal, Bannerman writes that he was 'initially of the belief that all the spectres of the Hollow were the product of an overactive feminine imagination, whipped up in the unhealthy atmosphere that must inevitably arise when a woman is denied all contact with the outside world, chained to an elderly relation and forced to consider only the thoughts and feelings of the dead.' He believed Susannah and Primrose were faking the haunting in a lengthy psychological campaign against each other. The mother deemed her daughter somehow to blame for her husband's long-ago death and the daughter was convinced life had been robbed from her by enforced devotion to the cause of a man she had little memory of and no affection for.

The cleric eventually became as convinced of the reality of the haunters of the Hollow as I was to be a half-century later. Prevailed upon to remain into the evening on his third visit to Mrs and Miss Maitland-Middleton, Bannerman experienced a rare and complete immersion in the Hollow. Besides the transparency of the house and the celestial transformation noted above, he writes of 'figures in antique costume parading before my startled eyes' and of a 'conviction that I was in danger of harm to my person and mind'. His handwriting careless, he mentions that 'icy points pressed to my cheeks and forehead, as if long, invisible fingers were touched to my face, exerting considerable pressure… my looking-glass tells me that the marks left by this touch have not faded completely. Two fingers apiece touched my forehead and my left cheek, while the impression of a thumb, down to a half-inch scratch that might be made by a raggedly cut nail, marks my right cheek. The spacing of the impressions is such that my own hand, nor I would wager any but the most gigantic of human hands, could not have made them.'

Upon the death (in the orchard, purportedly of a bee-sting) of Mrs Maitland-Middleton, Bannerman ceased his regular visits. He mentions briefly that (somewhat against expectations) Primrose went on to marry a widowed schoolmaster in Wells and quit the Hollow. She sold the property in 1883, to Major Tolliver Brough, a retired officer of the Indian Army who was well aware of his new home's reputation. Bannerman paid a courtesy call and was told 'bogeys were not needed in this billet'. The parson reports, with obvious relief, that he could 'sense none of that queer, weird atmosphere so apparent about the place during the time of the late Mrs M.-M. and her unhappy daughter'. It appears that the haunting went into abeyance while Major Brough devoted his declining years to the cultivation of a rose garden.

He trained flowers to stand in neat rows like soldiers at attention, but his efforts somehow lacked the romantic qualities which we care for in such things. The Hollow passed from Major Brough's son to Miss Teazle's parents shortly before the First War, whereupon the other residents again poked fingers through the veil.

Bannerman concluded that the Maitland-Middletons had brought upon themselves the supernatural visitations to which he bore witness. This suggests he was unaware of the history of the Hollow, a circumstance that in itself lends weight to elements of his account which parallel those of 1824. The *Blackwood's* article makes it clear that the Hollow was already a notorious haunted site, and collects statements from Sutton Mallet residents who describe incidents from their own childhoods. Two dotards of the locality were engaged in a spirited argument, in accents that put the 'Gentleman' in mind of 'Olde Englishe', as to which of them had been in youth the swain bereft by the defection of Apple Annie to the ghostly lover conjured up under the spell of her phantom fruit. He translates (or manufactures) passages from a Latin manuscript he claims to have been shown at Glastonbury Abbey, though no such document resides there now or has ever been noted by anyone less anonymous than this worthy.

In the record, which *Blackwood's* dates as written in the 1240s but describing events of some thirty years earlier, a monk, Brother Crispin, confesses that he was of a party assembled by the then-abbot after a 'desperate petition' from the lord who was master of

Sutton Mallet and the surrounding wetlands. Though the fruit of the orchard was plentiful and of high quality, none of the lord's vassals could be persuaded to gather it for fear of the 'imps and goblins' that dwelled among the trees. The fiends would pelt 'with apples hard as stones' any intruders of whom they did not approve. Crispin, who went so far as to mention 'dragons and worms of the earth', took part in an exorcism, but admits it did not take. Though the quality of the spectral persecutions changed, the orchard was still so haunted as to be useless and fruit rotted where it lay until the ground was thick with 'insects and wasps'.

The lord and the abbot were not thereafter on good terms and, according to *Blackwood's*, the orchard was not farmed until 'it became the property of a free Englishman'. A record does exist from 1322 of a special grant, whereby the property known as 'the Hollowe' was detached from the holdings of the manor of Sutton Mallet and gifted to one William Tin, in recognition of 'his boldnesse during the late floode'. After that, the spirits allowed honest Will to have all the apples he could eat (or turn into *syddur*, 'strong drink'), though the tributes he paid yearly to the manor and the church rotted when they were removed from the property, and so went for compost. Throughout its history, it seems the Hollow has been particular about the living folk who are its custodians, treating them well or ill according to criteria that remain obscure to Miss Teazle. Though she follows Primrose Maitland-Middleton in identifying several particular ghosts – Apple Annie, the 'Tudor lady in some distress', Honest Will Tin, 'the Damp One' – she believes them relatively recent additions to a company that arose in the mists of the past. Oddly, Ronald and Susannah Maitland-Middleton, who died suddenly on the property, have never made themselves manifest in the home Ronald explicitly prepared for his afterlife. Were they black-balled by an exclusive order of spectres who found them tiresome?

'There were ghosts here before there were people,' Miss Teazle says, with a twinkle in her eye. 'And, my dear, there will be ghosts here long after the people have gone.'

Though it has not always been so, the Hollow is a happy spot. In researching this book, I have visited many places where the terrors of the past linger like fog in a ditch, where the unquiet spirits of those violently expelled from earthly shells walk in anger or fear or cruel hatred. The Hollow is not like that; I have claimed it as 'the most haunted spot in England', but I believe it also among the most magical, the most enchanting. It has supported one of our national treasures and gained from her benign proprietorship. Long may it continue so to do.

After Midsummer

The family didn't need a book to tell them they were not alone at the Hollow. They weren't sure if what was in the paperback really applied to their situation. Much of it came from earlier, perhaps unreliable, sources. Only the conclusion, when the author called the Hollow 'a happy spot', seemed to be about the place where they lived. They weren't guests, but recognised they shared tenancy and resolved to be respectful.

August wore on. Jordan had a birthday, which the family celebrated in the orchard. The first red appeared early among the green, like spilled drops of heart's-blood.

The night before, when she phoned, Rick was out. Enjoying a last night of freedom with his mates, Jordan supposed. She hoped he wasn't too hung over to follow her map. She'd worked hard on it, illustrating the turn-offs with pointing hands, depicting the city as a smoky ruin, putting in a little flying saucer to represent Rick and sketching herself in a pin-up pose at the end of the trail. It was fun, but also usable.

If he got on the road early, he should be at the Hollow by mid-morning. She found a floppy hat and Jacqueline Bisset sunglasses, and gave some thought to how she wanted to be discovered. Outside, obviously, so she would be the first thing Rick saw as he drove up, weary and dusty from the trek, smitten all over again by a vision of cool welcome.

The lawn furniture was in the wrong place, round the back of the house. She had to be out front, visible from the drive. And she had to be doing something, not obviously waiting for him. She thought about being found reading. He'd lent her an Iain M. Banks novel she hadn't got to yet. Reading that would suggest she was thinking subliminally about him while concentrating on something else. But it seemed forced, somehow: something anyone might be doing, not something specifically her. She had read more Louise Teazle, the first Weezie story and two more Drearcliff Grange books, but repetition – all those girls and ghosts – wore thin. She had dipped into the book of West Country ghost stories Mum had been sent. Without the frisson of personal acquaintance with the sites (Which tower had Mr M-M fallen from? Hers or the other?) she found the other chapters too inconsequential to hold the attention. It was hard to take seriously the ghost monkey of Athelhampton Hall, the evil priest of Sandford Orcas Manor, the burning angel of Alder or 'the gruesome black figure' of Creech Hill.

No, she would not read. She would do something. Something country. Something Jordan-in-the-country.

Some of the tassels on her shawl – *that* shawl, though it had not danced since the night of revelation – were missing. She thought she could crochet replacements. A restoration project she'd planned to do anyway. She only hoped it wouldn't get done too quickly. The point was to be found doing something, not snoozing in the sun having done something.

A sward of lawn by the drive was perfectly positioned, looking down a gentle slope at the front gate, which she'd made sure was open. A striped deck-chair could be set up casually, as if it usually lived there. She sat in it and sank alarmingly. No way she could crochet while wobbling in this contraption. She spread a picnic-blanket and set out her sewing basket. She could arrange herself prettily, showing off her newly tanned calves, and still be able to work.

There would have to be music, of course. His or hers? He tolerated her tastes and even, away from his mates, could be prodded into admitting that she had made him listen to things he secretly liked. His official music choices ran to rap and metal, though she thought it was only because the crowd he hung about with were into that stuff. Asked who his favourite artists were, he waffled. She settled on alternating Nancy Sinatra and Fun Lovin' Criminals CDs. Either would be apt, but not too overwhelming.

When should she tell him? About the Hollow?

Since midsummer, the family hadn't had another real discussion. It seemed pointless. They had re-read the chapter in the book, but its haunting was not theirs. No icy hands or wailing women. There were no further major displays, but every day something tiny reminded them of the other tenants. None of the family were afraid of the Hollow. Jordan had come to her own understanding and was happy with it. She had always lived with imminent cataclysm: nuclear war, the IRA's mainland bombing campaign, asteroids and comets in the sky, AIDS, the ever-threatening possibility that her family would burst apart. She was used to uncertainty. The real shock was that things had turned out to be gentle.

Rick would understand. He'd read all that science fiction and fantasy, watched all those episodes of *Star Trek* and *Babylon 5*. Terry Pratchett and Jean-Luc Picard had prepared him for the Hollow.

Still, she was looking forward to his face when she told him and he thought she was mad, and then again when the first *thing* happened, when the Hollow revealed a secret to him, taking him in too.

It would be delicious.

Maybe tonight, in her room, snuggled together afterwards, candles melting and hissing out around them, she would drop the first hints.

'Lunch, darling?' asked her mother.

Mum had come to the front door. Jordan looked down at her watch. Half-past twelve.

'Couldn't we wait for Rick?'

'It's soup and salad. You can have it when you want, but Dad wants to take Tim out this afternoon to look for the stone circle.'

Rick must have set off later than expected. He had

been out last night. It was just like him to oversleep or get a skull-cracking hangover. He might be only just on the outskirts of London, looking for the motorway west. Her best bet was to get lunch over with quickly. When Rick turned up, in early or mid-afternoon, she could show off her growing kitchen skills by whipping up something for him, all the while dropping arch remarks, raising an eyebrow as he was overwhelmed by the Hollow.

She got through her soup and salad in under three minutes.

'You *have* changed,' Dad commented.

She had gone through a not-eating thing last year. She wasn't Ana or Mia. If anything, she had been decidedly chubby. She'd just lost her appetite. Mealtimes stretched into Spanish Inquisition ordeals, hardly helped by the bad ozone crackling between Mum and Dad and – God help them – the Wild Witch.

'No Rick?' said Mum. 'Has he called?'

Jordan shrugged. 'He's on a long lead, Mum.'

A lump of unsquashed chickpea soured in her mouth. She scraped it out on a napkin.

Dad and Tim hurried off on their expedition of discovery. She slipped out to resume her post, leaving Mum to clear away and wash up.

Jordan finished her crochet tassels and couldn't listen to the Fun Lovin' Criminals for a third time. She darted indoors to have a pee and lingered in the Summer Room, by the telephone. Mum was on the big sofa, reading a Drearcliff Grange book.

'No calls, darling,' she said.

There was a knot in her throat. Did she detect just

the trace of a gloat in Mum's tone? In the city, her parents had been too mired in their own problems to pay much attention to Rick. They liked him more than Phil, her original semi-boyfriend, but there was still a reserve. That was understandable. They didn't see him alone, as she did. They only saw the Rick of Rick-and-His-Mates, not the real boy. Dad sometimes called him 'Precious Rick', with a feral grin that gave bite to the joshing. Jordan had once called Rick 'Precious', a private name. When it got out, she dropped it. To be fair, Dad had only used the expression a few times. He liked Rick, really. They had conversations, utterly mysterious to her, about comics, which she hadn't realised Dad once had a craze for. When Dad told the story of how his mother gave all his Marvels to a jumble sale, Rick won major points for cringing sympathy. Dad's tatty Hulk and X-Men comics, bought for old pennies, could have been sold today for enough to give Jordan a car.

She considered going up to her room and calling Rick's father's flat to find out when he'd left. But Rick's father would be at work, not at the flat. He wouldn't know the exact time Rick set out anyway. Unless he'd left a note, and there was no reason for that.

Settling on the lawn, she read the opening page of the novel seventeen times without quite catching what was going on. Someone seemed to be floating in a septic tank. She put the book down and flicked through her portable CD wallet, fingers lingering on Patsy Cline before she came up with Connie Francis.

Heat built inside her. Her skin tingled from the sun. Was she getting a burn? Rick would probably arrive just as she completed her transformation into a red-faced alien with Klingon forehead ridges.

Rick's mates must have taken him on a real bender, like a stag night. She knew he wasn't as comfortable with them as with her. His alleged best friend Walker – whom Jordan thought of as Veronica incarnated as a teenage boy – called him 'Spockears'. When he was ten, he'd entered a fancy-dress contest got up as a Vulcan. He stuck with Walker's lot because they'd been a gang since infants' school. Most of them hadn't gone on to college. They sniped at him because he was on his way to uni while they were driving vans or bouncing from one government scheme to the next. None of them, without exception, liked her. Their girlfriends were even worse.

Here, at the Hollow, where it would be just Jordan and Rick, things would be better.

A car turned into the drive and her heart leaped. She screwed her eyes shut and thanked invisible presences. She cleared her throat, adjusted her hat to unstick it from her radiator-warm forehead, settled her dress about her lap, and reached for the cast-aside book.

'We got lost,' shouted Tim.

Her heart went cold, as if she'd been shot with a snowball bullet.

Tim ran up from the car and through the house, to tell Mum about the search for the stones.

Dad parked the car in the garage – she had reminded him to leave a space for Rick's banger – and strolled across, smiling wisely.

'No Precious?'

She wanted to spit venom into his face.

It had all been an act, a bland, seductive, calculatedly cruel act. A long set-up for a quick, nasty pay-off.

'Summer holidays,' he said. 'Motorway is probably clogged. And it's a tricky navigating exercise. Remember how much trouble we had finding Sutton Mallet that first time. Almost like it's trying to get away from you. Maps are useless. I just found that out again.'

Every word was calm and barbed.

'Would you believe it? We drove around for hours but couldn't find those blessed stones.'

Dad stood on tiptoe in the spot and shrugged.

'Well, there they are,' he said.

Suddenly, oddly, she knew he was lying. He had never seen the stones, not even from the spot. He probably didn't believe in them.

'It's another blooming mystery. I half-think it's an optical illusion.'

She was in control. Every fibre of her body was knotted, but she would not give anything away.

'I sent Rick a map.'

'There you are, then,' he said, cracking a smile. 'He's doomed to wander.'

He went indoors.

Her face was burning now. Not just her forehead, imprinted with the weave of the hat, but her cheeks and chin. Her forearms looked orange through her sunglasses. Grass stuck to her legs like green veins.

Rick must have stayed in London for lunch.

Could they have done anything to delay him? His mates, her parents, his dad? Walker, slipping him an

E? The Wild Witch? Rick said he'd seen Veronica. Could she still be stalking the family, working on Rick now she had given up on Mum?

Jordan would be strong, determined. If it came to a fight, she was a far more dangerous opponent than Dad. She wasn't tied down by strings of emotion, by inner weaknesses. There was no money involved. She was free to inflict untold punishments. She was a seventeen-year-old girl, a saint in the eyes of society. She could play any game Veronica chose, and win.

She thought about Tim's catapult. You could have someone's eye out with that, if you weren't careful. You could have someone's eye out with that, if you *were* careful. The Wild Witch could do with a black eyepatch, on a string that wound through her nest of hair.

Was Mum in on this? The Wild Witch had been puppet-mastering her for years. Even Dad had danced to Veronica's whim more often than he'd like to admit.

It made a horrible sort of sense.

Connie Francis sang 'Where the Boys Are'. The high, clear voice reached into the murk of Jordan's mind and tugged, pulling the real her free.

She was being silly.

Her boyfriend was a few hours late. That didn't mean there was a vast conspiracy against her. Let's face it, his car was off the road more often than it was on. He'd been worried about the trip from the first time she mentioned it. London to Somerset was a longer haul than the rattletrap really liked.

(Rick had a mobile. He would call.)

His phone was probably still programmed with the number of the old flat, two on the autodial after his home number. He might not have the new number entered.

(There was an automatic redirect on the old number.)

Conditions here were strange. Everything worked at the Hollow, but not necessarily on the moors or in the village. Dad was right about the weird ways of the West Country. Rick might be driving in circles around Sutton Mallet, her map upside down, stabbing redial over and over, getting only a dead-air whine out of the phone.

(No.)

It was likely. More likely than anything else.

'Dinner's on the table in ten minutes,' said Mum. 'I've set an extra place. I expect Rick'll have a story to tell.'

(He's not coming.)

'Not hungry,' she said, to herself.

'Jordan?' asked Mum.

Mum stood in the doorway, wearing an apron with a busy-bee design over a short summer dress. She'd hidden her city spikiness behind this housewife act, but it was still there. If you looked closely, there were holes in her cheeks. Once, long before Jordan was born, she had pierced herself with safety-pins. Also, the dark holes in her eyes, which she shared with the Wild Witch, were still there.

'I'm not hungry,' Jordan said, clearly, loudly.

Mum looked distressed.

'Darling,' she began.

'Don't, Mummy. Just don't.'
Jordan sat outside until it was dark.

He noticed a blip on the radar. It could be left for the moment.

Jordan's precious boyfriend hadn't appeared. Not exactly a crushing disappointment. However, Steven knew all too well how much store she set by the carrot-headed clod and was dutifully concerned some harm might have come to him. From his unblinkered experience, it was much more likely Rick had just plain forgotten. Not only was he capable of that, he was capable of not feeling guilty about it.

If Rick never showed up, it might even be for the best.

The Hollow had accepted the family, but Steven still wasn't sure how inclusive its welcome was. Explaining the place to anyone outside the circle would be hard. If they hadn't all found out together, the family would have ripped each other's stories apart. What if a logical Vulcan gaze killed the magic dead?

Jordan had come in and gone to bed hungry.

Kirsty said it was best not to press their daughter, and he went along with his wife. He wanted to do some work after supper. While Kirsty read Tim a slightly too babyish bedtime story (*Weezie and the Spooky Something*), he went into the study and fired up the computer.

He looked at the ceiling, imagining Jordan in her room, in the dark, headphones on. When things were bad, she didn't sob but became this frozen, glum, glowering thing. No, that had been back in the city. Here, things would be different. Jordan was not alone. None of them were alone.

The family had found a strength he hadn't fathomed yet.

The modem shrilled and burbled. He opened his e-mail and scanned a dense message from Tatum, with an attached file of figures and facts. She was pressing him gently, because a client wanted to meet in person rather than deal with an intermediary. He was glad to be indispensable but knew the chauvinism must grate with Tatum. The client should be over thinking of her as just a PA with great legs. But he could do with a cash injection to cover the outlay on Oddments debts and home improvement expenses. He wanted to have the thatch looked over before autumn rains gave them a nasty surprise; that would take some sort of country crafts specialist (i.e. it would not be cheap).

Kirsty knew he had taken care of her debts. She didn't much regret the loss of her business. In the past, she too often mistook crazes for careers. Now, she was in the grip of a mercifully practical enthusiasm. He hadn't given up the mystery collection, and her Louise Teazle researches might turn up answers.

He replied to Tatum, telling her to bring the client to shore and call him in for a lightning deal-clinch when she had landed him. Should he ask her to check on Precious Rick? No, that was well beyond her remit.

Ten minutes later, as he was marking up an investment prospectus he distrusted more with each glossy fold-out, his screensaver cut in. A single green word slid across the black.

CAREFUL.

He looked again and the word was just a software logo.

It might have been in his mind, but was good advice nevertheless.

The MP had been reading him the little books by the lady who had lived at the Hollow before them. They had seemed non-essential at first, but Tim now recognised vital intel. The stories, which were about a creepy little girl called Weezie, contained a wealth of coded reference points.

It was strange to hear something from an old book and know the exact tree it came from. Weezie had a hidey-hole in Green Base, too, and also received tributes from the IP, whom she called ghosts. Features of the land and the house turned up in the stories. Almost every piece of furniture or corner of the Hollow had been fitted into the books somehow, as if the lady were leaving messages for him.

Had the Weezie woman given him the U-Dub?

He listened carefully to each story, sensitive to coded orders. The MP didn't understand half of what she was passing on, but that was the point of cipher.

The story finished and Mum shut the book.

He gathered the MP had read to Jordan when she was littler than he was now. But she'd never read to him until the Hollow. This was part of their lives now. Routine, SOP – a comfort.

'Is Jordan going to London?'

'No, Tim,' said the MP. 'Why do you ask?'

'She had her London face on tonight.'

The MP thought a moment. 'Yes, I suppose she did. It's just a mood. We all have them in this family. More than most people, I should say.'

'But it's different here.'

'Better. Yes. Jordan will be her new self again.'

'When?'

'Soon, I'm sure. Have you brushed your teeth?'

'Yes, ma'am.'

'Good night then.'

The MP withdrew. He heard her going down the twisted tower staircase to her own room.

Tim stretched out in his bed, lying flat but to attention. The U-Dub was under his pillow, as close to hand always as the football, the case of launch codes that went everywhere with the American President. A smooth pebble was nocked and ready, in readiness for the first report of hostile activity.

He turned his mind to tonight's story, *Weezie and the Dancing Stones*, and tried to puzzle out his orders. He thought he was to hold fast and make no sudden moves.

Sleep crept over him.

In the dark, in *her* dark, Jordan was cold with fury. She knew she should be concerned. It was possible, likely even, that Rick had only been killed in a traffic accident. But she'd grown beyond that worry. She knew this was the worst-case scenario. He just plain hadn't come.

(That's what he thought of her, she was worthless.)

She thought back, replaying each of their conversations, in person before the move, by phone after. She realised she had worked everything out and Rick had done no more than give silent assent. He never contradicted, never said anything wouldn't be possible, that he wasn't interested or had other commitments. She had even picked the date for his visit. He'd had no opinion, never contributed to the plan she'd formulated.

That was the most despicable thing. At any time, he could have spoken up. He could have said no. There would have been fireworks, but it would have been honest.

Instead, he had done the easiest thing. He'd let her leave the city, let her witter on about the future, and gone about the quiet, vicious business of forgetting her.

(He could be dead in a ditch, corpse trapped in a crumpled car.)

No. He was back home, with his Dad cooking his tea and Walker goading him about Spock ears.

Rick was content to lean back and let other people fix things for him, giving a silent nod to carefully worked-through plans he was then somehow not quite able to carry out. In his gang, Walker had all the ideas (bad ones, usually). With her, Rick was plasticine. He went along with whatever she said but didn't contribute anything really. He would nod agreement but not lift a finger. If you sent five people to different shops to gather the ingredients for an omelette, Rick would be the one who forgot eggs and came back with a plastic dinosaur with flashing lights in its eyes.

Was anyone else involved in the betrayal?

(The Wild Witch, Veronica.)

Ghastly, impossible. She was old enough to be...

Old, anyway. It was hard to tell with Veronica.

She reeled in that line of thought.

Blaming the Wild Witch for everything that had happened to the family, from Tim's bout of whooping cough to the failure of Mum's businesses, was too easy. Veronica's 'homoeopathic remedies' never worked and she was useless as representative-at-large for Oddments. But she was just a grown-up looney. Not Dracula in a dress.

This wasn't about the Wild Witch. This was about Rick.

(This was about Jordan.)

She put one last CD into her player, pulling her headphones on like a helmet. She injected Lesley Gore into her brain: 'It's My Party'.

Carrying the CD player like Red Riding Hood's basket, she left her room, went downstairs and stepped through the unlocked kitchen door into the orchard. There was no moon and no light from the house, but the needle-points of stars glinted above, four hundred million jabs of venom. She looked across the moor. There was a dark shimmer to the wet fields, as if something under the ground were stirring in sleep.

Tears wet her cheeks, but she didn't sob. It was just her eyes leaking.

The Lesley Gore of 'It's My Party' was hysterical, crying from shock. That wasn't Jordan's way. She knew what was a silly song and what was real.

The track finished. Next came the sequel song, 'It's Judy's Turn to Cry'.

Listening as if for the first time to the ill-thought-of quickie follow-up record, Jordan realised it was a far deeper work. Lesley was reaching for a truth she could only flirt with in the original hit. Because Judy has left the party with Johnny, Lesley kisses 'some other guy', and when Johnny finds out, he *hits* him... because he still loves her. In the triumphalist gloat, Gore wasn't the self-pitying reject of 'It's My Party' but a teenage Medea, coldly joyful to have her feckless and violent boyfriend ('he *hit* him') back, but plotting revenge. Lesley would never forget being left for Judy. She had taken Johnny back because she could, and because Johnny was weak, a fool, a man. Later, she would make him pay.

There should be a third song, she realised, to complete the trilogy.

'It's My Baby, And I'll Take It If I Want To.'

'Johnny's Turn to Die.'

'Everybody Run, the Homecoming Queen's Got a Gun.'

Instead, the next track was 'You Don't Own Me'.

She turned the CD off and stood in the dark, fire in her empty stomach, brain swarming.

She'd had it. She had tried, but it hadn't worked out. No regrets. It had been a nice dream, but that's all it was, a fairy story for children, like the Weezie books. Things weren't different in the Hollow. She was still who she had been in the city. She had allowed herself to forget for a while, to be lulled into a party mood. She'd been giddy with fizz and wishes.

Just another wrapping for desperation.

It wasn't just Judy. Now, it was everybody's turn to cry.

There had been an incursion in the night. Green Base was compromised, ivy curtains torn away and trampled, his reserves tampered with.

Tim nocked a pebble in the U-Dub and scanned the horizon. He detected no possible breach of the perimeter. He looked up at the house. The curtains in his parents' room were still shut. It was well before breakfast hundred hours.

The BS's curtains were open and she sat – asleep? – in her rocking chair, head hanging, nodding slightly. Tim took aim, in case the shape was a hostile in disguise. Over the sights of the U-Dub, he recognised her only too well.

Could it have been the IP?

So far, they'd been nothing but friendly. He had made no move to upset the balance, had always respected their need to stay in the shadows, had striven to watch out for their interests.

He looked back into the hollow tree.

There were scratches in the soft wood inside, like an animal might leave. But this was not the work of an animal. It had taken hands to wrench away the ivy.

Tim was alert, mind clear.

He needed to focus. It could be that the peace was ending.

All his life, he had strived to be ready for war. If this was it, he would not be caught by surprise.

Mentally, he stepped up to DefCon 4. He would not attack unless directly threatened, but then he would respond with all he had, expecting no quarter and demanding no surrender. He would fight until the victory was won, and – if that were impossible – until there was no one left standing.

He took stock. Supplies would have to be replaced. There was no telling what had been done to them. They might have been turned against him.

He pulled back on the rubber of the U-Dub and did a slow three-sixty, hawkeye out for hostiles. His trained arm did not ache with the tension of holding the locked and loaded U-Dub. This might last a long time.

It wouldn't be over by Christmas.

In the kitchen, Kirsty whisked. They had got into the habit of eating breakfast together. Today, only Steven came down in time. She was irritated to have broken too many eggs. Steven sat at the breakfast table, warming his neck in the early morning sun, reading the financial pages of the *Independent*.

It hit her how weird this was, like something from those hideous old films Jordan liked: housewifey slaving over cooked breakfast while hubby sits back and thinks money-making thoughts. She wasn't supposed to bother her pretty little head with man's business. Steven used to confide in her about deals he was putting together, soliciting her uninformed opinion. Understandably, that had changed. After Oddments, she was lucky not to be bankrupt. She could hardly expect to be treated as a financial consultant.

Still, when the Jordan thing was resolved, she'd broach the subject. With Tatum Hoyle – Tate 'n' Lyle, they called her – in the city, Steven needed things done here that Kirsty could manage easily. Her perfectly good degree (in journalism) had never really been put to use. She could at least type reports (word process, rather).

The Jordan thing, though.

She'd been whisking for several minutes. Butter sizzled brown in the pan. Concentrating, she scrambled eggs.

Tim wasn't at the table, either. She'd heard him going out at some unholy hour.

She took two plates of scrambled egg on toast to the table and sat opposite Steven. The table caught the sun at just the right time.

He was absorbed in the paper.

'Steven,' she said.

'Uh-huh.' He didn't look up.

'About Jordan?'

He folded the paper with an almost subliminal sigh. A tiny thorn shifted in Kirsty's chest. Her spine started to prickle. She had flashes of other mornings, sullen or shrieking. Behind her husband's bland expression, she glimpsed the twisted, spittle-flecked mask his face had become during the worst of it.

'She's chucked, right?' he asked.

She was guarded. 'We don't know that.'

'Yes we do,' he said kindly. 'We knew Rick wouldn't come, remember? You even said so once.'

'That was before we moved, before everything changed.'

'Rick didn't move. So he didn't change.'

That made sense. At least, it made Steven-sense. It was entirely inarguable, backed up with facts and figures and confirmed by rumours downloaded from a dozen Internet sites.

There was something she couldn't trust about Steven-sense.

'Would you call his father?' she asked.

Steven performed a mock shudder, waving his knife and fork over his plate.

'Could you imagine anything worse? What if your dad had called mine to ask about us?'

He was right. Probably.

'It's the uncertainty,' she said.

'What uncertainty?'

'Aren't you even concerned? Your daughter is upstairs crying her eyes out because of this bastard.'

'That doesn't sound like Jordan. You're stereotyping.'

Kirsty remembered Jordan in her skeleton phase. She *was* stereotyping, she admitted, but only because she really didn't want to think in personal, realistic terms about her daughter's reaction to this soap-opera tragedy. She'd hoped all that was over with, left behind in London. Surely, it couldn't happen again, not at the Hollow, not in the charmed place, not after the magic. Everything was changed.

'Darling,' Steven said, 'Jordan's too good for him, remember? Rick wasn't as bad as all that, but he hardly had much in the way of gumption. She could run rings around him. She needs someone with more up top, more going for them. That's always been her problem. She can't find anyone to challenge her. When she's bored, she turns in on herself, eats herself up from the inside.'

Who was good enough for Jordan? Kirsty had no answer. Did Steven? Or would no one ever be good enough for Daddy's Little Darling?

Tim came in through the kitchen door, catapult in hand, as always.

'Not at the table, Tim,' she said.

Tim paused on the threshold, considered it, and slipped back outdoors, without a word.

Steven had the paper up again. Had he even looked at his son?

She had just eaten, scoffed down breakfast without tasting it, but felt empty, as if the two uneaten breakfasts fuelled her own burning hunger.

For the first time at the Hollow, she was frightened. She wanted to talk to Vron, but couldn't. Her friend wasn't at their café, a bus ride away, or prepared to make a house call. Vron was left behind, with all the bad things. There were no postcards with cryptic answers to questions only just forming in her mind. Kirsty hadn't told Steven Vron had sent the books, had allowed him to give her credit for sleuthing them out on her own.

Vron was still out there, still in touch. That might be a lifeline soon.

Because things were going to have to change. Again.

Kirsty was not going to let herself be sucked into someone else's dream. Support for her husband and concern for her kids were all very well, but what about her? Who supported and was concerned for her?

Steven hummed as he looked at the sports section. She understood she was on her own.

Very well. So be it. Watch out.

She rocked in her chair, not fast but evenly, foot up on the low window-sill. She left the photograph of Rick up on the mirror, preserving her room at a precise moment in history. From now on, she wouldn't let anything change.

Jordan was inside herself, deep. She'd been here before. It was a comfort on some level, if only in the sense that she recognised the impossibility of comfort, the illusory nature of happiness.

It had all been a trick.

It wasn't magic, it was conjuring.

She recognised she'd been rooked by Rick, by her parents, by the Hollow. She had been sold a lie, and now didn't want to have the shreds of that lie clinging to her for the rest of her life.

She would devote herself to the cold, stark truth.

Behind her, the door opened a crack. She heard the small sound, as before. It wasn't Mum. It was no one, just the Hollow.

'Go away,' she said firmly, not shouting, not whispering.

The door clicked shut.

'Good,' she said, settling that.

The family was *wrong*. As individuals, they were acceptable, even decent. Potentially good people. But they were mismatched. Like kippers and custard,

Stravinsky and Sinatra. If ever a man and woman shouldn't have married each other, it was Mum and Dad. If ever a marriage shouldn't have had children, it was theirs. And if ever children could make a bad situation worse, they were Jordan and Tim. Each of the four was incompatible with the other three. Cross-currents of tension were doomed to grow and grow until there was an explosion. Yet, they stayed together. As a family, they were so inner-directed that splitting up, even for the sake of sanity, was never an option. You couldn't divorce parents or children. If those ties remained, severing others wouldn't make much difference.

It was a miracle Jordan wasn't sucked into repeating the cycle with Rick. She saw how easily she could be turned into a replica of her mother, or even of her father, with mismatched kids of her own and future generations of misery in the offing.

Finally, when her knee began to scream, she stopped rocking. She had work to do.

She stripped off yesterday's musty dress and stood in front of her mirror. Her coral knickers, the only underwear she'd been wearing, were the colour of her skin. Her tummy bulged over the elastic and her thighs were huge.

How had she let herself bloat like this?

It had been part of the trick, the cruellest trick.

She turned round, recognising a definite waddle, and looked over her shoulder at herself.

She was a pudgy monster. A disaster.

Everything swelled or sagged.

She didn't let herself despair. She held her mind

rigid. She'd have to set herself right. Her next project. She was alone in this, utterly.

She concealed her horrible body in an ugly dressing gown – one of Dad's cast-offs – that hung to the floor and could be clutched around her chin, collar up to cover the furry beginnings of jowls.

Poking her head out of her room, she found the coast clear and darted across the corridor into the smaller bathroom. She locked the door behind her and let the blind fall with a rasping rattle.

She hooked up the shower attachment and let the water run, as hot as it could get. She would need to scald off a layer of dirty skin

(that Rick had touched)

and start to scrub away some of the subcutaneous fat.

It would not be enough, but would be a start. She needed to scrape the fluffiness out of her hair, get rid of the conditioner. Later, she might hack it all off. For the moment, she would just pull it back.

She looked hard into the mirror over the sink, watching herself become ghostly as hot fog swarmed on the reflective surface. Her eyes finally disappeared in the murk.

That was that. It was over.

The fake Jordan, the one who had come out in the Hollow, was banished.

This was the real girl. She might not be as biddable, as beddable. But she was herself and herself alone. She didn't have to pretend. She didn't have to fake anything to please other people, to gull those who would gull her.

A droplet ran down the mirror like a tear, cutting a clear line, showing the reflection of her cheek. The fake Jordan was crying.

She smiled, savagely.

Good. It was good that the girl cried. She was the 'It's My Party' girl, the helpless blubberer, the girl who could do nothing but whine and feel sorry for herself.

Wiping the tear away, she glimpsed bared teeth in the hand-shaped reflecting patch. Fog gathered again, swift and efficient, and grey moisture blotted out her snarly grin.

She stepped into the tub and let the wet pain fall on her, holding herself rigid under the torrent, broiling her skin lobster-red, scourging the last of the fake Jordan.

She was the 'Judy's Turn to Cry' girl now.

Steven sat in his study, warm inside from breakfast, mind alert from two cups of fresh-ground coffee. He looked out of the window at his son playing in the orchard. Tim was happy. Kirsty would come round soon, when the penny dropped. Jordan was seventeen: breaking up with a useless boyfriend was part of the process. She'd mope a bit and play misery records. He'd happily lend her his Smiths CDs when she wore out her oldies. In a week or so, she'd snap back and be ready to break hearts when she met a whole new crowd at college in September. It was like the old Kirsty to overreact and treat every minute fluctuation of adolescent mood as a harbinger of apocalypse.

If anything, he was more concerned about Kirsty.

He was looking at an e-mail from Tatum. The Oddments debts were more substantial than they'd thought. Tatum was suggesting that someone had been dipping into the account, basically stripping the business before it disappeared entirely, leaving the mess for someone else to tidy up. Tatum didn't say who she thought that person was, but he assumed her number-one suspect was Kirsty herself. His wife had been buying things for the house but Steven had seen the paperwork on everything – the money had come from his own temporarily flush accounts. No, it could only be one person.

The Wild Witch. Veronica Gorse. Vron.

Kirsty was the main signatory for her business account but she had drafted Veronica as an alternate co-signee. She had complained it wasn't convenient to wait until Steven was there – he had been travelling much more than now – to pay for anything. Veronica had a lot to do with the business as it was, so Kirsty brought her in as a semi-partner, whatever that meant. Things had been going awry before then, but the addition of the Wild Witch to the set-up hadn't helped at all.

Steven was sure it was Veronica. Kirsty had once asked him to scribble signatures on a book of blank cheques. His refusal had been the thing that made her bring Veronica in. Had Kirsty been foolish enough to do something like that herself and give the chequebook to Vron?

He would have to be careful about how he brought it up. In the city, this sort of thing had been like lighting the blue touch paper. At the Hollow, all that was behind them but he remembered only too well what Kirsty had been like.

It wasn't so much her business – which she accused him of never treating seriously – as the combination of her business and Veronica. The woman was a menace and everything she touched came apart at the seams. Even now, he wasn't sure whether she was dangerously inept or actively malign. She was supposed to have trained as a therapist, but her methods seemed closer to New Age voodoo.

Veronica wasn't here. The Hollow would never let her near.

There was only Kirsty. And Kirsty was free of all evil influences. She'd been rescued from the brink, reclaimed for the good. He couldn't claim the credit. It was down to the house as much as him, down to the establishment of a real home for the family.

He composed a reply to Tatum. She was to transfer enough funds to settle the Oddments overdraft to the penny, paying all bank charges, then close down the account – ironically, he would need to get Kirsty to co-sign a letter to make it official – so that any cheques still floating around could not be drawn on it. Ideally, he wanted this implemented today, to cut off the wandering witch and her cash-sucking ways.

The e-mail went off and he thought about how to sell the move to Kirsty. She'd be free of all debts to anyone but him, but the last vestige of her independent business would be gone.

It shouldn't bother her, but he would be cautious.

* * *

Steven emerged from his sanctum mid-morning with a sheaf of papers. He wanted Kirsty to witness his signature on a batch of contracts and fed them to her one by one, efficiently getting white space under her scribbling hand. Once signed, each document went in an envelope and was sealed with a deft lick and press. He told her what they were about but she didn't take it in. From experience, she knew his business was endlessly fascinating to Steven but atrociously boring to anyone else. Just now, she was too preoccupied even to fake interest.

Mission accomplished, Steven gathered his envelopes and announced that he would walk into the village to the postbox. She let him go.

Jordan hadn't come down, though noises had been heard. Poltergeist-clattering in her room.

It struck Kirsty as funny.

Ghosts lived at the Hollow but Jordan was haunting it. Her daughter was the stick-thin spectre in the black shroud, huge dead eyes accusing, bony fingers reaching out to clutch. The ghosts were more normal, just...

Just what?

Feelings, mostly. And objects. Warm winds and invisible caresses. The secure world of a little girl before the War, surviving in a bubble.

The ghosts would help Jordan, if only Jordan would let them.

Just as the Hollow would help Kirsty.

As he walked to the village, Steven's insides unknotted. He'd slipped the letter past Kirsty, avoiding a possibly hairy scene. She need never know, since he suspected she didn't quite realise he needed her signature to close her account. She had turned it all over to him verbally. He was just taking care of the clearing-up without troubling her. If she knew, she would be grateful for his consideration.

The further away he got from the Hollow, the surer he was.

Even in this age of electronic communication, some things had to be sent by snail mail. Legal documents that required physical signatures and matters where confidentiality was a priority.

Small chores that got him out of his study were good for him. He was working long hours but not seeming to feel tired. The Hollow was a nurturing environment and brought the best out of him, but he had to get away sometimes. Once every few days, he walked the mile or so to Sutton Mallet. It wasn't much of a village. There wasn't even a post office, just a red pillar box. There never seemed to be anyone about.

He popped the letters in the box.

There. That was done. No going back on it.

He promised not to beat himself over the head about it. He had done a kind deed, not a cruel one. A certain degree of sneakiness was involved, but subterfuge was a neutral tool. It wasn't wrong to dissemble – to lie – if you were keeping a surprise party from someone. The outcome was what was important.

Nothing stirred around the triangular green. Heat haze made the air shimmer at knee-height. There was a pub, The Lady, but it never seemed open. There was a church and a graveyard. No signs of life. Maybe the village was like Paris: everyone headed to the seaside in the summer. Some cottages were shut up, the weekend retreats of yuppie city-folk who were abroad on their hols.

It had been hard to convince Brian Bowker that they planned on living full-time at the Hollow, rather than merely occupying it at two- and three-day stretches. Already, Steven thought of the absentee owners as incomers and city-folk. The Naremores were local, landed.

He walked back home.

With a Burt Bacharach Collection – 'I Just Don't Know What to Do With Myself', 'Always Something There to Remind Me', 'Anyone Who Had a Heart' – on loud in her room, Jordan sat at Miss Teazle's antique PC and drafted a letter to Rick. The document was up to twenty-two pages, which she would have to cut down to a manageable size. If there were too much of it, the effect would dissipate. This communication was designed to stick in the mind.

Simple abuse wouldn't do. If he had nerved himself up to make the break, he was ready for that. After all, he'd got out of their relationship at the lowest cost by simply not turning up. His cowardice was the weakness she had to home in on, and his susceptibility to outside influence. She laced the letter with disparaging comment on his taste in television and recreational literature. To him, *Star Trek: The Next Generation* was a sacred text.

She wrote a memoir of their life together, listing

each of his many failings. She stirred a little fiction into the mix and claimed to have slept with three of his friends and a member of his family. Five pages on, still mentioning no names, she said that she had slept with two of his friends. The discrepancy was a stroke of genius. His question wouldn't be 'Have you really slept with my friends?' but 'How many of my friends have you slept with?' The other thing would shred his family. Presumably, he'd rule out his twelve-year-old brother – though she had caught Benny looking at her breasts – and home in on his dad, with whom he was always rowing but who'd always played flirty games with her, or start wondering about her and his sister Marilyn, who was just a bit dikey.

Even if Rick didn't believe a word of it, he wouldn't be able to resist digging around for evidence. That sort of suspicion – as she knew only too well from the Veronica Wars – could destroy relationships as easily as any actual trespass.

By the end of the letter, she believed it herself. She had a physical memory of sex with Walker, with Rick's dad, with Marilyn. She knew about their birthmarks, their hidden tattoos, the looks on their faces when they came. She heard the little laughs that clogged their throats afterwards as they looked at her lying there naked, and smiled hard at what they'd just done with precious Rick's precious girlfriend.

If she was learning anything at the Hollow, it was that wishing makes it so.

'The Look of Love' came on, one of the lying songs that insinuated everything was all right, but she deftly zapped with the remote, skipping to 'Blue on Blue'.

Even that didn't quite do it for her. She was beginning to resent all the whining in these songs. Why couldn't there be more like 'Judy's Turn to Cry'?

She laced in choice quotations from Rick's friends, telling him what they really thought about him. She had twigged at once to the resentment Walker and his mates had around Rick. He was going to college and university while they were just going to kick around nowhere being bullied onto training schemes that never led to jobs. Rick might be clever, but that didn't make him smart. It was true: Rick's mates wanted him to fall on his face. Persuading him not to come to the West Country was probably a part of it. When he read her version, he would be sure Walker – she knew he had to have been the one who kept nagging at him about it, calling for one more drink and upping him from beer to spirits – had worked a trick on his head so he could himself have a chance at her.

Maybe she *wasn't* making it up? Walker was nineteen and had had a succession of skanky thirteen-year-old girlfriends. He had a streak of Rick's cleverness but had been chucked out of school for vandalism and now spent most of his time at other peoples' flats, stealing their paperbacks to sell down the market so he could buy club drugs. Maybe Walker really did have a thing for her.

It was credible.

She put in several mentions of Walker, noting (truthfully) that his favourite sentence opening when talking to Rick was 'The trouble with you is…'

This was a letter bomb. It would go off and destroy the bastard.

Her knuckles ached from typing. Her shoulders were knotted from hunching over the keyboard. She was cultivating a hump.

Cold fingers brushed her hackles, like the first touch of a masseur. An electric shiver ran up her spine and she writhed in black pleasure.

Thumb-like ice spots worked against her shoulders, numbing the knots.

She felt her hair rise around her in static tendrils.

The friends she had made at the Hollow were with her. She understood they were her real friends now, her family.

He hated it, but there was only one conclusion. They had a traitor in the outfit. The IP disavowed any knowledge of the attack on Green Base. They were in a lather about it too.

Tim worked to secure the violated facility. Strictly, he should abandon the position and relocate to the Fall Back Point under the bridge, but he had put too much into his HQ. A line had to be drawn and here it was.

In the dark hollow of the tree, he met with the IP rep. She looked like a little girl in a straw hat. Earlier, she'd shown herself in light. Now, she kept to shadow. The incursion had spooked her people. He couldn't blame them.

The U-Dub was loaded and ready.

He held at DefCon 4.

Over and again, he ran through the possibilities. Mum, Dad, Jordan. Each possible betrayal was a kick in the guts. He couldn't afford to be queasy or sentimental. The IP assured him the perimeter had not been breached. The attack had come from within, from someone at the Hollow.

Mum, Dad, Jordan.

Tim thought back to before, to the trying times. He'd had to train himself up sharpish to stay out of the fire, when the flat turned into a combat zone and battle raged all around.

They had seemed different people in London. Or was it here that they seemed different?

Had the city been the truth?

It could have been any of them. They'd have had to get up before him and carry out the attack, then sneak back. The MP and the PP were in the kitchen afterwards, having breakfast or pretending to. The BS was still in her room.

Could they be working together?

In London, the three had formed shifting alliances, one out and two in, unstable enough to collapse within hours. He had always been under pressure to compromise his neutrality by pitching in with one or other of the factions.

This felt like a solo attack, a rogue mission.

That usually meant the BS.

But he wasn't ruling anyone out.

He had no choice. He had to escalate, to show he could not be intimidated. He shifted up to DefCon 3.

She had crept up the tower stairs and lingered outside Jordan's room, several times. Music leaked from inside, not the muffled tinkle that came from earphones but bone-shaking full-blast stereo easy listening. For about the thousandth time, Kirsty wondered how her daughter had come by her musical tastes. It was like a mutant throwback, the most repressed aspects of the past surging up again.

Steven was probably right: Jordan was better off without the wretched Rick. But Kirsty knew all too well what it was to live through this sort of trivial despair, either at ground zero or within the blast area. That it was a teenage-magazine problem-page cliché didn't make it hurt any less. Jordan was an extraordinary girl; to have such an ordinary heartbreak made it all the worse.

Kirsty hovered in the passage for the fourth or fifth time, looking at the door, taking comfort from the light around the jamb. At least Jordan hadn't sealed herself inside with black masking tape (she had done once). That time, she had taped around the window as well and blocked up a ventilation panel, presumably intending to breathe herself to death. With the old Jordan, the Jordan Kirsty was afraid would come back, it was hard to distinguish between a suicide attempt and a performance art piece.

A floorboard creaked under her. Had Jordan heard that? Unlikely, through the lounge aria.

She rapped a knuckle to the door.

'Some tea, dear,' she offered, the Englishwoman's cure-all.

A groan communicated a negative.

'Will you be down later?' she asked, hating the high landlady's wheedle that crept into her voice, fake cheerful but horribly nagging. 'You haven't eaten.'

'Not hungry,' came a reply, perfectly enunciated.

'Darling?'

'Leave me alone.'

'Are you sure?'

'Crystal.'

'I can bring you something on a tray, leave it outside.'

'I'll be fine.'

Kirsty was pricked by things unsaid. If she forced her way in and imposed care and attention on her daughter, she wouldn't be thanked. At least, not this week. Maybe later, when they were both more grown up and Jordan had children of her own, they would smile, thinking back, and hug, remembering their closeness at this moment.

She put her hand against the door.

Other possibilities flashed at her. Facing the cold fury of her daughter, watching her carve patterns in her forearms or hack off all her hair with a breadknife. Kirsty might be that last element in the compound, the one that created the volatile substance. It'd be like watching Jordan go out the window.

That was a possibility, too.

'All right dear,' she said. 'I'm going.'

'Thank you, Mother.'

On the stairs, Kirsty was seized by the chills. The further away she was from Jordan's room, the more wrong things seemed. It wasn't the Hollow, could never be that. She worried her daughter was cutting herself off from the magic, detaching from the glow the family shared here, throwing herself back into a dreary world of disorders and disappointments.

Her knees were shaky, as if a weight were humped on her back. She reached out with both hands to lean on the walls. The tower stairs were narrow. A pleasant, appley-woody smell was unique to this part of the house. The stairs seemed narrower, the walls nearer. Light spilled into the gloom from a window at the end of the landing.

She found herself sitting on the stairs.

The back of her brain buzzed with the beginnings of what Vron diagnosed as 'complex panic attacks' but the rest of the family just called her 'turns'. It had been months since she'd felt this. Even in London, she had got over these episodes. Their return was not welcome, could not be allowed at the Hollow. She got over it now, by force of will. Closing her eyes, gripping the cool brass rails, inhaling the appley-woody smell, she quelled the buzzing and overcame the incipient turn.

The Hollow made her stronger.

This was something Vron would never have been able to prescribe, even in her witchiest moods. Though Vron had reached out, sent messages. Were the two books supposed to be instruction or a warning?

Kirsty opened her eyes and turned round.

From where she was, halfway down the flight of stairs, she could see only six inches or so of the landing. Tassels hung over the top stair, from a long carpet that ran down the centre of the landing, a faded red and purple strip which left grey-white boards bare at either side.

She saw a pair of shoes.

Not Jordan's shoes. These were smaller, a child's,

and old-fashioned. The heel was high. Rows of buttons rose above the ankles.

She didn't need to ask if there was anyone there.

She didn't need to crane to see if anyone stood in the shoes.

There was a strange flood of relief.

'Weezie,' she said aloud.

A ripple of laughter sounded. Giggly, girlish, carefree, innocent. It poured over Kirsty like a warm wave. The appley-woody smell surged and became almost overpowering, like a lungful of dope smoke. The aches in her knees and elbows were taken away.

Kirsty felt a spark in her chest and was grateful.

Then, she was angry. It wasn't fair. Everything had been going well for her, but now Jordan was demanding again, taking up her attention even as she whined about being left alone. The daughter crisis diverted Kirsty from what she wanted to do, what she wanted to be. Why should the selfish girl's sulky moods – self-destruction laced with blatant attention-getting – make her the centre of the universe? Kirsty resented being shunted aside into a cliché trembling on the stairs. Here, in the Hollow, she mattered too, and had a right to her share of the magic.

The girl on the landing was angry too.

The wardrobe in her room was built into a corner and, for some reason, disguised. A pair of brass flowers concealed a hook and eye arrangement.

Jordan lifted the hook and pulled the door open.

An old-lady dress hung before her, scented with

violets and medicine, a striped cardigan on the same hanger. She took it down and tossed it on the bed. Another dress hung behind it, much like the first. She reached in with her whole arm. Stiff, taffeta-like material scratched her bare skin. She pulled out an armful of dresses. The wardrobe still seemed full.

The musty collection of old-lady outfits went back and back into the wall. Louise must have kept every dress she had ever owned. Eventually, Jordan found a layer of middle-aged clothes – an evening gown with a silk flower sewn to the shoulder – and then the dresses she'd been looking for.

They were all the same, white and elegant and simple. Audrey Hepburn-style evening wear, with matching arm-length gloves and court shoes. In different sizes.

The first was a balloon. She held it against her body and looked in the mirror. Flaps and folds hung loose. The next dress was a better fit. She slipped it on over her T-shirt and knickers. It was limp on her hips.

The next dress fitted. She had to take off her T-shirt and hold her breath to get into it. The material was tight, too tight, over her ribs and bottom. She looked at herself in the mirror, holding up her hair and angling her neck, disapproving of the chubbiness growing around her chin and even under her ears.

The next dress in, a size smaller, was the one she fell in love with. It shone somehow, not like the drab thing she had on, and would be her second skin. She stroked it, with longing, and anticipation.

It was not beyond her. A year ago, before she got fat, she could have got into the dress. She couldn't wait another year. It would take serious work, but she had a goal and Dad said that goals were important.

Eating only the right things. And fewer of them.

Careful exercise. Tummy and bum exercises, not arm and leg exercises. If she gained muscle mass, the dress would split at the hips and have ridiculous Popeye arms. She needed slim arms, a velvet sheath of skin over bone and wire.

She looked at herself in the dress she would make do with until then. She saw the wobble of her stomach, navel outlined against the silk, and was repulsed by the pads of fat on her hips, around her nipples,

...That's not fat, Rick had once said, those are breasts; they come with the gender...

under her arms, on her thighs.

They would go. She had banished Rick with that letter, which she must put in the post immediately. She would forget every misleading thing he'd said, every wrong turn he had passive-aggressively let her take.

She breathed out and saw her ribs move, emphasising the pear shape she was determined to lose.

The dress, her goal, hung at the front of the wardrobe, a white tube. Behind it, she saw with a frisson, was another dress, lovelier still and a size smaller; and behind that...

'What news from the front?' Steven asked.

Kirsty glanced up at the ceiling.

'All quiet,' she said.

Tim sat by the fireplace. He had disassembled his catapult and was cleaning and testing every component, using a rag and a tin of shoe-polish.

'Has the little shit even phoned?'

His wife shook her head.

Steven was genuinely angry, though he thought this was a lesser evil than having Mr Precious around. If the toad were beating his daughter up, he couldn't have done her more harm. If Rick were here, he'd be tempted to slap him silly. But if he were here, this wouldn't be happening.

'*Should* I call his father? Just to get things settled?'

'I think things are settled,' said Kirsty.

'So do I.'

He sat in his favourite armchair – high-backed, well-padded, by the fireplace. Come mid-winter, it would be the place to be in the Summer Room.

'Did you go to the postbox?' Kirsty asked.

How could she have known? His stomach knotted and he found himself gripping the chair's arms.

'Yes,' he said. 'Anything you wanted sent off?'

'Jordan's written a letter.'

'Ah.' He eased inside. This was something else.

'Yes.'

Tim restrung the rubber of his catapult and tested the give of the material. Steven wasn't sure whether his son had found the thing or made it. It was always with him. He slept with it under his pillow. When Steven was a boy, Dr Spock's followers called such things fetish objects – he had prized a bright-red fire engine, and his best friend Jimmy Dee always carried an old, pea-less brass whistle – and were strict about weaning kids off them. He didn't see the harm.

Maybe he'd just never changed. As a grown-up, he suffered terrible fire-engine-type withdrawal symptoms if he ever left his Psion organiser behind on even the most trivial or recreational venture beyond his office.

'I've been talking with Mr Wing-Godfrey. A deputation from the Society are coming at the end of the month.'

'I suppose you'll have to feed them Weezie cakes and high tea like at Drearcliff Grange. I bet none of them have kids.'

'You mustn't be a bore about it,' she chided, not smiling. 'They take Louise Magellan Teazle seriously.'

'I wonder if Louise would have wanted that. She might have been trying to be funny.'

He had looked at a Weezie book as a boy and shuddered at the twee overdose. He had read American superhero comics. He could remember every detail of every panel of certain Fantastic Four or Daredevil issues, though he'd not physically seen them since his Mum gave his collection to War on Want during his first term away at university.

'I want to do something special for the Society,' Kirsty continued. 'I've been thinking a lot...'

'Uh oh... Danger, danger, warning, warning...'

'HH, VF,' Kirsty said, quelling his sarky tone.

Had he overstepped the mark? At the Hollow, they'd relaxed so much he'd forgotten how sensitive she was about the way her last big plan turned out

(though not so completely that he hadn't pulled that SS – Sneaky Switcheroo – with the bank letter)

and only now did the blazing meltdowns come back to him. When Oddments was going down in flames, so – it had seemed – was the family.

'There might be a percentage in looking after the house, putting a bit of money into restoration.'

'All mod cons?'

'More like all old cons. With advice, we could get the place exactly as it was when Weezie was here.'

'Which, if you remember, was only last year.'

'Not Louise, Weezie. This is the house in the books, Hilltop Heights. We could get a replica made of the sign over the door, maybe change the name.'

That was a bad idea. He felt it deep in his water, reacting strongly even before he could think about why Kirsty was wrong.

'We're on a moor, not a hill,' he said. 'This is a Hollow, not a Heights.'

Kirsty angled her head on one side. She was also trying to say something she couldn't put into words. They were venturing further out onto the ice. He recognised her incipient smouldering.

(When angry, she was terrifying, a biter and a breaker.)

'I know, but it's as if the Hollow wants to rearrange itself.'

'And we're merely keepers of the flame?'

'I wouldn't say that, but we have to respect the house. This is not an ordinary place.'

'You'll get no arguments from me on that, Kirst. But, with respect, Weezie was never real and Louise is gone. We live at the Hollow now. Us, the Naremores. It's our home. If it's rearranging itself, it's to suit us. We can't live and work in a museum of childhood chintz.'

'There are grants available for sites of interest.'

Kirsty had always been keen on grants and loans

and start-up schemes. Oddments had been puffed up with every hand-out going, and hadn't been able to survive after the dole dried up.

'It's all very well to have Wing-Weirdie and his pals over for tea and buns, but you can't cover the walls with Weezie paper to keep him happy.'

'I knew you'd take it like this.' Kirsty's face was in shadow. 'It's a threat to you, OMB, isn't it?'

OMB. O Mighty Breadwinner.

Tim looked up sharply, catapult at the ready.

'Is this an argument?' he asked.

'It's a discussion,' Steven assured him.

'That's all right, then. You promised. No arguments.'

'So we did, soldier.'

He looked at his wife and still couldn't see her face.

'It's all right,' she said in precisely the tone that implied that nothing was all right or ever would be again. He couldn't tell which of them she was failing to reassure. 'Mum's just off her head, as usual.'

'But it's such a nice head,' he said, getting up.

He wasn't going to let ill-feeling last till bedtime. He was going to crawl to Kirsty, give her some ground (or at least seem to) and make things right again, in this room, at this instant. The move to the Hollow proved he could change, that he was not trapped in the patterns of the past.

He stood up and walked to the long table. A splay of Weezie books was laid out like prospectuses in a travel agent's. He pulled Kirsty up out of her chair and held her to him.

'I'm sorry, darling,' he said. 'You're right. The

Hollow is a responsibility. Get what you can out of Wing-Godfrey's Society, only don't let them run our lives.'

'They won't,' she said, still cold. 'They can't.'

He kissed her.

'And, darling, think of the ghosts. How much do you want outsiders to know about them?'

She closed her eyes.

Tim wasn't fooled. His parents cuddled, but he stepped up to DefCon 2. There were definite signs that the peace was breaking. It was a strain to keep to treaty terms.

The U-Dub was stripped, cleaned and back together.

Something he could depend on.

He would have to be careful. Negotiations with the IP were at a delicate stage. It wasn't a question of going over to their side. He would always owe primary allegiance to the family unit. No state of hostility existed between the IP and the FU. He wasn't sure such a state was even possible.

Of them all, he was closest to the IP. Perhaps it was because he was physically nearer the ground, used to looking up at faces and paying attention to skirting boards. He was small for his age, shorter than most of the boys in his old class at school.

Did his parents not see the girl standing in the fireplace, still as a statue? Dressed all in black, all black herself. Not like West Indian children in the city – they were brown, really. This girl was coal-black, down to her lips and eyeballs, camouflaged against sooty bricks.

He saluted the IP officer.

The black eyes passed approvingly over him and fastened on his parents.

They're five by five really, he thought at her, with a tiny, half-embarrassed shrug. Mum and Dad were doing that grown-up kissy stuff most kids were obsessed with. Unhygienic and surplus to requirements, but it was not his place to criticise.

The black face didn't smile or frown. Nothing was given away.

The little girl stuck out her arms and legs, fastening toes and fingers into crannies in the walls at either side of the chimney, and scuttled upwards swiftly, like a big spider, climbing silently out of sight.

A fine rain of soot fell, unnoticed by anyone except him.

There were others in the room, but he was used to them. Dad's chair was one, a set of dents and impressions in its back resembling a scowling face. A single pane of glass set high in the French windows was an eternal smile, which showed only in the afternoon when you stood in the doorway (and were four feet tall). The smile had eyes in other panes, but they were fixed like a painting; the smile could change from a close-lipped friendly crescent to an almost-ferocious grin, displaying rows of pearly whites.

The IP were good people, Tim knew. Rock solid and reliable in a world where everything was always shifting. Men to go into the jungle with and have at your back during the thickest firefight.

But there was something about that smiling window. Like a smirk in the ranks at inspection. Nothing against regulations, but Tim knew something was being put over on the sly. He had that one marked down as a potential discipline problem.

Tim would keep an eye out in that direction. At the first sign of trouble, he would lodge an official complaint with the IP C.-in-C.

The MP and the PP were dancing close together, without any music.

Time to fade into the scenery.

After midnight, in her new dress, Jordan came down from her room, gliding silently so as not to wake anyone (they were all off in their tower, anyway). She went out into the orchard. It had been a hot day, stuffy in her room, so the chill of night was welcome, like feathers brushing her bare shoulders and arms. In the dark, she wasn't such a grotesque frump. If she kept to shadows, the dress would make her seem slim.

It was tight for walking, but a hidden slit, up to the thigh, meant she could make her way. The shoes were a problem. She had kept her trainers (silly as they might look) because she knew walking along the unlit road to the village in heels was an invitation to disasters, from feet chafed bloody to a dunking in a ditch.

In her right hand, the only part of her which was as slim and pale as she wanted to be all over, she held the Letter. Eighteen pages of perfect venom. Posting it would be a significant juncture in her life. The end of Rick and the birth of the new Jordan, the thin girl.

She walked down the drive, opened the gate a crack, and tried to slip through. Her hips caught and she had to push the gate open wider to escape. Her cheeks burned with humiliation but there was no one to see. The night breeze stroked away her blush with a sympathetic touch.

Cold caresses and whisper kisses.

There was no traffic at this hour. She walked down the middle of the road, trainers flapping, her dress hiked up around her thighs to keep it from trailing along the tarmac. The Letter was tucked warm under her armpit, to impregnate it with the scent of her body, to remind Rick of what was lost to him for ever.

Out of sight of the house and not yet within sight of the village, she wondered what she was doing. She was all alone on the face of a dark earth. Only the paved road distinguished this landscape from the moors King Alfred had known. The stars were fixed above her, glinting messages from a million years ago.

What was she doing?

She wasn't fat and she was being silly.

The caresses and chills were withdrawn. She was hot inside, almost with a fever. She spun around and around, dress skirling out like a flamenco dancer's. The Letter slipped out of its flesh-nook, sailing over the verge and a rhyne. It fell, a shining white oblong, in dark grey-green grass.

Her head buzzed.

She looked at the black marble water of the ditch. A full yard across, unfathomably deep. Its verges were overgrown with sharp reeds and grasses, suggesting a patch of marsh into which a whole person could sink and be stuck.

She was not dressed for fording the rhyne.

Her fingers still tingled with the effort of typing the letter, the pads of her forefingers flattened from repeated jamming against the keys.

She called the Letter to her.

And it was in her hand.

Yes. She shouted silently, holding up the Letter like a winning lottery ticket.

Even the moor sided with her.

She found a box set into a drystone wall. Black in the night, red under daylight. She posted the Letter.

Done.

She must be in the village, though no buildings loomed in the dark. She also had the idea that she hadn't taken the usual road here.

It didn't matter.

She walked back to the Hollow and was home in a trice.

From his observation post, he saw the truant return. He would have preferred to take a position inside Green Base. A sleeping bag could easily be jammed into the trunk, making a nicely padded foxhole. That would involve leaving the house, which meant negotiating the creaky stairs outside the parental bedroom. However, his OP would do. He had picked his room in the first place because it commanded the high ground.

Once the night's story was done and the MP had

seen him safely tucked in bed, he had counted slowly to a hundred, then got out from under the duvet and fixed up his OP. By the window was a half-sofa, a couch about his length with a rail-like back and single side. Mum said it was probably the survivor of a pair, but its broken-off arrangement suited him. He could get back support and let his legs stretch out, feet dangling. With his duvet wrapped around like a blanket and two pillows under his head, he was cocooned in a space by the tower window, close enough to the glass that his cheek felt the cold coming off it. The window faced the other tower, the smaller one. He had a view of the drive and the road and the orchard and the moor.

He caught quick naps during the day and night when he could, to be alert when he needed to be. Any wrong movement snapped him out of a doze.

The truant had left the Hollow less than an hour ago. He'd watched her trudge down the drive to the road. She came back walking differently, her arms not awkwardly clamped to her sides, as if she had got the hang of wearing her new dress. She didn't return by the road, but appeared out of the orchard, startling him. He couldn't work out her route, and was annoyed with himself that he hadn't spotted her the instant she breached the perimeter.

What was the BS doing?

The U-Dub was in his hand. A detachable pane in the window made a firing port. He would not normally have cocked the weapon for a routine watch, but at DefCon 2 it was vital to be prepared for any attack.

DefCon 1 was war.

He pulled back the U-Dub and sighted on his sister.

The BS didn't immediately come into the house, but lingered in the orchard – passing out of his sight for tense seconds – and wandered, with apparent lack of urgency, out to his HQ.

Tim had concluded his sister was behind the first incursion. The MP and the PP were too caught up in their own protracted peace talks to risk an incident over mere territoriality.

What would she do?

His arm was tense.

The BS stood among the trees and curtsied, raising her skirts and dipping like a dancer, bowing her head. Was she communicating with the IP or anyone else? He didn't want to believe she'd gone over to the hostiles, but she had form. In London, she'd always been an iffy prospect, weak and strong at the same time, hard to predict. At times, she was in his corner with commitment and vehemence, shielding him from the fall-out. At others, she was on his back like a vulture, jabbing and clawing with words and fingers. Seventy-five per cent reliable wasn't good enough.

He was sorry, but that's the way it was.

A vital truth that the IP had conveyed to him was that people didn't change, they just became more themselves. As time went by, it got harder and harder to pretend.

The BS seemed to be dancing with herself. Innocent enough. Not a week ago, the FU had all danced together, with the IP, during the grand summit. That had felt like permanent peace. Now, it looked like a mere armistice, and a shaky one at that.

Suddenly, his sister stopped dancing, pulled up her dress and squatted by Green Base. He saw the shining stream. She was pissing where he lived.

Anger made him loosen his hold on the U-Dub.

He nearly fired the first shot. He would have been within his rights.

But he took the advice of the IP C.-in-C., the Ipkick.

Not yet. He wasn't resourced for all-out war. But at DefCon 2, a guerrilla campaign was permissible.

He rolled away from the window, having seen enough, and let himself go to sleep, plotting…

Her old bank phoned in connection with the Oddments account. A stray £35.79 in charges needed to be paid before the account could be closed. Kirsty was puzzled for a moment when the woman referred to 'your letter of yesterday', then went utterly cold. She promised to send a cheque for the outstanding amount and hung up.

That was the end of that.

She couldn't remember a letter. There had been so many back-and-forth recriminations. It was probably something from last week or last month that had only just got to the woman's desk. If she could bring herself to sit through the inevitable lecture, she would ask Steven; the mess had been turned over to him to sort out. As a little boy, had he seen *Mary Poppins* and identified with the stuffy bankers who suggested pocket money should be invested rather than going to feed the birds?

She sat in the Summer Room, surrounded by real antiques (in shocking, unrestored condition which made her love them more than the waxed and show-polished pieces her elves had sought in lock-up garages under railway arches) and said a private goodbye to Oddments.

It had seemed like an escape, an opportunity, but turned out to be a disaster, a millstone. But it had been hers, a real business. She had a degree, she had work experience, she was not a housewife. After all, she wasn't exactly an ideal home-maker, so she had to be something else. There must be something at which she was excellent. As a girl, she'd been told that everyone was outstanding, everyone a star. You just had to find that thing at which you shone, and the world opened up its glories like a vault when the correct combination clicks.

Steven never said how much Oddments had cost him. Whenever he went through the fiasco, he talked about how much debt 'we' were in. But she knew what he felt. It was Kirsty being silly, running up frivolous debts, never thinking it out. If it hadn't been for the surprise pay-off that had let them buy the Hollow, his business might have gone under with hers. Then, she was sure, he would have cut her and the kids loose, and set himself up with Tatum Hoyle in a new partnership.

Before antiques, she had done other things: run an indie label that hadn't put out its first record because Vron could never finish mixing her debut album as a singer-songwriter, invested in the importing of a Czech beer whose shelf life was up by the time the first vanload was in Britain. Once Tim was old enough to go to school, she'd taken courses in business studies, law (when she had wanted to be a lawyer, specialising in child custody cases) and radio production (when Vron thought she could get a community broadcasting licence). She'd even completed some.

Repeatedly, she had tried to make a space that was hers alone. She knew Steven thought of these projects as crazes. When she was setting up Rose Records, just after Jordan was born, he was enthusiastic and helpful, even securing some investment from his clients. The label's long, unproductive fizzle bled his belief in her out of him. Subsequently, he was polite but elaborately long-suffering. He'd never shoot her ideas down, instead sabotaging them with a few tiny phrases. Vron said Steven's favourite sentence was 'Yes, but we have to be practical.'

Everyone was right: Vron could be a monster and had wrecked lives. But Vron was her friend, her healer, and always ready to commit to anything Kirsty thought of. She missed Vron, missed having her around for coffee, endless gossip and the occasional joint (last gasp of her student habits), missed having someone outside the family to complain to. If she were here, Vron would be nagging Kirsty to go through with her ideas about the Hollow, not imposing caution on her. Steven was her husband and said he loved her without conditions, but a sensible part of him shut her out. Vron would encourage her in anything, no matter how 'impractical' or even insane. She understood how important it was that Kirsty have a life of her own. Steven's downer attitude had passed to Jordan and Tim. Flat expressions came on the kids' faces whenever Mum was going mad. They'd just get out of the way until it blew over.

To Vron, nothing ever would blow over.

She hadn't talked with Vron since before the move. It had been a condition of what Tim called the peace treaty, that her best friend be cut forever out of their lives. They were all making sacrifices; but why had hers been a person, rather than a thing? The office Steven left behind had no feelings of its own. Kirsty had been expected to drop Vron as easily as she let her subscriptions to motivational magazines lapse.

Vron and Kirsty had spent some part of the day together for over twenty years, since they first met in the fifth form.

She must be in an agony. Or was she?

Vron always asked about other people's feelings, never confessed to any of her own. She had exes, a daughter, a sister, other patients, an extended network of friends and pick-ups. When she was with Kirsty, she never thought of them, never talked about them. She would always focus exclusively on Kirsty. She said Kirsty should have a sealed-off compartment in her mind, to keep her own self separate from her family.

Which would be worse? Vron wandering the streets bereft, fading to ghostliness without Kirsty, or Vron continuing as normal, occasionally reminded of her lost friend but getting on with the tangle of her own life?

Vron didn't have a telephone. The twentieth century was nearly over, but she didn't believe in phones or faxes or e-mail. She said machines got in the way of real communication. Aside from face-to-face meets, at which her eyes would unnervingly fasten on Kirsty's and penetrate her heart, Vron's preferred means of communication was a postcard. Kirsty had been getting postcards almost every day for years, with notes reminding her of appointments, visits and things to do. Vron would send cryptic clues which took hours to solve (at school, they had both been crossword-puzzle and Agatha Christie fiends) or runic symbols whose meaning was only clear when they were added up and looked at sideways and sometimes not even then.

Apart from the books – words from other people endorsed by Vron – there had been nothing. They were both cold turkey.

The books, though. They meant Vron hadn't forgotten. The second, *Ghost Stories of the West Country*, meant she was thinking of Kirsty and the Hollow. She wasn't completely shut out of new developments. Without having set foot here, she'd made discoveries.

Kirsty knew Vron understood this place. Perhaps better than any of them did yet.

She was keeping Vron in reserve, knowing she might need to summon her in the end. There were powers in the Hollow and Vron was used to dealing with powers. Steven and Jordan called her a witch, though that wasn't true. It was funny that her husband was trying to cope with their magical house by deploying all his Steven-sense. This place was made for the intuitive, logic-defying, lateral-thinking mind of women he would call witchy. If she was to make the best of the Hollow, she needed to be more like Vron and less like Steven.

It hit her that she would have to tell Vron about the Oddments account; she was an additional signatory and might still be getting letters from the bank. There was the matter of that £35.79. If Vron were here, she'd tell Kirsty not to pay, to let the bank yowl for their pennies. They weren't going to sue over the price of a few bottles of shampoo.

'I need someone', she said, out loud, 'to talk to.'

The room hung there, solid, empty.

She had thought there might be friends here. Like the friends who worked the magic chest of drawers. The presences who had called them out into the orchard at midsummer. The girl in the little shoes who had shared her rage.

'I'm sorry,' she said. 'It's just Kirsty being silly.'

'You shouldn't say that.'

She jumped, almost out of her skin, and turned. 'Jordan?'

A woman had spoken. It was not her daughter.

Her friend was in the fireplace, in shadow. A little girl in Drearcliff Grange uniform, with an adult's head, deeply lined face and waist-length, grey-dusted black hair. Her straw hat hung around her neck. She had Vron's eyes, which glittered in the dark.

'Who are you?' Kirsty asked.

'Who you need me to be.'

The voice was a little like Vron's, a little like Jordan's, a little like the woman who had read the Weezie books on the wireless when Kirsty was a little girl. Her friend also sounded like that voice Kirsty was always embarrassed by and refused to recognise: her own, recorded and played back. Herself, not as she was in her own head, but as others heard her.

This was a ghost. Not Apple Annie or the Gloomy Ghost. The ghostness was more important, somehow, than of whom she was a ghost.

'Are you Louise?' Kirsty asked, wondering. 'Her ghost? Or are you Weezie?'

The old girl shrugged. That was who she was, the Old Girl. Not Louise or Weezie, but something of both and something older. And, in the echoes of Vron and herself, she was Kirsty's ghost. Shaped especially for her.

She ought to be scared, she supposed. Even after all that had happened at the Hollow, this was unexpected. Back in the city, Steven would have written it off as the type of weirdness Vron was always polluting her with. But the family were settled here.

Kirsty sensed an escalation. Her earlier communications with what Tim called the IP were through the things in the drawers or in wordless wonder. The Old Girl was talking with her, adopting her means of communication, taking a step out of the shimmering to be with her.

'Why have you come?' Kirsty asked.

'I am here for you, Kirsty.'

The Old Girl knew her name. She was not just a hologram or photograph, cast off by strong emotion, but a being who could think for herself. This creature had a personality, a mind, a purpose.

'You need me,' the old girl said. 'You know why.'

The Old Girl kept to her place, but Kirsty saw her more clearly.

'You are my special friend,' she said.

The Old Girl nodded, gravely.

Kirsty felt a melting burst of relief and love. She would never be alone at the Hollow, alone in her family. Always, there would be someone in her corner, giving her strength.

She wasn't haunted. She was protected.

Jordan woke up, not knowing what time it was, and crawled out of bed. She still wore the dress, which hung loose on her like the skin of a dieting sumo wrestler. It was her reward. She wriggled out of it, bundled it up, and threw it into the wardrobe, pushing it to the back. She wouldn't need it again. She was ready for the next size in, the lovelier dress still. A look in the mirror revealed she was still unsightly. Flesh still moved independent of her bones, but there must be some improvement. Posting the Letter had been like shedding a burden. Evidently, it involved losing weight too.

She remembered something the Wild Witch said about not being able to fix your body until you'd fixed your mind. One thing you had to give her was that she was slim. She hadn't put on a pound since her teenage years. Mum's weight went up and down like a yo-yo, along with everything else, but Veronica – even as a child, Jordan hadn't liked to call her Aunt Vron, as Mum sometimes insisted – never changed. Perhaps there was something in witchery after all.

At the Hollow, there was magic. Jordan knew and accepted that. It had surprised and delighted her at first. Now she lived with it every day and wanted something more. The mere fact that there were wonders in the world, that she was privileged to see the curtain of reality lifted a little, had been a passing distraction but nothing was changed. She still had to live, to better herself, to cope.

It was mid-afternoon by her clock. She'd slept away the morning. She popped a couple of aspirin for her head, washed down with Evian water from her secret stash. No one could say she hadn't had breakfast.

She patted her belly. It was grossly huge, but didn't feel empty. During her first great struggle with her body, hunger had been like a rat chewing inside her stomach. This time, she had help. She felt fine. Even the headache was gone, as if she were living in an advert.

Rick would not yet have the Letter. She'd missed yesterday's last collection, but it would have been picked up from the postbox first thing this morning, hours ago while she slept, and was now in the trusty hands of the Royal Mail. Tomorrow, Saturday, the letter bomb would go off.

Then she'd never think of him again.

She found jeans – too tight, argh! – and a floppy T-shirt with thin-making vertical stripes. It was time to leave her room and recommence negotiations with the rest of the family. They'd take some selling, but she had everything straight in her mind. Her only problem was a need to lose a little weight by the end of the summer. She wanted to be presentable by the first day of her new college. She did not have a disease, she had a goal.

To compromise, to lull her parents along, she

would accept a cup of tea. But no biscuit. Custard creams and chocolate digestives were *streng verboten*.

She opened her bedroom door. A semi-circle of dead shrews greeted her, red showing in stiffened grey fur, toothy blank-eyed heads pointed at her doorway, ratty tails carefully extended. She hesitated to step over the fan of tiny corpses.

It was a sign.

She shut the door and sat on the bed, feeling sick.

Tim conducted a series of U-Dub test firings, sighting on a diamond-shaped pattern of knotholes in the wooden door halfway up the side of the barn. After five shots, he was accurate to a hundred feet. He pulled back a further ten feet, deeper into the orchard, got the range again, set his stopwatch going, and fired off, rapidly reloading between pulls, another five pebbles in sixteen seconds.

Three hit within the diamond. Worth ten merit points, easily, but he wouldn't rest until all five shots went true. It was down to him now, not the magic. He couldn't let his allies be a crutch.

The Ipkick was pleased with the start of the guerrilla campaign. Tim hadn't been sure but had gone along with it. Psychological warfare was effective, but his simple soldier's ways would have preferred something that did a goodly amount of concrete damage.

The birds killed the shrews, or they were squashed under tyres on the road and scraped along the verges. Nasty little creatures anyway, like mutant mice with sharp teeth and constant aggression. The Ipkick warned him away from live shrews. They could open a serious wound with a bite, and had the habit of locking their mouths in flesh and not letting go until their heads were cut off.

A shrew was a kind of nasty girl, too. That was what made the action appropriate.

The BS was under notice now.

If she chose to escalate, it would not be his fault.

He thought about DefCon 1. All-out war. He dreaded it, of course. No soldier *wanted* war, no matter what the conchies and civvies said. But it was the duty of all soldiers to be ready.

Careful, he had been told. Warned. The word had come up on his screen again, several times. He saw it sideways, in the folds of curtains, in newspaper headlines. If he looked straight on, it was gone, but that wasn't the point.

He sat in his study, looking away from the screen, adjustable chair leaned back. He considered the ceiling, the room above.

He knew he must not let it happen again.

It.

The things with Jordan. They so easily led to the things with Kirsty, the things with Tim. He saw the first signs already, the backward steps. His stomach burned when he remembered the worst of it.

Steven was not going to let his family come apart again. It had happened on his watch before, too many times. At the Hollow, he was stronger, swifter, smarter.

He saw the invisible ties that kept them together, not just the fault-lines that cracked when they were on the outs.

As he saw it, everything came down to Jordan, though she was blameless. It was her useless so-called boyfriend, Rick. He had given the Naremore family a good thump and run off like a coward.

Steven was not going to let him get away with it.

If his daughter wanted the bastard's head on a plate, he'd buy an electric carving knife and clear space in the freezer.

How to do it?

He could wait until he had business in London and make a point of finding Rick. But that wasn't immediate enough. Maybe he should make a special trip?

No. That was going too far.

A phone call would do it. But not now. Jordan had to be a part of this.

Later.

The shrews were still outside her door. By evening, the hallway was gloomy enough that she didn't have to see the tiny corpses in detail. Their dull eyes reflected. Were they all completely dead? She'd seen too many films in which supposed corpses spring to life.

Jordan wore her heaviest boots, with thick winter socks that made her feet sweat, and this evening's dress. It was stretched around the hips. Should she wear a butterfly-bow sash – one was provided – to cover her huge bottom, or would that just draw attention to her ridiculous shape?

In the end, she left the sash off and hoped the dress hung loose enough over her waist – which she wasn't happy with either – to make some sort of silhouette.

The dress bit into her under her arms, around her shoulders and across her chest...

(That's not fat, those are breasts.)

...pinching nerves and cutting off circulation.

Her white arms felt frozen.

They were the part she was best pleased with, slim but not bony, ice-white with delicate blue lines inside her elbows. Her hands were beautiful. Her feet were patties of fat, though.

Soon, all of her would match her hands. She would be statue-perfect.

With her boots, she kicked the shrews away.

Time to go downstairs. She was determined not to put up with any harassment from Mum and Dad. She was a woman now. They had no right to interfere.

She made an entrance, into the Summer Room.

Dad, from his chair by the unlit fire, turned to look. Tim, at the table, glanced up from a war comic. Mum, coming in from the kitchen, stopped to stare.

Jordan felt her cheeks burning.

Silence hung in the air. There were others in the room, applauding her. Only Mum and Dad (and her brother) were aghast, eyes popping. The others threw phantom flowers and rose to their feet to give acclaim.

'Where *did* you get that dress?' asked Mum.

She walked across the room, taking tiny steps, hobbled by the gown. She arranged herself on a tall stool, the only piece of furniture in sight she could use without fear of overstraining the dress.

'It was in my wardrobe.'

'It's… ah, old.'

'Yes, Mum.'

Dad inspected her, getting up and walking around. Jordan felt icy fury grow as Dad's smile cracked. She remembered the expression, from when she was little and dressed up for Hallowe'en as a tiger or Madonna. She was being treated as a sweet little curiosity, not a person. A lift of his eyebrows said she was not taken seriously. She was being indulged.

It would have been better if Dad raged at her and sent her back to her room to strip out of that ridiculous, indecent thing and come back to table in proper clothes. That would show awareness of what was changing, of the threat her parents should feel.

She was growing up. They would have to move over.

But no. To them, she was growing down. They wanted to turn her into one of those ageless, sexless Drearcliff Grange girls.

'Are you sure it's comfortable?' Mum asked.

Jordan nodded.

'It's awfully tight up top,' Mum said. 'You should probably let it out under the arms. There's a sewing machine in one of the spare rooms.'

'I'll change,' Jordan insisted. 'Not the dress.'

'You won't change that much. It's a child's dress. It's only long enough to reach your ankles because it's supposed to be a train, held up by attendants.'

'Rat coachmen,' put in Dad.

'Exactly,' said Mum. 'It's Cinderella's ball-gown. In *Weezie and the Phantom of the Pantomime*, she dresses up as Cinderella.'

Jordan felt the walls closing in. She was being trapped. It was a plot. She was being forced to stay a little girl. She looked at her parents' faces, and even at her brother. Tim was fixed on his comic, all hatches down like in the old days, tensed up to ignore the argument.

She would not cry. That was babyish.

'We've been talking about Rick,' Dad said.

It was all she could do not to explode.

Mum looked startled. She had been talked to, not with. This was one of Dad's decrees.

'I should call him, or his father.'

Jordan was speechless.

It was as if she were five years old. She had sorted out the Rick thing; he would get the Letter in the morning. Anything Dad did could only undermine her work.

Dad took the cordless phone from its cradle. Jordan was cold throughout. Rick's number was still stored. The whole family got to nominate numbers.

'Seven, isn't it?' Dad said, stabbing the auto-dial.

She couldn't believe it.

'Daddy, don't,' she said, inside her head. Her throat was stretched and dry. No words came out.

She was close enough to hear the ring at the other end of the line.

Please, nobody be there. That would be a mercy.

The ringing shut off and a woman's voice sounded.

'Might I speak to Richard, please,' Dad purred, with his hard-as-steel phone voice, suitable for defaulting creditors or absconded boyfriends.

Dad briefly covered the mouthpiece and said, 'He's coming.'

Who had the woman been? Rick's parents were separated, and he lived with his Dad. His brother and sister lived with their mother.

'Is that Rick?' Dad asked, into the phone. 'This is Mr Naremore, Jordan's father. You're a callous little git, aren't you? I'd like you to know Jordan's been through hell because of you. Did you even think of what it would do to her? Of all the progress she's made that you were pissing away?'

Jordan shut down inside and toppled from the stool. As she fell, she heard a ghastly renting sound as the seams of her dress came apart.

'Jordan's not wearing any underwear,' Tim said.

She lay on the floor, feeling cold flagstones through the carpet, impossibly and comprehensively violated.

'I hope you're satisfied, Richard,' Dad said. 'Jordan's just dropped dead.'

Click. At last, Dad had rung off.

She wished she had fainted, that she was unconscious. The waking world was too, too dreadful to bear.

Her face was on fire with a blush that was permanent, that would turn to the worst kind of weeping acne. Her dress was ripped apart, exposing vast stretches of her grotesquely swollen flesh. And Dad had wrecked everything.

She wanted to dwindle to nothing. And stay there.

There, that was done. Drastic measures, extreme results. But the trouble was over. Now, things could be fixed.

Steven stood up, letting Kirsty wrap Jordan in a shawl from one of the chairs. He twirled the phone like a gunslinger's smoking Colt.

He'd heard the little wretch squirm. He had settled Mr Precious's hash in a way that the kid wasn't going to forget in a hurry. In the background, as Steven said his piece, the woman who answered the phone was laughing. It had almost put him off.

Who was she laughing at?

Jordan sat up a little, holding her strange dress over her chest, hair over her face. Kirsty was comforting her, stroking her hair, murmuring into her ear.

Tears all round.

The womenfolk were in shock, but they would appreciate what he had done. A threat had risen, a threat to the balance of the family, and he had faced it, slain it and come home in time for supper.

Kirsty looked up at him, face pinched.

'Steven,' she said, 'how could you be such an idiot?'

Jordan eating tonight was a lost cause. Helping her daughter up to bed was all Kirsty could manage.

Steven was no help.

This was another example of what Vron called her husband's fondness for 'chainsaw microsurgery'. He would walk away satisfied that he'd done a good job, leaving her to cope with the wreckage.

God, she would have to call Rick's father and apologise. Without choking on it.

Her first priority was her daughter: the zombie.

By the time she got Jordan to her room, the dress

she was wearing had turned into a tabard. The stitching had rotted through, splitting the dress up the sides. When Kirsty was Jordan's age, she'd bought a similarly ancient frock at Oxfam and carefully unpicked the seams, replacing them with safety-pins. That was the only thing that could rescue this rag. She lifted the remains of the dress off over her daughter's head.

Jordan dived under her duvet and held it over her head, booted feet sticking out.

Kirsty should give her advice.

She was better off. She'd get over it. Things would rearrange themselves.

It was what her mother would have done.

The trouble was she didn't believe it. She still carried all her emotional scars, from kindergarten on. The hurts didn't loom large in her mind, but – if she thought of each individual heartbreak – they were as real, raw and bloody as the day they happened.

If Steven wanted to help Jordan, he'd have Tatum do something useful for a change and run Rick down in the street. It was about the only thing that would make any difference. Kirsty would feel a glow of cold secret pleasure if any of her old boyfriends were mysteriously murdered. She smiled to imagine them being killed in one night, all over town, long-stemmed roses left by the corpses to sign the deed. Vron would have done it for her.

She touched the bed, where she thought Jordan's shoulder was. The Jordan-shaped lump was wracked with silent sobbing. Kirsty withdrew her hand.

This was the first time she'd really been in Jordan's

room. She had been trying to let the girl have her own space, especially since she'd let Kirsty have the magic chest of drawers.

Jordan hadn't put up the posters from her tiny room at the old flat, which Kirsty knew she had carefully rolled into cardboard tubes for the move. Her CDs were arrayed in clear plastic racks.

She had set up Louise's old word processor, which Steven said was a prehistoric flint implement, at a desk by the window. Jordan had boxed her paperbacks in London. Few of the books had made it out of the boxes to the shelves.

Where was the wardrobe Jordan had mentioned? There was none in the room, not even a fitted cupboard. She probably meant a wardrobe in one of the spare rooms. Goodness knew, there was enough treasure trove to keep them supplied in oddments forever.

(Oddments, a Kirsty project, not lost after all...)

The Old Girl came in and sat in the rocking chair.

Kirsty shrugged a 'what can you do?' shrug. The Old Girl's outsize head nodded.

Steven shouldn't have his office in Louise's old study. This was the female tower of the Hollow. Men were unwelcome here. One had been killed during its building, a sacrifice to consecrate it to womanhood. Here, in Louise's lifelong room, the circle – strongest, most female of all shapes – held.

It was important that this be shared.

'Jordan,' Kirsty said, gently.

She tugged the duvet away from her daughter's head, wrestling it out of Jordan's fingers. The girl whined in the back of her throat and screwed her eyes shut.

'Shhh, my love, look at me, look at our friend.'

She got Jordan to sit up in bed. The cover fell away from her bare chest. With a pang, Kirsty saw how womanly her little girl had become. She dabbed the tracks on her daughter's face with a spit-damped thumb-knuckle.

Eventually Jordan opened her eyes, blinking.

Kirsty put her head next to her daughter's and they both looked at the Old Girl.

She felt Jordan's body tense with fear.

Objectively, the Old Girl was a scary apparition. It took a moment to realise she was on their side. Her scariness was directed away from the women of the Hollow and against those who would harm them.

Kirsty shushed soothingly.

'You are your mother's daughter,' said the Old Girl.

'Everything will be fine,' Kirsty said.

'Fine as spring rain and thrice-sieved flour,' said the Old Girl.

(Something Cook said in the Weezie books.)

The Old Girl's face creaked into a smile.

Jordan gulped out a panicky laugh, clinging to the last of her fear.

'If she's a witch,' Kirsty said, 'she's a good one.'

'I should hope so, my lovers,' said the Old Girl, with a West Country burr. 'Tears have been spilled. Wet water dries in a trice, but ghost tears tarry until cast out. This you can do. It is in you to rid yourself of these pest ghosts.'

Kirsty understood. Sadly, she realised, her daughter didn't.

His allies were wearing the BS down. The incident in the Summer Room was proof of that. Jordan was trailing the curse of the shrews when she came down. The little animal spirits nipped her ankles and shins, poisoning her until she came apart

(Tim had seen her naked, her boobs and everything) and fell over.

The MP had taken her upstairs and Tim was on solo guard duty. The PP didn't see the big board yet. He was always the last to catch on.

Jordan knew, now. And probably Mum.

There was a war on.

Tonight, he could sleep soundly. The Ipkick would take the watch.

Tomorrow, he would think of victory.

In the end, the women would thank him for it. Steven was master in his own home. Everything came down to him. He must consult – make a show of democracy – but it was his decision, his risk, his triumph. He'd always known it was how his business worked. Now he understood the world outside his office was exactly the same.

Kirsty had come to bed after he'd fallen asleep. She'd done her part of the job, calming down Jordan after the necessary shock. He let her sleep on after he was up, planning to reward her good and faithful service with a lie-in and a late breakfast. He'd cook for the family. A man should be proficient in the kitchen, to show he was not a shirker, that he could cope.

Steven thought of himself as an all-rounder,

adaptable and multi-skilled. This was underlined at the Hollow. In its many rooms, the house itself contained his whole life, business and family. It was like a castle, a community unto itself. Each room, each part of the grounds, was a different section of his life, connected by secret passageways and sliding doors. It was all one, all his realm. At long last, after the turmoil of the city, he had risen to the top and become master of his own life.

Last night, he had done battle for his daughter's honour and prevailed. Precious Rick was routed.

This morning, he would cook. The family would assemble, blearily, at table. He would serve them, joshing them out of their sleepy fug with light banter. They would divide the Saturday newspapers into sections and discuss items of interest to them all.

Later, he would sit in his favourite chair and watch football on satellite TV. Tim would sit at his feet, asking questions about the game. Kirsty would bring him beer and shaped potato nibbles. Jordan, understanding at last, would pop in at half-time and, unembarrassed, kiss him on the top of his head, then dart away like a sylph.

All was right.

He left his wife in her half of the bed, strode to the bathroom, brushed his teeth, washed his face and shaved (as he did every day, except Sunday). He dressed in jeans and a rugby shirt.

No one else was stirring in the house.

In the kitchen, he found last night's washing-up in the sink. What with all the drama, it had been forgotten. When Tim showed his head, Steven would assign him the chore. The sight of encrusted pans and plates put him off the idea of cooking breakfast. There weren't any urgent customers.

He went outside and blundered (again) into the wrought-iron chair Wing-Godfrey had insisted Kirsty put smack in the way of anyone leaving by the kitchen door. The fabled spot from which the standing stones could be seen.

He had never managed the trick of hunching himself to see through the tree telescope – though he had made a show of pretending, with a delighted 'Ahhh'. It had made him think there was something wrong with him. He tried again now, letting his knees slacken, twisting his spine, shifting focus.

There was a blur beyond the branches.

He saw a hillock, but not the stones. Figures – men or animals – moved in the early haze, revolving in a slow circle.

Something Kirsty had read out sparked in his mind. He had caught the stones dancing. He remembered the image but not what it meant. Was it a privilege or a sign of impending doom? If it was in a Weezie book, it couldn't be too threatening. As Kirsty had said over and over, Louise Teazle wrote about the Hollow and her ghosts were friendly. Even the Gloomy Ghost came round. The Kaye woman's book of ghost stories

(where had that paperback come from?)

was piffle, haunted house rot made up to spook a gullible public.

It was a shame none of the others were up.

The shapes, which might have been men of stone or stone-age men, whirled faster, raising a cloud of misty white smoke.

His back was cricked and painful. He couldn't hold this position much longer.

This was for him alone. The others had their personal revelations.

In the centre of the circle was a fire. Under sunlight, the flames were visible only as a shimmer, but smoke poured upwards. The stone men leaped over the fire in turn.

Someone was with the tall, stone figures. Someone small and flesh. He was compelled to dance but wasn't as skilled as the stones. Steven was momentarily sorry for this comical character who couldn't keep up. When he – it seemed to be a he, little more than a lad – leaped the fire, his clothes singed and smoked.

Sharp pain climbed Steven's spine.

The stones came together at last and lifted the lad above the fire.

Steven bent over double, holding his back, and lost the image. The spasm passed. He looked again, twisting his head from side to side. Branches were in the way.

Unaccountably, he was rattled by what he'd seen. Its character was different from everything else at the Hollow. There had been a sacrifice, he knew. The stones hadn't been dancing just for the joy of it.

He had to sit down. His back still had twinges.

It was the middle of August. How long had they lived at the Hollow?

Kirsty really couldn't remember.

Not more than two months, though. Not even six weeks.

It might have been years. Long enough to forget what came before, then begin to remember it again.

The old pattern showed under the new whitewash.

Last night, the Old Girl had initiated her, showed her how to make the Hollow work. This morning, the ghost's words were hard to recall. Often, Kirsty's friends from the other side were maddeningly vague.

She tried the chest of drawers.

She was tempted by the middle drawer that was always a jumble of surprises, but hesitated. Life in this family was always a jumble of surprises. She was scarcely the happier for it.

She pulled out the bottom drawer, hoping for a present, and found a school exercise book with a home-made cover of stiff wallpaper decorated with Braille flowers. She took it out and shut the drawer.

Was this a present? Or, as sometimes in the Weezie stories, a thing so long lost it had been forgotten? Opening the first page, she saw a child's writing, copy-book neat but with the odd scrawled correction.

'Once, not so long ago and not so far away, there lived a good little girl named Weezie. Actually, she was not so little as all that any more and perhaps not so good either…'

In the first sentence, the two 'so's had been crossed out, then inked in again. In the second sentence, 'as' had originally been written twice, and replaced with 'so'.

It was a draft of *Weezie and the Gloomy Ghost*. The book was published when Louise Magellan Teazle was just twenty, but this seemed the work of a child. There were spelling mistakes, corrected. In a flash, Kirsty knew this had been written when Louise was Weezie's age – when Louise *was* Weezie – and revised a few years later.

How had the teenage Louise – only a little older than Jordan – felt about coming back to this story, written in innocence to fill one of the devil's idle hours? Was she embarrassed, as Jordan would be if surprised by an old photograph of her dressed up for a primary school pageant? Or did she recognise a purity she would devote the rest of her life to recapturing?

This was a priceless find. Wing-Godfrey's Society would be giddy.

She should approach Louise's publishers. Or, better still, set up her own imprint. How difficult could that be? Her experience with Rose Records would be an advantage. There should be a facsimile edition of the original text, with the amendments. At the back of the exercise book were unfamiliar illustrations for the familiar story. Some were childish, some skilled; the girl Louise and the teenage Louise, visibly developing another talent. A few were rough sketches of the famous Kees Van Loon pictures. Others – mostly of the ghosts – were unique.

She sat cross-legged on her bedroom floor and read the whole thing.

The original version was simpler. None of the ghosts, except the Gloomy Ghost, had names or characters. And Hilltop Heights was baldly the Hollow. There was a confusion about grammar, with the odd first-person sentence slipping in.

A tiny droplet of ice slithered between Kirsty's

shoulder-blades. Was this supposed to be a story? Or was it a diary?

Suddenly, she didn't want to share the discovery.

The smile in the Summer Room window was fixed and fanged. Tim tried to avoid looking, but whether he was inside the house or out, the smile would catch his eye.

The Ipkick didn't like to talk about the smile.

It was one of the IP, all right, but not with the programme. Tim thought he knew who to trust, but even a single joker in the pack made him suspect other cards of hiding caps and bells.

He took up a position in his tree, U-Dub at the ready.

The BS was defeated, but the threat wasn't done. Behind her were other hostiles. Faces unknown, motives mysterious. At least his sister was out in the open, where he could mark her down.

Tim kept scanning the orchard, U-Dub cocked, watching for the tiniest tell-tales. He no longer felt he was a part of the landscape. That had been an illusion.

He was an alien, an intruder, a ravager. He could be nothing else.

The smile was there, above it all.

He was certain the smile was hostile brass, but there was no proof, no sign beyond his feeling.

He would let loose, eventually.

Steven looked at the Hollow and thought, How many animals can you see in this picture?

Tim was in the orchard. He had spotted his son's face, brown and green as usual, peering out of the tree he had made into his secret cave.

Who did his son play with all day?

(Not the stones, thank heavens.)

Kirsty and Jordan were in the towers, not having come down from their rooms all morning, sleeping it off. Jordan's pillow stiff with tears.

Dozens of jobs still needed doing, but he was at a loose end. It wasn't the same without an audience, without someone to talk to, to show off his prowess for.

Tim would do, but he was the one who could take care of himself. Steven didn't want to intrude into his son's private world. It would last a short enough time as it was. He wanted his women around him as he fixed up the work-bench in the barn or sorted through the junk in the spare rooms, reclaiming space for the family and unearthing the treasures left behind.

He looked at the tree again. No sign of Tim.

The last time he had spent alone with his son was the day they'd gone to find the standing stones. Tim had dashed about the circle, hiding behind each stone, playing visual tag with his Dad, peeking out to catch and be caught.

At the centre of the circle was a depression

(a fireplace)

where no grass grew. Both Tim and he had instinctively not stepped on that bare spot, keeping within the shadows of the stones.

It was a big clock, he thought, an arrangement of phallic sundials. A masculine place, concerned with measuring and ritual, with fire and blood. Then, it had impressed and even excited him.

Now, he was a little frightened.

He could never let the women know, of course. It was important he show no fear, that he set an example they could live by.

Tim would never find his way back there on his own.

Steven's head buzzed. The memory had been so vivid, and yet...

It hadn't happened, had it? Tim and he had driven all over the moor and not found the standing stones. He remembered that peculiar rubbery smell the hunchback's inside got after a few hours in the sun. In the end, they had just come home, disappointed and puzzled. What he had just recalled, down to the smoothness of the stones and the sponginess of the turf, was a phantom memory, a scrambled patch of *jamais vu*.

From it, he learned a lesson. He must warn his son not to go alone onto the moor in search of the stones. But in such a way that the warning would take and not be interpreted as a dare.

Things would have to change. Lulled by the charm of the Hollow, he'd let things drift, surrendering to forces beyond his control. Now, he would put his foot down.

He walked to the French windows. A pane, high up, flashed at him, setting his teeth on edge. He looked again but couldn't tell which pane it had been, or even what he had seen. Just reflected sunlight.

The Summer Room was empty, cool after the heat of the outside. For a moment, he thought something was standing in the cold fireplace. When he looked, there was nothing but a fall of soot which needed to be swept away.

He sat in his chair, and waited.

Rick was settled, one way or another. But the weight was not lifted. Anger still sprouted inside her like a seed. That was good. Anger burned fat. Anger made her lean. Anger was the road to her goal.

Jordan didn't need to wear the next dress. She wasn't ready for it in any case. She needed no outward sign of the woman she was becoming. That person was carried in her burning heart. Best she show only her girl shell.

She put on clothes she didn't know she had. Grey skirt, white blouse, magenta blazer, knee socks with tartan tags, striped tie, stout-toed shoes. A straw boater went with the outfit, its bow matching the sock-tags.

Jordan went downstairs.

Dad was in the Summer Room, sunk in shame as well he should be. At her entrance, he looked up, puppyish and eager, then shuddered.

He was repelled by the old shell, the sluggish thing Jordan was outgrowing. Even he was that sensitive.

'I wondered where everybody was,' he said.

She shrugged. There was nothing to be said to him.

'No one came down for brekky,' Dad continued. 'Or lunch. I thought I was home alone.'

She wished he would stop dropping oh-so-subtle hints. Everything he said came back to meals, to food, to her.

'Can I get you anything, doll?' he asked.

'Once and for all, Dad, *I'm not hungry!*'

She intended to speak with quiet force, demonstrating cool command of the situation, warning him off from further badgering. Instead, she shouted. Her voice reverberated in the chimney and came back at her.

Dad, startled, shrank in his chair as if she'd cracked a whip.

She liked the effect.

Was this what it meant to be grown-up? Being able just to shout and have people pay attention? She'd been speaking softly ever since she could make words, humbly beseeching and wheedling. From now on, she should issue demands.

'No need to bite my head off, doll.'

She hated it when he called her that.

Mum appeared in the room like a ghost, dust smudges on her forehead and hands. She wore a ratty old dressing gown.

'Darling,' said Daddy, still not getting it. 'That's better. I was worried you'd vanished too.'

Mum held her dressing gown together with a knotted fist.

In a dream last night, Jordan had seen Mum with another person, someone frightening and wonderful.

'You've got her clothes,' Mum said.

Jordan realised Mum was right. The outfit she was wearing was what the other person, *the Old Girl*, had left behind. The Drearcliff Grange school uniform, complete with blazer badge. Her whole body writhed inside the clothes, as if everything she wore, and the top layer of her skin, turned to slime. The sensation lasted long seconds.

She hated to be made a part of something without being fully consulted.

'I'm glad you're both here,' said Dad, missing what had passed between 'his womenfolk'. 'We need to talk.'

'That's true,' said Mum.

Jordan smelled treachery, an alliance forming against her. Last night's After Lights-Out all-girls-together session was forgotten, and it was back to the implacable tyranny of the parental junta. Orders handed down from the mountain.

'It's more than that,' said Dad. 'I need to talk and you, both of you, need to listen.'

His voice, even when not raised, echoed. He sat close to the fireplace. His words were sucked up the chimney and broadcast back at the room as if they came from everywhere.

Mum, shocked, let her dressing gown gape, showing her bra.

'There's nothing to be afraid of,' said Dad. 'I'm in control. That's what I want to tell you. Things have been slipping, going to hell again. I'm stepping in to protect you. I'm suspending democracy in this house, taking up the reins of government. For your own good. It won't be for ever. When I think you're ready, I'll let you back in. But there's a real crisis. I'm the only one who fully understands it and is competent to face it. We have a chance for something good here at the Hollow, something precious and perfect. I wouldn't be much of a man, much of a father and husband, if I didn't fight for it. I may have to be hard, make firm rulings you won't agree with, but you must believe me that it's all for the best. I'm doing this because I love you. There, now that's settled and we all feel better. Kirst, love, go into the kitchen and make us all a big pot of tea.'

Kirsty didn't know whether to howl or scream. It was as if a series of jabs were aimed at her stomach, punches pulled so she felt only anticipated pain. She couldn't look at Steven. With his talk of taking the reins and making firm rulings, he wasn't on the same page. Or in the same book.

'Tea all round would hit the spot right now,' Steven said, rephrasing the order as a suggestion.

How could she have married this man? How could the man she'd married turn into this fool?

'Come on, Kirst, hop to it.'

She didn't want tea. She wanted a divorce.

'You don't want tea, Steven,' she said. 'You want your head examined.'

She expected a flare of rage. Instead, he smiled indulgently, like her own father a million years ago when she first dyed and spiked her hair.

'You don't mean that,' he said, insufferably. 'I feel your anger. It's good that you give it vent…'

(Give it vent? Where did he get these things?)

'…and I can take it. That's what I'm here for. To take it all and soak it up, so you can get it out of your system and over with. Come on, love, give me some more.'

He stood and made a beckoning gesture with his fingers.

She was sputtering, incoherently.

How could anyone misunderstand so much? Steven was not only acting like an insane person, but was going dangerously against the will of the Hollow. She knew now that this place was not just populated, but was itself alive. The wonders they had taken for granted were provisional. There was an equilibrium. If it overbalanced, it would be his fault.

'That's better, dear,' said Steven, thinking the explosion over. 'Come and have a cuddle. Then pull yourself together and hie thee to the kitchen, wench.'

Horribly, Kirsty found herself wanting to give in, accept a hug and a tissue and turn into the creature Steven wanted. Helpmeet-supporter-confessor-servant-drudge-spermbucket. It would be so easy to give up and let someone else – no matter how misguided – run everything.

No. That wasn't going to happen.

Red afternoon light poured into the Summer Room and gave her strength.

'I said "no", Steven, and I mean it.'

Her own voice sounded truer to herself.

A flicker of doubt crossed his face. Did he realise how insanely he was acting? No, he just wasn't sure what to do next.

'Jordan,' he said, 'make the tea. Your mother and I need to have a lengthy discussion.'

Jordan didn't move. Steven looked at her, eyes dark. After a moment, she lowered her head and began to drag herself towards the kitchen. It was the films she was always watching, those horrible fantasies of hooking your man and chaining yourself to his stove, of twin beds and twinsets, of bridge parties and lawns and American chrome-finned suburban nowhere. Her daughter's spirit had been sapped by that bad influence, and was now broken by the cruelties of the penis-bearing sex.

Her husband smiled. His order was being obeyed.

'Jordan, don't,' Kirsty said. 'This is your argument too.'

Jordan paused. In her uniform, she looked barely twelve, agonisingly young and lost.

'It's in the school rules, Mummy,' she said. 'Whatever a master says must be so, or else it's the strap across the palm.'

Steven was triumphant.

Kirsty laid a hand on Jordan's shoulder, stopping her dead.

'Don't leave this room,' she said.

Her daughter's face screwed up, preparatory to a burst of tears.

'It's not fair,' she said. 'You're both picking on me, tugging me from either side.'

Kirsty withdrew her hand.

'Tea,' said Steven.

At this point, Kirsty hated tea. Its taste was constantly in her mouth, stronger than toothpaste or pepper. Throughout her life, there'd been no disaster that wasn't supposed to go away after a swig of char. That stopped here. Tea. It was what was wrong with England. She would never again prepare or consume the vile stuff.

It was happening again. Just when she had something going, something that looked like it would work, Steven went behind her back and took it over. If he couldn't, he would pull it apart, subtly at first and then blatantly. Rose Records, Oddments, Kirsty herself. Her interests, her projects, were threats to his pole position. He always reacted with decisive, destructive action.

She wouldn't let him get away with it this time.

The Hollow, and all it contained, was hers. It had revealed its magic to her first. This time, she was at the heart of it and he the periphery. He couldn't stand it. This was just a sneaky play.

He didn't really want tea. He wanted to break her spirit.

This was only to be expected. He'd grasped the nettle and knew he'd be stung. The thing was to get it over with, to ignore the momentary pain. It was best done quickly. Later, he'd smooth it over and butter them up. What was important was that he make them realise this was where the slide stopped, where the weakness ended.

His wife and daughter stood together, close but not touching, eyelines divergent. He had to keep them apart. They were bad for each other, enabling each other's weakness.

There was a natural division of labour. One to make tea, one to make the bed.

Tim should be here. He should see this scene, learn this lesson. It was in the way of things that Tim would rise in the family

(fight and kill his father)

and become the man.

Resistance was crushed. He had been firm, for once. There would be no more straying from the path. He was satisfied, confident.

(He had a half-erection.)

'I'm glad we've talked this through,' he said. 'You'll soon see it was all for the best.'

He let out the breath he had been holding.

Kirsty wheeled around, dressing gown falling open, red flush of anger on her chest, her hands claws. Surely, she wouldn't make a punch-up of this? If she did, she would regret it. She would lose.

'Steve, it's time you listened to someone else,' she said. 'You've gone absolutely, barking…'

'Are we early?'

Jordan's head hurt from the current of ill-feeling flowing between Mum and Dad. It was like the old days. For a second, as the new voice filled the Summer Room, she was sure Veronica had come back too. A jagged shadow crept into the room, twiggy arms extended to embrace them all.

But it was a man.

'I say, we *are* too early,' he said, coming through the French windows like a comedy vicar.

Mum's face went as red as her chest. She appeared to have trouble breathing. She looked a complete hag, hair a-straggle, dressing gown limp over her mostly undressed body. Her bra and knickers weren't even a pair.

'The minibus is parked in the drive.'

It was the brown man, Bernard Wing-Godfrey, dressed nattily in a beige cardigan with matching scarf and beret. People came in with him.

Mum held her robe over her body. Jordan stood still, afraid her parents would fall like dervishes on this poor interloper and hack him to pieces.

Others crowded in eagerly behind Wing-Godfrey, looking around, eager to be admitted to the sacred turf. Jordan took in a group of mannish ladies and womanly men, mild and apologetic, unsure how to behave.

'Oh, bravo, Miss Naremore,' said Wing-Godfrey, spotting Jordan, clapping softly. For a moment, she didn't understand. 'What a welcoming touch, the Drearcliff Grange colours.'

Her uniform was uncomfortable for a midsummer day.

A pair of tiny Japanese women in kimonos stepped forward and snapped off photographs on twin cameras. The flashes burst in her head.

Mum bolted, without a word, rushing for the safety of her tower.

It was left to Dad to cope. The man of the house, he had called himself.

'Come in, come in,' he said. 'Jordan, dear, could you get the tea going?'

The sentence took a long time to strike a spark in her brain.

'Yes, Daddy,' she said, finally.

As Jordan walked to the kitchen, the Japanese women snapped more photographs, a study of her in motion. She let her hair hang over her face and skulked rather than glided out of the room. Dad was

going to get his way after all. Someone else – Jordan
– was making the tea.

'Will Kirsty, Mrs Naremore, be rejoining us?'
Wing-Godfrey asked Dad.

Good question, Jordan thought.

From the tree, Tim saw non-combatants wander
onto the field of fire. A platoon-strength group
had come round from the drive and were infiltrating
the house through the French windows. The smiling
pane was laughing. With these hostages in its power,
Tim could do nothing. Or so it thought.

If it was the only thing to do, Tim was prepared
to be ruthless, to make sacrifices. He would cry later,
after the war was over and the victory won.

The U-Dub was cocked. The aches in his shoulder
and elbow had been there so long he was used to
them, would miss them if they were gone.

DefCon 1. At least the waiting was over.

He fixed on the smile and smiled right back.

Dressed hurriedly, hair at least combed, Kirsty
dashed downstairs. She paused outside the
Summer Room and caught a low rumble of chat. A
blurt of genuine laughter startled her. She must have
made a lasting impression on Wing-Godfrey's Society.

She took a deep breath and pushed the door in.

Steven was playing host. Jordan meekly served tea,
dreadful simper plastered on her face, eyes suggesting
she was screaming inside.

'Ah, Kirst,' said Steven. 'Come in and meet the Society.'

Attempting poise, she entered the room. Wing-Godfrey smiled at her, raising a mug in half-salute.

'This is Mrs Twomey,' said Steven, indicating a horsey, bluff middle-aged woman – Drearcliff Grange's Angela the Boss grown up. 'Miss Hazzard, Mr and Mrs Bullitt, and Cynthia and Megumi Kanaoka, from Japan.'

Miss Hazzard was young, blonde and angular enough to suggest spinal deformity. The Bullitts were an enormous woman and a tiny man, their matching mulberry cardigans studded with enamel badges of Weezie, the Drearcliff Grange coat of arms, the Gloomy Ghost and other Teazle characters. The Kanaokas, obviously, were the camera twins.

'This is our After Lights-Out Gang,' said Wing-Godfrey.

They all dutifully laughed and smiled. The Japanese women bobbed and bowed, which set the rest of them off again, like nodding dog car ornaments.

They must be expecting Kirsty to go mad again. With an axe.

'It's just as I always imagined it,' said Miss Hazzard. 'Hilltop Heights.'

'Except it's not on a hill,' added Mrs Bullitt. She had a very strong Birmingham accent.

Kirsty thought of the exercise book upstairs on her dressing table. She was horribly tempted to tell them Weezie lived at the Hollow before Louise disguised it as the Heights, but kept quiet. She still needed to think out what to do with the relic.

'Drink up,' said Steven, 'and you can take the grand tour. We have another child around here somewhere. Don't be surprised if he pops up out of a hole in the ground.'

'Like the Wiggy-Wig,' ventured Miss Hazzard.

'Indeed,' said Steven, who had no more idea than Kirsty who or what the Wiggy-Wig might be. These people had their Teazle memorised.

'You've a lovely day for it,' said Kirsty, unclenching her teeth. 'We've been lucky with the weather.'

Wing-Godfrey smiled sagely.

This was not down to her being her usual inept self and forgetting that the Society were coming. They really hadn't fixed a date. This was a total surprise. Wing-Godfrey had said *a* Saturday, not *this* Saturday. A big appointments diary lay beside the telephone; nothing was written in it until Tim's first day of school in September. If this visit were arranged, she'd have noted it in red. Despite what Steven thought of her, she wouldn't forget a concrete arrangement and let it creep up on her.

This was a trap. Somehow, she had been set up.

God, she hoped there were enough biscuits. They probably expected cucumber sandwiches with the crusts cut off, or baskets of Drearcliff Grange tuck. Not just tea, but high tea. She wasn't prepared.

'Shall we start in the orchard?' said Steven, standing to one side to let the guests use the French windows.

The Japanese women led the expedition. Wing-Godfrey hung back.

'That's better, Kirsty,' he said, looking at her clothes.

The brown man went to join his comrades in the orchard.

'I swear I didn't know,' Kirsty insisted.

Steven's face was shut.

'We've got to make the best of this,' he said. 'Jord, get to work in the kitchen. Root out some provisions. We've got enough apples, at least. They'll like apples from the orchard. For the associations. And we'll need gallons more tea. These are what you might call tea people.'

He had got his way about that. Kirsty wasn't inclined to protest.

Jordan looked to her for confirmation of orders.

It broke her heart, but immediate needs meant she had to back Steven up.

'If you could, darling,' she said. 'We'd owe you a tremendous favour.'

'Tremendous,' Jordan repeated.

Kirsty nodded.

Her daughter began collecting empty mugs from various surfaces and coasters.

'United front,' said Steven, offering Kirsty his arm.

Damn it, he had won. He was master here. She was just a bubble-headed ornament.

She would not let this rest. Inside, she boiled like a kettle.

Composed and smiling, they stepped into the orchard and found the Society looking up with awe at the house, exchanging Teazle tit-bits. The Japanese women used rolls of film. The Bullitts were canoodling; Kirsty overheard Mr Bullitt call his wife 'Head Prefect' and shuddered to think of their sex life.

(She and Steven had played that game.)

Miss Hazzard looked through the tree telescope, at the standing stones. Wing-Godfrey stood by her, proprietarily, lightly holding her head as he had held Kirsty's. He was overly prissy about touching anyone. Perhaps that came from so long a confinement, removed from human contact beyond the occasional beating.

She didn't want to feel sorry for him. She was angry at his imposition. She wasn't even sure there wasn't some sinister purpose to this visit.

Steven, who knew nothing about Louise Teazle, led them around the outside of the house, spouting like a tour guide, running through the original features they'd left alone and pointing out what they were doing with each room.

The Society were especially interested in the East Tower, where Louise had lived.

'I've occupied her study,' Steven said, 'and Jordan, our daughter, has the bedroom.'

Miss Hazzard sighed out loud, trembling with ecstatic envy. The girl couldn't be twenty. Shouldn't she be interested in clubbing, drugs and wild boys? What had driven her to seventy-year-old kids' books? She wasn't really deformed, just a victim of bad posture.

'What of your plans to open the place to the public?' squeaked Mr Bullitt. 'Bernard has been telling us about Mrs Naremore's exciting ideas. I dare say this could be quite a tourist trap.'

Steven looked as if he'd been shot but tried to cover up.

'Kirst is getting ahead of herself there, I'm afraid,'

he said, darting a venomous glance at her. 'We're not really set up for that sort of thing. Short on reliable staff. You might have noticed. Oh, we try, of course, but we're proper ones for the odd spot of bungling.'

'Still, such an opportunity…'

Mr Bullitt looked up to his wife for support.

'We're certainly not ruling anything out at this stage,' said Steven. 'It's early days yet.'

He would never let Kirsty make anything of the Hollow. Any time she raised it, he would bring up this incident as a humorous justification for stamping on her projects. Had he somehow contrived the situation? Set her up for a humiliation so he would have unlimited ammunition?

'A museum,' Mrs Bullitt said. 'That's what this place should be, for the public trust. It's a national treasure, a resource. Teazle belongs to us all, you know.'

'But the Hollow belongs to us,' said Steven, uncomfortable but firm.

'Yes,' said Mrs Bullitt.

When the place came on the market, why hadn't these people put in an offer? It wasn't as if it had been overpriced.

'I don't know that I could live here,' said Miss Hazzard. 'Too many…'

'Associations?' suggested Kirsty.

'…ghosts,' the girl said.

When the fruitcakes left, *if* they ever left, he would strangle Kirsty. Slowly. This disaster was down to her failure to share information, to keep track of important things. She'd given a vague invitation and not remembered when the Society got back to her. Now, the Hollow was invaded.

Steven was handling the crisis with consummate diplomacy and skill. After the spectacle Kirsty made of herself when they arrived, Wing-Godfrey's weirdies knew something was wrong. He exerted his powers of persuasion to make them forget the fright in her knickers and project an image of normality. He gritted his teeth as if clamping an imaginary pipe and talked bollocks about the house and grounds. He was a spellbinder; they'd all go away idiotically happy, privileged to have been shown around by such an expert. He also dropped a few digs to let them know he wasn't completely a subscriber to their daft religion. The Hollow was his home now. He wouldn't be pushed about because of their devotion to a fusty spinster whose books only sissies would have read at his school.

Keeping the group together was hard. Their subtly different enthusiasms pulled in different ways.

'There's a division in our ranks,' Wing-Godfrey explained, in the hayloft above the garage, 'between those who primarily prize the Weezie books and those who rate Drearcliff Grange above all.'

This empty space was a Weezie site.

If this went on and on, he would have to *read* the blasted books. He could never trust Kirsty, who had actually read Teazle as a girl and again recently, to guide parties about the place. Maybe now things were better with Jordan, she could be trained up and fed full of the information. She had always been good at passing exams. The uniform had gone over well. Just the sort of frill that sold a prospect. Putting this together was just like assembling a big money deal.

Steven was ready to move on, but the Weezies – Mr Bullitt and one of the Japanese women – were exploring a shadowed corner that was a lair for some species of twee creature. Mrs Twomey, he gathered, was a lifelong 'Grange Gel', and impatient to get on. She wanted to see 'the West Wing'.

He ran a head-check. The Society had seven members, present and accounted for. Or was it one president and seven members? He had an idea the Bullitts had a family member with them, dragged along unwillingly on this expedition. Or was it Wing-Godfrey who had a shadow?

He counted again. Eight heads, excluding Kirsty. Fine.

This space had changed. He'd thought of turning the hayloft into a suite of offices. There was room for serious computer and communications equipment. He had envisioned a grown-up version of the Steve caves he'd made as a kid, with a bar and a pool table. When he first climbed up here, he knew it was a man's preserve, just as Jordan's bedroom and the spare room Kirsty called the sewing room were female spaces.

Now, with the Society pottering around, the hayloft was spoiled. Even at the height of summer, there were draughts. A rotten smell suggested parasite problems which hadn't showed up in the sinister survey. The roof was too low. He kept scraping his head on beams.

No. There would be no office-suite here, no den, no Steve cave. He just didn't like the hayloft. He didn't know why.

Did something live here?

To keep calm, he counted again. Nine heads, including Kirsty. Ten, with himself.

He must be wrong.

No. He knew enough about the Hollow not to be fooled. They had another guide on this tour.

He counted, slowly this time.

By opening the bale-door, Steven let in enough light to see everybody clearly. If only they wouldn't drift around the place so much. What was so fascinating about empty corners?

Nine.

Or ten.

He looked at each one in turn. There was no one left over, no stranger.

'Let's see if tea is ready,' he suggested, his voice sounding weak in this echoey space. 'Then, we can tour the inside of the house.'

He wasn't sure he wanted this lot traipsing through his office and bedroom, but anything was better than staying in the hayloft.

'That's too much to ask,' said Wing-Godfrey, sincerely.

'No,' Steven said, hating himself. 'I insist.'

'We are fortunate that custodianship of the Hollow has fallen to such sympathetic and congenial persons,' said Wing-Godfrey. 'I propose you both for lifetime honorary membership…'

'Seconded,' said one of the others.

'No opposition? I should say that's the easiest decision this thorny little group has ever made. Congratulations, Mr and Mrs Naremore. Welcome to the Louise Magellan Teazle Society.'

Steven really wanted to get out of the hayloft. He couldn't believe he had contemplated working in this hideous, oppressive space. His jaw hurt from smiling. His gut churned with the strain of keeping so much inside.

'You'll have to take the Drearcliff entrance exam, of course,' said Wing-Godfrey. 'But that should be no problem for you. Miss Hazzard sets the paper. She's the ranking mistress of Teazle Trivia. When *Mastermind* had Teazle as a specialist subject, the BBC came to her to set the questions.'

The shadows were getting thicker. Steven was going to scream. A trickle of sweat got in his eye.

'Tea,' he creaked.

'Just about now that would be most welcome. What say we, girls?'

The After Lights-Out Gang chirruped enthusiasm.

Steven tried not to fall off the steps on the way down. He dashed out of the garage, not caring what these loonies thought, and filled his lungs with fresh air.

'Are you overcome by the closeness?' Miss Hazzard asked.

'Something like that,' he said.

'I quite understand.'

The young woman laid a hand on the crook of his elbow and squeezed, like a very old relative.

'You should wear a crystal to earth the power, or it'll build. In the end, something will go *pop!* and there'll be tears before bedtime.'

He felt better already. It had just been the hayloft. Something in the hayloft.

It took engineering to get Mrs Bullitt down the ladder. One of the Japanese women asked if she could spend a penny. He gave her the choice between the outside loo and the ground floor inside toilet.

'It's glands,' Mrs Twomey said, nodding at Mrs Bullitt. 'She's a martyr to her glands.'

Jordan appeared from the kitchen, wearing a straw boater with a tartan band.

Tea things were set out on the garden table. Jordan had made a pile of sandwiches and arranged biscuit selections into mandala mosaics on three large plates.

Dare he let these people eat or drink anything Jordan prepared? She could have laced the tea with weed-killer or spread drain-cleaner on the sandwiches. He didn't pretend to know what went on inside her head and this had been such a day of disasters he almost expected another explosion.

Jordan picked up the large tea-pot – it looked like an oversized *Alice* prop – and posed, like a giant tea-pot herself, arm crooked like a handle, pot held like a spout.

'Shall I be mother?' said his daughter.

They survived tea. Kirsty would never again underestimate Jordan. She'd acted as if this whole farce was expected and planned. *Had* Jordan known about the surprise visit in advance? And kept quiet to bring about just this situation? A disaster which made her look better than her parents? Kirsty hadn't expected a challenge from that direction, but behind her daughter's retro timidity was dangerous steel.

Kirsty sat, gripping her tea-cup like a fetish, as Jordan talked knowledgeably and amusingly about living in Weezie's room. The Society were won over by the girl in school uniform. Kirsty didn't realise her daughter had read so much Louise Teazle.

Jordan looked younger, yet more poised.

The crises were not over. Once Wing-Godfrey's crowd were persuaded to depart, the family still had a great sorting-out to go through. Kirsty didn't expect all of them to be still standing when it was over.

Whatever else, the After Lights-Out Gang had saved them from a titanic row. That was a mercy. Steven hadn't exploded, so he must have been forced to cool down. Jordan had proved by her actions that she was not a pushover.

A settlement would be reached, a division of power. Nothing permanent. Something workable until the next quake. Kirsty was not going to let the others get away with this. If it looked unliveable for her, she'd call Vron.

She smiled at the thought. No matter what they had found in themselves at the Hollow, Steven and Jordan were no match for Vron. Beside her, they were amateurs. Vron played with people's heads the way most folk played patience, to pass the time and keep her hand in. There were Vron stories Steven didn't know.

Kirsty forced herself to pay attention to the chatter.

Jordan was coaxing personal, human things out of

Miss Hazzard – Harriet Hazzard, she turned out to be, which made her sound like the heroine of a girls' story. She had an open place at an Oxford college, but couldn't take it up at the moment because she was carer for her brother, who had AIDS.

It had never occurred to Kirsty before, but Jordan didn't have visible friends. Not even – or especially not – Rick. Seeing her chatting with a girl more or less her own age was odd.

Steven was stuck between Mrs Twomey and Mrs Bullitt, who gave the lie to his male master of the universe act of an hour or so ago. She saw how sad and funny her husband was, if pushed, and remembered she loved him. There was a chance the family would come through this afternoon without blowing to bits.

'Now,' announced Bernard Wing-Godfrey, whom she would find hard to trust again, 'this fine repast consumed, shall we repair to the interior of the Hollow, to ferret out its secrets and savour its scents?'

He stood and the tour was on again.

Tim knew this was it. The balloon was up. The French windows shut, almost by themselves. His family was trapped in a killing box, along with unknown non-combatants. There must be a fifth columnist or two in the crowd. Typical of the hostiles to send spies or saboteurs.

The smiling pane showed its fangs.

At long last, the moment came. Tim let go of the elastic. The U-Dub unloosed its payload.

He scored a direct hit.

One of the windows burst. A shower of sparkly fragments fell on them.

Jordan's whole body went taut. She wanted to curl up in a rioter's protective position.

The sound, like a gunshot, reverberated in the Summer Room. Other windows rattled. She was seized with a panic that more attacks would come. A blast-wave would roll through the orchard, against the side of the house, smashing the big windows. The room would become a blizzard of razor-fragments to shred them all.

'Something is in my eye,' said Mrs Twomey, evenly. 'I don't want to touch it.'

A missile pinged off the ceiling and fell to the floor.

Jordan's ears rang. A final diamond of glass fell and broke on the flagstones. She was still on her feet.

Harriet, tentatively in charge, held Mrs Twomey's head and looked professionally into her eye. The stooped girl had a lot of strength. Jordan liked her.

'I see it,' Harriet said.

The injured woman winced.

'Can I help?' Jordan asked.

Harriet told her to fetch water.

Mrs Twomey screamed as Harriet's spit-wet finger neared her eye. She screwed up her face, which made her pain – real or imagined – worse, and screamed again. Her screech was high, shrill, girly – not at all what Jordan expected from such a solid barrel of a woman.

She nipped to the kitchen and came back with a shallow bowl of water and a sheet of quilted paper.

'Wash it out,' Harriet said. 'Here, let me.'

The girl dripped water into Mrs Twomey's eye.

'All gone, Mrs T.,' she said. 'You were brave.'

Quieted, Mrs Twomey blinked a lot, panic over and the shard gone.

'It was a window,' said one of the Kanaoka sisters, picking up a piece. 'Smashed.'

This was not an accident. There had been a missile. She had heard it fall.

She rooted around and found what she was looking for. Gripping the object, she approached the others. Opening her fist, she showed them a pebble.

She knew who had fired the shot, knew

(in a flash of insight)

who had left the shrews outside her door, who had been campaigning against her.

'Someone's playing silly buggers,' she said.

It was not an expression he'd ever heard his daughter use. It sounded strange, though he had to agree with the sentiment.

'What happened?' someone asked.

He didn't know. He was acutely embarrassed by that. He was supposed to be on top of things. This was his house and he should have an answer for every question. It was about confidence. Even if you didn't know, you weren't supposed to say so. There were ways of waffling with conviction which usually worked with his clients. Just now, he had lost the knack.

Steven stepped towards the French windows, determined to act.

'Don't do anything stupid,' said Kirsty.

He ignored her and went into the orchard.

No one around. He hadn't expected there to be. He made out a sightline from the smashed window to the fallen tree.

Tim's fallen tree.

After firing, he felt an exhilaration, a freedom. The tension in his shoulder, elbow and wrist was gone. The missile was in the air. This was unknown territory.

Now, with the PP on the warpath, he was afraid.

Something had gone wrong. The window-pane was gone, the gap as black as a missing tooth, but the smile still hung there, like a twitching cobweb.

Screaming had come from inside the house. Collateral damage. It happened in wartime, innocents falling to friendly fire.

'Tim, come down,' the PP shouted.

He squirmed inside the tree, squirrelling back away from the knothole, compressing his body into a small space, willing himself to become part of the wood.

'I know you're there.'

He had another pebble. The U-Dub was ready for reloading. The situation was desperate. He slipped the missile into the thong and pulled back.

He sighted through the hole, on the lawn.

The PP came into view and looked up. The U-Dub targeted on his forehead.

Tim listened out, for suggestions from the Ipkick. Comms were down. He was on his own, here. It would be his snap decision.

Was his father a threat? A covert hostile?

'Come on down, Tim,' the PP said.

Tim's fingers wavered. He remembered the freedom of letting go.

Caught, he wished he had a hollow tooth full of cyanide. At the back of his mind, it had always worried him that Green Base, while defensible, had only one safe entrance and egress. It took only one man to besiege him. He could hold the position indefinitely – he was provisioned and the space was too small for anyone larger than him – but there was no easy escape.

'I'm not angry,' Dad lied.

Tim knew the PP's moods. This calm, loud one meant he was very angry indeed, close to losing control. That had happened only a few times, but was terrifying, a betrayal of the non-aggression pact between them. Up until the last, Dad would be rational, cool and insistent, then it would all fly apart and he would lash out with everything he had.

Could Tim take the PP out with one shot?

No. That was not an acceptable loss. He relaxed the U-Dub and slipped it into its holster-pocket

Tim climbed, up past the knothole. The tree was hollow, open at top and bottom. If he couldn't get out at the bottom, he would have to try the top.

He worked his way up. The interior contours of the tree seemed to change from moment to moment. He saw a patch of leaf-shaded daylight above. Previously, he had only been able to poke his head out. Now, he would have to get his whole body through.

The IP lined the ridges of the inside of the tree. Tim felt hands grasping his wrists, helping him heft up higher, clearing obstacles. This much they would do. His knees were rubbed raw. Something twiggy lashed across his face.

'Tim,' the PP shouted.

He reached the egress and slipped through. His head, shoulders and arms made it, but his hips caught. He could cry with frustration. But crying was for babies, for kids. He wasn't going to cry again.

It was the U-Dub, sticking out. He let himself go limp, reached back with one hand and took the catapult, then slipped it out of the tree. Now, armed, he could escape easily.

He stood on one branch and grabbed a higher one. Both sagged, creaking under his weight, but didn't break.

Apples came loose and bombed the ground.

Tim looked down through leaves and branches. Dad hopped out of the way, a ripe apple splitting at his feet. Other apples fell. The PP dodged comically, getting out from under the tree.

'Tim, I see you,' he shouted.

Tim had expected that. His plan was to clamber along the sturdiest of the branches and make it to another tree, then the ground, then dash for the perimeter and the fording place at the corner of the property.

Once off the Hollow, he would be safe.

(Why? What would stop Dad making an incursion into neutral territory to bring him back?)

The sturdiest branch wasn't as sturdy as he had thought. It normally brushed against the finger-like outlying branches of the nearest tree, but with his weight, it bowed out of reach and towards the ground.

Tim had nowhere to go.

'Your son?' asked Wing-Godfrey, mildly. 'Some boyish jape?'

Kirsty was knotted inside.

Steven was capering like a slapstick fool. Tim dangled from a branch like an overripe fruit, twenty feet above unforgiving ground.

'Excuse me,' she said to the Society.

She seemed to wade through broken glass to get to the French windows. Surely one small pane couldn't make so much debris? The glass had been shattered as if by a bullet. If the pebble had been aimed at a person, there might have been a fatality. It was a mercy Mrs Twomey, whose shrieks had let the school down, was not blinded in one eye.

No one had consulted her about whether a killer catapult was a suitable toy for a young boy. Now, the answer was only too obvious. It wasn't as if a written constitution decreed all male children had the right to own and operate projectile weapons. Steven indulged the boy, delighted his son had the man-skills to make and use such a horrible instrument of harm.

If they lived through today, her foot was coming down.

No matter what the catapult lobby argued, there was going to be a confiscation.

'Tim,' she said, 'don't move.'

Her son heard her and went slack. With one hand, he held a branch that yawed alarmingly; in the other, he clutched his catapult.

'Drop that bloody thing and hang on with both hands,' she said.

Tim shook his head, imperceptibly. He would

rather fall to his death than be disarmed.

Where had he learned such values?

'Tell him,' she told Steven.

Her husband was no use here. He didn't listen to her.

'Come down,' he shouted.

Tim was frightened. His legs shook. His footing was unsure.

Did Steven want their son to fall? Was he so angry with Tim that he had forgotten to be frightened for him?

One of Tim's soles slipped off green bark and his leg dangled in space. The trainer came off and took an eternity to fall. Her heart and breath stopped until the shoe bounced on the grass, then she melted inside.

She could not cope with this any longer.

She wanted to tell Tim to go back, to climb down safely, to run up to his mum for a hug and promise never to endanger himself like this again. She wanted a long, sensible family talk about the dangers of the catapult. She wanted everyone – Steven as much as Tim – to say sorry and promise to do better in the future.

But wanting didn't mean moving. She was frozen.

Bernard Wing-Godfrey and his Society stood on the crazy paving outside the French windows, a goggling audience for this tragic stupidity. Despite his inconvenient arrival, she still thought he might be important to her plans for the Hollow.

She knew she should be thinking only of her family, but couldn't. It wasn't fair. Every time she had something going on her own, Steven or Jordan or Tim would barge in demanding attention. That was why her projects fell by the wayside. The worst thing was that the others wrote off the failures as her fault. It was her woolly-headedness, her ineptitude, her impracticality, her lack of commitment. Not their interfering, their jealousy, their nagging need to be at the centre of her world every moment of the day.

A sound came from the back of her throat. She had no idea what the word she was trying to get out might be. Her vocal cords were dry sandpaper.

Tim dangled like a monkey, from one hand, by one foot.

Someone was going to die.

He had gone as far as he could. The branches swayed as if in a strong wind.

Tim wasn't the only weight in the tree.

He clung to his branch, feeling it bend. The IP were with him but he needed them to back off. He couldn't see them but knew they were there.

They were filing out, one by one. humping along the branch.

The tree creaked and cracked. It wouldn't have fallen in the first place if it were healthy.

Branches bent. Tim's fingers were greased by sweat. One of his trainers was gone. His socked foot kept slipping off a bark-skinned patch of wet wood.

People shouted from below, but he couldn't make out their words.

The Ipkick squatted safely, a few branches up. Tim saw her position. A faded school tie was knotted around the branch, greened with moss to blend in. Her marker.

'What now, soldier?'

Tim wondered if it would be best if he stopped playing soldiers.

The branch he was standing on came away from the tree-trunk. Though still connected by pulpy strands, the bone of the wood was broken. It scythed downwards in a rush of leaves, snapping off twigs, thumping against the hollow bole. Someone – Mum? – screamed, but was shut up halfway. He hadn't fallen with the branch. He heard the thumping impacts of a dozen apples.

Hand clamped around the surviving branch, he hung on. His wrist burned. His shoulder, strained from holding the firing position, yanked painfully.

He tried to let go of the U-Dub, to bring his left hand into play, but the catapult was holding him rather than the other way round. The smile came up in his mind, mocking him.

He reached up, ignoring the hot pain in his shoulder, and hooked his left arm over the springy branch. If he pulled himself up, he'd have a secure perch up by the Ipkick.

His ally gave him no encouragement.

Was the Ipkick his ally? Had it all been a trick? Had he unknowingly given everything away to the commander of the hostiles?

With that thought, he lost his hold.

A deadweight fell out of the sky. Steven had no time to cradle his arms. His son landed on him like a sack of horseshoes. Knocked off his feet, he thumped against the ground. A tooth went and salt blood leaked onto his tongue. The fingers of his left hand bent the wrong way.

Kirsty was screaming. And so was he.

Tim was still moving. He tried to get away. Steven made a grab with his injured hand. As he made a fist around a fold of Tim's T-shirt, liquid agony jolted his whole arm.

His son was terrified.

And well he might be. If ever a boy deserved a sound, pants-down smacking, Tim was that soldier.

Kirsty dashed in and swept Tim up in her arms, hugging and sobbing and kissing. He still clung to his blessed catapult as if it were a sacred relic that could protect him from the storms of his father's rage.

Steven was too angry to be relieved.

He got up and saw his trousers were marked by Tim's muddy heel-prints. He tongued around inside his mouth and found a chip of enamel like a piece of grit. One of his front teeth had a corner snapped off. His blood-red left hand was swelling to the size of a football. Other parts of his body were jabbed by pains.

The After Lights-Out Gang stood by the house, bewildered by the show. Worse than any of his injuries was that he had to bottle the rage that wanted to explode from behind his eyes and pour in a rain of fire over his misbegotten son. The audience meant Steven couldn't let off steam the way he would have if the family were alone. This called for serious effing and blinding.

What had Tim been thinking of?

* * *

The boy was safe. Kirsty gave thanks and hugged Tim closer than she had since before he could walk. He had come out of her and her responsibility was to protect him.

The tree was coming down. Steven, the tool-using man, would be renting a chainsaw and the rotten tree would be ten years' worth of firewood. It had nearly killed her darling and she was not going to let it stand.

In the house, the telephone rang. It connected to a fire-bell mounted over the kitchen door, so it could be heard throughout the orchard.

What now?

Kirsty checked Tim's face and hands, his limbs and trunk, frisking him for hidden wounds. The boy was white and quiet, startled out of himself. He probably couldn't believe he'd lived through the fall. His catapult, unbroken, was still firmly in his grip.

He looked up at the branches. She tried to get him to look at her, but his gaze tugged upwards, eyes jittering from side to side as he scanned for something. She looked up too and saw a green face.

No, just leaves and a knot of branches.

The after-image of the face stayed with her.

That telephone jangled her nerves.

She hugged Tim close and shouted to Jordan to get the phone and get rid of whoever it was.

Her daughter stepped inside the house.

Tim tried to say something. Spittle came out of his mouth. She wiped it away with her wrist.

'I think my hand's broken,' said Steven.

That didn't matter. Her husband would live. If he didn't, she could get another. Tim was irreplaceable.

If she let him come to harm, she was worth nothing.

'It's just a sprain,' she said, not looking. 'Put cold water on it.'

The shadows of the tree seemed to crawl over Kirsty's skin, tickling like a hundred thousand insects. The shadows of leaves were like dark blemishes on Tim's face. She picked him up, his arms around her neck, her arm under his bum, and carried him out of the shade, holding him up to the sunlight as if late afternoon warmth could wash away the hurt.

There were people by the house. For a moment, she couldn't remember who they were.

Those moments replaying in her mind – her son losing his grip, plunging through empty air, limbs waving – blotted everything else. It took a second or two for her to recall her own name, her immediate circumstances. Her life was divided in two by the shock. She saw reality for the first time, understanding she was on a high-wire without a net. How could she ever take a step again, knowing what might happen? A hundred feet below them were the jagged rocks.

Steven was still in the shadow, right hand clamped around his left wrist as if his left hand were a dead bird. She looked above her husband but couldn't see the green face. Still, she was afraid for him.

'Come out, Steven,' she said.

He didn't understand.

'Away from the tree,' she insisted.

He looked above him. She clenched inside, certain something like a green monkey would fall on his face, limbs and tail wrapping around his head and shoulders, teeth and fingers chewing for his eyes and tongue.

'*Now*,' she said, as if he were her child.

Steven stumbled out into the light.

The tree waved in a wind, sighing. She had beaten it, rescued her men from the thing. When it was sawed down, she'd make sure the roots were dug up and burned. Nothing would remain, not one apple pip.

'How is he?' Steven asked.

She would remember for ever that she couldn't trust Steven to look after the children. She had to be certain at all times that she knew where they were. If she didn't watch over them, no one else would, no one else could.

(Such a burden, such a distraction, the children.)

Steven reached out, with his good hand. She took Tim out of his way, ignoring the hurt in her husband's eyes. Just now, she didn't want him near her.

Tim took his face off her shoulder. There was a shallow graze on his cheek and forehead, like the mark of a twiggy finger.

'Mum, Dad,' he said, 'they're not our friends.'

Her blood was ice.

Just behind Tim's flushed, streaked face was a paler, calmer mask. She saw him dead and alive at the same time.

'Not our friends.'

Not *his* friends, perhaps.

She put Tim down and stood away. She wasn't sure he wasn't dead. He was like Steven and Jordan, set against her. He had always been their secret weapon, smallest and most demanding, yet least rewarding, of the FU. He had come along unexpectedly – Tim, not Jordan, had made her give in to Steven's pressure and get married, abandoning her law course – and cemented the hated transformation of Kirsty, the individual with potential for personal growth, into Mrs Naremore, the doormat of all time.

Now Tim – if this was even Tim, and not something wearing his shape – wanted her to reject even the magic.

She was over her fear for her family.

'The Hollow,' said Jordan, into the phone.

'Mrs Naremore?' asked a man's voice, familiar.

'This is Jordan. Mum's...' What to say? This was no time to give details. '...caught up in something.'

'*Jordan*,' said the caller, with loathing.

The voice slipped into her ear and coursed around her body, like a shudder. 'Jordan Naremore,' the voice insisted. 'I'm looking at a letter. A letter from you.'

The Summer Room was dark. It had lost the light.

'Who is this?' she asked.

'He read your letter.'

It was Rick's dad. He didn't sound himself. There was no distortion on the line. It was as if he were speaking clearly for the first time.

'My boy's dead,' he said. '*Bitch*.'

Click. Dead air.

She held the receiver, needing to say something, knowing no one would hear. She couldn't put the phone down. Her arms were iron, her stomach was water.

Through the French windows, she saw Mum and Dad with Tim. She was cut off from her family. The visitors were in the way, keeping out the light.

'My boy's dead. *Bitch*.'

Rick. Dead. *Bitch*.

Dead.

She barely remembered her Gran, Dad's mum, who'd died before Tim was born. She had just been a presence, gone without making an impression. Last year, Melanie Staples, a girl she knew slightly from school, was killed in a fire caused by faulty wiring. For days afterward, Jordan had only been able to think of Melanie, someone she'd once sat three desks away from in Geography, getting used to the idea of Melanie not having a future, not being even a peripheral part of Jordan's life. She hadn't especially liked Melanie, who was friends with some girls who gave her a hard time, but hadn't really had anything against her. It had been a matter of indifference to Jordan whether Melanie was in the room or not, but for a while she found it hard to continue everyday life. She kept remembering that someone she knew couldn't drink tea, walk to school, do homework, watch television... and wouldn't ever do those things again. Days after, Melanie had a dreamlike quality she'd expended thousands of words in her now-abandoned diary trying to define. When Rick made a joke about Melanie frying, she broke up with him for two days, unable to believe his callousness, eventually writing it off as just bravado.

Now Rick.

Letter. Dead. *Bitch*.

She fumbled with the cordless receiver, not cradling it properly. She was in a standing-up swoon.

The only boy she had ever made love with was dead.

Secrets she had shared were hers alone now.

Their arguments would never be settled.

It was over.

Everything was over.

What to do?

Suddenly, the Summer Room was full of people and shadows, all talking at once. The words were a babble, an aural blur like static. She had lost the ability to distinguish between voices.

Kirsty saw Steven pick up the telephone. He listened briefly, heard nothing and put it back in its cradle. Jordan had been careless. She stood in the middle of the room, eyes unfocused.

Teazle Society members fussed.

They were solicitous. Was she all right?

Of course she was. It was her family they should worry about. All of them.

'What was he doing up there?' asked Mrs Twomey.

Trying to get attention, she thought. Undoing any chance his poor old mum might have of making even a small space in her life for herself.

The telephone rang again. This time, Steven picked it up. Jordan must have been unable to make sense.

So many distractions. People around when she wanted to be alone. There seemed more visitors than she had counted. As if the shadows of the Society were a separate gang.

Was there a polite way of getting rid of them?

In the end, she'd wind up shouting at them to sod off.

Even Harriet Hazzard, the carer, was no use now.

Steven nodded, listening to the caller, mumbled, held the receiver away from his ear, flinching from tinny shrieking at the other end of the line, and hung up.

Jordan looked at her father with horror. She covered her face with her hands and ran out of the room.

Kirsty clung to Tim, protecting him.

'Bad news, old fellow?' asked Wing-Godfrey.

'Uh, yes,' Steven said. 'Afraid I'm going to have to cut short the tour.'

Wing-Godfrey was stricken. Mrs Bullitt yelped with disappointment. The others were similarly aghast. Children told there would be no more ice cream. Ever.

This was wrong. She had been wrong. If anything, Wing-Godfrey's people should stay and her family should leave, trot off to hospital or something and let her get on with it. The outsiders understood the Hollow better, understood what Kirsty wanted to make of the place.

'Tim's fine,' she said, forcing a smile that made her cheeks hurt. 'We shouldn't be rude because of a little tumble.'

They hadn't seen the inside of the house yet, really. There were sacred sites to visit. Weezie's nooks, Louise's study, Louise's room. The collection of Teazle memorabilia.

Steven's face screwed up. Whatever he wanted to say, he couldn't get it out.

It mustn't be very important.

Tim's fingers unhooked from her blouse and hair. *They're not our friends*, he had said.

She looked at the nodding Society members.

Loving Louise had kept them children at heart. This was their special treat. Only a monster would withhold it.

It was time to be firm. She was mistress of the Hollow.

'Shall we look at the East Tower first?'

He hadn't got anything coherent out of Rick's father, beyond bald facts. The boy was dead and he was blaming Jordan. There had been a letter. And something about a crash, on a bike or in a car. He could not stop thinking of what he had seen through the tree telescope. The dancing stones, the figure thrown into the fire. He had wished the boy dead, as flatly as that. Rick had hurt his daughter and Steven had focused his hatred on him. He had forgotten the sort of house he lived in, hadn't imagined the Hollow might take him seriously and do something about his wish.

After everything else, he had no doubt that the Hollow could do it. Powered up by his desires, it could strike across the country, executing his wishes.

Be careful what you wish for.

He must think of Jordan. This would be dreadful for her. To be shouted at by the man – he'd been incoherent when ranting at Steven – must have been a profound shock. With this on top of her breakdown this morning and the scene under the tree, the poor girl must be wrung out.

'We can look in on the study first,' Kirsty said to the After Lights-Out Gang. 'Where Louise wrote. It's almost unchanged, except for Steven's things.'

Kirsty and the Society were like a television on in the background. He caught a few words out of context and mixed them with the rising swirl of fear overtaking his mind.

'Then, if my daughter will let us, we can peek in on Weezie's room.'

No. He mustn't let that happen.

'Best not,' he croaked, sub-audibly.

Kirsty and the After Lights-Out Gang flowed towards the East Tower. Kirsty even took Tim along, leading him solemnly by the hand. The Summer Room was empty but Steven didn't feel alone. The telephone rang again, assaulting his strained nerves. He pulled the jack out of the wall. The noise shut off but persisted in his head. No, not in his head; in the kitchen and up in their bedroom, where there were extensions. The phone in his office and the car phone were on different numbers.

A spasm of dislike for Rick's father overtook him. They'd met a few times. He seemed a better sort than his son, separated from his wife and struggling to pay for everything. He was boring about some odd hobby horse – fishing? Portugal? Real tennis? – and had a succession of short-lived, unattractive, much younger girlfriends. Just now, Steven had no sympathy to spare. He had yet to cope with his own terror and guilt and would then have to deal with Jordan's cobweb of complexes. Rick's Dad would have to get by on his own, or not at all.

The distant phones stopped ringing. He let out a breath. Then they started jangling again.

Curse the man.

No. He tried to take back the thought, but it was out of his head. He looked up at the beams, and imagined ultraviolet energy swarms passing up through the plaster ceiling into the space under the thatched roof. His casual impulses were a whirlpool of power, gathering force to strike again.

He sucked in mentally, trying to pull in every thought he'd ever let leak from his skull. He clenched his hands, ignoring screaming pain, and begged the Hollow not to kill again. He had no idea whether he had any control.

The phones stopped ringing.

His heart skipped.

He imagined the man lying dead, shut off like a phone bell, another victim.

A dreadful compulsion came to him. He should plug the phone back in and use the call-back facility. Just to make sure he was wrong, that Rick's father was still alive, that this whole thing was nothing to do with him. The precious stupid bastard had pranged himself, a drunken teenage-accident statistic. Steven's brain was not hooked up via this house to some orbiting spiritual laser weapon that could zap anyone on the face of the globe dead in their boots.

He looked at the white phone cord, lying like a thin worm on the carpet.

Clattering came from the East Tower. Kirsty was taking the tour group up to Weezie's bedroom. Jordan's room. It would be easy to sit down on the sofa and wait for the screams. It had been a truly horrible day and the evening was shading into nightmare.

He couldn't.

At a run, he left the room and dashed for the stairs.

They had to go up the stairs in single file. Mrs Bullitt found the steps a trial and needed a rest halfway. Her wide hips plumped against the rails on both sides. Kirsty was worried the woman would get stuck, like Winnie-the-Pooh. She had the idea Mrs Bullitt was extremely strong inside her bulk, but needed constant moments to recoup. The other After Lights-Out Gangers were used to such pauses. How had Mrs Bullitt made it up the hayloft ladder? The trick must have been managed without too much fuss or Kirsty would have noticed.

Jordan had darted up to her room after taking the phone call. She must be carrying out an emergency tidy-up procedure to make the place suitable for show. The After Lights-Out Gang would have to go into Weezie's room – Jordan's room – in twos and threes. It was cosy rather than spacious.

Tim still held her hand. He was a deadweight. Kirsty was tired of dragging him around. After today, he would have to grow up.

The day had been a trial, but would be over soon. These nice people would leave, then…

She would think about things.

She drew out the tour – to give Jordan time to get her underwear off the floor or whatever – by showing the view across the moor from a slit window. It was dusk, which meant it must be past eight in the evening. Where had the hours gone?

The Japanese women shot more photographs. Their cameras seemed to be fixed to their faces like cyber-attachments. They must see everything through viewfinders and only get to look at places they visited when the film was developed.

When Tim was falling from the tree, one of the sisters had taken photographs, clicking four or five times as the boy was plunging, presumably adjusting focus all the way.

These people, the lot of them, were aliens. Their lives and loves were beyond her comprehension. What was it they shared? What was it about Louise?

She rapped a knuckle on Jordan's door.

'Darling, the Society would like to see Weezie's room.'

She heard a mumble and opened the door.

The cameras clicked again and again. Her daughter, surprised halfway into a dress, screamed. Kirsty shut the door, swiftly.

She opened her mouth but couldn't get an apology out. The After Lights-Out Gang looked at her, all smiling, eager, infuriatingly bland. Wing-Godfrey hemmed and hawed like an imbecile.

Jordan's face was scarlet, not from embarrassment but because the choker collar of the child's lilac dress she was putting on was sizes too small.

No one made a move to troop downstairs. They'd come all this way to see Weezie's nook and would bloody well get to poke around inside. Or else, as Miss Hazzard said, there would be tears before bedtime. Their eyes were like the blank lenses of the sisters' cameras.

Kirsty had the door at her back. She barred their way. They were uncomfortably close to her.

The door opened and she stumbled in, taking Tim with her. Jordan shut the door again, against the After Lights-Out Gang.

Kirsty looked at her daughter.

How had she managed to get into the dress? Apart from the floppy strangling bow at her neck, the short sleeves were cinches which made her upper arms look like bloated sausages. The hem, only a few inches below her waist, barely covered the top of her knickers. The bodice shrunk onto her torso like some wet leather torture device. Fastened at the back by an interlacing set of hooks and eyes, it was strait-jacket tight, squashing her breasts flat.

Jordan passed a hand over her hair, prettying herself. She had put clownish red lipstick circles on her cheekbones. Brown freckles made with an eyebrow pencil dotted her face.

Tim was keening, almost too high-pitched to hear, terrified still.

'Do you like it?' Jordan asked.

Kirsty choked.

The landing was crowded. Steven made it up the stairs three at a time and blundered into the After Lights-Out Gang.

'Kirst,' he said.

His wife wasn't there.

'Mrs Naremore is with your daughter,' Mrs Twomey told him.

'She was not decent,' said one of the Kanaoka sisters, politely.

'We've been minutes waiting here,' said Mrs Bullitt, in one of those Brummie accents which makes every casual comment sound like a whined complaint. 'My ankles will punish me for this.'

'You've done very well so far, Head Prefect,' her husband told her. 'Gold star in your report book.'

Mrs Bullitt simpered, tiny mouth almost disappearing into her chins.

Steven shoved his way decorously through to the door. He knocked.

'Kirsty? Kirst?'

She was with Jordan. Did she know about Rick yet?

What about all these people?

He found himself doing what he had done in the hayloft, counting heads, always getting a different figure. Seven, excluding himself. So, eight.

No: seven, including himself.

A Society member had gone astray.

He put his ear to the door and heard nothing. That was probably to the good. He couldn't take another screaming fit from anyone.

He turned to the After Lights-Out Gang.

'I'm afraid I'm going to have to ask you to cut short your visit.'

There were moans of disappointment and 'Come-comes' of disbelief. No one made any motion to back off and leave the house. An explanation was needed, to make them go away. He plumbed his mind for the appropriate phrase, then hit on it.

'There's been a family emergency,' he said.

That was it. A family emergency.

Only one?

'Oh dear,' said Mrs Twomey. 'I am so sorry.'

Steven tried a reassuring smile, but took it back. If reassured, they might stay. He needed to go against his instinct to keep his business to himself, to let them know that this was beyond an emergency.

'A family catastrophe,' he elaborated.

'Can I do anything to help?' asked Harriet Hazzard, keen to show off her Guides' badge for first aid.

He shook his head.

'We just need some space. You might telephone in a –'

(week? No.)

'– month or so, to reschedule.'

(Never. He would *never* let these people back. If it meant sending Kirsty to a deprogrammer, the Louise Magellan Teazle Society – of which he was now an honorary lifetime member, he remembered – would never get back on the property. The Hollow was out of bounds.)

'Some of us have come a long way,' complained Mrs Bullitt, not needing the accent to emphasise the whine.

'I'm sorry about that,' he said.

(Not sorry, never sorry, don't use the word.)

'It can't be helped,' he settled for.

No one moved. He stood between the After Lights-Out Gang and the door, protecting his family – Tim must be inside with Kirsty and Jordan – from these afternoon-tea fanatics. His whole body was tense, even his agonised left fist, as if he expected them to charge him.

With enough momentum behind her, Mrs Bullitt could splatter him and smash the door in. The Kanaoka sisters would get it all on film, click-click-click.

'I'm afraid I have to ask you to leave.'

How often had he heard that said? In pubs and bars after drinking-up time. In films where the dissolute relation has disgraced himself in the gentleman's club and the senior member expresses ultimate disapproval. It always struck him as false. What 'I'm afraid I have to ask you to leave' meant was 'bugger off out of here'. It was always used when politeness was an absurd pretence.

He wasn't afraid, he wasn't sorry; he was delighted. Before the (family) emergency, he would have welcomed any opportunity to get shot of the lot of them. He would have wished for any excuse, idly assuming the imaginary emergency would be something that could be settled in a few minutes with enough of the evening left over for a film on telly and a late supper. Not this, not these: not Tim and Kirsty and Rick and Jordan. Not broken dolls which could never be glued back together.

'Please,' he added, a last resort.

The After Lights-Out Gang communed among itself, wordlessly. Again, he was sure they would jump him, some pinning him to the floorboards while the others forced the door open.

'Very well,' said Mrs Twomey, 'but I hope you understand what a disappointment this is. It's not the done thing to treat the Society in such cavalier fashion.'

There was a cavalier in those bloody Weezie books, wasn't there? And a roundhead.

'Not done at all,' emphasised the tiny Mr Bullitt, stern with knitted brows.

'Custodianship of the Hollow involves responsibilities,' Mrs Twomey continued. 'You'd do well to remind yourself of them constantly.'

He wanted to cry, to show shocking weakness, to frighten them out of the house. People were hurt, people were dead. That was more serious than whatever it was the After Lights-Out Gang wanted. He had to take care of his family first.

'I'm sorry,' he said again, despising the word.

Miraculously, one by one, they withdrew. Harriet and the Japanese women first, then – with a strain – the Bullitts. Finally, he was left trading fixed glares with the vice-president. Mrs Twomey saw him as a wrong 'un, unworthy of the trust he'd unwittingly taken up by moving into this place.

'Good evening,' she said, devastatingly, and left.

Alone in the passage, there was more light. The sun was almost down, but red poured in.

He tried the door again.

'It's just me,' he said. 'They've gone. We're rid of them.'

No answer.

He tried to rattle the handle. No give. It was as if handle and door and wall were cast from the same piece of iron.

Inside the room, what could he do or say to make it better? It wasn't as if he could reverse his earlier wish and bring Rick back to life. Or was it? If the Hollow could kill at his orders, couldn't it take back what it had done? It was merely another step into the impossible. There were ways it could be done.

Maybe Rick wasn't dead? He only had a voice on a line to go by. He remembered the word 'careful' scrolling across his screen. That had come from the Hollow, from the haunt. In this house were presences and faces and sounds. There could be voices too.

The Hollow might have lied to them.

That was what he must wish for. Not a 'Monkey's Paw' return as a mangled living corpse, but a false report, later retracted. The body burned beyond recognition would be someone else – a no-good who'd stolen Rick's car and trashed it. Rick would be off somewhere drunk and useless, not realising what had happened. That would explain his no-show at the Hollow, too.

He thought hard, trying to make it so.

The door handle gave and Kirsty let him in. She was white, even her lips. In bed, covers tucked up around her neck, Jordan looked like a five-year-old.

Tim sat in the rocking chair, with his catapult. When this was over, Steven would be decommissioning that little implement of death. He would brook no resistance.

'What's the matter?' he asked Kirsty, to find out what she knew rather than to learn anything. 'How's Jord?'

Kirsty shook her head, furious. 'Don't listen to her, she's full of rubbish.'

'It doesn't like us any more,' said Jordan, quietly but firmly. '*They* don't like us any more.'

'You're telling me. I've just had that Mrs Twomey shooting death rays out of her eyes at me. We're not having them back in a hurry, I can tell you.'

'Not them,' said his daughter, disgusted with him. '*Them*. Those who were here before us.'

'The ghosts,' said Tim.

'Them. It. The ghosts. The Hollow. They were all right before we came, but we drove them mad. No surprise, really. We've been driving each other mad all along.'

Steven looked at Jordan, understanding but wishing he didn't. It was his fault. He had done a terrible thing, made a terrible thing happen. He'd got his wish and found no joy in it. Now, the family were paying for what they had got, paying with pain and fear and worse.

They weren't charmed any more. They were haunted.

The family spent the night together, in Weezie's room (it could not be said to be Jordan's any longer). Kirsty and Jordan lay cramped on the bed; Tim curled up in the rocking chair, eyes fixed on the black beyond the uncurtained window; Steven huddled by the door, duvet tented around his shoulders. They warded off sleep for as long as possible, but each in turn succumbed to exhaustion, numbness and the dark.

They all dreamed. They were in the house, at the Hollow, looking for the little girl, who was always in the next room, on the next landing, just outside the door, just beyond the window. She led them a solemn chase, leaving doors to swing slowly closed and curtains to shift like ivy in the wind.

Each, in their dream, was alone, terrified.

From the
JOURNAL
of a
VICTORIAN
GENTLEWOMAN

8 February

The Reverend Mr Bannerman is blind. He does not – *cannot* – understand the Hollow. No one who has not spent night after night after night under its roof can hope to fathom this place. The Mama understands, only too well. But not half so well as I.

13 February

I barely remember Father, yet I am certain the portrait which hangs in the Summer Room, painted from his death mask, is not a good likeness. I have read every word he ever set down, but still he is a stranger. The Mama has devoted her life – *and mine!* – to his sacred memory, but she despises him. His first great sin was dying so carelessly. His second, more unforgivable lapse was not to *manifest* thereafter. The parade of mediums and sensitives and psychics and charlatans who have passed through the Hollow bear witness to the Mama's desperate need that Father linger here as a ghost. These people, without fail, commence by stating that they sense his presence, that they are sure they can coax him out of his shadows of concealment with their especial – *expensive* – services. Then, after a period of various mumbo-jumbo, they take fright. Even arrant frauds swiftly realise that the Hollow is capable of trumping their manufactured illusions. Some flee in panic, some swear to quit their professions, a few even return monies given over to them. Father is not here, not any more, but others are… earthbound spirits and goblins damned!

20 February

The Mama is a worse monster than the others. She is petitioning Bannerman to perform a rite of exorcism. She wishes to be alone in the Hollow, with Father. I am never mentioned. She half-believes an exorcism will cast me out too, I think. She cannot tell the difference between her own living daughter and Apple Annie. That song, heard all too often hereabouts, has stuck in her mind. None of the ghosts we have seen or heard – ghosts are not all people, some are things or sensations or transformations – resembles in the least the wailing girl of the song, but the Mama has taken it into her head that Father has deserted her for this chit of a spirit and dallies with her in the orchard. She has fixed upon the tallest of the trees as their amorous nest and loiters by it, tutting and fretting. If Bannerman doesn't allow bell, book and candle, she will have sawmen in and bring down the tree. The prospect horrifies and saddens me, though I know her beliefs about the tree are baseless. It is a living thing and spirits do cling to it. Apple Annie is a creature from a song and Father is gone. The Mama cannot accept this. Bannerman, no less than her charlatans, is not helping her, or me.

28 March

Bannerman will not come back. The Hollow took against him as soon as he started to believe in it. I have seen it do that before, to the worst of the sensitives. The wonderment of levitating crockery passes rapidly when a heavy tureen smashes against a man's face. The Hollow can mark those it deems enemies. It can kill. It killed Father, I am sure. Then it cast him out. I wish it would kill again. Truly, I do.

2 April

The Mama is worse in spring, as apple blossom thickens the air. She wavers between decreeing an execution order for the tall tree and having the whole orchard destroyed. The 'school' attracts fewer and fewer pupils as the fad for Father's works passes from the public memory. Our only real income is from the apples. 'Apple Annie's, they call them. It is believed that the fruit has bewitching properties. Girls who set their caps at lads make them gifts of Apple Annie's. It falls to me every year to arrange the picking and sale of the fruit. The Mama sometimes takes to calling me 'the farm girl'. I have caught her out several times in her claim that 'her Primrose' died soon after Father, and that I am a jumped-up pupil who has become a servant. When the mood takes her, she threatens me with dismissal, accuses me of stealing items (in truth, I have had to resort to the pawnshop in Taunton to pay for household necessities) and upbraids me for my many mismanagements. Her Primrose would never be so ungrateful, she shrieks. She carries with her a riding-crop, though she has not set herself on a horse these past twenty-five years. She lashes out, inflicting what she calls her 'sting'. My hands, as I write, are striped with repeated stings. Some who I employed last year to bring in the apples will not return because of her habit of doling out instant punishments for 'liberties'.

24 April

I dread death, not as most do. I have no terror of the great unknown. For I know only too well what is to come. Bannerman's heaven and hell are comforting lies, just as Apple Annie's enchanted orchard or the Spiritualists' 'other side' are fairy tales. What comes after is eternal torment, here on earth. When the Mama sits at her place at the end of the long table, I see the rows of shades in all the empty places along either side. As she is in this life, so are they in the life to come. Cold, dark, damp, alone, spiteful. Each carries their own miasmic hell, like a shroud or one of Mr Dickens's chains. A Christmas Carol is a lie. People, like ghosts, cannot change. All are trapped, as in aspic or amber. I have stripes on my back and shoulders. This last week, since her stroke, the Mama's right arm is frozen. Her fingers cannot hold her sting, but still the lash falls on me when she is near and angry. It is as if her arm is dead but its ghost extends from her shoulder, invisible but supple and with a sting – a flint-studded length of ghost leather

– as an extension of the phantom fist. The pain will last, will extend into the twilight beyond death. The Mama will be there first, awaiting me. I should leave this place, but have known nowhere else. Sometimes, I find it impossible to step over the boundary of the Hollow. The world outside is haunted and tormented too. At least here, I...

3 May

The orchard has blossom and apple-buds. Soon, fruit will swell. I can hardly walk for the whipping I have taken. Since the Mama has had to use a stick, the lashes have always been at my legs. It is as if I were being stroked with stinging nettles. I have angry red blotches. Tonight, we had the full company at dinner. The Mama talks to them, lectures on Father's greatness, with outrageous outbursts of abuse at him, myself and the assembly. It seems the seated figures grow less shadowy. I can make out faces, all as twisted and shut as the Mama's. They nod at her whim, humouring her. They have stings, too. Mother does not want to join them before me. I fear for my life.

31 July

The tree is to come down. In a week's time. The anticipated victory has given the Mama strength. She has left her bed and hobbles about, lashing with her tongue and sting. She quibbled with Adam Cobb on the price, but finally settled the matter. We cannot afford the loss of the tree, can barely afford the price of its murder. It is no use talking with the Mama. I cannot sleep. Fingers like twigs rake at me. I fear for the Hollow. Without the tree, it will change again.

2 August

I have done it! I have talked with Adam Cobb and told him the Mama has changed her mind. He would have argued, but – though it pains me to let the matter go – I allowed him to keep the portion of the fee he was gifted. I, Primrose, am true mistress of the Hollow. My decision is that the tree should remain. Returning from the village, with angry sky boiling overhead and the heat crackling, I felt straighter than in months. The stings do not bother me. They seem to change quality, almost to become caresses. Almost. In the evening, the first drops of rain spattered against the windows, pellets the size of thumbs. Penny-sized dark splashes marked the bleached stones of the orchard paths. A summer storm, long predicted, is upon us. Thatch lets in trickles of water. The house fills with a damp straw smell that is a ghost in itself, a presence which only makes itself known in heavy rain.

Later

The Hollow has cheated me! As the storm smote the countryside, I sat at table and informed the Mama of my decision about the tree. I was prepared for anger on a level of the storm, but knew she was too feeble to lash in a way that would hurt. I am mistress here, not her. But the Mama smiled, cunningly, and said I had not the power to overrule her. She laughed, cruelly. At that moment, an arc of lightning lanced down and struck at the base of the very tree I had sought to protect. In a white moment, I saw everything. Flames, instantly extinguished by the torrent. The earth that bound the tree's roots seemed blasted out of existence. For a heart-smiting moment, I was afraid the tree would fall towards the house, smashing through the wall and the windows, an apple-pimpled fist coming down on us. But no, it fell outwards, away from the house. It took a long time, I think. Other lightning strikes seared my eyes with lingering images of the great living thing tottering, branches shaking and snapping, fruit raining and rolling. I dare not go out to see what damage the felled titan has caused. The Mama laughs still, not alone.

3 August

The tree has smashed a copse of smaller trees, at the edge of the property. Adam Cobb's labourers are at work, hauling away the ruins, costing money I cannot spare. Girls pick up the shiny, wet apples. Each must be accounted for and sold. If so much as one is eaten, it shall come out of their wages. I must be strict, for we are desperate and only I can cope. The miracle is that the tall tree still lives. It is on its side, but enough of its roots are in the earth for it to survive. Adam says it will adjust to its new position and continue to fruit for a hundred years or more. The Mama called down the lightning, but has not won. She is talking with Adam now, insisting he bring axes and saws. She will not be stopped. I write in the Summer Room, surrounded by ghosts who dare not venture out into the sunshine. Everything is clean and dripping. Insects buzz and swarm. Insects have stings, too. Some of the insects are not living things. Generation upon generation has lived and died here. They all remain. The Mama has just clapped her hand to the back of her neck.

7 August

It is over. The Mama is not here. I was afraid she would linger. The others remain, silent, at attention. I am uneasy around them. They have grown used to the habit of cruelty. It is hard to break.

10 August

She tried to kill the tree; I did kill her. That is how I see it. Everyone knows. I should hang for it, but I will not. She was old, bodies grow weak, wasps sting, people must die. We must wish what we must and cannot be held accountable for it. If Bannerman's God answers a parishioner's prayer, He, not the supplicant, is given the credit; therefore, I cannot be blamed. And yet, a voice of doubt.

13 August

The ghosts are hooded, like wigged judges or hangmen. A black rope of slimy stuff hangs from the chandelier in the Summer Room. A verdict has been passed, which I must agree with. It will come soon.

14 August

The fallen tree, which thrives, is a bridge over the rhyne. That part is dead, and will be cut away soon. But now it is a way out of the Hollow. Tonight, I will escape justice, crawl across the tree bridge. This will stay behind, with the ghosts. The Mama is murdered, and I can be free. I shall be stung no more.

Towards Autumn

Dawn came, August early, to the Hollow, creeping across the moors like a poacher. Long black shadows dwindled, going underground for the day. No birdsong, no wind. A summer Sunday: no commuter's car growled on the road, no insect moved on the glassy rhynes. Fruit lay where it had fallen. The topmost leaves had gone from green to red overnight.

The family awoke in the East Tower, wrung out by dreams and unrefreshed by sleep, nagged by aches and pains and memories.

They were all alone, together.

Loose pages, covered with faded ink, lay at the foot of the bed. They got underfoot.

Jordan drifted through the hours. Voices were faint and buzzing. Making out the words wasn't worth the trouble. Her only sensations, heartache and the bloat of her belly and limbs, were inside. Her skin was nerveless – thick, unfeeling cloth. She saw in sharp focus, as if through Weezie's stereoscope. Figures were flattened and dark-rimmed, separate and distinct, each on their own plane. A sourceless ozone tang persisted high in her nose, like the beginning of a sneeze, clean but shocking. She felt like a condemned murderess in the electric chair, living an eternity in the split second between the switch being thrown and the juice hitting her spine.

Someone was dead. A long time ago, she thought. She was guilty, though not too sure of the details. Perhaps she had been murdered herself and was now a ghost.

No. *They* were the ghosts.

She was pestered by apparitions. A stern, old-fashioned couple and their silent, big-eyed child.

And others.

A terrible hunger clawed inside. She must not eat, for she was full to bursting, but she wasn't satisfied. She thought of stripping paint off her furniture and eating that.

How had she come to this house?

What had gone before?

If she concentrated so much that it hurt, she knew. Her name was Jordan Naremore; her Mum and Dad were Kirsty and Steven; her brother was Tim, the pest. Her boyfriend was Rick. No, Rick was out of the picture.

The first jolt hit her, through the eyes.

Rick was dead. It was Rick who was dead. His dad had told her, just as everything was slipping away, just as the ghosts were taking over the house.

She remembered the ghosts. A brown man. Twin

oriental imps. A crooked girl. A giantess and her dwarf. A woman-man. They wanted to haunt this house. They had tried to drive Jordan and her family from their home. But the ghosts were gone, and she was still here.

Had she won or lost?

She could not tell. It hurt to remember, made her eyes like hot coals in her skull. She held the family picture in her mind, like the dozen tiny pieces in the right depressions in the hand-held Drearcliff Grange game. Eyes in sockets and smiles on mouths. Then, she let the game drop and the picture fell to pieces, features falling from faces to leave only blank dimples.

She let herself be carried along, through the day.

Later, while rearranging the mess in her room, she found the pages. They were old, but the handwriting was legible, almost like a child's. She read what was written, not following the fragmentary story or understanding the provenance of the pages. They seemed to be torn from a book. Ruled blue lines had faded away almost completely while the inked words stood out all the more. Was what she read a message, an inside-out retelling of the story of her recent life?

As if scouting enemy territory, Steven searched the Hollow, going over the route he had guided the After Lights-Out Gang through yesterday. Tim stuck close by, not speaking, catapult in hand. Kirsty had decreed Tim could keep the weapon only if he didn't carry ammunition.

His son had learned the truth about this place

before him. The boy had been playing soldiers so long no one noticed when it stopped being a game and became a survival strategy.

He checked every room, not knowing why, and saw nothing. By day, the house was on its best behaviour. Broken glass glittered in the Summer Room. Tim, terrified of a punishment Steven hadn't yet decided, wouldn't go near the scatter of shards. Kirsty should sweep that up, before someone got hurt.

In the orchard, the tree still stood, broken branch dangling like a hanged man. Kirsty wanted the tree cut down, but Steven wasn't sure that was possible. He was wary of attacking anything around here. It might well attack back.

He put the barn-garage off till last.

Inside, was a surprise. They had inherited a car. Next to the hunchback was a brown Volkswagen Beetle, patched with rust. Through the windscreen, Steven saw an Ordnance Survey map spread out on the passenger seat. In the back was a dead little girl.

Tim screamed and pulled back his catapult. Without a stone, the worst he could do was twang someone with the rubber.

The girl wasn't a corpse but a large doll, dressed in a pinafore and a straw hat. A Weezie doll, with a wide painted smile. The stubby lashes of the round eyes looked like the sun's rays in a kindergarten picture. The hair was a bunch of blonde ropes, like dreads.

Steven wanted to burn the thing.

For the first time today, the telephone rang in the house. The bell above the kitchen door clanged like a fire alarm.

He knew it would be bad news. It always was.

In the Summer Room, Kirsty looked at the telephone. Louise's old – antique, now – black rotary dial phone was on the stand. Its woven, threaded cord snaked to the wall-jack. Steven had unplugged their push-button cordless phone yesterday, but she didn't remember him fixing up the old apparatus. Its ring was piercing as a toothache. The receiver jiggled in its cradle with each jangle.

Other things she'd done to the room were unpicked. The dangerous three-bar heater was back in the fireplace, where she'd cleared a space to burn wood come winter. Pictures she had replaced had returned. Even a hideous scowling Victorian that Louise must have relegated to a junk-room. A dusty old television cabinet replaced their home-entertainment stack.

The telephone didn't stop ringing.

She dreaded picking it up. Yesterday, Jordan and then Steven had taken calls which shattered them the way Tim's stone shattered the pane above the French windows. Jewels of glass still lay on the floor. Looking up, she couldn't find the missing piece in the puzzle. Where was the gap where the pane had been?

It was Sunday. She shouldn't have to answer.

Spectres appeared at the French windows. Steven and Tim.

Her husband looked at her and at the telephone, understanding. She almost wished Tim would pick up and put the caller off. Then, her son made a motion towards the phone-stand. Steven grabbed his shoulders to stop him.

Kirsty scooped up the receiver to save her son.

Noise reached her ear. Submarines pinging under arctic ice and satellites beeping in deep space. Having stepped off a precipice, she was suspended for a long moment, waiting for gravity to reach up and tug her downwards.

'Mrs Naremore, it's Harriet. We met yesterday. Miss Hazzard.' She remembered. The carer. 'Sorry to trouble you on a Sunday, especially with your, um, you know, *troubles*... but it's a bit, well, awkward, odd. The other Society members thought I should phone, because of what happened before, to Bernard. In the Middle East.'

'He was a hostage,' she remembered out loud.

'Yes. He doesn't like to talk about it, but we all know. He was chained, in the dark. He acts all the time as if he's over it, as if the past doesn't bother him but, well, it *does*, doesn't it? It could hardly not.'

Steven craned to hear what she was being told. He had something to say.

'We were all in the minibus, except Bernard. We were halfway home before we realised he wasn't ahead of or behind us. Eleanor thought we'd just lost him on the road.'

Which one was Eleanor?

'His sister says he hasn't come home. We were wondering if he'd broken down and made his way back to you? Or got in touch in any way?'

Kirsty didn't know what to say to the girl.

'Bernard Wing-Godfrey is missing,' she told Steven.

'I think his car's in our barn,' he said.

She opened her mouth to pass this on, but he shook his head. She wasn't to tell an outsider. Not yet.

'Leave your number, Harriet. We'll call if we have news.'

The girl gushed a little relief and recited a number twice. Kirsty didn't have a pen or paper to hand, but repeated the number back as if she were writing it down.

'Good luck, take care,' Harriet said, ringing off.

Kirsty listened to the buzzing phone for a moment, then set it down.

Jordan was in the room, having appeared silently, barefoot. Her hair was over her face like a pair of drawn curtains. A long black T-shirt hung on her like rags on a scarecrow, bottom hem just above her knees.

'I found these,' she said, holding out some pieces of paper.

Kirsty couldn't be bothered with her daughter's scrawling. Probably another of her letters.

'I think they're for us,' Jordan said.

Kirsty took the papers and put them down on the table.

'There's a Volkswagen in the barn,' Steven said, elaborating.

'And a little girl,' said Tim, afraid.

'A doll, in the back seat,' Steven explained.

'No, a little girl,' Tim insisted. 'A *dark* little girl.'

'A golliwog?' Kirsty asked, incredulous.

'Regular blonde. What's her name? Weezie.'

Steven knew perfectly well what the girl in Louise Teazle's books was called. He just didn't want to admit it out loud. To him, it was embarrassing. Girly.

'The car's brown,' he said. 'It must be his.'

'He left, surely. With the others.'

'I don't know, Kirst. I wasn't keeping track. What with everything else.'

She understood. 'He's still here.'

'Not on the property,' he snapped. 'He can't be. I've just searched the place, with Tim.'

'Why? You didn't know he was missing until now.'

'I wasn't searching for him. I was…'

'What?'

'Patrolling, checking, making sure we were alone.'

'We know we're not alone, Steven.'

He shook his head. 'I know what it was like last night, after dark. I know what it's been like. But I'm not buying any more. It's just not part of the world I understand.'

'This is where Daddy says "there must be some rational explanation",' sneered Jordan.

Like lightning, Steven slapped their daughter.

'Enough,' he said.

The slap echoed. Jordan's cheek was red, strands of hair plastered to it. Her eyes were large with tears and her underlip wobbled.

They never smacked their kids. It wasn't policy, but they had a horror of that kind of punishment. Steven had been caned at school, for minor offences. He still got angry when the subject came up, fantasising about tracking his now-enfeebled headmaster down and paying him back with extra lumps for interest. When the troubles were at their worst, they had hit each other

(twice, shockingly, an unbidden memory, the unforgivable set aside) but they never took it out on Jordan or Tim.

Christ, if Jordan deserved a slap around the face for a snide comment, what punishment did Tim want for nearly blinding a guest?

'There are no ghosts at the Hollow,' said Steven. 'There's only us.'

'Isn't that bad enough?' Jordan asked.

Everything was back on an even keel. Steven had it all stacked up, stowed away and tethered down. The facts were at his fingertips, the figures added up with nothing left over.

It had just been a game.

They had enjoyed pretending that the Hollow was a haunted house. Oooo-ooo-oooh, *spoooky*. But the game had gone too far, stopped being funny, stopped being fun.

It was time to get serious.

'I need some support around here,' he said. 'It's been sorely lacking. You're all grown up enough to pull your weight. We have problems. We have to be man enough to accept that, to look beyond that. Only by pulling together and taking direction will we get through this.'

They looked at him as if he were mad. Mouths frozen open and eyes goggle-round, like baby seals waiting for the club.

'Steven,' said Kirsty, 'you're an idiot.'

Her nose looked like a target. His right hand knotted into a fist.

One punch and it would all be over.

He could *feel* the give of cartilage under his knuckles, see the scarlet blood-spurt. One sharp, swift jab and he'd be undisputed master of the tribe.

He raised his hand, letting her know, giving her a chance to back down, to yield. He didn't want to hit her, but it was his duty.

Even now, she could avoid this.

The bitch-cow. The stupid bitch-cow.

Kirsty stood up to him, idiotically defiant. Why couldn't she see? Was it so hard?

It wasn't the Hollow. It had been like this before. Maybe worse, with the Wild Witch bobbing about behind the scenes feeding his wife demented ideas, with all the hells of the city shifting under their feet. The point was not to let that happen again.

He would do anything.

'Steven,' she said, like his mother, like a teacher. 'Think.'

That was it.

He let fly, putting his whole body into it. This was going to connect hard and lift Kirsty off her feet, flattening her snub nose into her face.

A body slammed into his side, knocking him off balance. His fist passed Kirsty's head harmlessly. Knees and fingers and feet and teeth sank into his side and arm and neck. He fell badly, drawing his legs up to protect his groin and belly. His already-sprained hip thumped against hard flagstone. Blows came at him.

He glimpsed his daughter, hair flying, as she tried to kill him.

* * *

S he kicked the monster, stubbing bare toes against the staves of his ribs. She shifted balance and stamped, bringing her calloused heel down on his chest.

No one tried to stop her.

He flattened out, letting his knees and elbows unkink. She squatted on his chest, T-shirt riding up around her waist, and sliced at his face with her fingers, hooking into his cheeks with nails, working towards his eyes.

She spat at him, each hawk racking her whole body.

She focused everything she felt, at him.

It was Judy's turn to cry! She recited under her breath, emphasising each word with a slash. Judy's turn. To cry, cry, cry…

When she was finished, so would he be.

B lood on the floor, on the carpets. Kirsty worried the stain would never come out of the old weave, then squirted out a giggle at the thought.

Jordan rode Steven like a horsewoman and pounded on his face like a drummer. Her hair whipped like wet rope. Her eyes were huge with anger.

Kirsty didn't know what to do.

This hadn't been covered in the meeting. This wasn't on the agenda. This wasn't in the user's manual.

Jordan wasn't alone. Shadows danced with her, winding around her arms and torso. She was a priestess and an executioner.

Steven might die.

Steven *should* die.

Finally, Kirsty admitted it to herself. The best thing

would be to wipe the slate. Get rid of this family and start a new one. There was no hope. She had been pretending since for ever that it could be pulled together, but it couldn't. If it came to this, she would stand back and let it happen.

Jordan would be taken away.

That just left...

Tim.

(The top drawer. He would fit into the top drawer.)

The boy was on the other side of the room, also watching. He shouldn't see something like this.

She wanted to go to him.

Instead, Tim came forward and slipped the loop of his catapult over his sister's head. He pulled back. The rubber went tight across Jordan's throat. She was bent back. Her hands lifted from Steven's face. She turned, *growling*...

It was only his sister. Jordan. Not the IP, not the hostiles. It had probably been her all along.

Now, she was distracted from Dad.

He twisted the U-Dub in his hands, noosing the rubber. He had the reins on her, but she was bigger than him, stronger than him, and mad.

Jordan stood, the rubber rope stretching between them. Tim had to keep hold of the U-Dub.

'What did I ever do to you, Timbo?' she asked.

'It's not me,' he said. 'It's us.'

Jordan had friends among the hostiles. They were with her. As she towered over him, they pressed behind her shoulders, peering over and down. The Smile was among them, and the Ipkick, and the Brown Man.

She took hold of the twisted strand of rubber and yanked. He held fast.

Dad rolled out of the way. He was hurt.

'Children,' said Mum, bored. 'Don't fight.'

That wasn't going to help. Mum had long ago resigned any authority. The last battle would be between Tim and Jordan.

And Jordan would win.

She was closest to this place, to the Hollow. He had tried, but she'd found the way.

She tugged. The sweat-greased handle of the U-Dub slid out of his fist. The wooden Y-fork hung around her neck like a pendant. It revolved as the rubber string unwound.

Jordan wiped her hair away from her face. Her head looked like a skull in a wig, with rolling marbles for eyes.

Then she was just his big sister.

Tim wanted to cry. He wanted this game to stop now.

This wasn't the way. Jordan's throat was almost closed and her eyes hurt. She wasn't angry. She didn't feel better. Nothing had changed.

Except Tim.

Dad was a monster and had to be stopped. But Tim was a kid. Nothing was really his fault. He was just susceptible to outside influence.

Tim was blinking, mouth going in and out, bubble forming in one nostril. He wasn't a soldier any more.

She remembered the shrews.

What had that been about?

No matter how she turned, the knots got tighter. She couldn't trust her parents or her brother not to hurt each other or themselves.

Could she trust herself?

Dad had hit her. She still felt the clap against her jaw, shaking her whole head.

And she had lost her temper.

Attacking Dad to save Mum, she'd not been herself. She had shown the Drearcliff Grange spirit, sticking up for the bullied.

The worst thing was that she was losing herself.

Who was she? Jordan. Really?

As the room grew dark, she was afraid. Now she had to be strong for everyone.

She knelt in front of Tim and tried to form a smile, tried to project reassurance.

'You're scaring me,' he said.

'What time is it?' Steven asked.

It hurt to talk around his broken tooth from yesterday and loose tooth from just now. He had other pains, though he didn't think Jordan had broken any bones. Just covered him in bruises.

Kirsty looked at the inside of her wrist, frowned, then shook her watch.

'It's dead,' she said. 'It can't be later than three. We've lost lunchtime.'

That frightened him. He was hoping he'd blacked out for hours. That would explain what was troubling him.

'Why is it dark outside?'

Kirsty looked through the picture windows. The orchard was dusklit, greens and reds turned to greys. The sky was slate.

'Summer storm,' Kirsty said. 'It'll bucket down soon. It hasn't really rained since we've been here.'

He didn't think she was right. It was nightfall.

That didn't mean it wouldn't bucket down, though. He thought it would, and more than rain.

He was on the chaise longue, sticking plasters over the cuts on his face. He wanted to scratch them away, but kept his hands down.

Jordan's fury was burned out for the moment.

He didn't know what to do about her. Or to her. He had struck first and she'd fought back, subscribing to the theory of massive retaliation.

She stood by the French windows, gazing out at the gathering dark as if it were calling to her.

Tim flicked the light switches by the door. The three bulbs strung from the beams came on, fizzed and popped. Tim flicked the switches off. Fragments floated down. Smoke curled around the beams, pooling on the ceiling.

The overhead lights were a Naremore addition, to replace Louise's dreary standing lamps. Those were back, exactly where they'd been before he shifted them into a junk room. Steven nodded to one and Tim went to it. He reached up, on tiptoes, found the pull-cord and, nervously, gave a tug.

The lamp came on and didn't pop.

There were three other lamps. Tim went round to each, turning them on. This made for a brightly lit area, but a cavern of dark above. Looking up, Steven no longer saw the beams. Louise's useless chandelier hovered like an ornate flying saucer. The Summer Room felt like a primitive campsite, mammoths and sabre-tooths prowling beyond the circle cast by the fire.

The picture windows became a dark mirror, reflecting the room back at them. The trees beyond were the merest ghost-shapes, standing among furniture and people.

In the window-mirror, they weren't alone. Some reflections were familiar. Others weren't.

He tried to count heads, but couldn't.

Bernard Wing-Godfrey was in the crowd. When Steven looked at the window, the brown man was there, somewhere in the room, but when he tried to find him this side of the looking glass, Wing-Godfrey was gone.

Steven forced himself to ignore the window-mirror, drawing mental curtains. He concentrated on the room.

Louise's antique telly was back. His equipment was piled up by the fireplace, like wood. The VCR was plugged in, but its timer flashed 88s. The heavy clock on the mantel, which they had left where it was, had no hands.

Tim was the one he could count on.

'Go round the house, check all the clocks, everything with a timer. The central heating box, the fax machines, uh, the microwave. Find out what time it is.'

Kirsty put a hand on Tim's shoulder.

'Not alone,' she said. 'He doesn't go alone. Steven, I mean it.'

'I don't think we can be alone here.'

'Yes. That's why one of us goes with him.'

The problem was Jordan. She might go off at the slightest provocation. Obviously, she couldn't be trusted with Tim. But if Steven or Kirsty went – and he wasn't sure he could get up some of the stairs in his state – then the other would be left with their daughter.

They couldn't *all* go.

Maybe it didn't matter. Whatever the clocks said, it was nightfall at the Hollow.

'The television, Tim,' said Mum. 'Turn it on and go to Ceefax for the time.'

Tim nodded and went to their big-screen TV, which was shoved back by the fireplace. He reached for the on-switch. He'd need the handset to look up Ceefax, but it was in its holster by the screen.

'No,' shouted Dad. 'What if it goes off like the lights?'

Tim hesitated. He could still hear the popping of the light-bulbs. Inside the television set was a kind of a big bulb. It could explode with killing force, projecting glass shrapnel.

'The Hollow isn't comfortable with anything new,' said Dad. 'It likes Louise's things.'

'I don't think that's true,' said Mum. 'It's not the house. It's you. All of you. You've turned against it and it's wary of you.'

'Try her telly, Tim,' said Jordan, sounding normal. She meant the strange contraption that had reappeared in its old place. It was the size of an oven, wooden, with a small convex screen, rounded at the corners.

Tim stood in front of the box, which was taller than him. When they first moved in, he'd switched the TV on experimentally. Mum and Dad had laughed when he jiggled knobs trying to make the colour come on.

Once upon a time, before the War, television was black and white.

He turned a dial rather than pushed a switch, and stood back.

It took long moments for the TV to come on, 'to warm up', Mum had said.

A blurry, harsh black-and-white vision formed.

Two strange puppets bobbed around a giant plant with a face. Was this television a Punch and Judy show, with a midget concealed inside, working the strings?

'Bill and Ben,' Dad said.

'...the flower-pot men,' Mum finished.

Tim found the two puppets frightening. Men made out of flower-pots, with girlish faces. He switched the channels and found a still picture of circles and squares in a pattern, then wrestling, then nothing, nothing, nothing, nothing.

He turned to his parents, dismayed.

'Where are the other channels?' he asked.

Mum and Dad wanted to laugh again, but couldn't.

He kept clicking. No Ceefax. Nothing with a clock.

'What time is it?' he asked, babyish tears in his eyes.

'"Time to go home, time to go home",' Mum crooned, horribly.

'"Time for bed, said Zebedee",' said Dad.

This was something adult, hidden from him. It

frightened and annoyed him. Whenever Mum and Dad tried to act like kids, they were creepily *wrong*, like the flower-pot men.

White static washed across the screen. Tim stepped away from the old TV.

He was afraid of what it would show him in black and white.

Mum and Dad had lost it. And Tim. Jordan had to be on her guard every moment, in case they struck at her. She'd been forced to fight back, much as she hated it.

It was night-time again.

Dad was right: it had come too early. But the Hollow wasn't the rest of the world. It had its own time, its own climate, its own rules.

She hated the family's rules but at least she knew them. Here, she didn't know from moment to moment who her friends were, what everyone was playing at.

She had only herself.

(Was that enough? Wasn't she weak, fat, useless? In the end, wouldn't she let herself and everyone down?)

She couldn't see the orchard through the windows. They could have been painted black.

Her own face, flabby and unappealing, gawked back at her. Spots were showing up, around her mouth and on her forehead. No wonder she'd been dumped. No wonder no one cared about her.

As she looked, her face flowered, bloated.

She touched her cheeks, not feeling the weeping blemishes, then put her fingers on the cold glass of her reflection. She turned away, putting the image behind her.

The telly was tuned to nothing. Snow.

Mum tried the phone. Jordan heard static across the room. Mum jiggled the cradle, the way people did in films after losing a connection or when the wires were cut. Did that ever work? Mum listened for a minute, failing to get a dial tone, and put the telephone down, sadly.

'I guess the modem and the mobiles are out, too,' Dad said, angry.

'Or they're dangerous,' put in Mum. 'Damn things.'

It wasn't fair. Their things blew up, but Louise's didn't work.

The telephone rang, once. Then, again. It kept ringing, each pause between bell-jangles long enough to make her think (hope) the caller had given up.

Who could it be? Someone phoning from a long, long way away.

'You better answer it,' said Dad, relying on his invalid act to keep him on the couch and out of danger. Mum looked horrified.

Again, plucky little Tim stepped in.

'The Hollow,' he said.

A serious, miniature-adult frown creased his face as he listened to the insect buzz on the other end. He nodded, not saying anything, then held out the receiver.

'Jordan,' he said. 'It's for you.'

Her skin chilled, sweat turned to frost.

Tiny breathing sounds came from the receiver.

Slowly, as if wading through mud, she walked across the room. Lightbulb splinters stuck to her bare feet, pricking not stabbing. The distance between her and Tim narrowed but lengthened.

Tim's outstretched arm extended, unnaturally.

A thousand miles of carpet and flagstone passed under her. She tuned out the television and whatever Mum and Dad were saying. As if in a space-suit, she heard only her own breath and tiny sounds from the telephone. Impatient tutting and tapping.

She took the phone and put it to her head, hooking her hair out of the way, turning her back on her family, the cord winding around her.

'It's Jordan,' she said.

'Kiss kiss kiss,' hissed the phone.

Ice bullets exploded. She dropped the receiver. It plunged slowly, then broke on the stone floor. Bakelite fragments and cardboard and metal discs.

It had been Rick.

The mood of the Hollow was changing. The exploding lightbulbs, the telephone call that had shocked her daughter. Until now, it had all been a magic show, put on to delight and amaze, perhaps even awe and terrify. But the bulbs could have hurt someone – Jordan's dirty bare feet had splinters in them – and the call was worse. Curled on the sofa, Jordan hugged her knees, hair over her face, shuddering uncontrollably.

'You're in danger now,' said Kirsty.

Steven looked at her as if she'd said something stupid.

'Before, you weren't, not really. It was exciting,

wasn't it? Intriguing. As if you were all feeling it out, the Hollow. Now, it's darting at you, like a snake, or like a cat with a mouse.'

Her husband looked around the darkened Summer Room.

'What do you mean, "you"?' Steven asked.

Kirsty didn't need to explain. The Old Girl was still on her side.

'Come out, you chickens,' Steven shouted.

There was no reply.

'Don't, Steven,' she said. 'Don't annoy them any more.'

'Them?'

'Them. It. The ghosts. The Hollow.'

He looked at her, paying attention. Was she getting through?

'This place is not alive, Kirst. We're not the only people here.'

No. He didn't understand.

'They want us out of here. Well, we shan't be shifted. This is my house, my home, and I will not be intimidated in it.'

Had she ever known what Steven was thinking? Really?

'Come on out,' he shouted. 'It's all over. We know your game.'

Jordan peeped up through her hair, eyes rimmed with red.

'It's them, Kirst,' Steven said. 'The After Lights-Out Gang. You know what gave them away? The name. The bloody stupid Weezie Louisey name. After Lights-Out. That's when they go to work and that's exactly what they've done. They've put the lights out. Now, Bernard Wing-Godfrey is up there somewhere, in the eaves and attics. He knows this house better than we do. They've all studied the place, in the books and probably in the floor-plans. I don't know if it's just Wing-Godfrey, but he's certainly here somewhere. I'll bet a couple of the others are lying in wait. They'll have white sheets on with eyeholes cut out, and chains to clank, probably dogs with luminous paint-masks.'

Kirsty was appalled at the way her husband's mind worked. It would do no good to ask how the After Lights-Out Gang had managed to make the sun set at three in the afternoon. He would have an explanation. The lights were rigged to explode, the phones were tricked up with high-tech gear, and the sun was on a dimmer-switch.

'They want our house, Kirst,' he continued. 'Always have. They want to turn it into a shrine. We must have got in before they could put their bid together. Now, they think they can run us off the property and pick it up for a song. They've made a huge mistake, Kirsty. Oh yes they have. This might have worked on someone else, on someone superstitious, on someone stupid. But it can't touch me, it can't touch us.'

'The bulbs exploded, Steven,' she said.

'And your point is?'

Dad was convinced. His cracked explanation solved everything, which meant he didn't have to be afraid any more.

'It doesn't matter who's doing this, Dad,' said

Jordan. 'Or how it's being done. It doesn't matter how you're haunted, whether it's by ghosts or men in sheets. Mum is right. The bulbs exploded. That could have hurt us. Before then, it was all us. Tim broke the window. You hit me. I, ah, hit you. We were only hurting ourselves. All the ghosts ever did was pick up on the way we were, prod us into being more extreme. The worst they could do was haunt us, frighten us. That's all over. This isn't about frightening us any more. This is about hurting us, harming us.'

'Killing,' said Kirsty.

The word was there. In the room, between them. Tim was at attention, fidgeting now he no longer had his catapult.

'Yes,' Jordan said. 'That. Killing us.'

She looked around the room. What else was tricked up, ready to explode or attack? The light was different from the old lamps, soft and amber, with deeper shadows. Colours were faded pastel, like an illustration in a Drearcliff Grange book. The ceiling was a canopy of dinge. Anything could be up there, beyond the light, looking down on them.

Dad took her by her shoulders and forced her onto the sofa, next to Mum. She didn't resist, allowed him to sit her down.

'Stay here,' he said, 'and look after Tim and your mother. I'm going to find them and put a stop to this nonsense.'

A stab of terror struck her. She held his wrist.

Should she let him go? There were dangers out there, in the rest of the Hollow. But he had slapped her, prompted her to fight him. He might be as much of a threat as the ghosts. He was close to the edge, building up frustrations he'd have to take out on someone or something. The house was pouring the volts into him just as it had into the lightbulbs. She didn't want to be there when he went off.

She let go of him. She let him go.

'You'll see, Jord,' he said. 'I'm right.'

She turned to Mum, who had nothing to say and seemed happy to watch telly. She was right next to Jordan on the sofa, but a million miles away in her head.

He left the Summer Room by the secret passage and found the rest of the house dark. It didn't matter. Now he knew what he was up against, he had no reason to be afraid. To be cautious, yes. There was no telling how desperate Wing-Godfrey's Louise loonies might be – Kirsty had been right about that, given him pause for thought – but he was on to them. He'd take back his property, prove he was master here. He was the owner, not some sitting tenant in the way of a development scheme. This was his ditch and he would defend it.

His feet caught up in something and he stumbled, falling against the rack of coats. He grasped thick cloth and found himself hanging onto a long garment he couldn't recognise by its feel. It wasn't one of his coats and he didn't think it could be Kirsty's or Jordan's. It was another of those things brought out of storage and used to decorate this haunting. He smelled mothballs and old lady.

The trap he had blundered into was an arrangement

of boots, set across the passage. He let go of the coat and kicked his way through wellies.

His eyes were not adjusting to the dark.

Some light was in the passage, from under the Summer Room door. The further away he got from the room where he had left his family, the darker it grew. There were windows in the passage, but nothing shone through them.

He had planned to go to his office – not Louise's study any more, but *his* office – first, knowing he could find his way there with his eyes shut. But he didn't know, he realised, how far he had gone down the passage. Was he past the doors of the spare rooms? He let his hand trail the wall, at the height of the door handles. Paper and plaster. He walked forwards, feeling his way. Ten steps. He must have missed the rooms.

The East Tower door should be in front of his nose, almost touching. Looking back, he saw the faint fan of light under the Summer Room door. A fire on a distant hill. It couldn't be more than twenty feet away, but seemed like twenty yards.

In the dark, it was impossible to get oriented.

But if he couldn't see, then neither could Wing-Godfrey. It was up to him to prove he knew the house as well as the invaders. He was not afraid of the dark, he was not afraid in the dark. This was *his* dark. He owned it, as much as he owned the walls of the house and the trees in the orchard. The dark, he knew with electric certainty, was on his side.

He had walked up to his door. He could open it with his eyes closed.

He stuck out his hand to grasp the door handle.
Nothing.

He looked back, at the light, and ahead, where the door should be. A more solid blackness hung there, where the passage ended. He pictured the door in his mind, remembering it was varnished brown wood, with a ceramic handle. The handle was chipped, a rough slice out of the smooth shape.

He reached again, further, bending over, extending his hand. His fingers inched through empty space. He was close to overbalancing. He took a step forward, expecting to collide clumsily with the door, skinning his knuckles, banging his nose.

Nothing.

He reached out with his left hand, to balance. His fingers brushed cold glass and he flattened his palm against the pane. He knew exactly where he was, by touch. This was the window at the end of the passage, which was shuttered when his door was open. The door, actually to the stairwell of the East Tower, opened outwards like an exterior door, and faced the door that opened inwards, to his office.

He closed and opened his eyes, detecting no difference. Functional blindness didn't matter. He had his bearings, and was confident.

With a sense of quiet triumph, he reached out, took the door handle, and turned.

The door handle took his hand and turned the other way.

He had hold of something cold, a hand of ice in a leather glove. Fingers interlaced with his and held him fast, thumb pressing the inside of his wrist.

The hand was fixed in space, as if stuck out of a wall rather than at the end of an arm. As it turned, slowly and with great strength, he was bent over. The grip crammed all the bones of his hand together, but the cold numbed any pain.

His head bumped the wall. His forehead scraped against the ridges of the raised-pattern wallpaper.

He jammed the heel of his left hand where he judged that the face of the person holding him was and slammed against solid wood. The impact ran up his arm. All the pain that had faded since his fall yesterday came back. He was sure again that he had broken fingers. He scrabbled against what finally felt like the door.

The hand was a solid cage around his fist, closed like a snare. He'd lost all feeling in his fingers but his arm was chilled to the elbow and tingles of numbness ran up to his shoulder.

His knees kinked and he lost his footing. His legs kicked and he fell to the floor, arm wrenched upwards, shoulder-socket yanked.

He was fixed to his door.

Looking back along the passage, the light of the Summer Room was a thousand miles distant. Something got in its way, blotting it like a curtain being drawn. With a faint slushing, dragging noise – what *was* it? – it came down the passage, towards him. A smidgen of light behind it outlined the shape. It had a head and arms, and long skirts that trailed – that was the noise! – on flagstones.

His throat wouldn't work.

The light was gone and he couldn't see the shape.

He still heard the skirt scraping across the floor. This passage had been carpeted with rush matting, but it was gone now. He felt only rough, cold stone under him.

The grip on his hand was less like another hand than it was a vice, closing slowly but inexorably.

The cloth-scraping was close.

He smelled mothballs and something else.

Points of ice came out of the dark and touched his face, then fell to his chest, pressing his shirt to his skin – did they cut through, sink into his flesh? – and stabbing hard against his heart.

D ad had been gone for a long time.

Mum and Jordan sat on the sofa, as if watching the old telly. A blizzard buzzed on the screen. White static light made ghosts of them.

Tim's hands wouldn't stop moving.

Without the U-Dub, he was bereft, naked, vulnerable. It hung around Jordan's neck, like an amulet. His sister was hunched up on the sofa, knees against her chin, long hair like a dust-sheet. The U-Dub was out of sight, between her knees and chest. He saw a loop of the rubber outside her hair.

He put his hands in his pockets but his fingers wriggled like worms, as if they weren't part of him. Frightened, he pulled his hands out again and looked at them.

The grain of the U-Dub was in his left palm. The pull of the rubber was a line on his right forefinger.

The weapon had been given to him. By the IP. He should have known he could never trust it.

Dad thought there were smugglers or pirates behind it all, like on *Scooby-Doo*. Mum said there were real ghosts; one had talked to Jordan on the old telephone.

It was darker than night outside.

She hadn't believed – *really* believed – Rick was dead until she heard him. Before that call, it could have been a cruel prank, getting back at her for the Letter. But the voice that hissed at her, distorted by distance yet close enough to be inside her ear, could not have come from a living person.

…Kiss kiss kiss…

She kept hearing it, even though the telephone was smashed. It had got into her brain like an egg-laying insect. Whispers hatched and swarmed and ate inside her skull. She jammed fingers into her ears and pressed her shut eyes against her knees, but was only trapped in the dark with the kissing voice.

The taste of Rick was in her mouth.

Kissing her, invading her, winding around her.

She was stuck in endless night with the shade of her dead boyfriend. He would be with her for ever. And yet they were broken up. Nothing changed that.

An eternity chained to a hateful person. That was her lot.

She remembered Primrose and the Mama, shut in this house, tied together by fear and hate. She understood horribly how the diarist and her mother fitted into the picture, as much as Louise and Weezie and the Drearcliff Grange spooks.

A cold wind riffled her hair, slipped into her T-shirt by the loose neck and slithered across her shoulders. Cool air blew between skin and cotton.

She looked up and let the breeze part her hair away from her face.

Mum sat beside her on the sofa, watching dead television. Tim sat on the floor, off to one side. Both were awake but dulled, still as statues, not alerted by her movement, not feeling the wind. That was just for her.

…Kiss kiss kiss…

It wasn't just inside her head. It was in the room, on the air currents, in the rustle of the slightly shifting curtains and the slushing buzz of the television.

…Kiss kiss kiss…

She felt them. Cold caresses and whisper kisses.

Rick's lips had brushed hers within the last few minutes. She recognised the tang of his toothpaste, the aftertaste of the lager he drank, the press of his attempted moustache. The touch had come when she was out, on holiday from her head, directing her fury at Dad. How could she have missed it?

She felt a yearning, a need for more kisses, yet a dread of them. It was like being a virgin again, wanting to go on but certain – despite the boiling cauldron of desire – it would be a mistake, that this was not the time, that the time might never come. Ahead was an unknown country, of wonders and terrors, a prospect of pleasure and the certainty of pain.

If she had known Rick would be first and last, she might have warded him off.

…Kiss kiss kiss…

That layer of air remained with her, even as she sat up straighter, as if her skin were repelling her T-shirt with an anti-magnetic force. The cool was in motion, like a stroking palm. The cold spot touched between her shoulder blades, then worked her neck muscles under her hair, as if massaging. The touch was too icy to be pleasant, but she didn't fight it. The cold made her feel alive again.

The chill touch ranged over her back like a searchlight and slipped around her side, under her armpit. She lifted her arm, and shivered as the ice circle pressed against her swollen tummy and ran up between her breasts...

(That's not fat, those are breasts.)

...then fell again and pushed sharply at a spot that *gave*, passing through her skin and ribs, settling around her heart like permafrost. For an instant, she believed her pump was stopped, that she had only seconds of consciousness before brain death.

The terrible thought was that she would go on, trapped in her body, a puppet of the dead.

No. She was alive. The ice wasn't just her heart. It dissipated throughout her.

Her T-shirt clung to her back now. She shivered with proper cold, wishing for a shawl or a blanket. The ice was in her veins and her vitals.

She wanted to reach out to Mum.

But Mum was in the zone, static whitening her face, tiny screens in her eyes.

...Kiss kiss kiss...

The French windows were open a crack. The draught came from there. Beyond the glass, the orchard was dark as midnight.

It *was* night. Real night, now. Hours had passed.

Out in the orchard, the voice was in the trees and the ditches. There were no birds at the Hollow, no insects. Just Rick's voice.

She stood, pins and needles pricking her legs, and walked to the French windows. Tim's gaze followed her like a security camera. Mum didn't seem to notice.

Was she being called or warned?

She took the brass handles and pushed the French windows open. They swung outwards, panes like mirrors flashing old images, and hung completely open.

Beyond the French windows, there was nothing.

The trees, the ditch at the end of the orchard, the lawn, even the patio just outside the windows... in such deep darkness, they might as well be gone. She looked at the floor. The flagstones extended to an inner jamb, a raised metal draught excluder. The light from Louise's lamps similarly stopped at the rim, as if it bordered a sea of black ink.

How deep might that sea be? An inch, or a thousand fathoms?

She stood exactly at the centre of the open windows. Her bare toes stubbed against the draught excluder.

Looking straight in front of her, she saw nothing.

But she still heard the voice.

...Kiss kiss kiss... kiss kiss kiss... kiss kiss kiss...

Was that even what it was saying? Or was she just finding words in a susurrus?

She opened and closed her eyes. There was more light inside her head than out.

She wavered in the doorway.

If she stepped across the threshold, would she plunge from a cliff-like overhang

(from Hilltop Heights)

to an unimaginable pit of spears a mile below?

Or would she just feel patio stone under her feet, and then soft, damp grass?

She swayed back and forwards, only by a few millimetres, with each breath.

Ki...

...sss sss sss... sss sss sss... sss sss sss...

The cold was in her, a part of her. She had accepted it, was ready to work with it. But it was out there, too, waiting for her, wanting her.

Her hair rose around her, stiff with static electricity, crackling as it lifted. Tiny hairs on her arms stuck up like quills.

She reached for the window-catches, mind made up.

Looking back, she saw Tim's face oval with horror and Mum distracted from the television.

She would shut out the ghosts.

But her hair wouldn't turn with her head. She felt a painful tugging at the roots. A blast of wind from *inside* the house pushed her and she missed her footing.

Her hands fumbled the catches and her arms waved about, windmilling.

'Mum,' she said, pleading.

Her mother ignored her.

Instinctively, she hopped over the draught excluder and tried to stand upright, to get her balance back.

She stepped into cold, black, running water.

He was in a confined space. If he moved, he banged his head. His numb right hand was in his lap. For a moment, he didn't know whether it was attached to his wrist. He felt with his swollen left hand and found it was still there. The bones were under the skin and meat, though they might as well have dissolved. The muscles just weren't obeying orders. His nerveless right hand wasn't particularly cool to touch, but the sensation of the icy grip lingered. The memory of pain was scarcely less sharp than the pain itself.

Steven was alone in the dark.

He wriggled into a half-sitting position, trying to cross his legs but banging his knees. He smelled wood and mothballs. Was he bundled into a cupboard or under the stairs?

As a kid, he had made Steve caves, lairs in his parents' houses where he stashed comics, torches, tools, supplies. He disappeared into them for hours on end, not noticing the passage of time.

He had an adult's body now and was less comfortable in his Steve cave. Not only was he bigger, shoulders hulking against the sides of the space and neck bent over so his chin jammed against his breastbone, but his arms and legs didn't fold up the right way. When did he get so creaky?

There must be an exit – a latch or a catch. If he just rolled hard, he should be able to burst open the door or lid.

He had loved his Steve caves. He never wanted to escape from them.

There were worse things than being alone in the dark.

Like being in the dark, but not alone.

The smell of mothballs was fainter here. He remembered, with terror, the shape that had advanced on him, its indistinct silhouette and distinct smell.

The shape, the figure, the person.

The ghost, he admitted.

He was shaking, jamming his spine against wooden ridges. His fear spasm threatened to become a fit.

There were ghosts. The Hollow was haunted.

Who had it been? Louise? Rick?

Or someone older, ancient even?

Louise Teazle had been dead less than a year; Rick not more than a day or two. Whatever was going on at the Hollow had been about its business for much longer. The ghosts were too good at haunting to be newbies.

Something had held him fast as something else closed on him.

Two, at least. And they smelled *old*.

He was sure there were more, maybe many more. Tim acted as if a whole army of ghosts lurked in the Hollow, guerrilla spooks in every bush or shadow.

Here, in his space, was he safe?

Steve caves were always a refuge from the outside world. Once inside, nothing could get him.

He had the memory of fear, but not fear itself.

His right hand began to have feeling again. He could move his fingers.

In pitch darkness, he felt out the contours of his cave. He recognised the shape of the ridges above him. He was in a wedge of emptiness under a flight of stairs. There were cupboards Kirsty hadn't explored yet. This must be one of them. He'd got here first and it was his.

He could stay here, beyond harm.

Steve caves had mystic properties. Tim would understand, but not the women. The caves rendered him invisible to the monsters. They were equipped with life-support systems. Once inside, he was home free and safe. He never needed to go to the toilet.

He had his place and could defend it.

But what about his family? Kirsty, Jordan, Tim. It wasn't that he wished them harm. He had done all he could for them and they hadn't cooperated. If they'd listened, jumped when he said frog, they might be safe now too. Instead, they'd gone against him.

He could weep with frustration. Nothing he had done got through to them. Now they were out there, at the mercy of the ghosts, probably lost for all time.

There was nothing more he could do.

Jordan didn't know how long she'd been walking. This was still the Hollow, though. She was seeing the place from a different angle now. The house and grounds contained this unending dark land, tucked into a fold which usually went unnoticed. In *Weezie and the Lands of Mayhap, Perchance and Might-Be*, doors led to different gardens depending on how they were opened.

She waded through shadow that came up to her calves. More than darkness and less than liquid, cold and feathery, cleansing not staining. She wished she'd worn shoes and socks. She'd gone barefoot because her fat feet wouldn't fit into even her oldest pair of trainers. In her nose and mouth, she had that tang she'd come to associate with the ghosts.

There were no stars or moon but the black sky had a violet underglow. Trees and stones made distinct silhouettes. Aside from her bare, white arms, everything was a flat, unreflective black.

She trudged up a bank and found herself in a copse. She was not alone.

The ghost Mum had introduced her to sat on a low branch, solemn old-lady face on a child's body. She had her own After Lights-Out Gang, dark girl-shapes in boaters and skirts, with green and violet cat-eyes. None were Rick.

'What are you?' asked Jordan.

'That's a question,' said the Old Girl.

It was like talking to herself.

'I think you're a ghost,' she ventured, 'that you're all ghosts.'

The Old Girl slipped off her branch. Pale light came from above, casting harsh shadows. She had blonde braids, like Weezie. Her face, what Jordan could see below the visor-shadow of her hat brim, was withered and dry, like fruit left too long in the bowl. Brown patches wept on her cheeks.

'What are ghosts?' the Old Girl asked.

'Dead people,' Jordan said, swallowing water from her mouth. 'People who've lived in a place and stay on after their bodies have gone, tied to a house or a piece of ground. By unresolved feelings.'

The Old Girl smiled, showing yellow teeth. Apple pips were caught in her gums.

'Maybe they – maybe *you* – died suddenly,' Jordan continued, shuddering to think. 'Before you could finish everything in your life. A violent death, murder or suicide or a terrible accident. Perhaps if your life is cut off, you have things left to do in your mind. It keeps you here, binds you to – what would you call it? – the earthly plane.'

'Earthly plane?'

'There might be better reasons to stay, not to go on to wherever you go on to. A long, happy life lived in one place. Perhaps that puts down roots, means you stay where you were most loved. The tie doesn't have to be a terrible thing, does it?'

She looked into the Old Girl's face, hoping for a nod that she was on the right track.

'Do you believe in personal survival after death?' the ghost asked.

The question brought her up sharp.

It was asked in a man's voice. Still in the register she had heard earlier, but different. A master's question, not a schoolgirl's.

'Do you believe,' the voice continued, 'human personality survives the passing of the body? Can a coherent mind, with memory and intent and all the rest of the package, exist without corporeal form?'

Was the Old Girl even speaking? The ghost's mouth was in and out of shadow, shining when opened.

'I suppose I have to,' Jordan replied. 'You're here.'

'Who am I?'

That was what had been puzzling her.

'Are you Louise?'

The Old Girl turned away. Her braids hung down

the back of her school blazer.

'I think you look the way you do to me because Louise lived here for so long,' Jordan said. 'Are you not a person at all, not someone who ever lived, but something else, something given shape by what people expect to see?'

One of the others shifted closer to the Old Girl, enveloping her in a dark cape. It was like a scene from an opera, a tableau held long enough for the aria to finish.

'Or are you just a recording? Set off by the presence of an audience? Something that happened here once, playing over and over, with no more intelligence than a video? A tape that's been played too often and stretched and corrupted. If there's no personal survival, then you've no mind to listen with. If you seem to react, that's just an interpretation I put on it. Are ghosts like the weather, something you just have to work around?'

Was the Old Girl listening to her?

Were any of them?

There were a dozen in the copse, but she could be alone, as silly as an old woman giving advice out loud to characters in afternoon soaps. It frightened Jordan to think she was arguing with herself.

She shut up, sobered. She thought of Mum and Tim back in the Summer Room, spellbound by the black-and-white fuzz of old television. And Rick, off there in the night somewhere, a ghost or a hoaxer.

She worried about Rick. If he was a ghost now, was he a mindless replay loop or a conscious, aware thing? If he was just a shadow-echo, they couldn't hurt each other any more. If he were a person, he could have feelings for her, either way. Love or hate. Again, which would be worse?

The Old Girl turned round, shrugging off the taller, shadow-cloaked ghost. She had green eyes, like Weezie and like Louise.

Jordan couldn't tell. She couldn't tell if anything was behind the eyes, a mind or a blank.

The thought made her want to cry.

Was she wasting her tears on someone long gone?

She had asked the wrong questions. What are you? Who are you?

The words wouldn't come. All the moisture was gone from her mouth. Her tongue was dry.

The Old Girl's eyes were liquid.

A person's? An animal's? A portrait's?

Finally, Jordan croaked, 'Who am I?'

'That's a question,' the Old Girl said, in the female voice so like and unlike those she knew. 'That's a question, indeed.'

They all stepped back, joining the tree-shadows. Jordan was alone and out of the copse.

His sister was gone. Tim was left with Mum. From her face, he wasn't sure she was here really either.

There were others in the Summer Room.

They came in through the French windows and down the chimney, from out of the shadows and from behind the sofa and chairs, through the television screen and in the light from the old lamps.

The IP.

The hostiles.

There had never been any difference. They'd just picked sides and played a game.

Now the game was nearly over.

He thought Mum couldn't see the hostiles. The Ipkick was in the cold fireplace. Black light fell around her, making her straw hat shine but shading her withered face except for an orange slice of chin.

She looked like a real child. Her soldiers were with her, the hostiles. Savage, creeping things, with twig fingers and hooded eyes.

Tim hugged Mum and watched. The Ipkick came out of the fireplace and walked across the room, at the head of her column. She paused by the television and turned the off switch. The screen shrank to a light dot which died, leaving only an after impression, which squiggled as Tim shook his head.

When the television turned off, so did the ghosts. Apart from the squiggles, Tim saw no one else in the room. Just because you couldn't see them any more didn't mean they'd gone away.

Tim clung to Mum.

The Summer Room was quiet, but every shadow was cover, every light deceptive.

It was an indoor jungle.

'They're watching,' he said.

Mum held him tight. She knew too.

They had always been watched at the Hollow. The smile was back, where he had broken the window, cracked across but crueller than ever.

Mum's hold relaxed. Tim didn't understand why.

'I know a game,' she said. 'A good game.'

Her eyes were too bright and her smile twitched. Mum was very, very frightened, and that killed something inside Tim, pushing him into a world without rules and regs. The tunnel wasn't shored up, and could fall at any time.

Tim had to be brave for Mum.

But he didn't know if he could.

Frightened people were scary in themselves. You never knew what they would do

(Jordan and Dad had fought, really meaning it, hurting each other)

and what they meant.

'Do you want to play?'

Her eyes shone with unshed tears. Her smile put deep creases in her cheeks and around her eyes. It made her look much older.

Tentatively, he nodded.

'Come on then,' Mum said, getting up, holding his hand too firmly, yanking him off the sofa. 'I want to show you some magic. It's in my room.'

Turning back to look, she couldn't see the copse or the house. The Old Girl and her After Lights-Out Gang were gone.

She had been given something to think about. She wasn't out here for herself but for Rick.

Whatever sort of ghost he was.

Rick's voice was still with her, hissing like an old record winding down. It was more than a memory of the voice she'd heard on the phone. It was in the wind that stirred gently against her legs and arms, raising the fine hairs she hated which no one else could see.

She had come out to meet him, to confront him.

This was nothing to do with her parents; this was between her and her ex-boyfriend, the ex-boy.

'Rick,' she called, not loud.

Her voice didn't echo, but the name hung in her mind a few moments before popping like a bubble.

'Ri-ick,' she tried again, hating the whining.

Then, he was there.

'Jord,' he acknowledged.

His face shone like a shirt in a detergent ad. Death hadn't marked him. At least, not where she could see.

She was weak with relief. Finally, after all that waiting and grief, he was here! He had kept his word after all, gone along with the plan.

'What are you playing at?' she asked, remembering to be angry with him. It was well past his deadline.

'It's you, Jord. I couldn't stay away from you.'

'You might have thought about that before...'

He shrugged, trying to get round her with a grin she'd once mistakenly told him was adorable. For ever after, he put it on when he wanted to make up for something unforgivable or get something unobtainable.

'...before...'

'Before you *died*, you bastard.'

She hauled around and slapped him, half-expecting her hand to pass through smoke. She connected and raked her nails across his cheek.

He bent with the blow, but stood up and wiped the mark off his face.

'Kiss kiss,' he said. 'Kiss kiss?'

She was not going to kiss a ghost. Not yet. Not until things were straightened out.

'What happened to you? Why didn't you come when you said you would? How did you die?'

He waved away her questions, infuriating her.

'It was your bloody mates, wasn't it? They talked you out of trotting off to the country for the old ball and chain. Probably talked you into some stunt that got you bloody killed. One thing about this, you're better off without them dragging you down all the time. Though what they did is about as bad as it could be. Which one of them was it?'

'Which,' he repeated.

Or had he said 'witch'?

They stood in a rough circle. Stonehenge-height megaliths, like giant battered speakers at a death metal festival. Dark mist had given way to blackened earth and shrivelled grass, as if there had been a fire here long ago.

'Love you, Jord,' said Rick.

He was a real presence, who could be slapped and felt. He displaced air. His clothes moved when he did. He was not just a hologram or a vivid memory.

Rick reached out for her, hands long and white.

She backed away, grazing her feet and ankles on black brambles. She did not want to be touched.

'Love you,' he repeated.

He had never been able to form a sentence with both 'I' and 'love you' in it. She only just noticed that.

'Kiss kiss,' he implored.

There was something moronic about the repetition, as if he were a three-dimensional photocopy of the original, a degraded image that would never be a substitute for the real thing.

'Are you really there?' she asked, suddenly sorry for him

(hating herself for that, he had deserved to die for dumping her so sneakily)

and for herself.

He came close to her, angling his head to kiss her. His fingers touched her shoulders. She was colder than him. His grip was familiar, fingers and thumbs lightly holding her, arms drawing her near.

She was an open-eyed kisser. He was not.

His eyes fluttered shut as his lips closed on hers. She felt the tip of his nose touch her cheek and opened her mouth, sucking air to clear a spit bubble.

Rick stopped and stepped back, letting her go.

He was still a bastard. It had all been a trick. He didn't want a kiss, he just wanted to prove he still owned her.

They were not alone in the circle.

Rick had a gang. She could not see the others clearly, as if their images were smeared or blurred, but she recognised the way Rick fitted in with them, head cocked to one side, hunched over so his hands reached the gorilla-pockets halfway down his jeans.

'You've made new friends?' she said. 'Not much improvement on the last lot.'

Rick shook his head.

'Jord, you shouldn't.'

Puffs of flame burst in the darkness, making the circle into an arena. A bonfire rose around a flat black stone, like a cartoon witches' cauldron. She felt the warmth of the flame. Firelight had reddened her legs and arms.

Rick's friends had faces now. Some wore reflective motorcycle helmets or mirrored sunglasses, others badly knotted Drearcliff Grange ties and kilt-like skirts. One, a tall woman, wore full-length robes and a pointed hood which showed only her vicious eyes.

'What happened to you?' Jordan asked, not of Rick but of his gang. 'Why have you changed? You weren't like this when we came to the Hollow. You were kind, you were nice.'

'It's not us,' said Rick. 'It's you.'

She wanted to strangle him, sink fingers into his throat until his eyes popped out of his head and his blackened tongue stuck out between his teeth.

'It's because of you all,' Rick said.

She had made fists. Rick sounded like Dad at his worst.

'Because of what you're like, because of what you are,' said Rick, 'we can hurt you.'

'Not "can",' boomed the witch woman, '"must".'

How long had he been here? He had been unconscious – or had he? – when bundled into the Steve cave. Comfortable in the dark, he must have dropped off, if only for moments. Or maybe longer. Time wasn't behaving itself at the Hollow, anyway. Had he been dreaming or thinking? What was the difference?

Steven perfectly fitted into the cave under the stairs. It was cosy, not cramped. He no longer banged his head or elbows if he turned. He relished the dry, woody under-the-stairs smell.

If he thought of his family, his wife and children, they seemed like the ghosts. As a child, as soon as he understood he would grow up, he had thought of the wife he would have, the children who would come along. Those imaginings hadn't had names or faces, but were like the real people in too many disturbing details.

At once, he knew why it seemed so strange.

He *had* been dreaming. Kirsty, Jordan, Tim. He had made them up. He had expected them, and there they were.

This was waking life, in the dark under the stairs.

Out there in the house, *Watch With Mother* was on television. *The Flower-Pot Men.* His Meccano set was in a box under his bed, with his neat stack of comics. Dad was out at the office and Mum doing the housework. He was home from school for the long, long holidays, happy to be at a loose end.

Everything else, he had made up.

He had been fuzzy, but his head was clear now.

Where had he got the names from? And the faces? They were vague now, like a damp magazine cover. The advertisement on the other side showed through in reverse. A black-and-white car erupted across the colour face of a smiling woman.

It was time to put his toys back in the box and have tea.

Already, with the aching melancholy of knowing they were just made up, he missed his dream family. He knew so much more about them that he hadn't thought of, little things and big things that just hadn't come up in the course of his latest dream.

Jordan had taken flute lessons, but given it up.

Kirsty used to have a habit of chewing a strand of her hair. Her mouth still scrunched up at one side when she was thinking, though her once-long hair was cropped and spiked when she met him and had never grown back. It had taken him years to work out what she was doing. He had never told her about it, knowing it would make her self-conscious.

They were gone. Those things were gone.

He found himself crying.

It was a chance to start over, to unpick all the mistakes. Steven and Jordan were gone of their own volition, wandered off into the dark. By now, they would have found their places, away from her, on their own. From her wrong turn in life, only Tim was left.

If he were to go she would be alone again, able to start afresh, free of the domestic coral that had accrued when she wasn't looking.

Kirsty couldn't believe she had pretended to be interested in washing machines.

Every time she'd tried to have something for herself, one of the terrible trio got in the way, demanding to be wiped up after, to have tea made, to be listened to. Her projects stood no chance with that oh-so-casual and oh-so-devastating undermining.

Vron had been trying to tell her for years.

Kirsty would be better off.

She didn't want to be a ghost in her own lifetime, the clanking spectre of all she could have been if only she hadn't given in to Steven and the kids.

The others had alienated the Hollow. She was the only one who saw the place as a resource as well as a home. This was her home and her world. Eventually, she would invite Vron to share in running the place. Marketing and packaging and exploitation. It was what the Old Girl wanted.

'It's for the best,' she said, over and over.

Tim didn't resist, but didn't help either. He was an anchor, a deadweight. It would have been easier to sling him over her shoulder in a fireman's lift and carry him upstairs. She had done it a hundred times when he was little and needed to be put to bed after playing himself to exhaustion and falling asleep in the living room. She didn't know if she could manage that any more; as he'd grown, she seemed to have shrunk. She wasn't yet forty, but years had been piled on her by the family, by their unending demands and needs.

Just for once, she considered herself first.

'Come on, Tim,' she said, 'nearly there.'

Had she thought this through?

No. That was a Steven thing: thinking things through. Code for putting something off and never doing it.

It was a simple matter.

And it was the top drawer for Tim.

Mum practically dragged him upstairs, step by step, cooing all the way. She was having a funny turn.

Tim told himself the ghosts had done it to her.

They had got into her head and made her strange.

But he knew that wasn't true.

Mum had always had the strangeness inside. The ghosts hadn't even brought it out, though Tim thought she wouldn't be as openly strange if the sun hadn't gone down early.

He didn't fight her on the stairs. He might need to save his strength, to fight her – or any of them – later.

'Here we are,' she said, as they stood on the landing, outside the door to Mum and Dad's room. 'Happy as can be.'

The way she treated him reminded him of Jordan.

Sometimes, in half-light or when surprised, Mum looked like Jordan. Now, she was acting like his sister did when she wanted something, usually that Tim be quiet and get out of the way so she could be with her creepy boyfriend.

Mum opened the bedroom door.

A Mum and Dad smell wafted out, not unpleasant, but strong. It was in the bedclothes and the curtains, even the dust.

'Magic, you'll see,' said Mum.

The bedroom was bigger than Tim remembered. He hadn't been in here more than twice since they moved in. It was parental HQ, and he was too grown-up to need to sleep between them even when he had bad dreams.

The furniture had been rearranged.

'This is Weezie's magic chest of drawers,' Mum explained.

It looked like ordinary furniture. The wood had been painted and stripped several times. Rinds of orange and blue were left in the deepest grain. A lamp shaped like a swan with a lightbulb in its mouth stood on a doily-like crochet cover. It was the only switched-on light in the room.

Mum knelt by the chest, coming down to his level. She held him by the shoulders.

'The bottom drawer always has a present,' she said.

She pulled out the bottom drawer, with a rasp. Something flashed.

'See,' Mum said. 'A present.'

She took out a piece of glass. The smile. There was an actual smile in the glass, not a flaw but a lipstick crescent.

Terror bit Tim.

'Something useful,' said Mum. 'It'll fit in place of the pane that was broken. How considerate.'

Tim couldn't look at the smile, which Mum held between thumb and forefinger, but couldn't look away either. When Mum held it up and put the light behind the glass, a tongue seemed to lick her hand. The lips pouted, wet and red.

'Do you want a kiss, Tim?'

Uncertain, Tim nodded.

Mum leaned close to his face, then slipped the cold glass between them and pressed it against his mouth. His lips stuck to it as to a frosted sheet of metal. His scream was gummed over. He felt a tearing as the glass was removed, as if patches of the thin skin of his lips stuck to the horrible thing.

'There now, that showed you were grateful.'

She propped the smile against the base of the swan-light, where it could gloat at him.

'You're not convinced?' Mum said, eyes wide,

smiling herself, holding him tight. 'You think the glass was there all along, not a present but waiting to be found. Maybe so, Timbo, maybe so…'

She closed the empty drawer and smiled like a fat cat with a stomach full of bird.

Tim was convinced. Of course it was magic. The broken smile was whole again.

Mum teased the drawer-handle, a brass teardrop dangling from a flower-face, and pulled the drawer slowly open again.

Glittery eyes looked up. Tim tried to back away.

It was some sort of stuffed animal, mounted on a base.

'I think it's a stoat,' Mum said. 'Like in *The Wind in the Willows*.'

It was a snarling, vicious thing. Mum took his hand and made him stroke its fur, which was stiff like a thousand needles. A shudder ran up his arm. The animal's green glass eyes suggested a trapped, frozen malignance. Tiny rows of exposed teeth were like sharpened pearls.

'Don't like it,' he said.

'No, I should think you don't,' she said. 'But there's a way to give back presents we don't want. Here, you do it. Pull out the top drawer and pop the stoat in.'

She let him go, picked up the stuffed animal by the base, and sat back on her heels, holding the thing in her lap.

Carefully, expecting to set off a tripwire, Tim opened the top drawer. It was empty, which was a relief. Mum handed him the stoat, which he reluctantly accepted.

'Just put it in and close the drawer.'

'It won't fit.'

'It's the size of the drawer it came out of. It must fit.'

That was true. Holding the base, careful not to let his fingers touch the animal itself, he lowered the stoat into the drawer. Though it was too big outside to go in, it fitted perfectly once he dropped it into the drawer.

The stoat looked up, angry red points in its green eyes.

'Go on, Tim,' encouraged Mum.

He shut the drawer. It slid smoothly home.

'Now peep inside again.'

He did. The drawer was empty.

'Can we make the smile go away?' he asked.

Mum was horrified. 'The glass? We need the glass, Tim. It's not like the horrible stoat.'

It was worse. The stoat had been trapped. The smile was free. Couldn't she hear it chuckling?

The magic chest of drawers only gave nasty presents.

'Here,' Mum said, opening the bottom drawer.

A large, curly-horn seashell. She took it out and set it next to the smile.

'And...'

She shut the door swiftly and pulled it open again, grinning with excitement, her lower lip sucked into her mouth, her eyes glistening.

A pencil box, with an inlaid jester on the lid, his face scratched away.

'The top drawer always has the same thing in and the bottom drawer never has the same thing twice and the middle drawer is always a jumble of surprises,' Mum recited.

Rapidly, she pulled out a series of items from the

bottom drawer, the drawer that never has the same thing twice.

A long bone. A rusty pocket-knife. A tea-cup filled with webs of mould. A brown wooden human hand. A long-tailed, live rat.

The last made them both gasp.

Mum didn't want to touch it. The magic had betrayed her, which didn't fit in with her way of seeing things.

Tim preferred the rat to the smile.

(And the hand, which he found really repulsive, seeming to be real until it was picked up.)

'Get rid of it, Tim,' she said.

He gripped the tail and held the animal up. It twisted around, trying to get its teeth into his hand, but was too heavy to upend itself in the air.

He groped for the drawer handle and pulled it out, dropped the rat inside and shoved it shut.

There was a whirring and a strangled bleat.

He rubbed his thumb and fingers together, to get rid of the rat scum.

'Wrong drawer, Tim,' Mum said.

He realised what he had done. He had put the rat into the middle drawer, the drawer that was always an interesting jumble. That sounded nice, until you thought about it.

Mum touched the handle of the middle drawer, then thought better of it.

The smile, surrounded by the other treasures from the bottom drawer, was exultant. Tim didn't like any of them, really. There was something horrible about all of them.

Actually, the rat had been the pick of the prizes.

The middle drawer didn't make things go away, like the top one did.

Tim pulled it open.

The rat was still there, but it was an interesting jumble.

She shut the drawer, quickly. The worst thing about the rat was that it was still alive.

Tim was badly upset, and no wonder.

She should just have popped him into the top drawer and forgotten about him. But she felt the need to share, to let someone in on the magic, if only because they wouldn't be here to share for long.

'I don't like this, Mum,' he said.

She wanted to reassure him, but couldn't. He was right not to like the chest. It was hers, not his.

Tim had come from her and she was sending him back. Like Steven and Jordan, he hadn't worked out and there was no shame in admitting that. Kirsty always knew when to give up, to let things drop. She had done it too often to have a complex about it.

She pulled open the top drawer. It was empty, always the same.

'We should put the rat in here,' she said.

Tim agreed, nodding.

'Please, Tim.'

He pulled out the middle drawer, which he couldn't see into because the top drawer was in the way. The jumble shifted, with a skittering and scratching.

'You'll have to take out the whole drawer and pour it in.'

Tim shook his head. He would go no further.

'So, as usual, it's down to Mum, is it?'

She was irritated. It was just like Tim to make a mess and pretend paralysis when it had to be cleared up.

Shifting Tim aside, she took hold of the middle drawer by its corners and yanked it out of the chest. Without looking, she upended its contents into the top drawer. A wriggling and thumping made her cringe.

She set the extracted drawer on its side and shoved the top drawer shut, then pulled it open. With relief, she saw it was empty. There was one utterly reliable thing in her life, one drawer she could count on not to give her a nasty surprise.

The middle drawer slid easily back into place.

'Well, Tim, it's been lovely,' she said, standing up, 'but it's time to go home.'

He looked up at her, not knowing what she meant.

She picked him up in her arms. His legs, longer than she remembered, hung loose. He was quite a weight. She felt the strain in her shoulders.

'Mum?'

'It's not you, dear,' she said, laying him in the top drawer, 'it's me.'

She admired the fit. He folded up so well and filled the drawer completely, not uncomfortable or broken and with nothing sticking out or left over.

Kirsty had never loved her son more, not since he was born.

She blew him a kiss and shut the top drawer. It didn't feel heavy or awkward and slid home smoothly on runners that might have been freshly oiled. The drawer was a perfect fit with the chest.

Perfect.

Something cold and wet, like a tendril of pond-weed, slid across Jordan's face. It stung softly, like a jelly-fish tentacle or a nettle. Her hand went to her cheek. No swelling yet.

She was slapped again, across the shoulders. Then on her bare legs.

Rick's friends circled around her, lashing out.

They used whips she couldn't see. Whips more alive than those wielding them.

Rick was in the circle, whirling his own whip.

The lashes forced her to her knees. She drew in her head and arms.

The witch woman darted forward on long legs and gave a delicate flick of her wrist.

Jordan waited a moment, following the invisible uncoiling with her eyes, and was struck on the crown. The blow shook her skull, rattled her brains.

No blood. Just pain.

She had mindflashes of the frenzy that had fallen on her after Dad's slap. Then, she gave in to anger; now, she just gave in.

This was her punishment and she would take it.

Could they kill her? Could ghosts do that? Were they like vampires – who could kill her and make her one of their kind?

She was curled in a foetal ball, on her side, knees tucked in. A slithering lash fell across her shins, opening the skin with tiny hooks.

She shrank inside herself.

She might as well let go. She could be with Rick for ever, with his friends. There was a place for her and the hurt would be over.

It was all about sacrifice.

The whipping continued, but hurt less. Numbness spread, like dental anaesthetic.

She uncurled and lay flat, arms out, legs together.

They stood around and over her, more like stones than people. Leaves fluttered out of the black sky and piled up on her, an autumnal quilt.

She couldn't feel her legs or arms. She closed her eyes.

She was ready to be kissed now, though her lips wouldn't be able to feel it. She would be a closed-eye kisser if that was what Rick wanted.

But... tiny voices bothered her.

Her friends Ana and Mia. Anorexia and bulimia. Not eating, or eating but purging. Jordan always insisted, fiercely, she didn't have a problem with food, no matter that she had sometimes gone weeks without solids. Anas only thought they were overweight; Jordan definitely tended to chubbiness

(self-image might be unreliable – everybody's was: Mum and Dad certainly weren't the people they thought they were)

and had to watch what she ate.

Not eating was a unique addiction, a disease you had to work with. Work hard. On a day-to-day basis, to have Ana to stay, you had to be strong like an athlete on a brutal training regimen, not weak like alcoholics or problem drug users. Alkies and junkies had no will-power... with an eating disorder, *all you had* was willpower. And Ana was Jordan's special friend, not Mia. Next to Ana, Mias were pushovers. Mias were about momentary lapses and hating yourself. Ana was the real path of pain to perfection. You had to subscribe to a vision of the world and hold to it with fanatic devotion. Against all reason, all persuasion, all logic. It was more like a religion than a condition.

If Ana really lived with Jordan, she had a firm friend. A second self, in her corner, on her side. And, now, Ana was *howling*...

Jordan had chosen who and what she wanted to be. Against peer pressure, successive advertising blitzkriegs and parental expectations, she dressed the way she wanted and listened to the music she liked. No one could tell her different. That went for the shape she was and wanted to be too. She would go to agonising lengths to be herself, the self she saw in her mind. She would fight to the death to prevent others moulding her into their own image of what Jordan Naremore should be.

The leaves stopped falling.

She could not give in. It was not in her character. Not after all this fuss. She was who she was, and she had to stick by that.

'No,' she said, simply.

She opened her eyes. The figures were stone. Rick was gone.

He could stand up in the Steve-Cave now. When he napped, it expanded. He could shape the dark space and everything within it.

Steven had friends here.

His old friends and his new friends. His family were here somewhere, but improved versions: a wife who supported him and never got into trouble on her own, children who were obedient and cheerful and a credit to him.

It wasn't a tyranny. Everyone followed his lead, but only because he was invariably right.

He explored the cavern.

Under his feet, he found a small tube. A tin torch, with a serrated plastic toggle which fit snugly under his thumb. A familiar thing, something he'd never actually thrown away but hadn't seen in ages. Even in the course of packing and unpacking everything he owned for the move to the Hollow, he hadn't noticed this. It wasn't too surprising that it should be here when he needed it.

He flicked the switch.

Tiny light grew. The batteries must be old, rusted. He remembered the lemony, acidy smell of old batteries. The non-renewable type they didn't make any more.

He pointed the torch upwards. A column of orange light failed to reach the ceiling.

The ground was black and featureless, gritty but not earth, grainy but not board. He let the light swing around in a circle, then flicked the torch off.

No use wasting what little light he had if there was nothing to be shown.

He paced his cave, losing count of his steps, unsure where he started. He had no idea of its size.

Something got caught up in his feet.

He shot a flash of light down. He was hobbled by a twisted bundle of wire coat hangers. Ribbons of white plastic, the remains of a shopping bag, wound around the tangle of wire and hooks.

He kicked himself free, scattering the contraptions, breaking them apart.

The hangers disturbed him. They weren't his, and he didn't know why they were in the Steve cave. The torch *was* his and had its place here. He expected it.

But the hangers, bent together like a clawed cushion, were an intrusion. A man-trap set where he was the only man who walked. He resented them, was slightly afraid of them.

The cave had been breached.

She sat up and shook out her hair. Leaves fell from her chest. The tingling memory of pain was dead and going.

Jordan stood.

Her stomach groaned. She was hungry. It had been days since she'd eaten properly.

Ana might have taught her a lesson, but wasn't her friend, really. It took strength to know that too.

She touched one of the stones. It was smooth, as if exposed to the wind for centuries. Trees stood beyond the circle.

Something white, like a bird, fluttered against a low, dark bank, beckoning.

She walked towards the scrap, arms and legs prickling with cold. Before she was close, she recognised the thing. Her mind stretched the wrong way again.

It was the Letter.

The dark bank was a stone wall with a cavity in it. The Letter lay below. Jordan looked closer and saw the cavity was a hole stopped with a piece of iron. In the iron was a slit.

She picked up the Letter. The envelope had been neatly slit but the sheets of paper were still inside, all in order. It had been received, but by whom? She slipped the envelope down the back of her knickers. Later, she'd destroy the cursed thing.

She scrambled over the wall and lowered herself on the other side.

No matter how close she put her face to the iron plate, she couldn't tell its colour. It could have been red. Equally, it could have been black or anything. Was it a pretend postbox? Or did things posted here make their way to unintended addressees?

She looked into the dark. In the distance, she saw lights.

Suddenly, she was afraid again. Not for herself.

She pulled out the top drawer. Empty. Tim had been a good boy and not screamed or made a fuss.

Kirsty was a little light-headed.

So this was freedom.

She experimented with it, thinking of a life she now had to herself. No meals to cook, no clothes to wash and iron, no mess to tidy, no warm bodies to work around, no schedules to fit into. Now she could do what she wanted.

Nothing would get in the way.

Her first impulse was to call Vron, but that would bring someone else in. Vron was on her side, but was still another person, with opinions and enthusiasms of her own. Kirsty wanted to start out by herself, to get her ideas in working order and her business in shape before letting *anyone* else in. This time, she had to follow the advice she had devoured from her motivational magazines and be captain of her own ship.

She looked into the empty drawer and had no regrets. She slid it shut.

Wherever Steven, Jordan and Tim were, she hoped they were happy. They might even be together. She had no malice for them, not anymore. They were solved problems, part of her long-gone past. Without them hanging around nagging her with their complicated bundles of trouble, she had no need to resent them any more.

If they hadn't gone, she might have wound up killing them.

Her eyes were drawn to the brown hand on top of the chest of drawers. A perfectly crafted piece of work, of some material she didn't recognise. The nails were glassy, the skin dull. She saw veins across the knuckles.

A strange present.

She stroked the back of the hand. It had a give, a plasticity not like flesh but not stone either. Maybe soft wood.

To celebrate her liberation, she decided she deserved another present. Maybe another hand would give her a matched pair, for the mantelpiece.

She knelt down before the chest as if it were an altar,

wished for something nice, and pulled out the bottom drawer. Heavier than usual, it rasped on its runners.

Bernard Wing-Godfrey, folded up neatly, fitted into the drawer. He held his right wrist in his left hand, fingers a tourniquet. The brown man's hand was missing. His stump was clean, not leaking.

She thought he might be dead, but he expanded and contracted with breath. His clothes were creased from the folding. His legs bent the wrong way, like a crash test dummy. His eyes fluttered under closed lids, as if he were having a bad dream.

Kirsty stood up and looked from the neat stump to the hand.

She indeed had a full set now, though not the way she had imagined.

She took a blow to the heart. A curtain lifted and she saw everything with hideous clarity.

This was no fair exchange. A child for a stranger, a family for someone she thought sinister, her life for a perhaps-malicious intruder.

How had she ever thought it would be worth it?

After an investment of eighteen years, she couldn't just walk away from a loss. Her family might have been thorny and frustrating – they had ground her down by increments – but she couldn't blame them turning her into a monster. She had managed that by herself, without even Vron or a whisper from Weezie. She was worse than a murderess. She had thrown her children away, let her family go without fighting. How had she thought she could change her life by stripping people out of it like old wallpaper?

She wanted to scream.

She spun around and caught sight of her face in a mirror. She was pale and haggard, an apparition, a madwoman.

She pulled out the top drawer. It was heart-breakingly empty.

'Tim,' she said, 'come back.'

She shut the drawer and yanked it open.

Stray hair stuck to her cheeks, glued by tears.

'Tim,' she shouted, 'Mum didn't mean it. Come out, from wherever you're hiding, come out. I'm not angry. I'm sorry. I'm so so sorry, so so so sorry.'

Words didn't do it.

She worked the drawer back and forward, handling it roughly, splintering the runners.

Wing-Godfrey's eyes flicked open.

Why didn't the magic work in reverse? She wanted it undone, but the chest just lay there like a dead thing.

She kicked the bottom drawer, which was solid with Wing-Godfrey's weight, and jammed her toes painfully.

Nothing had ever come back.

She had put many things in the top drawer, the drawer that was always the same, the drawer that was always empty. Presents she'd tired of, messes she'd wanted out of the way, experimental objects like early capsules tossed into space to see what would happen.

But none of those things had been alive. Except the jumbled rat, and that hadn't had a mind.

They went somewhere, didn't they? Somewhere in the Hollow was a space where everything wound up. A storehouse where exchanges were made. Thrown-away things were piled next to the presents ready to go into the bottom drawer.

Wherever Tim was, he could still hear and think.

She called his name, loudly. It came back at her from the corners of the room.

Wing-Godfrey had vanished into the Hollow and returned. It could happen.

Of course, he hadn't gone into the top drawer. Or had he? She couldn't imagine why he would slip away from the After Lights-Out Gang and go into her bedroom, then hide in the top drawer of Weezie's magic chest of drawers. He had vanished some other way, like Steven or Jordan, walked through a door that wasn't usually there, and rattled around – a hostage again – inside the walls or under the grounds.

She took Wing-Godfrey by the lapels and hauled him out of the drawer. He didn't resist. He seemed to be somewhere between asleep and awake, pliable but unconscious. He kept his hand around his chopped-through wrist.

He was too heavy for her to manhandle easily. Stood up, he put a weight on the bottom of the drawer that strained the wood and threatened to pop it out of its joists. She had to work his knees for him to get him to step out of the drawer.

Wing-Godfrey was easy to move across the room and dump in a chair. She got him turned around and sat up straight. It was like dealing with a sleepy child... Tim

(agonising heart pain)

when he was so tired from playing soldiers all day and well into the evening that he couldn't unbutton his buttons

(or would pretend so Mum would undress him and put him to bed)

or lift his eyelids.

She turned from Wing-Godfrey to the chest and tried to slide the bottom drawer shut with her foot. It wouldn't go. The weight had buckled the drawer. She knelt and tried to force the drawer in with both hands. No use. She saw that the bottom of the drawer was detached, popped from its grooves, square-head nails pulled and bent. She'd have to get Steven to fix it, with a hammer and maybe a plane.

Would tampering with it affect the magic?

And there was currently no Steven.

Vron nagged her for letting Steven play Hairy Tool-Using Man Master whenever a shelf needed putting up or a door re-hanging, insisting a menstrual cycle did not rob women of opposable thumbs. It was usually easier to get Steven to do it. His smug superiority was more acceptable next to a well-put-up shelf than poured on her after her feeble effort had collapsed and he had to do the job properly.

She upended the drawer and bashed it, then tried again. It still wouldn't fit.

Was the magic broken?

She pulled out the middle drawer. An interesting jumble, but not organic this time. Nothing useful. A shifting sea of what looked like disassembled watch and clock parts.

This was no good. She got back to Wing-Godfrey.

She didn't think he could see her. His mind was back in captivity, in the dark. Had he held his wrist like that when he was chained by it? Did he think of severing his own hand to get free, like a trapped fox chewing off its own leg?

'Wing-Godfrey,' she said.

He might have recognised his name.

'Bernard.'

His head moved, a little.

'What happened? Where were you?'

The questions sounded useless, as soon as they came out of her mouth.

His eyes flickered to the chest. No, to the top of the chest. His hand. She had an idea he wanted it, though it could hardly be any use to him.

She picked the thing up and fancied he gave a croak of approval, of excitement.

It was limp now, less like a manufactured item than a body part. She didn't like holding it. She stepped quickly across the room and dropped it in Wing-Godfrey's lap. She rubbed her fingers, afraid they were coated with invisible oil, and had an urge to dash to a sink and scrub her hands.

Wing-Godfrey looked into his lap. Still on automatic pilot, but with purpose. He fitted the hand onto his wrist. It took, at once. He didn't even stretch and wiggle his fingers to test. He gripped the chair arms with both hands and pushed himself upright.

His eyes were alert now, alight. The whites were stained as brown as the rest of him.

He looked at her, intelligence directed, expression giving nothing away. She remembered what she looked like. A madwoman. She should explain, but didn't know where to start.

How could she say what had happened to her family?

Slowly, with a dignity and strength she had not noticed before, Wing-Godfrey moved around the room. He was comfortable – in the room, in the house, in the Hollow – in a way she could never be, though she was the owner

(the sole owner)

and mistress. He was more than comfortable. He was part of the furnishings that had passed from Louise Magellan Teazle to the Naremores, which the authoress must have got from her family and they from people lost to history. His colour, that strange uniform brown, was the exact stain of the panelling in the secret passage, the desk in Louise's study, the posts of the bed and the magic chest of drawers.

Before Louise, who? Those terrified people in the ghost story book, Apple Annie and the Maitland-Middletons.

'I've lost my Tim,' she said, pathetically. 'I've given him away, by mistake. A terrible mistake.'

'Wiggy-wig,' said Wing-Godfrey.

Was that something from the Weezie books? It sounded like baby-talk.

'Wyg-i-Wyg,' he insisted.

A name? A place?

Click. She realised. Not baby-talk, not a name, not a place. An acronym.

'What you give,' Wing-Godfrey said, 'is what you get.'

The statement made her weak at the knees with relief. He meant Tim would come back, that he wasn't given away. He was just hidden and could be found.

'What you *give*,' he repeated.

The relief was stripped away.

What he said did not mean what she'd wanted it to mean. What it meant was the worst thing she could think of.

'…is what you *get*.'

Now, she screamed. Not just in terror.

She couldn't tell how far away the lights were, or even if the source was the house. The ground underfoot was treacherous. The path disappeared as if by whim. Jordan waded through bramble and found herself sinking into marsh. She wished she'd worn shoes. Her feet were scratched and muddy. It was the hour of the night when – even in August – it is colder than comfortable, and she was out here in just a tatty T-shirt.

The ghosts left her alone.

It was useless. The light never got nearer and she had a terrible feeling it was moving. She was being misled, dragged through every thorn bush and mud patch on the moor, to be left empty for the rising sun.

She had no idea of time. The night was still pitch, moonless and starless

(though it hadn't been a cloudy day)

and without a red rind of approaching dawn.

She had no idea of direction. The easiest thing would be to sit down and wait for the ghosts. She had no doubt that if she stopped struggling, stopped moving, they'd come back and finish the job. Maybe that would satisfy them, satisfy this place? Her family would be saved by her sacrifice. She doubted that. It was too neat, too convenient. At the Hollow, everything had to be earned. They had to save themselves individually before they could be saved as a family. She had to do her bit, come through this weirdzone walkabout, before anything else.

Any number of shapes in the distance could be the house.

She had an idea that this was all still the Hollow, that she had passed through the tree telescope to the standing stones but not crossed the moat. By night, the land was elastic.

From the first, she'd noticed the Hollow was larger on the ground than on an Ordnance Survey map. She had just not realised how vast, how extensive. The property was a continent, with lost tribes and ruined cities and fallen civilisations and trackless wastes. The house was a many-roomed mansion, a folded-up city disguised as a single-family dwelling.

The Naremores had never had a chance of owning the place.

Jordan thought of the ghosts she had met here: the Old Girl, the Rick stone, the Witchy Woman. They seemed like people, with personalities, faces, voices. But she still wasn't sure of them. Even after her conversation with the Old Girl on the nature of ghosts, she thought it might be something like a clever interactive program. Was everything they said or did a set reaction to something she had said or done first? The Old Girl came from her reading of Louise's books... the Witchy Woman was the Vron she'd been afraid of when she was little... and Dead Rick?

With her Letter back, she wasn't even sure Rick

was dead. It seemed to her now that the voice on the phone – supposedly Rick's dad – had been slightly buzzy, slightly *off*. He said he was looking at the Letter, but that wasn't possible, was it?

It could be that, in daylight, she would get through to Rick's dad and learn her worthless ex-boyfriend was sleeping off a dusk-till-dawn *Deep Space 9* marathon. If he were called to the phone, there'd be an embarrassed, halting exchange as she got over her relief and remembered to be furious with him, unable to let loose as she wanted to for fear of jarring the world back onto the track in which he was shockingly dead.

Daylight?

Might never happen.

Dad and Tim had spent an afternoon driving around, off the property, looking for but not finding the standing stones. Now, she kept coming back to them.

Whenever she thought she'd made progress, and a tree seemed familiar or a patch of mown grass suggested the kitchen lawn, she pushed through bushes or stepped onto a gravel path to find herself on the edge of the circle again.

Where she had nearly died.

The stones were inert now. She didn't know which of them had been Rick.

She tried different ways of leaving, walking *away* from the light as often as towards it, but wound up back here.

She couldn't feel her feet. Which was a mercy.

She clutched at her neck and found rubber tubing. Tim's catapult. Her brother had tried to strangle her with the thing. She'd been wearing it like a pendant. How had that happened? How had it come to her brother trying to kill her to prevent her killing their father?

She took off the catapult. The rubber loop was limp, as long as a skipping rope. The forked wooden weapon was larger than she had thought, as if the arms were handles and the handle a pointer.

Holding the thing lightly, thumbs and forefingers loosely gripping the fork-ends, she felt it twitch, the extended handle rising and pointing like a needle.

It was not a catapult but a dowsing stick.

The pointer indicated an unpromising path, one she had taken and failed at already. At least once. The stick was definitely tugged, as if on a fishing line.

Jordan stepped out of the circle. The stick pulled her on. The line was being reeled in.

She didn't know if she was being saved or caught.

She stumbled but kept balance, then pulled back, resisting the tugging, and got herself in walking shape. She took a deep breath, feeling power gathering in the stick, and decided she was equal to the force, that she would collaborate in this.

Steadily, she walked on, fork in front of her.

A hedge came up to block the way, but the stick led her to the gap that was only there if you looked a certain way. She went through without so much as a twig brushing her hair. She passed between trees, along the edge of a stretch of still, dark ditchwater, across a nighted lawn towards a wall of blackness that might have been a towering cliff.

The tugging shut off and the stick fell out of her fingers, hanging like a pendant again.

She was on the kitchen lawn, close enough to reach out and touch the house. The garden table and chairs were out, leaf-curls trapped in the filigree. She looked around and, in the gloom, saw trees and buildings where they should be.

Jordan realised she was crying. For joy.

He was on his guard, which made unseen walls close in. Not daring to use his torch for fear of attracting attention, Steven kept tripping over detritus, bumping into things. Twisted hangers extended infinitely, a barbed tank-trap tangle. More jetsam was scattered among the hooks. Torn-up comics. Broken toys. Cast-off computer monitors with the plugs snipped off. Unusable Christmas decorations. Oddments.

He no longer felt secure, no longer a boy in his private domain. Old worries returned.

The strew of hangers was purposeful. Not a tank trap, but a Steve trap.

Blind in the dark, he listened out.

The space was quiet but there were tiny sounds. Animals scurrying in the distance. Something small, breathing. A tinkle of running water. The hangers shifted, clinking against each other, creaking as they bent and unbent into hook-headed stick-men.

He had his back to a wall, which felt like stone.

Time passed. The noises continued, unthreatening but disturbing.

A low whistle, not a bird but a bird-call. Kids playing Red Indian, scouting through imaginary caverns, tracking the wounded paleface.

An answering whistle. Another.

It was just kids. The thought was not reassuring. Children could have a dark meanness, an innocent malice. The memory of cruelty came back to mind in a hot, embarrassing rush. He'd made Steve caves to hide in, away from bigger boys. Playground bastard-bullies. The comic-rippers, the arm-twisters, the name-callers.

A fourth distinctive whistle, lazily extended.

All points of the compass. He was surrounded.

The quality of the dark changed, from warm and spongy to cold and thin. When he shut his eyes, the neon patterns inside his lids were centipedes not sunbursts.

His thumb brushed the torch-switch.

One burst of light would end the game. A flare, marking his position. He could be found and dealt with.

In return, he'd have a mental image of his situation. As it was, he had no idea what was in the dark beyond the reach of his arm. He had lost all sense of the size of the space he was confined to.

Against his back was stone. He could be in a snug coffin or a vast cavern. He couldn't tell from the sounds, which could be loud and distant or quiet and close.

The dark was stasis and eventual decay.

He was tired, hungry, thirsty. He needed to pee. He missed Kirsty and his own kids. He wanted to shower, fall into his bed, let go of consciousness.

But he was here and had to be alert.

A whisper breeze brushed his face, riffled his hair, shocking as the cold touch of a razor.

His whole body was tense.

He would not call out. That would be as much a giveaway as turning on the torch. If he gave his position away, they could converge on him, pressing out of the dark with fists and boots, teeth and claws.

Did he believe that?

Was he alone in the middle of nowhere, forgotten and ignored, frightening himself with bogeys? He felt abandoned, insignificant, obscure. There was no real reason for the ghosts to have anything against him.

Not the ghosts.

But there were others, the whistling tribe.

He thought of his family. They were strangers, aliens almost. How had that happened? It wasn't as if they had changed much, just dropped the masks.

His ribs hurt where his daughter had hit him. His left hand was useless, since his son had fallen on him.

He had a flash of Jordan's frenzied attack and flinched.

Another whoosh of wind passed, like a near-miss guillotine blade.

Steven chewed his lip. He knew he had to look.

He held up his torch and stuck his hand out. His thumb was frozen on the switch.

It was the only thing he could do.

He closed his eyes and exerted pressure on the switch, wanting the light but not wanting to see.

That was absurd. He stopped, opened his eyes, calmed himself. He heard his own heartbeat, waited for it to slow. He breathed deeply and normally, told himself this was not important, and turned on the torch.

An orange face glared at him, close to his own.

Small, round, merciless. Tiny hands, fingers hooked, reached out.

Screaming, he shut off the torch.

He awaited the touch of the hands.

The orange face hung in his vision, streaked with movement, eyes glittering with malice.

The worst thing was that he had recognised it.

His son, Tim, transformed into a fury. And yet as terrified as he was terrifying.

Beyond the face-flare had been other child-sized figures, in blazers and straw hats, faces all angry eyes and war-paint. Another After Lights-Out Gang.

Steven shrank against the wall, and skittered sideways to avoid the touch, feet tangled in coat hangers, palm scraped bloody on the rough stone.

He heard Tim slam against the wall, with incredible force. He felt the impact in the stone.

It was no use talking.

He had to get away.

Launching himself away from the wall, kicking free of the hangers, he ran into the dark.

After five steps, he slammed his face into a low, solid object.

He clutched the torch, turning it on, but lost his hold on the thing.

The space was a passageway, a corridor, recognisably part of the house though he couldn't say where. A cone of light showed the painted ceiling and a moulded picture rail, then fell to show a twisted, surreal tangle of hangers on a carpeted floor.

The torch rolled away, taking the light with it.

Tim's face shone orange again. He was on all fours,

eyes intent on Steven, lips drawn back.

Hanger-hooks tore at Steven's clothes. He worried that he was punctured.

Tim edged forward on his hands and knees, intent.

The echo of Steven's scream hadn't yet dissipated.

Steven squirmed backwards, away from his son, away from the light. Behind Tim were the After Lights-Out Gang. Cigarette glow-worms burned, red phantom faces glowed in the dark. They were girls. Not schoolchildren, but ancient-eyed, primal creatures. These were the goddesses those long-ago bastard-bullies had worshipped, made sacrifice of smaller boys to. This was their shrine of pain.

Tim crawled to the torch and picked it up. He shone the beam directly into Steven's face. The dazzling flare blinded him.

Then, Tim turned the torch off.

Darkness. And crawling.

Jordan stepped into the Summer Room. No one was there. She lifted her T-shirt from her stomach and bent to wipe her face with the cloth.

There were lights on. Louise's lights.

Should she search the house for the others? Or wait here? Everything revolved around this room, the heart of the Hollow. Everyone came back here eventually, as she had.

She thought she had an idea now, how the place worked.

If she concentrated, she could keep things stable. She could walk down the corridor, go upstairs to her room

(Louise's room)

and not get lost on the way. Not this time.

She left the Summer Room.

The corridor was shadowed but not unlit. She didn't know if she could trust the light switches (they were new). After her venture out into the vast nightlands, she should be able to walk ten feet in the gloom.

She made it to the stairs and went up, eyes lightly closed, feeling her way along the bannister. She reached the landing. The moon, visible from inside the house if not the orchard, shone through the landing window, whitening the walls and patterning the carpet.

Her door hung open. She stepped into her room.

The lamp on her bedside table was lit. Her room was filled with soft, jungle light – the lampshade was patterned with tiger stripes and turquoise foliage. The wardrobe door hung open.

A dress hung there, a satin sausage skin for someone with no hips or bust, a tall famine refugee. Jordan felt a yearning, an excitement. She could get into that, and become the creature she had thought was inside her.

She shut the wardrobe door, firmly.

There was water in the wash-stand. She stripped off her smelly shirt and cleaned her face and legs, working the dirt out of her scratches, combing water into her hair.

She dropped the Letter on the bed. It lay like a used knife.

Then she pulled on a baggy pair of jeans and a jumper that smelled of fabric softener. She unrolled thick socks over her feet and massaged life into her toes, then slipped on comfortably loose trainers.

She caught sight of herself in the mirror.

Lit from below, she was a strange being, with jungle stripes on her face like Tim in camouflage. There was a dresser lamp, a slim tube over the mirror. She tugged a beaded pull-string and the stripes went away.

She lifted her jumper off her tummy. It was soft, but not bloated. As she breathed, she saw her ribs move, the knitted bones clearly outlined.

If anything, her face was gaunt. She had one or two spots and some fresh scratches. But she wasn't a monster, wasn't a freak. She'd never be a supermodel but, with care, she'd be at least average. Above average.

A tear welled and dribbled.

She had wasted so much worry, hurt herself and others so much, over nothing, a fancy. Having Ana to stay was a waste of time and energy. Jordan lamented cooked breakfasts and chocolate bars and cream pastries she had passed by.

Over her shoulder, in the mirror, she saw the Old Girl.

She wasn't dressed as a schoolgirl now, though she did wear a pinny and a straw hat. She was a little old lady.

She turned, but there was no one there.

'Louise?' she asked the mirror.

Louise Magellan Teazle must have looked into this mirror every day of her long life. It wasn't surprising some of her remained in the glass.

The Old Girl smiled. She was faint, not transparent but blended in with the light and shade.

'You kept this place well, but we've wrecked it.'

The apparition showed sadness but understanding. 'We didn't understand. How could we?'

Jordan realised there had been an instruction manual for the Hollow, but they hadn't recognised it. Mum had come the closest.

Even in the mirror, the Old Girl was just a shape on the wall, the shadow of a hat stand.

It was time to go back to the Summer Room.

R espect the Enemy. But track him and kill him.

Tim advanced stealthily through the dark. He was point-man, but his squaddies backed him up. In Country, he trusted the IP.

Night-vision gave him an edge but the Enemy was twice his size, victor of a thousand skirmishes.

They had a fix, and worked forward patiently, following spoor. Anything that came to hand could be an ally or a traitor, a weapon or a trap.

The Enemy had stumbled off, deserting his position, routed by Tim's surprise attack. This was now a mopping-up operation. However, that didn't mean he could slack off. The Enemy had nothing more to lose but his life. He would be more dangerous now he'd broken military discipline and was fighting only for survival, like an animal.

Track and kill.

The company were practiced night-fighters. Their minds were sharpened, stripped of all excess thought. They had been in this dark for a thousand years.

Once, he'd had a family, a home, friends. But Tim had been taken away from all that, out of the world and into the combat zone. He had fallen a long way without a parachute, but landed on his feet and come out fighting. He had joined the IP, the best fighting unit in the night-world.

He didn't hate. The Enemy wasn't a man, but a stone that must be broken so the road could go through. You didn't hate a stone, just shifted it out of the way.

It helped to focus on that.

The Enemy had scurried up to the next level, leaving blood on the ladder. Tim stood back while one of the IP checked the ladder for loosened crossbars or wire-traps. It was clear. Good. The Enemy was sloppy, thinking too much of getting away and not enough of stalling his pursuer.

There was a silent discussion. Tim was point. His squaddies fell back in a half-circle as he mounted the ladder, but were behind him all the way.

He climbed to the next level. Hanging just under the top of the fixed ladder, he poked his head up over the edge. The quality of the dark was different, as if the sky were lower, and there was a woodier smell, more enclosed.

The Enemy was in the distance, retreating.

Tim pulled himself up onto the next level and stood up straight. His squaddies made it over the edge too and regrouped. He was part of a fighting unit, a cog in a well-oiled killing machine. He took a silent breath and recalculated.

He turned on the torch he'd requisitioned and cast its beam across the wooden plain. The Enemy froze in the light, then picked up his feet and ran into the dark.

One of the IP, a blonde girl with a tiger-striped face, pointed, snarling.

Tim turned off the torch, course fixed in his mind, and began to run.

Jordan found her mother in the Summer Room with the brown man, spotlit by lamps which burned with unholy fire. Neither were in a fit state to have a conversation. Mum had panda-eyes from crying hard. Mr Wing-Godfrey was pliable but unresponsive, a sleepwalker.

Through the French windows, she could see the patio and the barn and as far as the orchard. It was still dead of night. All the clocks and watches she'd checked were stopped somewhere between midnight and two.

She was too exhausted to stay awake but too wired to sleep.

They were not alone and they were not safe.

A wind rattled the window-panes and disturbed the curtains. Mum and the brown man were on the sofa, surrounded by Louise's things. The television set and the standing lamps had advanced by inches, rucking up the rugs with wooden paws. Jordan picked up one light, an old-fashioned pole with a cream coolie hat shade, and carried it back to a corner where it wasn't in the way. As she moved it further from the sofa, its bulb dimmed and fizzed but did not die or burst. From the corner, it cast little light.

'Mum, where's Tim? Where's Dad?'

Her mother didn't say anything, but reacted to

the mentions of her son and husband as if they were darts thrown at her. Her face grew paler and brighter as if under an interrogation light.

Jordan turned and saw the coolie light was out of its corner.

As long as she kept it in sight, the thing stayed put. When she looked away, it was on the move, growing brighter. It had hopped forward a yard. She looked at Mum and then back and it was a yard nearer and five candles brighter. She wanted to snap it over her leg and throw it away. Instead, she picked it up and put it firmly back in its corner.

'You,' she said to Wing-Godfrey, 'keep watching this lamp.'

The brown man's head moved slowly but his eyes were open.

Jordan patted the coolie hat and felt a smug sense of victory.

There were four other standing lamps, identically shaded but a few inches shorter. She had dealt with the general, and now must take care of the privates. There were nooks and alcoves for them all. She shifted the lamps, damping down the painful, bleaching light which made the Summer Room into an overexposed moonscape.

Wing-Godfrey couldn't look in five directions at once.

Except he could. Jordan shifted his head and pointed at the big window. Five fixed lights reflected there.

'If one of them moves, call out,' she said.

The television set was on a trolley with rebellious castors. Trundling it was a job, but she managed. She humped the big box over the fireguard and put it in the fireplace. It should be happy there.

Knee-high occasional tables piled with vintage magazines and high-backed armchairs with lace antimacassars had occupied spaces they had been banished from earlier, but Jordan left them alone. Anything that couldn't cast light was less likely to be a discipline problem.

She drew up a stool and sat down, by the sofa.

Mum had stopped sniffling. She was at least responding to her.

'I put Tim in the top drawer,' Mum said, and sobbed.

Jordan had no idea what that meant, but it was evidently a terrible thing.

'He's lost,' Mum went on.

Jordan found a tissue in her pocket and wiped her mother's face, cooing that she would find Tim soon, that Dad would come back, that it would all be all right in the end.

Did she believe it? Was she was just feeding back the speech Mum used on Jordan when she woke up from a bad dream.

(The good old days? When all they had to fear was each other?)

Mum tried to smile and laid a shaking hand on her hair.

'We have to be strong, Mum,' said Jordan.

Mum began to stroke, then grabbed a fistful of hair and yanked hard. A patch of Jordan's scalp hurt, badly. She yelped. Tugged off the stool, she landed hard on her knees.

All the lights flared, turning Mum's face into a snarling skull with deep black eye-pits. Then the room went dark. Light-ghosts swarmed in Jordan's eyes and aftershocks of pain shot through her.

Mum was still pulling her hair.

The lights came back and Mum stopped pulling. Jordan looked up and around. The five lamps were in a tight circle around the sofa, towering overhead, hats angled forward in threat, cords stretched across the floor.

She stood, knocking over two of the lamp stands. They tumbled like tall trees and lost their shades. Their filaments still burned.

Jordan was outside the circle. Mum and Wing-Godfrey were trapped.

She put her hand to her head and found wetness.

The mad bitch had pulled out a chunk of hair by the roots.

After all she had done! Ungrateful cow!

She should leave her here to stew but knew she couldn't. Striking out on her own had been a mistake. And Mum's attack hadn't been as bad as other things. Jordan remembered she had seriously assaulted Dad after he hit her. Out in the night, the ghosts had almost killed her.

Mum wasn't herself.

Though, God knew, Mum's own self wasn't always a comfortable person to be around. She'd never been one for smoothing things over. That bad-dream speech Jordan remembered *wasn't* from Mum, but a film. It was something a 1950s movie mother might say. Mum didn't notice nightmares, unless they were her own.

This, however, was the whole family's nightmare.

Jordan resolved to wade back into the fray, to get through the encircling lamps, the layers of hurt and shock, and reach her mother.

The lights fizzed.

When Tim flashed the torch, Steven knew where he was. The upper level of the barn, in the hayloft. Even when the light was off again, he smelled straw and dry wood and remembered this place as uncomfortable.

His instinctive dislike of this corner of the Hollow wasn't because of anything that had happened in the distant past, but because of what was to happen in the near future. He'd never liked the hayloft because it was where he would die. Ever since the barn was built, hundreds of years ago, it had been assembling the props for his death scene.

How could he fight against his murderers?

Tim was just a child, his son. No matter what, Steven couldn't turn and fight Tim, as he could if someone else – Mr Precious Rick, the Wild Witch, even Kirsty – were coming at him. He wanted to save his own skin, but not at the expense of hurting his son. Even before she flew at him, he had learned from slapping Jordan. There were wrongnesses which couldn't be lived with.

If Tim won and left him dead, would he learn from that too?

Tim was with the After Lights-Out Gang. Of them all, he'd grown closest to the Hollow, found it easiest to go over to the others, to join the ghosts.

Was Tim even alive? Didn't you have to die to become a ghost?

No, Tim hadn't died. There was a tie between father and son, a two-way wordless communication. If his son were dead, Steven would have known.

However this turned out, the survivor would carry a load of pain and guilt that might be worse than losing the struggle.

Perhaps the best would be to turn around, walk up to Tim and toss him through the ladder-hatch? Then, he would take on himself the pain to come, the torment and the agony.

(Do that.)

If only for a moment. Physically, he could cope with Tim. He was not sure about the After Lights-Out Gang. Those savagely painted girlish ghosts would burn him at the stake and be back in their dorms in time for breakfast.

He stopped running. Surely, he must have crossed the space? No: distances were greater in absolute dark. When you weren't looking, when you couldn't see, the Hollow was as big as you could imagine.

'Turn on the torch, Tim,' he shouted.

No light came. But he heard footsteps, getting nearer.

'Tim, it's Dad,' he appealed.

The After Lights-Out Gang had their inner glow, dark violet. Steven made out their shapes, or their shadows. Big girls, taller and broader than him, they were still proportionally children.

They stood in a circle, like the dancing stones. In their centre, where the altar-piece should be, was his son. Steven was more afraid for Tim than of him.

'They're not our friends,' he said, biting down on the crack in his voice. 'Come to me. I'll look after you.'

He was not convinced by his own promises.

The After Lights-Out Gang just stood, menacing blocks of dark. They held hooks. Twisted coat hangers gleaming at the sharpened points, old agricultural implements with fresh edges.

'Go home, girls,' he shouted. 'This is our house now.'

The whistles began again. Slow, drawn-out, shrill, mocking, like wolf-whistles.

One of the gang lifted a long, thin shape to her lips. A recorder? A schoolgirl instrument, a flute for weeds and babies. She aimed it at him. A sharp report came, and a muzzle-flash. A dart stung in his shoulder.

Not a recorder. Some kind of blow-pipe gun.

The stinging was mostly shock. Touching his wound, he felt cold wetness. The girl had shot him with an icicle. A silly weapon, but still a killing thing.

The After Lights-Out Gang stood between him and the ladder-hatch. He was trapped.

No. There was another way out of the hayloft.

In the wall, somewhere behind him, was the bale-door. That opened out twenty feet above the ground. The crane-arm jutted above the door, but there was no chain or rope. Still, if he leaped outwards and landed on the soft grass, rolling properly, he could take a twenty foot drop.

In his panic, he had no idea which direction he was facing, no sense of the nearness or farness of the walls. Or the ladder, or the door. He could be inches away from falling through the ladder-hatch. A dead drop to solid concrete or the roofs of the cars in the garage space.

All the gang had blow-pipes ready.

He stood up, blood buzzing in his head.

'Tim,' he said, loudly but evenly.

A flash. A shot. Close enough to startle badly. He felt the icicle whoosh past him. This time, he had been missed.

But he had what he needed. A sense of where he was.

The bale-door was ten feet or so away, exactly to his left.

He turned and judged that he was facing the door.

In the dark, he heard the jiggle of a pipe being pumped or reloaded or locked or whatever. He took three precise steps and reached out. He did not touch the bale-door.

For that, he needed light.

He put his hands up and said, 'I surrender.'

No reply.

'Here,' he said. 'I'll give you a fix.'

He began to whistle.

He heard the steps behind him. Not the After Lights-Out Gang, but Tim.

He looked down, still in utter dark. He made out the top of his son's head.

'Tim,' he whispered.

He didn't know if he was getting through.

One of the girls nodded, a kill-him-and-get-it-over-with nod, justification for a massacre.

That nod hit him worse than the ice dart.

* * *

She had been wrong. Her daughter hadn't been faking it, wasn't the threat in this room. By pulling Jordan's hair, Kirsty had lost a chance, squandered an opportunity to make things right. She had thrown away both her children.

Awful despair gaped inside her.

The Hollow.

It might as well snuff her out like the lights. She would be saved from more mistakes.

She was numbed beyond fear.

After all, she was on her sofa in her front room. How could that not be normal?

The lights wavered, casting spider-armed shadows on the ceiling and walls.

Jordan stood, hurt, outside the circle of lamp stands.

Kirsty breathed slowly, becoming calm. If she let herself be taken, perhaps it'd all be over. She had thought it best her husband and children go, but it was simpler to remove herself from the situation, to throw *herself* away.

If she gave in, the others might be saved. That was the sacrifice of this circle.

'Goodbye, love,' she said.

'Mum, no,' Jordan shouted, understanding.

Kirsty looked at the brown man, who had already been away and come back. Bernard Wing-Godfrey held out his hand and she took it. In her grip, his hand came off again, at the wrist. Then his forearm came loose at the elbow and slithered out of his cuff, and his upper arm detached at the shoulder and hung loose in his baggy sleeve. His head lolled to one side. Kirsty saw the join around his neck, skin stretching as the bones unlocked.

The president of the After-Lights-Out-Gang came to pieces inside his suit.

Then he stood up.

None of his pieces were completely free, just let out on a long lead, loosely strung on cobwebby matter. His torso bobbed eight feet in the air, wrapped in his jacket. His head hovered on a yard-long ectoplasmic snake neck. His limbs jittered in the air, hips trapped in trousers. His independent calves and feet, arms and hands strained for the points of the compass. Strands glistened between his component pieces.

His left hand whizzed out of the air and took hold of Kirsty's chin, forcing her to look up. His face was beyond the corona of the light, but his eyes shone brown, liquid with contempt.

The right hand shot across and slapped her.

She felt the impact in her teeth. Her vision filmed over red.

The hand circled her head, looping a garrotte string about her neck. The noose went tight. She gasped, but couldn't take a breath. Trapped blood pounded in her temples. The thin strand was strong as steel wire, and ratcheted like a cheese-cutter.

Kirsty did not fight.

She had offered herself. It was a fair exchange. If she joined the ghosts, Tim and Steven would be given back. She would have to stay, become one of the haunters of the Hollow.

Fair enough. She deserved it.

She was lifted into the air, ghost-strings about her wrists and ankles.

Wing-Godfrey's head bumped against the ceiling, like a neon-eyed balloon. She was raised close to its expanded face, as if he were drawing her to him for a kiss.

Jordan was shouting.

Kirsty had said her goodbyes.

The closer she got to the head, the less it looked like the brown man. The mouth was six inches wide. The teeth shone as brightly as the eyes. The ears were bat-wings.

It didn't matter.

At the last, with all the arguments over, she thought only of Steven, Jordan and Tim. No one and nothing else had ever come close, not Vron, not any of the projects or problems or distractions. All she would leave behind of value was family.

Ten minutes ago, she wasn't sure she even liked her husband and children, now she knew with iron certainty that she loved them. She was prepared to die for them.

She was fuzzy from the loss of blood to her head.

It would not even hurt.

A burst of light came into her mind and she was floating gently, released from her bonds.

Suppressing any thought about what the girl's nod might mean to Tim, Steven grasped his son under the arms and picked him up, hugging him. Too surprised to struggle, the boy adjusted his weight, pressing his face to Steven's neck. His son's teeth were like ice against his throat.

The blow-pipes fired, puffs of light in the night.

Steven saw the bale-door up close, in a flashbulb instant. He threw himself against it, trusting it to be unlatched.

(The estate agent had suggested they keep it bolted, to prevent accidents; had they ever acted on his advice?)

His shoulder jarred but the door gave way. He realised too late that he was throwing himself and Tim carelessly over a twenty-foot drop.

Below the bale-door was gravel drive. He needed to leap outwards. To land on the soft grass. Roll into a ball around Tim.

He was wrong.

They didn't fall far, just collided with floor where there should have been air.

It was dark again and the orchard wasn't beyond the bale-door.

Beneath them, a carpet slid in wrinkles over polished floorboards. Steven staggered onwards, finding his feet, reaching for Tim's hand.

He didn't know which side his son was on, but wasn't leaving Tim to the After Lights-Out Gang.

He ran, pulling the boy.

They were in a corridor, somewhere in the house, having passed through an impossible secret passageway. The darkness was not complete. Thin light seeped under shut doors.

He slammed against a wall, coming to a dead end.

Turning, his back to the wall, he hugged his son. Coming down the passage were four solid silhouettes, taller and more powerfully built than schoolgirls.

These were the creatures his son had made friends with, had perhaps joined. They all saw the ghosts – the After Lights-Out Gang – differently, Steven realised. These were unlike the spectres of his own dark; these were Tim's playmates, Tim's ghosts, Tim's death squad.

'Tim,' he said. 'It's time to stop playing.'

His squaddies would rescue him and put the Enemy out of the game with a shot to the head. Then, time for a well-earned leave.

The girls were close. Tim saw them, awaiting his order. The Enemy held him tight. If he kept his head low, the girls would all have clear head shots.

All he had to do was give the order, the universally recognised nod.

'The game's over,' the Enemy said.

Tim felt the words like bullets.

Something had changed in the combat zone. A peace treaty, signed in another country thousands of miles distant, meant this was not right. Killing the Enemy would not be heroism, but a crime.

Still, to let him free would invalidate the mission, toss away the hundreds of man-hours that had brought them to this final confrontation. Because of words on paper, this would never be settled.

Tim would never know which of them was best.

No one would ever know. Or he could just finish the war in his own fashion, with clean victory.

He was ready to give the nod.

But no. There was no enemy here. No victory was ever really clean.

'Dad,' he said, tears welling up.

He was more tired than he'd ever been in his life. He turned away from his squaddies and jammed his face against Dad's chest.

'Good job, son, good job, Tim,' Dad said, hugging him close.

'Mum,' Jordan shouted.

She was terrified that her mother couldn't hear her, that she was too wrapped up in the embrace of the brown man.

'Don't go,' she said, trying to project meaning. 'Don't.'

There was no need for this sacrifice. Another ghost wasn't what the Hollow really wanted. It would only taint the place more.

Jordan understood her family was not a good influence.

Her mother was floating, face discoloured, in Wing-Godfrey's coils.

Jordan could easily reach out and grasp Mum by the ankles, perhaps pull her out of the ghostly, murdering hug, haul her back down to the ground. But it wouldn't be enough.

Like everything in the Hollow, it was in the heart.

Mum had to want to come back… to the ground, to her family.

She had stopped struggling, looked almost peaceful.

Jordan tried to cast her mind back, think of something she shared with her mother, some private experience, some taste, some interest, some insight.

She needed to fix the connection between them that had been broken too early.

From Jordan's early childhood, Mum had been strange. Not like the mothers in the films she liked, but off on her own bizarre enthusiasms, touchy when Dad voiced even the mildest doubts about her latest craze, too eager to scurry off to the witch Veronica. She grew to resent the way Mum's preoccupations squeezed out everything else. Jordan had become who she was as a way of making a space for herself, even in starvation, in the family. She realised now why she fixed on heroines whose style was so at odds with anything Mum liked, because at heart they were all saying, 'You don't own me', 'Is that all there is?', 'Whatever will be will be' – the things her mother believed but found such a struggle to live out.

Mum's arms floated outwards, as if she were drowned, or ascending.

'I'm sorry,' Jordan said. 'I should have helped.'

She could have, she knew. For the last few years, she had been clever enough, skilled enough. She could have taken an interest in Oddments or the other crazes. If she had supported her mother, then Mum wouldn't have had to run to a sociopathic crone to be believed in.

'I love you, Mum.'

Simple. Direct. True?

God, yes. True. How could it not be?

'*We* love you.'

That was true too. Jordan knew it, with a growing calm.

If the family had a collective heart, it started to beat again.

The Summer Room changed. Through the windows, she saw real night, not utter blackness. Stars faded with the first pinkish wash of impending dawn. The lamp stands were just left-over furniture.

And the brown man, the strung-out thing Wing-Godfrey had become, collapsed like a puppet.

Mum fell.

Jordan pushed through the lamp stands, knocking them over, and was there, directly under her mother.

Mum landed heavily, knocking the breath out of them both. Coolie hats rolled free and lightbulbs popped. Jordan's knees gave way and she was driven onto the sofa, all her mother's weight on her.

They would both be bruised like losing heavyweights.

But they were alive.

Mum shifted, trying to escape Jordan's embrace.

They wound up on the sofa, hugging each other ferociously, looking beyond the felled circle of lamp stands, seeing Wing-Godfrey scattered on the carpet.

The brown man pulled himself together slowly.

The fear Jordan was used to was subsiding.

She sensed Mum had changed, come through the worst of it. That gave her the strength not to be scared. Or rather, not as scared as before.

The brown man stood by the French windows, head and limbs pulled back into place. Dawn light outlined him and came through him. He was a bubble inside a slack suit.

The windows were open. There was noise in the orchard.

Someone was coming.

Mum cringed.

'Don't, Mum,' Jordan whispered. 'Not this time. Don't give them the satisfaction. Don't be scared.'

She stroked her mother's spiky hair.

They were by the rhyne, beyond the orchard. Not inside the house. No After Lights-Out Gang in sight. In the moment of their embrace, of their mutual recognition, the girls were sent back to their dorm, stripped of the rank his son had given them.

Steven put Tim down and looked out over the moor. He saw no standing stones from here, but the horizon was picked out by light.

'In the water, Dad,' said Tim.

Something was bundled up in the pondweed, like an island with four peninsulas.

'Don't look,' Steven said.

A dead man lay in the ditch, head hanging under the water, puffy layer of air trapped inside the back of his soaked jacket.

Bernard Wing-Godfrey. He must have been at the bottom of the ditch since yesterday and just floated to the surface.

'Come away,' he said, leading his son by the hand.

Tim was upset, he knew. A boy shouldn't have to see such a thing. Steven was grateful for the twilight time, which concealed the details.

He would call the police when the sun was up.

They walked past the hollow tree, Tim's abandoned camp. The boy shrank against him, as if expecting an attack, but it was just an old tree, nothing that could hurt anyone. Steven rapped on the wood, barking his knuckles. The tree sounded like a drum.

'No one home,' he said.

Tim darted out from under his wing and kicked the tree.

'See,' Steven said.

Tim thought about it and nodded.

'Shall we see how the womenfolk are?' Steven asked.

'Yes, Dad.'

From here, they could see the French windows. Lights were on in the Summer Room.

Steven squeezed his son's hand.

The French windows were pulled open, wider. Jordan tensed, was ready for whatever was coming through. Then Dad and Tim, battered but unhurt, stepped into the Summer Room. Jordan unclenched, giddy with relief. The Naremores were together again, safe. They shouldn't have split up and hared off in all directions.

Tim looked at the brown man and shrank against Dad.

Dad was wary of Wing-Godfrey, though he hadn't been in the room when he came apart.

'He's in the ditch,' Dad said, nodding at the brown man. 'Drowned.'

The brown man was transparent, a man-shaped cloud.

'This is a ghost,' Dad said.

The word was like an exorcism. The shape moved back, into the fireplace, and came apart again, decoalescing into the shadows and the soot-falls.

'That was a ghost,' Dad said.

'Yes,' she agreed.

She understood Bernard Wing-Godfrey had made the Hollow his home, permanently. He had fixed on the place for years, from his stifling prison through all the time with the Teazle Society. He had read his Weezie closely and sensed a welcome here for a certain type of spirit. Jordan wanted to weep for the poor, sad man. She pictured him slipping away from the tour, weighting his pockets with stones, sliding into the rhyne as if it were a deep bath. It took willpower to drown in three feet of water, to resist the urges of the body to stand up and strike for the air. Like Jordan, the brown man had willpower to spare. The strength which had enabled him to survive carried him through the sacrifice of his body, to buy his way into the Hollow's company of ghosts.

She thought they'd seen the last of Wing-Godfrey, but he'd always be here, playing for ever with Weezie and the Wiggy-Wigs. He had marked out the boundaries of his heaven and stepped there.

Her father and brother tramped across the carpet and flopped down on the sofa, next to her mother and her. Arms slipped around backs.

They were together again, a family.

'What are ghosts?' Tim asked.

Dad tried to shrug, but his arms were occupied, holding them all.

'Pests,' Mum said.

'Not just,' Jordan contradicted. 'Not worse than us. The same.'

She saw it, completely. How the Hollow worked. How they fitted in with the ghosts.

'They're not real,' Dad said. 'Just a nuisance, like a lingering smell or bad weather.'

He was wrong.

'They have minds,' she said. 'Some of them.'

In the fireplace, where Wing-Godfrey had faded, another figure, smaller and slighter, came together.

The Old Girl.

She stepped out, into the room. The beginnings of dawn didn't bother her. She was an old woman with a pinafore and a straw hat, not a child with a withered face. She looked more natural now Jordan had a firmer idea of this place.

Tim pressed his face against Jordan's tummy, spreading himself across his parents' laps. Mum hissed, like a cat before a fight.

The hostility gave the Old Girl pause. She began to snarl back.

How could she expect anything else? After this long night.

Only Jordan understood, was without real fear.

'Hello,' she said. 'Hello, Louise.'

The ghost smiled, weakly.

Steven looked at the apparition. She was more solid than the brown man, like a real person in the room. She'd had more practice, living at the Hollow for so long before becoming one of the ghosts.

If this was Louise Teazle, she didn't frighten him. Why hadn't she shown up before? She reminded him of the way the Hollow had felt when they moved in, as if she'd left herself about the place, only to be shredded, twisted and torn by...

What?

'Why did it change?' he asked.

'Because of us,' said Jordan.

The ghost nodded, reacting. It was not a psychic hologram, a recording of a person who was gone; it was a presence, with an intellect and a personality.

'It's why this place is called the Hollow, Dad,' said his daughter. 'You said it yourself, it's an island not a hollow. This spot, the house and grounds, contains a power, a presence. It's been here for thousands of years, as long as feeling, thinking people have lived on top of it. Its natural state is neutral, formless. It has to be shaped by us, the living. When we came here, it was what Louise made it...'

'She cheered up the Gloomy Ghost,' said Kirsty, understanding.

'Yes, exactly. Before her, cold, frightened and lonely folk lived here, They were haunted because they made the ghosts cold, frightened and lonely. We should have known, from the books, Louise's and the ghost-story paperback. Remember the sad girl who ate the ghost fruit and was lost to the world, and the women terrorised after the man fell from the tower. You should have read those pages I found. There, on the table. It's Primrose's story. I thought it was ours, but it isn't. It doesn't have to be. Even the army officer who saw nothing was a clue, because of the kind of person he was. Every time people live here, they change the ghosts. In the end, it needed a child to change the ghosts for the better. And we ruined them again.'

'It's like a mirror,' he said.

'Wiggy-wig. WYGYWG. What you give is what you get. If the ghosts hurt us, it is because we hurt each other. This place catches how we feel, what we are, and shapes itself to suit. All they are is us. We made them. They have the shape they have because of Louise – all those straw hats and little girls – but we're changing them, driving them mad. You can see how our ideas – Tim's soldiers, my R-Rick – are starting to reshape them, to make them *our* ghosts. They come back at us and we blow up at them. It makes us monsters, but only if we are the beginnings of monsters already...'

He was too tired to be frightened all over again. But the concept was terrifying. Every resentment, every failing, every malicious thought that passed out of him – out of *them* – went into some vast swelling sponge. When it hurt them, they felt worse and fed it more, a cycle that could never be broken.

Except by a child, by a girl from a book.

'We have to stop tearing ourselves apart,' said Jordan. 'We have to be a family.'

Steven held his wife and children and hoped first of all that he could trust himself, control himself. Only then could he hope for his family to gather around him, to take strength from him rather than be sapped by him.

The Old Girl was still smiling.

The family were a family again.

The Hollow was inhabited. There was a new

ghost, a brown presence who was without form. His shape would be determined by the living, would join with the others who made up the spirit of the place.

The sun rose over the moor and flooded into the Summer Room. As light hit, the Old Girl did not disappear but became an arrangement of sparks, an intricate constellation which would always be there if looked at sideways.

After dawn, one by one, the family fell asleep.

Autumn

The evening before Jordan's first day at college, the family ate together on the kitchen lawn. A spell of late-in-the-year warm weather made up for the storms of the past fortnight, which had soaked the thatch and revealed a few drips that needed fixing. The last of the apples had been picked, stored for the winter or sacrificed in a day-long pie-production line that filled the freezer and occupied the entire family. Drifts of leaves gathered in the orchard, and Dad had held the first ceremonial bonfire. The sweet smoke of burning, crackling foliage wafted across the Hollow and out onto the moor.

Tim had been at school for a week; already, he was making new friends and picking up a burr that was on its way to being a local accent. Jordan noted instances of 'youm', 'not I' and even 'gurt' in his vocabulary. How long would it be until he sounded like a compleat wurzel?

The walking on eggshells was almost over.

Still, it was like living in a former battlefield with

a heavily armed UN peace-keeping force. Every time the impulse to snap at her brother or parents came, she had to hold anger in, reminding herself what might happen if she vented. The others were like that too, even Tim.

Mum and Dad disagreed about the wine to have with dinner. Each got a few words into their argument, then halted, eyes straying from each other, skittering towards the dark corners of the kitchen. Then, almost comically, each backed down so fast there was almost a real row over who would give way.

Always, Jordan knew the others were there. Mostly, it was a comfort.

After they had worked equally in the kitchen, dividing up the tasks with the minimum of fuss, they doled out their meals – she had decided to go vegetarian, which meant she had to take responsibility for an alternate main course at most family meals – and carried the food through in a procession and sat around the garden table.

The evening *smelled* wonderful. The bonfire of the afternoon was embers and ash, but the scent lingered.

The mood lasted, until it broke.

'A ghost,' said Tim, pointing, afraid.

They all smiled but Jordan's smile froze.

Beyond the orchard, beyond the rhyne, beyond the boundaries of the property, stood a scarecrow with long, tangled hair – midnight black, with a white lightning jag – and bare, red-nailed feet. She leaned at an angle to the ground, holding a tree branch that overhung the ditch, hair adrift on the breeze. She wore a velvet skirt so purple it was almost black, and had new blue tattoos up and down her bare white arms.

'Good God,' said Mum.

'It really is a ghost,' said Dad.

It was the Wild Witch, Veronica.

'Vron,' Mum breathed, yearning in her eyes. Then, suddenly, cold caution.

'Do you suppose she walked all the way?' asked Dad.

Mum stood up, pushing her chair away from the table.

'Kirst-eeee,' sang Veronica, bell-clear voice sailing across the water.

Mum didn't know what to do.

Jordan remembered to hate Veronica. Even after they'd moved to the Hollow, the witch had worked her black magic. The family were beyond her reach, but she'd got to Rick. Finally, Jordan got through to Rick's father on the phone, an embarrassed and embarrassing conversation. Now she knew the full sordid story of the Wild Witch and Rick the Not-Dead.

Just because they were alive and elsewhere didn't mean their ghosts hadn't numbered among the legions of the Hollow.

'What does *she* want?' Tim said, harshly.

Jordan, like Mum and Dad, knew exactly what Veronica wanted. Mum and the family, the Naremores, back. They had been her toys, an interactive soap opera.

No, that was harsh. This wasn't an evil mastermind, but a sad woman who'd messed up her own life so badly that she needed to infect someone else's.

'Kirsty,' she said, 'I can't cross.'

She let go of the branch and leaned forwards, over

the ditch. Jordan was sure she'd overbalance and fall into the water

(witches float, that's the test)

but she was halted in the air.

She hung, leaning against something invisible.

Jordan knew this place was barred to the woman, and was grateful. The family were settled enough in the Hollow to be protected.

Mum left the table and walked down the gentle slope through the orchard to the rhyne, moving between the trees without urgency. Dad got up and followed her.

'Come on, Tim,' said Jordan, taking her brother's hand.

The reddish sunset spread above. Their shadows were long as they passed through the orchard.

Up close, Veronica looked older than Jordan remembered. The white streak spread silvery filaments through her wild hair. Her long skirts were tatty.

Where was her power?

She smiled at them.

'You need me,' she said. 'So I came.'

Mum shrank against Dad. Jordan felt the others, all around. They were more than a family. They were a crowd.

'I know about this place,' Veronica said. 'Even from here, I can feel it. We can make something of it, Kirsty. You and me. There's enormous potential.'

Mum shook her head.

Jordan saw, for the first time, the loss in Veronica's eyes.

'Hi, Jord,' she said, directly to her, smile twitching.

'I've brought Richard with me. He's in the car. There are explanations. A lot of healing to be done. We all have to learn to share.'

She didn't want to see the boy. Along with everything else, she had outgrown him.

'Steven, you've never understood really, that it's not about owning Kirsty. It's about what we have between us. There's enough to go around, enough to share. If you listen, you can learn so much from the feminine, from the other half of life. Tim, little soldier, it's your Auntie Vron. Remember the talks we used to have, about tactics and strategy? I understand what you've found here, in the Hollow. I've found more out about the place, stories going back and back into the ages. I have so much wisdom to share, to give. This is my place, I'm certain, as much as it is yours. We've always been wound up together, even at the bad times, we've needed all of us, pulling every which way, to keep the show on the road. Without me, you've been through trying times, warping experiences. This shut-out, this barrier, is a tragic malformation of the energies of the Hollow. If only you'll let me in, everything will be perfect again. Perfect love, perfect chaos, perfect life.'

Veronica's hair started blowing away from her head. Her skin was pressed against her skull. Jordan saw ripples as the pressure grew. She was tilted upright and pushed back a few steps.

'Are you doing this?' she asked, trembling.

No one answered her.

'Goodbye, Vron,' said Mum. 'I miss you, but we've changed. We've all changed.'

Veronica's face darkened, a flash of the old malice.

'No one ever really changes,' she said, and stalked away, under blood-red sky.

They watched her go. The shadows grew softer. Knots inside Jordan loosened.

What would the rest of Veronica's life be like? She had other toys to play with, but none so cherished as Mum. She was the one who had always believed in magic, but the Naremores had found the real thing, shutting her out.

Jordan would not be sorry for her, would not not *not*.

What the woman had done with Rick, a shiny new toy, was beyond contempt. She knew Rick would be punished, that the journey back to the city would be torture. He and Veronica would lock claws, sinking venomous fangs into each other's hearts.

Never again would Jordan be tormented like that.

'I saw the Brown Man today,' said Tim. 'Near here. He likes the tree I used to have.'

'I hope he's happy,' said Mum.

The coroner had brought in a suicide verdict. Bernard Wing-Godfrey left a note in his inside pocket, sealed in a plastic bag. The investigation was uncomfortable, though. Everyone was on tenterhooks, thinking that the ghosts would show themselves and attract more attention to the Hollow.

Getting on as a family was hard enough. If anyone else found out about the Hollow, there was a risk that the balance would be upset. Already, Mum and Dad were unsure whether Tim should be allowed to have his friends over to play, though they were relenting.

Jordan worried that Veronica would be vengeful.

She had sent Mum the book of ghost stories – Mum admitted that now – and could make a fuss with the papers and television. It would be tiresome denying everything, especially with Wing-Godfrey still so much in the local news.

No, the Wild Witch was beaten. Even she knew that.

She was gone now. She stalked across the field until she found a path, and slipped along it, out of sight.

'I'm proud of you, Kirst,' said Dad, hugging Mum.

She was quiet. Jordan understood it was hard for her. Dad, she thought, didn't. Yet. Under the new family regime, things changed more slowly than they seemed. They had been acting like a family since midsummer, but only now – as habits were setting – were they really feeling like one.

'She's mad, isn't she?' said Mum, wondering.

'No,' said Jordan. 'She's not mad. That was why she was dangerous.'

Veronica would be back in Rick's car. Good luck to the both of them.

Mum and Dad were closer to the place and each other. They were better together, though Jordan recognised moments every day when each had to bite back words. But not fighting was habit-forming, and the Hollow was supportive.

Dad's business, as far as anyone understood it, was doing fine. There was a crisis-ette when he learned that Tatum, his assistant, was setting up on her own and poaching several of his clients. That was smoothed over, now. It might be that Dad didn't want to work so hard. Local interests might take up more of his time. Mum was writing sketches and stories, and had picked up an agent if not a publisher; the Hollow library was still growing, still changing. Tim didn't play soldiers any more. He was interested in animals and had got an *Encyclopaedia of British Birds* on CD-ROM for his back-to-school present. Jordan tried to spend time with her brother, not butting in but sharing his interests, giving him something of herself.

They all had the ghosts. Not seen so much, but constantly present. Rarely did an individual personality, like the Brown Man or the Old Girl, make itself known, but there was a kind of a light, even in the evening, a late summer warmth, a comfortable smell. There were fewer magic tricks, since the Hollow didn't need to impress them any more. But if there was any danger of spirits sagging, something came along to surprise them.

And, as they had just learned, they were protected. Some things would never bother them again.

Jordan was excited about college. She had seen so few people outside the family these last months.

The Hollow was wonderful, but was not enough.

Louise had been so enchanting and enchanted that she'd spent her whole life here, never marrying, never having children, with few living friends. Jordan understood how perfect a life that had been for her, but also sensed – in the corners of the room she'd inherited from Weezie – the ghosts of regrets. She would be different.

The Hollow would always be here for her, to replenish her, mend her heart, shelter her. The Hollow was her home.

But, eventually, she would leave.

They would mature in the Hollow, like apples in jam. Mother, father, daughter, son; warmed by the glow, their inescapable – and recently proved – love would thicken. As for years to come, the family were a whole, united by fiercely shared feeling. Things that had seemed important were trivial, and things that had seemed negligible were potent.

The Hollow enfolded the family with its welcome. It needed them. Populated, it was fixed. With people, it could withstand the winds. That evening, the place was on its best behaviour, autumn red promising winter white.

About the Author

Kim Newman is a novelist, critic and broadcaster. His fiction includes *The Night Mayor*, *Bad Dreams*, *Jago*, the Anno Dracula novels and stories, *The Quorum* and *Life's Lottery*, all currently being reissued by Titan Books, *Professor Moriarty: The Hound of the D'Urbervilles* published by Titan Books and *The Vampire Genevieve* and *Orgy of the Blood Parasites* as Jack Yeovil. His non-fiction books include the seminal *Nightmare Movies* (recently reissued by Bloomsbury in an updated edition), *Ghastly Beyond Belief* (with Neil Gaiman), *Horror: 100 Best Books* (with Stephen Jones), *Wild West Movies*, *The BFI Companion to Horror*, *Millennium Movies* and *BFI Classics* studies of *Cat People* and *Doctor Who*.

He is a contributing editor to *Sight & Sound* and *Empire* magazines (writing *Empire*'s popular Video Dungeon column), has written and broadcast widely on a range of topics, and scripted radio and television documentaries. His stories 'Week Woman' and 'Ubermensch' have been adapted into an episode of the TV series *The Hunger* and an Australian short film; he has directed and written a tiny film *Missing Girl*. Following his Radio 4 play 'Cry Babies', he wrote an episode ('Phish Phood') for Radio 7's series *The Man in Black*.

His official website can be found at

www. johnnyalucard.com